PENGUIN CLASSICS

Washington Irving (1783–1859), America's first successful professional writer, was born and raised in New York City. His literary talent manifesting itself early, he broke into print before he was twenty years old. In 1809, under the pseudonym of Diedrich Knickerbocker, he published the rollicking burlesque *A History of New York*, the first work in belles lettres by an American to catch the public imagination and endure. Although he had trained to be a lawyer, the urge for authorship long distracted him from a serious career in law or business. Yet not until he was approaching forty did he attempt to support himself exclusively by writing. *The Sketch Book* (1819–20), published almost simultaneously in England (where he was then living) and the United States, won him immediate acclaim on both sides of the Atlantic and established a demand for his work. Foreign travel inspired much of his writing. Between 1822 and 1832 he issued three more collections of humorous and lightly romantic sketches and tales, most of them evocative of European scenes and the European past: *Bracebridge Hall*, *Tales of a Traveller*, and *The Alhambra*. In 1828 a biography of Columbus appeared, the first of several historical works by Irving notable for their romantic coloring. After seventeen years in Europe, he returned home in 1832 a national celebrity. His later writings include *A Tour on the Prairies* (1835), *Astoria* (1836), *The Adventures of Captain Bonneville* (1837), biographies of Goldsmith (1849) and Mahomet (1850), and a five-volume *Life of Washington* (1855–59). Irving's sprightly and often half-mocking prose style, together with the felicitous blend of humor, pathos, and the picturesque in his fiction, made a major impact on the popular literature of his age.

William L. Hedges is the author of *Washington Irving: An American Study, 1802–1832* (1965) and numerous essays on Washington Irving. He is co-author-editor of *Land and Imagination: The American Rural Dream* (1980) and has written widely on writers, topics, and texts in American literature from Benjamin Franklin to Thorstein Veblen. He teaches English and history at Goucher College, where he chairs the program in American Studies.

WASHINGTON IRVING

THE SKETCH BOOK OF GEOFFREY CRAYON, GENT.

With an Introduction by
William L. Hedges

Penguin Books

PENGUIN BOOKS
Published by the Penguin Group
Viking Penguin Inc., 40 West 23rd Street,
New York, New York 10010, U.S.A.
Penguin Books Ltd, 27 Wrights Lane,
London W8 5TZ, England
Penguin Books Australia Ltd, Ringwood,
Victoria, Australia
Penguin Books Canada Ltd, 2801 John Street,
Markham, Ontario, Canada L3R 1B4
Penguin Books (N.Z.) Ltd, 182–190 Wairau Road,
Auckland 10, New Zealand

Penguin Books Ltd, Registered Offices:
Harmondsworth, Middlesex, England

This collection edited by Haskell S. Springer
first published in the United States of America by
Twayne Publishers, a division of G. K. Hall & Co. 1978
This edition with an introduction by
William L. Hedges published in Penguin Books 1988
Published simultaneously in Canada

1   3   5   7   9   10   8   6   4   2

LIBRARY OF CONGRESS CATALOGING IN PUBLICATION DATA
Irving, Washington, 1783–1859.
The sketch book of Geoffrey Crayon, gent.
(Penguin classics)
"The text of this edition was edited by
Haskell Springer, and originally published by
Twayne Publishers in The Complete Works of
Washington Irving."
Bibliography: p.
I. Springer, Haskell S.   II. Title.
III. Series.
PS2066.A2S6   1988   818'.207   88-22410
ISBN 0 14 03.9032 4

Printed in the United States of America by
R. R. Donnelley & Sons Company, Harrisonburg, Virginia
Set in Caledonia

CONTENTS

INTRODUCTION

The Sketch Book of Geoffrey Crayon, Gent. is a literary anomaly that keeps eluding strict classification and analysis. Seldom, if ever, out of print in the nearly 170 years since its highly acclaimed initial publication (1819–20), Washington Irving's loose assortment of essays, sketches, and tales has delighted large popular audiences in the United States and Great Britain and traveled worldwide in translation. Its critical reputation diminished as the nineteenth century waned: modern taste at times finds parts of the potpourri insufficiently seasoned, a bit thin and derivative, overly sentimental. Nonetheless "Rip Van Winkle" and "The Legend of Sleepy Hollow," on the basis of which Irving is generally credited with inventing the short story as a distinct genre, still stand as undoubted American classics. And for readers who relish irony and burlesque humor, the wry, self-mocking imagination of Irving's persona, Geoffrey Crayon, has a way of redeeming most of *The Sketch Book* from its apparent weaknesses.

Turning to the text, we find everywhere anomaly, irony, ambiguity. The book is Janus-faced, looking almost simultaneously back and forth across the Atlantic, fondly viewing selected English scenes, characters, and institutions, while voicing Crayon's loneliness and homesickness for America. Although addressed primarily to an American audience, it has English readers also in mind before it is finished. It was written, moreover, at a time when some Americans suspected British writers and critics of a concerted effort to denigrate the new republic and its literature.

Structurally the miscellany seems to aspire to be something more than its fragmented self. We continually notice Crayon's consciousness of himself as a writer or, we might more appropriately say, maker of books. Not that this alleged author/editor matches the blatant ego(ec)centricity of an earlier Irving persona, the addlepated Diedrich Knickerbocker, who keeps interrupting his own narrative, *The History of New York*, with ludicrous complaints about how hard it is to make a great book out of very little material. But Crayon's fantastic encounters with old texts in "The Art of Book Making" and "The Mutability of Literature" reveal a curious anxiety about authorship. Indeed we may ask ourselves what *The Sketch Book* would be without its quenchless flood of direct quotations from, and oblique allusions to, early authors (mostly British) great and small, to say nothing of the Bible (see the Notes to this edition), without its frequent comments on authors and texts, above all without Crayon's pilgrimages to the Boar's Head Tavern and Stratford-on-Avon, along with his need, in the face of the frequent reminders he has of the "mutability" of earthly things, to hold firm to the idea of Shakespeare's universal appeal.

Irving had been living and traveling in England for almost five years when he brought the work out, but his actual experience of the country is filtered through the screen of Crayon's obsessive bookishness. Surprisingly, contemporary readers in both the old world and the new responded positively to this nostalgic intertwining of imagination and reality, past and present, although being exposed to a past that republicanism had in theory discarded may have been disconcerting to some Americans of English descent.

Finally to all this oddity we must add the text's publishing history. As Irving explains in the "Preface to the Revised Edition," *The Sketch Book* appeared first in the United States in a series of seven installments or numbers, not all of which were in print before it was published complete in two volumes in London. The work was well received in both countries, but it was the British reviews, hailing *The Sketch Book* as the first genuinely distinguished specimen of imaginative writing by an American, that were decisive. British contempt for American literature had reached a climax in January, 1820, only two months before the first volume of *The Sketch Book* appeared in England, when the celebrated clergyman, reformer, and wit Sydney Smith asked in a great flourish in *The Edinburgh Review*, "In the four quarters of the globe, who reads an American book?" Sensitive to British opinion in cultural matters, Americans had long been angered and embarrassed by such taunts. Yet at that very moment British reviews were already praising Irving's work-in-progress. Only seven months later *The Edinburgh Review* itself was predicting that *The Sketch Book* would "form an era in the literature of the nation to which it belongs."

And so it did. An international celebrity almost overnight, Irving now found himself fully in the business of writing books. Previously no American author had been able to earn a decent living by literary labor alone. But with Irving's success, certain psychological barriers seemed to weaken. Having awarded high praise to one American author, British critics began to find other American books generally more acceptable, a development which encouraged American readers to take native authors more seriously. High literacy rates in the United States and a rapidly expanding economy gave magazine and book publishers a lucrative market. Before long other American writers were able to support themselves by the pen. Where they followed Irving's lead and secured a separate English copyright for their works, they had a good chance of increasing their profits. His accomplishment thus established professional authorship as a real option for Americans.

Thirty-six years old when the book came out, Irving had been a writer on and off since he was nineteen, though he had published nothing in his own name. It was an open secret in New York City, his hometown, that he was the author or coauthor of letters by "Jonathan Oldstyle" (1802–03) in the New York *Morning Chronicle*, of the comic periodical (*Salmagundi*

(1807–08), and of Knickerbocker's *History of New York* (1809). Richard H. Dana, Sr., reviewing the still incomplete *Sketch Book* in *The North American Review* in 1819, seemed to take it for granted that the quality and popularity of his earlier writings had made Irving an American literary "success" already. But he had not been able to make a living by writing. Indeed, he had not even made a serious attempt to become a professional writer until he began *The Sketch Book*. Few Americans at this point had. Prejudices in part derived from Puritanism still persisted in some quarters against the seeming frivolity of certain kinds of writing, fiction and drama especially. Those who wrote were expected to do so in their spare time, unless they happened to possess independent means.

Irving's father, a Presbyterian immigrant from Scotland, had subjected his large family to a heavy regimen of church attendance, Bible reading, prayers, and psalm singing. In his five sons he had tried, with mixed success, to instill the Puritan ethic of hard work, frugality, and temperance. All five ultimately became involved in one way or another in the family importing businesses. Two, however, including Washington, went into law first, and a third became a doctor. For Washington, the legal profession was a way of avoiding business, which he hated. But his writing in turn distracted him from the law. Two of his brothers were also partially addicted to the questionable habit of writing. Subject to pangs of guilt over his "idleness," the young Irving at times threw himself energetically into what bourgeois society considered real work. But he lived for years without a clear sense of purpose, unsettled, unproductive, and often dispirited. Recognizing his talent, his older brothers partially subsidized his literary labors, making him, after the publication of *Knickerbocker*, a business partner with only minimal responsibilities. But this arrangement did not work well. If the jobs he was asked to do—lobbying in Washington for the family enterprises, for instance—were not arduous, he somehow made them time-consuming; perhaps uneasiness at depending on his brothers stifled his muse.

In 1815, embarking on what was supposed to be an extended nonbusiness trip to Europe, he got only as far as Liverpool, where he found his brother Peter ill, and the family importing firm, under his charge in England, going bankrupt. Washington's gentlemanly leisure was abruptly terminated. He worked strenuously in Liverpool for two and a half years in an effort to mitigate the family's financial disgrace. Meanwhile, more appalled than ever at the prospect of a business career, he resolved to give professional authorship a try. The obstacles he faced were formidable, beginning with the low spirits and feelings of loneliness to which he was subject. He had never quite recovered from the death of his fiancée, Matilda Hoffman, in 1809. And in the middle of the bankruptcy he had learned of the death of his mother, to whom he was strongly attached. Living in a foreign country, he was cut off from what he knew best, the society he could write about as an insider. There were also the constraints attendant upon the need to produce a money-making work.

As an amateur, Irving had been a freewheeling, irreverent humorist. "Oldstyle," *Salmagundi* (on which he collaborated with his brother William and James Kirke Paulding), and *Knickerbocker* thrive on caricature, satire, even flagrant self-contradiction. The writing often mocks the literary conventions it uses, the periodical essay, for instance, or the figure of the whimsical gentleman (usually a bachelor) of the old school, emblem of an outmoded, narrow, arbitrary, ultrarespectable gentility, who nonetheless simultaneously provides a viewpoint for mocking contemporary fads and follies. Parody so pervades *Salmagundi* and *Knickerbocker* (especially the original edition, 1809) that at times they seem to amount to little more than the ludicrously pretentious rhetoric of individuals blinded by illusions. One of the prime targets of such ridicule is the self-aggrandizing vision of itself that the United States was developing.

Seeking to win broad acceptance from a paying public for *The Sketch Book*, Irving substantially transformed himself as a writer, closely watching popular tastes and experimenting with some of the milder, less threatening forms of romanticism—pathos, sentimentality, and fantasies evoking the remote and the supernatural. He began to look into German folklore, which he discussed with Walter Scott on a visit to Abbottsford in 1817. He deliberately chose the format of the miscellany so as to appeal to a diversity of tastes. No longer trying to startle and unsettle, he saw to it that he was less persistently and boisterously humorous than in his early writings. His style grew smoother, more ingratiating. The prose of *The Sketch Book* seems quite consciously crafted, the language at times clearly striving for poetic effects. There is a studied avoidance of vulgarity.

The new manner won over the British critics. *The Quarterly Review*, seeing "the hand of the master" in *The Sketch Book*, called Irving the "best writer of English . . . that America has produced since the era of her independence. He seems to have studied our language in all its strength and perfection—in the writings of our old sterling authors. . . ." *The Edinburgh Review* noted with pleasure that Irving had modeled his "diction" on "the most elegant and polished of our native writers." It hoped that other Americans would follow his example. Dana, however, in his essay in *The North American Review* noted above, voiced reservations about the new style. While he knew that *The Sketch Book* was going to be popular, his assessment of the new work was mixed. On the whole he seemed to prefer Irving's earlier writings. American literature, he believed, had needed the wit and humor of *Salmagundi* and *Knickerbocker* to counteract its excessive earnestness, a quality derived from the nation's "being rather raw in authorship" and thus fearful of being adjudged coarse and undignified. Dana discerned an admirable naturalness and freedom in the youthful Irving but found *The Sketch Book* a bit too *"dressy,"* too "elegant," slightly artificial or foreign.

Dana's strictures on Irving's new style take on added significance in the context of a debate that had been in progress in the United States for at least two decades, a disagreement related to American sensitivity to British criticism. With the American Revolution had come a conviction that the new nation ought to have a literature commensurate with its lofty political ideals. But the early results, particularly in *belles lettres*, disappointed many. In *A Brief Retrospect of the Eighteenth Century* (1803), for instance, the Reverend Samuel Miller of New York asserted that American writings were "in general, less learned, instructive, and elegant than are found in Great-Britain and some of the more enlightened nations on the Eastern continent." The causes were not hard to find, he maintained: American institutions of higher education were inferior; there was no system of patronage to provide authors with financial support and the leisure to write; the "spirit of our people is *commercial*"; and, "still connected with [Britain] by the ties of language, manners, taste, and commercial intercourse," Americans were inclined to consider "her literature . . . as ours." All in all, Miller found that Americans had few incentives to encourage the work of native writers.

Many American readers accepted British literary standards and consequently their own cultural inferiority. There were occasional complaints, however, on both sides of the Atlantic that American literature was insufficiently distinguishable in subject or style from English literature. In the United States these complaints increased noticeably after the War of 1812, especially in the pages of the *North American Review*, founded in Boston in 1815. Giving voice to a romantically oriented and more sophisticated form of literary nationalism, the new journal criticized American writers for undue subservience to the classics. Edward Tyrell Channing, for instance, declared in 1816 that war inevitably exists between individual genius and "rules for versification, laws of taste, books of practical criticism, and approved standards of language." He urged writers to keep faith with their own thoughts and feelings instead of imitating approved models. Obviously congruent with the democratic ethos, Channing's doctrine of aesthetic freedom and self-reliance was to begin to exert a strong influence on American literature after 1830, in the era of Emerson, Thoreau, and Whitman.

There is undoubtedly some validity to Dana's complaints about Irving's style. We need look no further than the third paragraph of "The Author's Account of Himself," where we find Crayon rhythmically extolling America's "mighty lakes, like oceans of liquid silver; her mountains with their bright aerial tints; her valleys teeming with wild fertility"—and so on and on. For all their glitter, these hackneyed generalities fail to convey a sense that the writer has had close encounters with the American wilderness. Such over-writing in the earlier Irving would almost certainly have signaled parody.

But "Rip Van Winkle" and "The Legend of Sleepy Hollow" give us all the proof we need that Irving was perfectly capable of depicting American landscapes in such a way as to create for the reader an illusion of being there—in the Catskills or on the bank of the Hudson. Or for a quick indication of this scenic talent, one can turn to the first several paragraphs of "The Angler," in which Crayon recalls boyhood fishing expeditions with his friends and in his quiet playful way demonstrates why the "piscatory tactics" recommended by Izaak Walton for "the velvet margins of quiet English rivulets" will not work on a rocky American mountain stream.

Irving's strengths as a writer were in humor and narrative. When he abandoned them, he risked trouble. He was not a very good essayist or moralizer. His thought is liveliest when it questions attitudes, doubts illu-sions, deflates pretensions—his own among them. At the same time the high authority of English taste in early nineteenth-century American culture obviously made him uneasy. In a prefatory "Advertisement" to the first English edition of The Sketch Book (see Appendix B), he claimed that he had originally intended not to publish it in England, giving as a major reason the "austerity" of "British critics" towards American writers. And in a far more remarkable admission in "L'Envoy," the book's final word (not a part of the original American edition), Crayon exposes his anxiety about "ap-pearing before a public which . . . from childhood" he has regarded "with the highest feelings of reverence." That public of course is the British au-dience, fear of which, he admits, has heretofore undermined his self-confidence and stifled his creativity.

Clearly the doctrine of America's cultural dependency on England made sense to Irving. He has Crayon speak eloquently and cogently on the subject in the following passage from "English Writers on America," one of the best known selections from The Sketch Book:

> We are a young people, necessarily an imitative one, and must take our examples and models, in a great degree, from the existing nations of Europe. There is no country more worthy of our study than England. The spirit of her constitution is most analogous to ours. The manners of her people,—their intellectual activity—their freedom of opinion—their habits of thinking on those subjects which concern the dearest interests and most sacred charities of private life, are all congenial to the American character. . . .

"English Writers on America" first appeared in the second number of the American Sketch Book, before an English edition was contemplated. But Irving clearly knew that the essay would be read in England. By confronting

the touchy issue of British condescension toward America and the conse-
quent American resentment, he sought to play the apostle of good feelings—
it was that "era"—between the two peoples, balancing criticism and praise
for both sides. That he was not entirely comfortable doing so is suggested
by the fact that at times his prose again rings slightly false.

Whatever his uneasiness, however, most of the writing of *The Sketch
Book* seems clear, uncomplicated, vivid, and relaxed when it is compared
with the ponderousness that characterized much American prose in his
time—the essays of *The North American Review*, for instance, or the fiction
of Charles Brockden Brown or James Fenimore Cooper. It is not difficult
to understand why selections from *The Sketch Book* were used as models
of style in nineteenth-century American schoolrooms. Irving prided himself
on being a stylist. The modern editor of *The Sketch Book*, Haskell Springer,
tells us that in revising the text for the first English edition, Irving reworded
and rephrased numerous passages in response to criticism, including specifically several passages singled out by Dana as marred by mixed metaphor.

In addition he made several structural changes, the most important perhaps being to move "Westminster Abbey" from near the end to the middle
of the book. He added three new selections to the second volume, including
reworked versions of "Traits of English Character" and "Philip of Pokanoket," originally written for *The Analectic Magazine* several years earlier.
And he rearranged many of the other sketches and stories in the second
volume. Thus, except for the brief "L'Envoy," "The Legend of Sleepy Hollow" now concludes the book. The first English edition is basically *The
Sketch Book* we know today, even though Irving made a final revision in
1848, inserting two more sketches, "A Sunday in London" and "London
Antiques," both apparently at least partially drafted thirty years earlier.

What Irving had when he was finished was a book with broad popular
appeal that could also claim the attention of more serious readers. He had
discovered popular culture for American (and perhaps English) literature
and brought the two together in the uneasy relationship that has existed
between them ever since. That is, he discovered a growing middle-class
audience, able to read, curious about art and fashion, eager for information
and entertainment, craving novelty and emotional stimulation, prepared to
pay good money for an attractive product. What it did not want was an
undue taxing of its intellectual faculties or an open challenge to its basic
values. It was in this market that American writers would henceforth chiefly
support themselves—the alternative, in the absence of patronage, being
literature as an avocation. American printers, publishers, and booksellers,
including some who doubled as hack writers, had made sizable profits from
this trade earlier, but not writers with serious literary pretensions. The
larger meaning of Irving's success was that it blurred for good the distinction
between the fine art and the business of literature in the United States.

That he was in England when he wrote *The Sketch Book*, that a good deal of it is about England, and that it was highly praised by British critics helped enormously to sell it. For although his American readers increasingly defined their society as new, democratic, liberated from an oppressive past, they were nonetheless curious about the theoretically repudiated old world. As Crayon says, speaking in "The Author's Account of Himself" of his own early desire to go abroad,

> . . . Europe held forth the charms of storied and poetical association. There were to be seen the masterpieces of art, the refinements of highly cultivated society, the quaint peculiarities of ancient and local custom. My native country was full of youthful promise; Europe was rich in the accumulated treasures of age. Her very ruins told the history of times gone by, and every mouldering stone was a chronicle. I longed to wander over the scenes of renowned achievement—to tread as it were in the footsteps of antiquity—to loiter about the ruined castle—to meditate on the falling tower—to escape in short, from the commonplace realities of the present, and lose myself among the shadowy grandeurs of the past.

Here one touches America's half-secret longing for knowledge of its counterself, of exactly what it professes not to be. Crayon will in due course offer much that is calculated to satisfy that longing. But readers may note a certain irony in the latter part of the passage just quoted. One suspects that in the heightened rhetoric of the long final sentence Crayon is slightly mocking his own interest in the past as a bit lugubrious, a not entirely healthy appetite for an up-to-date American.

As he goes on in the next paragraph to speak of his "earnest desire to see the great men of the earth," his facetiousness becomes fully obvious:

> . . . I had read in the works of various philosophers, that all animals degenerated in America, and man among the number. A great man of Europe, thought I, must therefore be as superior to a great man of America, as a peak of the Alps to a highland of the Hudson; and in this idea I was confirmed by observing the comparative importance and swelling magnitude of many English travellers among us; who, I was assured, were very little people in their own country.—I will visit this land of wonders, thought I, and see the gigantic race from which I am degenerated.

Crayon's sly wit thus asserts itself at the very beginning; he is not going overboard in adulation of the old world. It is in such irony as this that he keeps his balance, retains his good sense while catering to popular tastes. And as easily as he mocks the affectations of others, Americans or Europeans, he makes fun of excesses to which he himself is prone—antiquarianism, for instance, or (see "The Spectre Bridegroom") the sentimentalism which, as journals Irving kept while struggling with *The Sketch Book* show, plagued him in periods of depression and self-doubt.

To reduce *The Sketch Book* to the testament of a crypto-aristocratic anglophile and political conservative, as is sometimes done, is to miss its finer points and misunderstand Crayon. His England is admittedly only touristic, the product of "idle humour" and "vagrant imagination," something he half-laughs at himself for offering the reader. Fighting for his literary life, and fearful of British critics, Irving had no incentive to go far in exhibiting the harsh realities of contemporary English life, the hardships, social dislocations, and class conflicts being generated by the industrial revolution. But both he and Crayon know that their England is somewhat obsolete and idealized. Here and there we are made aware of the increasing restlessness not only of nouveaux riches capitalists but of people in the lower orders as well.

Fundamentally, Irving all his life was a political moderate, variously a Democratic-Republican, Federalist, Democrat, and Whig. He obviously found appealing the sense of order, social harmony, and stability embodied in the trimly laid out English countryside and the survival of old customs and traditions. But Crayon's gentle satire in the much revered Christmas sketches makes it quite clear that Squire Bracebridge—to say nothing of his parson—has somewhat lost himself in the English past and is out of touch with current reality. And Crayon obviously has fears of becoming an anachronism himself.

Geoffrey Crayon, Gent., is not just a fancy name for Washington Irving, even if, as middle-aged, bachelor Americans in England, as writers and avid readers, they have roughly similar temperaments. In Crayon the shy, pensive, slightly melancholy, and sentimental side of Irving exaggerates itself and becomes a fictional character, allowing the author to modify his own experiences or create entirely fictitious ones—as when Crayon's interest in old things leads him through narrow gateways and dark passages to momentarily frightening encounters with personages who seem oddities from a forgotten world.

Crayon's self-characterization begins with the title page epigraph taken from Burton's *The Anatomy of Melancholy*. It encourages us to view him as solitary, a "mere spectator of other men's fortunes and adventures." And there is self-mockery in his next epigraph, a few half-comic, half-pathetic lines from another old book, *Euphues*, by John Lyly, which precede "The Author's Account of Himself" and compare the homeless traveler to a "snaile that crept out of her shel" and "was turned eftsoones into a Toad." While Crayon in his traveling is not "transformed into so monstrous a shape," fear that he might be is never quite laughed off.

His homesickness is a part of "The Voyage," which ends with his exclamation upon disembarking at Liverpool, "I alone was solitary and idle. I had no friend to meet, no cheering to receive. I stepped upon the land of my forefathers—but felt I was a stranger in the land." And what he shows us of Liverpool (in "Roscoe"), a banker-author's struggle for artistic self-realization in "the very market place of trade," does not altogether cheer him. We do not know whether the next sketch, "The Wife," takes place in England or the United States, but again, as in "Roscoe," financial disaster and bankruptcy have to be faced. Temporarily forsaking his spectatorial role, Crayon intervenes directly to keep the newlyweds together, revealing himself a man of feeling and Irving a literary descendant of Sterne, whose *Sentimental Journey* casts a shadow over Crayon's tour.

Subsequently as he takes us through rural landscapes or out-of-the-way London neighborhoods, inspects ancient churches, castles, country houses, and libraries, we are almost always aware of Crayon's presence. Generally he is alone. In the "nooks and corners and bye places" that he sketches, his contacts with human beings are fleeting. In "The Stage Coach," before he is rescued for Christmas by Frank Bracebridge, he looks on wistfully as three boys, returning from school for the holidays, reach their destination, are reunited with their pet animals, and walk up the road "to a neat country seat," where their mother and sisters are waiting: "I leaned out of the coach window, in hopes of witnessing the happy meeting, but a grove of trees shut it from my sight."

In the immediately preceding sketch, walking by himself among the tombs in Westminster Abbey as the dusk gathers, Crayon has become aware of the interior of the church as a formidable emptiness, from beyond which the sounds of the outside world can scarcely be heard. This image comes too close for comfort to epitomizing his experience in general: not sufficiently anchored in the living world, he finds himself alone contemplating the dead. His sense of the past doubles as a sensitivity to the passing of time. Why else does he so often join passing funeral processions? Mutability is the shadow that walks beside him.

The Sketch Book persistently hints at a story about Crayon that is never fully told. But we may perceive it in "the fluctuations of his own thoughts and feelings; sometimes treating of scenes before him; sometimes of others purely imaginary, and sometimes wandering back with his recollections to his native country." These are Crayon's own words about himself in his "Prospectus" for the original American edition of *The Sketch Book* (see Appendix A). In explaining what his "writings partake of," he warns readers not to expect much coherence in the miscellany. Yet by presenting the

apparently random sketches as reflective of the shifting "thoughts and feelings" of a particular personality, the warning ironically suggests underlying
connections.

Irving omitted the "Prospectus" from the finished book. But what makes
it "finished" is the reader's sense that in the first London edition Irving's
seemingly aimless association of ideas and impulses may finally have gotten
Crayon somewhere. The story all along has hinted that his "vagrant" wandering in a foreign country is a quest of sorts. Irving has rearranged the
book so that after the morbidity of "Westminster Abbey," the emotional
nadir for Crayon, feelings become decidedly more positive. The English
sketches on the whole are lighter now, more humorous, giving the impression that Crayon is feeling less a stranger in John Bull's "family mansion."
True, there is pathos in "The Pride of the Village" and tragedy in "Philip
of Pokanoket." But the latter, with "Traits of Indian Character," helps pull
the book back toward America near the end, strengthening the image of
the new world, which both contrasts with and complements the old.

If we take "Rip Van Winkle" and "The Legend of Sleepy Hollow" as
instances of Crayon's "wandering back with his recollections to his native
country," then these stories become part of *his* story. And positioning
"Sleepy Hollow" at the end of that story (except for "L'Envoy") adds to its
poignancy. Not that "Sleepy Hollow" cannot stand completely on its own,
a self-contained fiction, needing no connection with the rest of the book to
be perfectly satisfying. It is the book that is enhanced by the connection,
not the reverse. The same is true of "Rip Van Winkle." There are many
ways of looking at these two stories besides what is offered in the next few
paragraphs.

Narrated by Diedrich Knickerbocker, though encountered in Crayon's
book, the stories suggest a kinship between the two personae. Knickerbocker is not the same writer in *The Sketch Book* as in *A History of New
York*. His rambunctiousness has been laid aside; he is no longer primarily
a parodist. Instead of exploding in words, he tells his stories in an easygoing,
unpretentious, oddly humorous way. His diction is that of a well-educated
person who feels no compulsion to prove it. Fond of colloquialisms, he tends
to use elegant words and phrases ironically. That Crayon should turn to
stories that he or someone with whom he is in touch has "found among the
papers of the late Diedrich Knickerbocker" suggests that there is a coun-
terforce working in him, balancing the attractions of England. The Knickerbocker stories give us specifically realized landscapes with figures in them
to whom we are brought much closer than we are in the English sketches.
Human beings relate to one another and to the physical environment more
informally. The narrator is at home in the land.

The disturbances that mar the idyllic composure of these localities ring
familiarly in the context of *The Sketch Book*. Either Rip Van Winkle or

Ichabod Crane might be a figure in Crayon's dreams. Both are collectors and tellers of stories. Rip, in conflict with the nose-to-the-grindstone mentality of his wife, has "an insuperable aversion to all kinds of profitable labour." Ichabod will work as a schoolmaster if he has to, but he would rather sing, dance, or tell stories for his supper—and his appetite is voracious. Although the aura of mystery and the supernatural in these two texts derives largely from Irving's reading in German folklore and romantic fiction, they seem nonetheless remarkably American, not only in setting and character but in their social or cultural implications as well.

Though sometimes hinting that Dame Van Winkle's shrewishness may be a function of her husband's reluctance to work his land, Rip's story is largely sympathetic to *his* "idle humour" and "vagrant imagination." Following them away from his marriage and into the mountains, he loses the prime of his life in a dreamless sleep. But when he gets over the shock of waking up, he finds himself, at an age when no one can expect him to work, comfortably provided for. And he has a fantastic story to tell.

If the issue in that story is a tension between imagination or artistic inclination and industry or industriousness, in "Sleepy Hollow" it seems to be between imagination and money. We find Ichabod Crane referred to curiously as a "man of letters." The remark is of course ironic. His one-room schoolhouse is called "his literary realm." In the village he passes for a man of "superior taste," a "kind of idle gentleman like personage." These phrases resonate ludicrously in the context of *The Sketch Book*. For Ichabod is "in fact, an odd mixture of small shrewdness and simple credulity," a superstitious, psalm singing Connecticut Yankee with an eye to the main chance. He uses his music and storytelling as a false front masking his more serious intentions. What his "imagination" truly "expanded with," we are told, was the prospect of winning Katrina Van Tassel's hand and thereby gaining possession of her father's ample acres. These he would convert into "cash," to be used in turn for speculating in western real estate.

In the face of this threat the community imagination seems to materialize and frighten the imposter out of the region. Later, it is rumored, he migrates to a "distant part of the country," probably to the west and closer to the frontier, where, by Yankee ingenuity and calculation apparently, instead of an advantageous marriage, he rises from schoolmaster and law student to lawyer, politician, and finally small-time judge. Oh yes, along the way he also *writes*, for the newspapers. Back in Sleepy Hollow there are no writers, but the people thrive on storytelling. A flourishing oral literature gives the locality a sense of itself and its past. It turns out that Knickerbocker is only the conveyor of the story we have read. He heard it in the city and wrote it down; Crayon apparently gets it into print. The man who told it at the "corporation meeting" in New York, which Knickerbocker attended, seems to have heard it from an "old farmer," who thus turns out to be the creator of the second "legend of Sleepy Hollow," that is, the legend of Ichabod Crane—unless, of course, Brom Bones had a hand in it.

Crayon's compendium finally becomes an artful comment on authorship or storytelling in a rapidly expanding democratic and commercial society, a comment, in effect, on itself, on the writer's effort to satisfy both a popular audience and himself. But Crayon the writer and Crayon the traveler are not easily separated. His literary longings and anxieties closely relate to what general readers of *The Sketch Book* are apt to be more aware of—the traveler's yearning for a home. Metaphorically integral to the work as a whole, the re-creation of old English Christmas at Bracebridge Hall is crucial in Irving's promotion of Anglo-American amicability. He is helping his compatriots discover what Hawthorne was to call in the title of his own book on England (1863) *Our Old Home*.

The Christmas sequence, a major event in early American popular culture, needs to be seen against the background of Puritanism's long-established hostility, especially in New England, to Christmas as a pagan and popish holiday. Here Crayon's felicitous style wraps the major themes and images of the book together in an attractive package, a special gift for the reader. The landscape, the manor house, the family, the servants, and the villagers unite, with Crayon, a welcome guest now in "the land of my forefathers," to form a glowing image of peace and good will. But what gives this Christmas its full meaning is the sense of tradition behind it, a tradition in which Christianity blends with vestiges of pagan rites and customs derived from the Druids, Romans, Saxons, and Scandinavians. Holly, ivy, mistletoe, the "yule clog," the lord of misrule, "an enormous pig's head, decorated with rosemary, with a lemon in its mouth"—such bows to the past adorn the occasion. Simultaneously Crayon draws copiously on English Christmas poetry that he has resurrected from his libraries.

In the juxtaposition of his writing to the earlier texts, readers may begin to sense the meaningful continuity between present and past that Crayon in his more joyful moods can count on as at least a temporary stay against the all-encompassing mutability. Irving had rediscovered Christmas for many American and even English readers. *Harper's New Monthly Magazine* in 1883 went so far as to call him "the laureate of English Christmas" because of the extent to which "the spirit of Dickens's Christmas, and of Thackeray's" and of the Christmas of the *Illustrated London News*—the emphasis on abundant feasting, quaffing, frolicking, and good cheer—derives from *The Sketch Book*. Or it may be more accurate to say that Irving had invented a new Christmas out of the old, invented the Christmas of modern commercial popular culture. True, it was to be a long time before the festooned Christmas tree became a fixture in American households, before Christmas cards were mass-produced or merchants began to promote Christmas buying the day after Thanksgiving. Yet only three years after *The Sketch Book* was published, a New York writer named Clement Moore, capitalizing on Irving's having made Americans aware of St. Nicholas in *Knickerbocker's History*, was to give Santa Claus his biggest boost with " 'Twas the Night Before Christmas" (officially "A Visit from St. Nicholas"). And in 1825, with the publication in Philadelphia of *The Atlantic Souvenir*, a new kind of literary product appeared on the market, designed specifically for purchase as a gift for Christmas or New Year. Soon similar annuals or giftbooks were available in most of the cities on the east coast, and gradually they spread westward.

Predecessors of the monthly magazines that were to flourish in the United States from the middle of the nineteenth century on, the giftbooks were miscellaneous gatherings of original literary pieces by a variety of authors. Unlike the magazines, however, they had cloth or leather bindings that were often elaborately embellished, gilded, for instance, or inlaid with mother-of-pearl. And many contained lavish illustrations. The annuals were designed, in other words, to be particularly appealing to the eye and the touch, as Christmas or Valentine boxes of chocolates are today, and were often bought by conspicuously consuming Americans as much for drawing room display as for reading.

The literary fare inside these volumes was generally light and entertaining, its prevailing moral sentiments appropriate to the season. Looking back, one is struck by the extent to which *The Sketch Book* in its format, style, tone, and domestic longing anticipated the miscellanies that Americans became so fond of in the decades before the Civil War. Not incidentally, the holiday annuals, as business ventures, helped support American literature. Editors paid good money for original contributions. Work by almost every American writer of any significance—including Irving himself—appeared in the giftbooks.

He had given form to both the literary sketch and what was eventually to be called the short story. Such major fiction writers as Poe, Hawthorne, and Melville benefited by his efforts. The "sketch" book became a recognized genre, as did the more-or-less Crayonesque persona who went with it in half-random assortments such as *The Idle Man* (1821–22), by Irving's critic, Dana; *Dreams and Reveries of a Quiet Man* (1832), by Theodore Fay; *Crayon Sketches* (1833), by William Cox; *Pencillings by the Way* (1832–36), by Nathaniel P. Willies; *Reveries of a Bachelor* (1850), by Donald Grant Mitchell; and *Leaves from the Diary of a Dreamer* (1853), by Henry Tuckerman. Women also compiled sketch books, and the domestic fiction written in great quantities by American women authors beginning in the 1820's was by no means unaffected by Crayon's style, sentiment, wit, and humor. The period from the publication of *The Sketch Book* through the early 1840's became, as Van Wyck Brooks aptly observed, "the age of Washington Irving."

No deep thinker, the new nation's first successful professional author tended to live, though rather uneasily, by relatively commonplace ideas that made headway in his time in the slackening of the harsher religious convictions that had prevailed in colonial America. Having rejected his father's Presbyterianism, Irving fell back, particularly for consolation in times of trouble, on a faith in the saving power of good fellowship, which, whether officially promoted by Protestant denominations or not, was the religious drift of many in the nineteenth century. Most fully realized in literature by his English heir, Charles Dickens, this was the underlying faith of Irving's miscellany. Only five years before its publication, the second of the two wars between Britain and the United States in a little more than a generation had come to an end. Though prompted largely by Irving's personal frustrations and financial distress, *The Sketch Book*, as the projection of Crayon's longing for peace and domestic tranquility, succeeded in giving literary form to an emotional need widely shared by Americans in what was coming to be called the Era of Good Feelings.

—William L. Hedges

A NOTE ON THE TEXT

The text of this edition is that established by Haskell Springer for the Twayne edition (Boston, 1978) of *The Sketch Book of Geoffrey Crayon, Gent.*, volume VIII of *The Complete Works of Washington Irving*. Based on modern editorial principles, the Twayne text is certified by the Modern Language Association's Center for Editions of American Authors. It is reprinted here with permission. The complicated publishing history of *The Sketch Book* made for many difficulties in establishing an authoritative text. For a complete explanation of the decisions made by Springer, the reader is referred to his "Textual Commentary" in the Twayne edition (pp. 340–79). Briefly, however, he has used Irving's manuscripts, where they survive, as his copy-texts, except where a sketch was later so much revised as to become virtually a new work. Such copy-texts are the basis for almost one-third of the book. Somewhat more than a third is based on the first American edition (1819–20). And the first English edition (1820) provides the copy-texts for the remainder of the Twayne edition of *The Sketch Book*, except for a few small sections added in the Author's Revised Edition (1848). The arrangement of the items in the book is that of the 1848 edition. As Springer observes, "This use of multiple copy-texts results . . . in some unevenness of texture in the book as a whole." The variation in spelling and punctuation, however, is apt to be scarcely noticeable to readers who are not looking for it. The compensation is that the text for each sketch or tale comes as close to being what Irving originally intended as possible.

THE
SKETCH BOOK
OF
GEOFFREY CRAYON, GENT.

"I have no wife nor children, good or bad, to provide for. A mere spectator of other men's fortunes and adventures, and how they play their parts; which methinks are diversely presented unto me, as from a common theatre or scene."

BURTON

PREFACE TO THE REVISED EDITION

The following papers, with two exceptions, were written in England, and formed but part of an intended series for which I had made notes and memorandums. Before I could mature a plan, however, circumstances compelled me to send them piecemeal to the United States, where they were published from time to time in portions or numbers. It was not my intention to publish them in England, being conscious that much of their contents could be interesting only to American readers, and in truth, being deterred by the severity with which American productions had been treated by the British press.

By the time the contents of the first volume had appeared in this occasional manner, they began to find their way across the Atlantic, and to be inserted, with many kind encomiums, in the London Literary Gazette. It was said, also, that a London bookseller intended to publish them in a collective form. I determined, therefore, to bring them forward myself, that they might at least have the benefit of my superintendence and revision. I accordingly took the printed numbers which I had received from the United States, to Mr. John Murray, the eminent publisher, from whom I had already received friendly attentions, and left them with him for examination, informing him that should he be inclined to bring them before the public, I had materials enough on hand for a second volume. Several days having elapsed without any communication from Mr. Murray, I addressed a note to him, in which I construed his silence into a tacit rejection of my work, and begged that the numbers I had left with him might be returned to me. The following was his reply.

My dear Sir,

I entreat you to believe that I feel truly obliged by your kind intentions towards me, and that I entertain the most unfeigned respect for your most tasteful talents. My house is completely filled with workpeople at this time, and I have only an office to transact business in; and yesterday I was wholly occupied, or I should have done myself the pleasure of seeing you.

If it would not suit me to engage in the publication of your present work, it is only because I do not see that scope in the nature of it which would enable me to make those satisfactory accounts between us, without which I really feel no satisfaction in engaging—but I will do all I can to promote their circulation, and shall be most ready to attend to any future plan of yours.

>With much regard, I remain, dear sir,
>Your faithful servant,
>JOHN MURRAY.

This was disheartening, and might have deterred me from any further prosecution of the matter, had the question of republication in Great Britain rested entirely with me; but I apprehended the appearance of a spurious edition. I now thought of Mr. Archibald Constable as publisher, having been treated by him with much hospitality during a visit to Edinburgh; but first I determined to submit my work to Sir Walter (then Mr.) Scott, being encouraged to do so by the cordial reception I had experienced from him at Abbotsford a few years previously, and by the favourable opinion he had expressed to others of my earlier writings. I accordingly sent him the printed numbers of the Sketch Book in a parcel by coach, and at the same time wrote to him, hinting that since I had had the pleasure of partaking of his hospitality, a reverse had taken place in my affairs which made the successful exercise of my pen all important to me; I begged him, therefore, to look over the literary articles I had forwarded to him, and, if he thought they would bear European republication, to ascertain whether Mr. Constable would be inclined to be the publisher.

The parcel containing my work went by coach to Scott's address in Edinburgh; the letter went by mail to his residence in the country. By the very first post I received a reply, before he had seen my work. "I was down at Kelso," said he, "when your letter reached Abbotsford. I am now on my way to town, and will converse with Constable, and do all in my power to forward your views—I assure you nothing will give me more pleasure."

The hint, however, about a reverse of fortune had struck the quick apprehension of Scott, and, with that practical and efficient good will which belonged to his nature, he had already devised a way of aiding me. A weekly periodical, he went on to inform me, was about to be set up in Edinburgh, supported by the most respectable talents, and amply furnished with all the necessary information. The appointment of the editor, for which ample funds were provided, would be five hundred pounds sterling a year, with the reasonable prospect of further advantages. This situation, being apparently at his disposal, he frankly offered to me. The work, however, he intimated, was to have somewhat of a political bearing, and he expressed an apprehension that the tone it

was desired to adopt might not suit me. "Yet I risk the question," added
he, "because I know no man so well qualified for this important task,
and perhaps because it will necessarily bring you to Edinburgh. If my
proposal does not suit, you need only keep the matter secret and there
is no harm done. 'And for my love I pray you wrong me not.' If on the
contrary you think it could be made to suit you, let me know as soon
as possible, addressing Castle street, Edinburgh."

In a postscript, written from Edinburgh, he adds, "I am just come
here, and have glanced over the Sketch Book. It is positively beautiful,
and increases my desire to *crimp* you, if it be possible. Some difficulties
there always are in managing such a matter, especially at the outset;
but we will obviate them as much as we possibly can."

The following is from an imperfect draught of my reply, which underwent some modifications in the copy sent.

"I cannot express how much I am gratified by your letter. I had begun
to feel as if I had taken an unwarrantable liberty; but, somehow
or other, there is a genial sunshine about you that warms every creeping
thing into heart and confidence. Your literary proposal both surprises
and flatters me, as it evinces a much higher opinion of my talents than I
have myself."

I then went on to explain that I found myself peculiarly unfitted for
the situation offered to me, not merely by my political opinions, but by
the very constitution and habits of my mind. "My whole course of life," I
observed, "has been desultory, and I am unfitted for any periodically
recurring task, or any stipulated labor of body or mind. I have no command of my talents, such as they are, and have to watch the varyings of
my mind as I would those of a weather cock. Practice and training may
bring me more into rule; but at present I am as useless for regular service as one of my own country Indians, or a Don Cossack.

"I must, therefore, keep on pretty much as I have begun; writing
when I can, not when I would. I shall occasionally shift my residence
and write whatever is suggested by objects before me, or whatever rises
in my imagination; and hope to write better and more copiously by
and by.

"I am playing the egotist, but I know no better way of answering
your proposal than by showing what a very good for nothing kind of
being I am. Should Mr. Constable feel inclined to make a bargain for
the wares I have on hand, he will encourage me to further enterprise;
and it will be something like trading with a gipsy for the fruits of his
prowlings, who may at one time have nothing but a wooden bowl to
offer, and at another time a silver tankard."

In reply, Scott expressed regret, but not surprise, at my declining what
might have proved a troublesome duty. He then recurred to the original

subject of our correspondence; entered into a detail of the various terms upon which arrangements were made between authors and book-sellers, that I might take my choice; expressing the most encouraging confidence of the success of my work, and of previous works which I had produced in America. "I did no more," added he, "than open the trenches with Constable; but I am sure if you will take the trouble to write to him, you will find him disposed to treat your overtures with every degree of attention. Or, if you think it of consequence in the first place to see me, I shall be in London in the course of a month, and whatever my experience can command is most heartily at your com-mand. But I can add little to what I have said above, except my earnest recommendation to Constable to enter into the negotiation."*

Before the receipt of this most obliging letter, however, I had deter-mined to look to no leading bookseller for a launch, but to throw my work before the public at my own risk, and let it sink or swim according to its merits. I wrote to that effect to Scott, and soon received a reply:

"I observe with pleasure that you are going to come forth in Britain. It is certainly not the very best way to publish on one's own accompt; for the booksellers set their face against the circulation of such works as do not pay an amazing toll to themselves. But they have lost the art of altogether damming up the road in such cases between the author and the public, which they were once able to do as effectually as Diabolus in John Bunyan's Holy War closed up the windows of my Lord Under-standing's mansion. I am sure of one thing, that you have only to be known to the British public to be admired by them, and I would not say so unless I really was of that opinion.

"If you ever see a witty but rather local publication called Blackwood's Edinburgh Magazine, you will find some notice of your works in the last number: the author is a friend of mine, to whom I have introduced you in your literary capacity. His name is Lockhart, a young man of very considerable talent, and who will soon be intimately connected with

---

*I cannot avoid subjoining in a note a succeeding paragraph of Scott's letter, which, though it does not relate to the main subject of our correspondence, was too characteristic to be omitted. Some time previously I had sent Miss Sophia Scott small duodecimo American editions of her father's poems published in Edinburgh in quarto volumes; showing the "nigromancy" of the American press, by which a quart of wine is conjured into a pint bottle. Scott observes: "In my hurry, I have not thanked you in Sophia's name for the kind attention which furnished her with the American volumes. I am not quite sure I can add my own, since you have made her acquainted with much more of papa's folly than she would ever otherwise have learned; for I had taken special care they should never see any of those things during their earlier years. I think I told you that Walter is sweeping the firmament with a feather like a maypole and indenting the pavement with a sword like a scythe— in other words, he has become a whiskered hussar in the 18th dragoons."

my family. My faithful friend Knickerbocker is to be next examined and illustrated. Constable was extremely willing to enter into consideration of a treaty for your works, but I foresee will be still more so when

> Your name is up, and may go
> From Toledo to Madrid.

————And that will soon be the case. I trust to be in London about the middle of the month, and promise myself great pleasure in once again shaking you by the hand."

The first volume of the Sketch Book was put to press in London as I had resolved, at my own risk, by a bookseller unknown to fame, and without any of the usual arts by which a work is trumpeted into notice. Still some attention had been called to it by the extracts which had previously appeared in the Literary Gazette, and by the kind word spoken by the editor of that periodical, and it was getting into fair circulation, when my worthy bookseller failed before the first month was over, and the sale was interrupted.

At this juncture Scott arrived in London. I called to him for help, as I was sticking in the mire, and, more propitious than Hercules, he put his own shoulder to the wheel. Through his favourable representations, Murray was quickly induced to undertake the future publication of the work which he had previously declined. A further edition of the first volume was struck off and the second volume was put to press, and from that time Murray became my publisher, conducting himself in all his dealings with that fair, open, and liberal spirit which had obtained for him the well merited appellation of the Prince of Booksellers.

Thus, under the kind and cordial auspices of Sir Walter Scott, I began my literary career in Europe; and I feel that I am but discharging, in a trifling degree, my debt of gratitude to the memory of that golden hearted man in acknowledging my obligations to him.—But who of his literary contemporaries ever applied to him for aid or counsel that did not experience the most prompt, generous, and effectual assistance!

W.I.

Sunnyside, 1848.

THE AUTHOR'S ACCOUNT OF HIMSELF

I am of this mind with Homer, that as the snaile that crept out
of her shel was turned eftsoones into a Toad, and thereby was forced
to make a stoole to sit on; so the traveller that stragleth from his
owne country is in a short time transformed into so monstrous a
shape that he is faine to alter his mansion with his manners and to
live where he can, not where he would.

LYLY'S EUPHUES.

I was always fond of visiting new scenes and observing strange
characters and manners. Even when a mere child I began my travels
and made many tours of discovery into foreign parts and unknown
regions of my native city; to the frequent alarm of my parents and
the emolument of the town cryer. As I grew into boyhood I extended the
range of my observations. My holyday afternoons were spent in rambles
about the surrounding country. I made myself familiar with all its
places famous in history or fable. I knew every spot where a murder or
robbery had been committed or a ghost seen. I visited the neighbouring
villages and added greatly to my stock of knowledge, by noting their
habits and customs, and conversing with their sages and great men.
I even journeyed one long summer's day to the summit of the most
distant hill, from whence I stretched my eye over many a mile of
terra incognita, and was astonished to find how vast a globe I inhabited.

This rambling propensity strengthened with my years. Books of voyages and travels became my passion, and in devouring their contents
I neglected the regular exercises of the school. How wistfully would I
wander about the pier heads in fine weather, and watch the parting
ships, bound to distant climes. With what longing eyes would I gaze
after their lessening sails, and waft myself in imagination to the ends
of the earth.

Further reading and thinking, though they brought this vague inclination into more reasonable bounds, only served to make it more
decided. I visited various parts of my own country, and had I been
merely a lover of fine scenery, I should have felt little desire to seek
elsewhere its gratification, for on no country have the charms of nature
been more prodigally lavished. Her mighty lakes, like oceans of liquid
silver; her mountains with their bright aerial tints; her valleys teeming
with wild fertility; her tremendous cataracts thundering in their solitudes;
her boundless plains waving with spontaneous verdure; her broad deep
rivers, rolling in solemn silence to the ocean; her trackless forests, where
vegetation puts forth all its magnificence; her skies kindling with the
magic of summer clouds and glorious sunshine—no, never need an

American look beyond his own country for the sublime and beautiful of natural scenery.

But Europe held forth the charms of storied and poetical association. There were to be seen the masterpieces of art, the refinements of highly cultivated society, the quaint peculiarities of ancient and local custom. My native country was full of youthful promise; Europe was rich in the accumulated treasures of age. Her very ruins told the history of times gone by, and every mouldering stone was a chronicle. I longed to wander over the scenes of renowned achievement—to tread as it were in the footsteps of antiquity—to loiter about the ruined castle—to meditate on the falling tower—to escape in short, from the commonplace realities of the present, and lose myself among the shadowy grandeurs of the past.

I had, beside all this, an earnest desire to see the great men of the earth. We have, it is true, our great men in America—not a city but has an ample share of them. I have mingled among them in my time, and been almost withered by the shade into which they cast me; for there is nothing so baleful to a small man as the shade of a great one, particularly the great man of a city. But I was anxious to see the great men of Europe; for I had read in the works of various philosophers, that all animals degenerated in America, and man among the number. A great man of Europe, thought I, must therefore be as superior to a great man of America, as a peak of the Alps to a highland of the Hudson; and in this idea I was confirmed by observing the comparative importance and swelling magnitude of many English travellers among us; who, I was assured, were very little people in their own country.—I will visit this land of wonders, thought I, and see the gigantic race from which I am degenerated.

It has been either my good or evil lot to have my roving passion gratified. I have wandered through different countries and witnessed many of the shifting scenes of life. I cannot say that I have studied them with the eye of a philosopher, but rather with the sauntering gaze with which humble lovers of the picturesque stroll from the window of one print shop to another; caught sometimes by the delineations of beauty, sometimes by the distortions of caricature and sometimes by the loveliness of landscape. As it is the fashion for modern tourists to travel pencil in hand, and bring home their portfolios filled with sketches, I am disposed to get up a few for the entertainment of my friends. When I look over, however, the hints and memorandums I have taken down for the purpose, my heart almost fails me at finding how my idle humour has led me aside from the great objects studied by every regular traveller who would make a book. I fear I shall give equal disappointment with an unlucky landscape painter, who had travelled on the continent, but following the bent of his vagrant inclination, had sketched in nooks and corners and bye places. His sketch book was accordingly crowded with cottages, and landscapes, and obscure ruins; but he had neglected to paint St. Peter's or the Coliseum; the cascade of Terni or the Bay of Naples; and had not a single Glacier or Volcano in his whole collection.

THE VOYAGE

Ships, ships, I will descrie you
             Amidst the main,
I will come and try you
What you are protecting
And projecting,
             What's your end and aim.
One goes abroad for merchandize and trading,
Another stays to keep his country from invading,
A third is coming home with rich and wealthy lading.
             Hallo my fancie, whither wilt thou go?

OLD POEM.

To an American visiting Europe the long voyage he has to make is
an excellent preparative. The temporary absence of worldly scenes and
employments produces a state of mind peculiarly fitted to receive new
and vivid impressions. The vast space of waters, that separates the
hemispheres is like a blank page in existence. There is no gradual
transition by which as in Europe the features and population of one
country blend almost imperceptibly with those of another. From the
moment you lose sight of the land you have left, all is vacancy until
you step on the opposite shore, and are launched at once into the bustle
and novelties of another world.

In travelling by land there is a continuity of scene and a connected
succession of persons and incidents, that carry on the story of life,
and lessen the effect of absence and separation. We drag, it is true, "a
lengthening chain" at each remove of our pilgrimage; but the chain is
unbroken—we can trace it back link by link; and we feel that the last
still grapples us to home. But a wide sea voyage severs us at once.—It
makes us conscious of being cast loose from the secure anchorage of
settled life and sent adrift upon a doubtful world. It interposes a gulph,
not merely imaginary, but real, between us and our homes—a gulph
subject to tempest and fear and uncertainty, rendering distance palpable
and return precarious.

Such at least was the case with myself. As I saw the last blue line
of my native land fade away like a cloud in the horizon, it seemed as if I
had closed one volume of the world and its concerns, and had time for
meditation before I opened another. That land too, now vanishing from
my view; which contained all that was most dear to me in life; what
vicissitudes might occur in it—what changes might take place in me,
before I should visit it again.—Who can tell when he sets forth to wander,

whither he may be driven by the uncertain currents of existence; or
when he may return; or whether it may ever be his lot to revisit the
scenes of his childhood?

I said that at sea all is vacancy—I should correct the expression. To
one given to day dreaming and fond of losing himself in reveries, a sea
voyage is full of subjects for meditation: but then they are the wonders
of the deep and of the air, and rather tend to abstract the mind from
worldly themes. I delighted to loll over the quarter railing or climb to
the main top of a calm day, and muse for hours together, on the
tranquil bosom of a summer's sea. To gaze upon the piles of golden
clouds just peering above the horizon; fancy them some fairy realms
and people them with a creation of my own. To watch the gently
undulating billows, rolling their silver volumes as if to die away on
those happy shores.

There was a delicious sensation of mingled security and awe with
which I looked down from my giddy height on the monsters of the
deep at their uncouth gambols. Shoals of porpoises tumbling about the
bow of the ship; the grampus slowly heaving his huge form above the
surface, or the ravenous shark darting like a spectre through the blue
waters. My imagination would conjure up all that I had heard or read
of the watery world beneath me. Of the finny herds that roam its fathom-
less valleys; of the shapeless monsters that lurk among the very foundations of the earth and of those wild phantasms that swell the tales of
fishermen and sailors.

Sometimes a distant sail, gliding along the edge of the ocean would
be another theme of idle speculation. How interesting this fragment of a
world, hastening to rejoin the great mass of existence. What a glorious
monument of human invention; which has in a manner triumphed
over wind and wave; has brought the ends of the earth into communion;
has established an interchange of blessings,—pouring into the sterile
regions of the north all the luxuries of the south; has diffused the light
of knowledge and the charities of cultivated life, and has thus bound
together those scattered portions of the human race, between which
nature seemed to have thrown an insurmountable barrier.

We one day descried some shapeless object drifting at a distance. At
sea every thing that breaks the monotony of the surrounding expanse
attracts attention. It proved to be the mast of a ship that must have
been completely wrecked; for there were the remains of handkerchiefs,
by which some of the crew had fastened themselves to this spar to prevent
their being washed off by the waves. There was no trace by which the
name of the ship could be ascertained. The wreck had evidently drifted
about for many months: clusters of shell fish had fastened about it; and
long sea weeds flaunted at its sides.

But where, thought I, is the crew!—Their struggle has long been over —they have gone down amidst the roar of the tempest—their bones lie whitening among the caverns of the deep. Silence—oblivion, like the waves, have closed over them, and no one can tell the story of their end. What sighs have been wafted after that ship; what prayers offered up at the deserted fireside of home. How often has the mistress, the wife, the mother pored over the daily news to catch some casual intelligence of this rover of the deep. How has expectation darkened into anxiety— anxiety into dread and dread into despair. Alas! not one memento may ever return for love to cherish. All that may ever be known is, that she sailed from her port, "and was never heard of more!"

The sight of this wreck, as usual, gave rise to many dismal anecdotes. This was particularly the case in the evening when the weather, which had hitherto been fair began to look wild and threatening, and gave indications of one of those sudden storms which will sometimes break in upon the serenity of a summer voyage. As we sat round the dull light of a lamp in the cabin, that made the gloom more ghastly, every one had his tale of shipwreck and disaster. I was peculiarly struck with a short one related by the captain.

"As I was once sailing," said he, "in a fine stout ship across the banks of Newfoundland, one of those heavy fogs which prevail in those parts rendered it impossible for us to see far ahead even in the day time; but at night the weather was so thick that we could not distinguish any object at twice the length of the ship. I kept lights at the mast head and a constant watch forward to look out for fishing smacks, which are accustomed to lie at anchor on the banks. The wind was blowing a smacking breeze and we were going at a great rate through the water. Suddenly the watch gave the alarm of 'a sail ahead!'—it was scarcely uttered before we were upon her. She was a small schooner at anchor, with the broad side toward us. The crew were all asleep and had neglected to hoist a light. We struck her just a mid-ships. The force, the size and weight of our vessel bore her down below the waves—we passed over her and were hurried on our course. As the crashing wreck was sinking beneath us I had a glimpse of two or three halfnaked wretches, rushing from her cabin—they just started from their beds to be swallowed shrieking by the waves. I heard their drowning cry mingling with the wind. The blast that bore it to our ears swept us out of all further hearing—I shall never forget that cry!—It was some time before we could put the ship about; she was under such headway. We returned as nearly as we could guess to the place where the smack had anchored. We cruised about for several hours in the dense fog. We fired signal guns and listened if we might hear the halloo of any survivors; but all was silent—we never saw or heard any thing of them more!—"

I confess these stories for a time put an end to all my fine fancies. The storm encreased with the night. The sea was lashed up into tremendous confusion. There was a fearful sullen sound of rushing waves and broken surges. Deep called unto deep. At times the black volume of clouds over head seemed rent asunder by flashes of lightning which quivered along the foaming billows, and made the succeeding darkness doubly terrible. The thunders bellowed over the wild waste of waters and were echoed and prolonged by the mountain waves. As I saw the ship staggering and plunging among these roaring caverns, it seemed miraculous that she regained her balance or preserved her buoyancy. Her yards would dip into the water; her bow was almost buried beneath the waves. Sometimes an impending surge appeared ready to overwhelm her, and nothing but a dextrous movement of the helm preserved her from the shock.

When I retired to my cabin the awful scene still followed me. The whistling of the wind through the rigging sounded like funereal wailings. The creaking of the masts; the straining and groaning of bulk heads as the ship laboured in the weltering sea were frightful. As I heard the waves rushing along the side of the ship and roaring in my very ear, it seemed as if death were raging round this floating prison, seeking for his prey—the mere starting of a nail—the yawning of a seam might give him entrance.

A fine day, however, with a tranquil sea and favouring breeze soon put all these dismal reflections to flight. It is impossible to resist the gladdening influence of fine weather and fair wind at sea. When the ship is decked out in all her canvass, every sail swelled, and careering gaily over the curling waves, how lofty, how gallant she appears—how she seems to lord it over the deep!

I might fill a volume with the reveries of a sea voyage, for with me it is almost a continual reverie—but it is time to get to shore.

It was a fine sunny morning when the thrilling cry of Land! was given from the mast head. None but those who have experienced it can form an idea of the delicious throng of sensations which rush into an American's bosom, when he first comes in sight of Europe. There is a volume of associations with the very name. It is the land of promise, teeming with every thing of which his childhood has heard, or on which his studious years have pondered.

From that time until the moment of arrival it was all feverish excitement. The ships of war that prowled like guardian giants along the coast—the headlands of Ireland stretching out into the channel—the Welsh mountains towering into the clouds, all were objects of intense interest. As we sailed up the Mersey I reconnoitered the shores with a telescope. My eye dwelt with delight on neat cottages with their trim shrubberies and green grass plots. I saw the mouldering ruin of an abbey over run with ivy, and the taper spire of a village church rising from the brow of a neighbouring hill—all were characteristic of England.

The tide and wind were so favourable that the ship was enabled to come at once to the pier. It was thronged with people; some idle lookers-on, others eager expectants of friends or relatives. I could distinguish the merchant to whom the ship was consigned. I knew him by his calculating brow and restless air. His hands were thrust into his pockets; he was whistling thoughtfully and walking to and fro, a small space having been accorded him by the crowd in deference to his temporary importance. There were repeated cheerings and salutations interchanged between the shore and the ship, as friends happened to recognize each other. I particularly noticed one young woman of humble dress, but interesting demeanour. She was leaning forward from among the crowd; her eye hurried over the ship as it neared the shore, to catch some wished for countenance. She seemed disappointed and agitated; when I heard a faint voice call her name. It was from a poor sailor who had been ill all the voyage and had excited the sympathy of every one on board. When the weather was fine his messmates had spread a mattress for him on deck in the shade, but of late his illness had so encreased, that he had taken to his hammock, and only breathed a wish that he might see his wife before he died. He had been helped on deck as we came up the river, and was now leaning against the shrouds, with a countenance so wasted, so pale, so ghastly that it was no wonder even the eye of affection did not recognize him. But at the sound of his voice her eye darted on his features—it read at once a whole volume of sorrow—she clasped her hands; uttered a faint shriek and stood wringing them in silent agony.

All now was hurry and bustle. The meetings of acquaintances—the greetings of friends—the consultations of men of business. I alone was solitary and idle. I had no friend to meet, no cheering to receive. I stepped upon the land of my forefathers—but felt that I was a stranger in the land.

ROSCOE

—In the service of mankind to be
A guardian god below; still to employ
The mind's brave ardour in heroic aims,
Such as may raise us o'er the groveling herd,
And make us shine forever—that is life.
THOMSON.

One of the first places to which a stranger is taken in Liverpool is the Athenæum. It is established on a liberal and judicious plan; contains a good library and spacious reading room and is the great literary resort of the place. Go there at what hour you may, you are sure to find it filled with grave looking personages, deeply absorbed in the study of newspapers.

As I was once visiting this haunt of the learned my attention was attracted to a person just entering the room. He was advanced in life, tall, and of a form that might once have been commanding, but it was a little bowed by time—perhaps by care. He had a noble Roman style of countenance; a head that would have pleased a painter; and though some slight furrows on his brow shewed that wasting thought had been busy there, yet his eye still beamed with the fire of a poetic soul. There was something in his whole appearance that indicated a being of a different order from the bustling race around him.

I inquired his name and was informed that it was Roscoe. I drew back with an involuntary feeling of veneration. This then was an Author of celebrity; this was one of those men, whose voices have gone forth to the ends of the earth; with whose minds I have communed even in the solitudes of America. Accustomed as we are in our country to know European writers only by their works, we cannot conceive of them, as of other men, engrossed by trivial or sordid pursuits, and jostling with the crowd of common minds in the dusty paths of life. They pass before our imaginations like superior beings, radiant with the emanations of their genius, and surrounded by a halo of literary glory.

To find, therefore, the elegant historian of the Medici, mingling among the busy sons of traffic at first shocked my poetical ideas; but it is from the very circumstances and situation in which he has been placed, that Mr. Roscoe derives his highest claims to admiration. It is interesting to notice how some minds seem almost to create themselves; springing up under every disadvantage, and working their solitary but irresistible way through a thousand obstacles. Nature seems to delight in disappointing the assiduities of art, with which it would rear legitimate dullness to maturity, and to glory in the vigour and luxuriance of her chance productions. She scatters the seeds of genius to the winds, and though some may perish among the stony places of the world, and some be choked by the thorns and brambles of early adversity, yet others will now and then strike root even in the clefts of the rock, struggle bravely up into sunshine, and spread over their sterile birth place all the beauties of vegetation.

Such has been the case with Mr. Roscoe. Born in a place apparently ungenial to the growth of literary talent; in the very market place of trade; without fortune, family connexions or patronage; self prompted, self sustained and almost self taught, he has conquered every obstacle, achieved his way to eminence, and having become one of the ornaments of the nation, has turned the whole force of his talents and influence to advance and embellish his native town.

Indeed it is this last trait in his character which has given him the greatest interest in my eyes, and induced me particularly to point him out to my countrymen. Eminent as are his literary merits, he is but one among the many distinguished authors of this intellectual nation. They, however, in general live but for their own fame, or their own pleasures. Their private history presents no lesson to the world, or perhaps a humiliating one of human frailty and inconsistency. At best, they are prone to steal away from the bustle and commonplace of busy existence; to indulge in the selfishness of lettered ease, and to revel in scenes of mental but exclusive enjoyment.

Mr. Roscoe on the contrary has claimed none of the accorded privileges of talent. He has shut himself up in no garden of thought nor elysium of fancy; but has gone forth into the highways and thoroughfares of life; he has planted bowers by the wayside for the refreshment of the pilgrim and the sojourner, and has opened pure fountains where the labouring man may turn aside from the dust and heat of the day, and drink of the living streams of knowledge. There is a "daily beauty in his life," on which mankind may meditate and grow better. It exhibits no lofty and almost useless, because inimitable example of excellence; but presents a picture of active yet simple and imitable virtues, which are within every man's reach, but which, unfortunately, are not exercised by many, or this world would be a paradise.

But his private life is peculiarly worthy the attention of the citizens of our young and busy country, where literature and the elegant arts must grow up side by side with the coarser plants of daily necessity; and must depend for their culture, not on the exclusive devotion of time and wealth, nor the quickening rays of titled patronage, but on hours and seasons snatched from the pursuit of worldly interests, by intelligent and public spirited individuals.

He has shown how much may be done for a place in hours of leisure, by one master spirit, and how completely it can give its own impress to surrounding objects. Like his own Lorenzo De Medici, on whom he seems to have fixed his eye as on a pure model of antiquity, he has interwoven the history of his life with the history of his native town, and has made the foundations of its fame the monuments of his virtues. Wherever you go in Liverpool you perceive traces of his footsteps in all that is elegant and liberal. He found the tide of wealth flowing merely in the channels of traffic, he has diverted from it invigorating rills to refresh the gardens of literature. By his own example and constant exertions he has effected that union of commerce and the intellectual pursuits so eloquently recommended in one of his latest writings;° and has practically proved how beautifully they may be brought to harmonize and to benefit each other. The noble institutions for literary and scientific purposes, which reflect such credit on Liverpool, and are giving such an impulse to the public mind, have mostly been originated, and have all been effectively promoted by Mr. Roscoe; and when we consider the rapidly encreasing opulence and magnitude of that town, which promises to vie in commercial importance with the metropolis; it will be perceived that in awakening an ambition of mental improvement among its inhabitants, he has effected a great benefit to the cause of British literature.

In America we know Mr. Roscoe only as the Author—in Liverpool he is spoken of as the Banker, and I was told of his having been unfortunate in business. I could not pity him as I heard some rich men do. I considered him far above the reach of my pity. Those who live only for the world and in the world, may be cast down by the frowns of adversity; but a man like Roscoe is not to be overcome by the reverses of fortune. They do but drive him in upon the resources of his own mind, to the superior society of his own thoughts, which the best of men are apt sometimes to neglect, and to roam abroad in search of less worthy associates. He is independent of the world around him. He lives with antiquity and with posterity. With antiquity, in the sweet communions of studious retirement, and with posterity in the generous aspirings after future renown. The solitude of such a mind is its state of highest enjoyment. It is then visited by those elevated meditations which are the proper aliment of noble souls, and are like manna, sent from heaven in the wilderness of this world.

While my feelings were yet alive on the subject it was my fortune to light on further traces of Mr. Roscoe. I was riding out with a gentleman to view the environs of Liverpool when he turned off through a

° Address on the opening of the Liverpool Institution.

gate into some ornamented grounds. After riding a short distance we came to a spacious mansion of freestone, built in the Grecian style. It was not in the purest taste, yet it had an air of elegance and the situation was delightful. A fine lawn sloped away from it, studded with clumps of trees, so disposed as to break a soft fertile country into a variety of Landscapes. The Mersey was seen winding a broad quiet sheet of water through an expanse of green meadow land, while the Welsh mountains, blending with clouds and melting into distance, bordered the horizon.

This was Roscoe's favourite residence during the days of his prosperity. It had been the seat of elegant hospitality and literary retirement—The house was now silent and deserted. I saw the windows of the study, which looked out upon the soft scenery I have mentioned. The windows were closed—the library was gone. Two or three ill favoured beings were loitering about the place, whom my fancy pictured into retainers of the law. It was like visiting some classic fountain that had once welled its pure waters in a sacred shade, but finding it dry and dusty, with the lizard and the toad brooding over the shattered marbles.

I enquired after the fate of Mr. Roscoe's library which had consisted of scarce and foreign books, from many of which he had drawn the materials for his Italian histories. It had passed under the hammer of the auctioneer and was dispersed about the country. The good people of the vicinity thronged like wreckers to get some part of the noble vessel that had been driven on shore. Did such a scene admit of ludicrous associations, we might imagine something whimsical in this strange irruption into the regions of learning. Pigmies rummaging the armoury of a giant, and contending for the possession of weapons which they could not wield. We might picture to ourselves some knot of speculators debating with calculating brow over the quaint binding and illuminated margin of an obsolete author; or the air of intense but baffled sagacity with which some successful purchaser attempted to dive into the black letter bargain he had secured.

It is a beautiful incident in the story of Mr. Roscoe's misfortunes, and one which cannot fail to interest the studious mind, that the parting with his books seems to have touched upon his tenderest feelings; and to have been the only circumstance that could provoke the notice of his muse. The scholar only knows how dear these silent, yet eloquent companions of pure thoughts and innocent hours become in the season of adversity. When all that is worldly turns to dross around us, these only retain their steady value. When friends grow cold and the converse of intimates languishes into vapid civility and commonplace, these only continue the unaltered countenance of happier days, and cheer us with that true friendship which never deceived hope nor deserted sorrow.

I do not wish to censure, but surely if the people of Liverpool had been properly sensible of what was due to Mr. Roscoe and themselves, his library would never have been sold. Good worldly reasons may doubtless be given for the circumstance, which it would be difficult to combat with others that might seem merely fanciful; but it certainly appears to me such an opportunity as seldom occurs, of cheering a noble mind, struggling under misfortunes, by one of the most delicate but most expressive tokens of public sympathy. It is difficult, however, to estimate a man of genius properly, who is daily before our eyes. He becomes mingled up and confounded with other men. His great qualities lose their novelty and we become too familiar with the common materials which form the basis even of the loftiest character. Some of Mr. Roscoe's townsmen may regard him merely as a man of business; others as a politician; all find him engaged like themselves in ordinary occupations and surpassed, perhaps, by themselves on some points of worldly wisdom. Even that amiable and unostentatious simplicity of character, which gives the nameless grace to real excellence, may cause him to be undervalued by some coarse minds, who do not know that true worth is always void of glare and pretension. But the man of letters who speaks of Liverpool, speaks of it as the residence of Roscoe. The intelligent traveller who visits it, enquires where Roscoe is to be seen. He is the literary land mark of the place, indicating its existence to the distant Scholar. He is like Pompey's column at Alexandria, towering alone in classic dignity.

The following sonnet, addressed by Mr. Roscoe to his books on parting with them, is alluded to in the preceding article. If any thing can add effect to the pure feeling and elevated thought here displayed, it is the conviction, that the whole is no effusion of fancy, but a faithful transcript from the writer's heart.

TO MY BOOKS

As one, who, destined from his friends to part,
Regrets his loss, but hopes again erewhile
To share their converse and enjoy their smile,
And tempers as he may, affliction's dart;

Thus, loved associates, chiefs of elder art,
Teachers of wisdom, who could once beguile
My tedious hours and lighten every toil—
I now resign you; nor with fainting heart;

For pass a few short years, or days, or hours,
And happier seasons may their dawn unfold,
And all your sacred fellowship restore;
When, freed from earth, unlimited its powers,
Mind shall with mind direct communion hold,
And kindred spirits meet to part no more.

THE WIFE

The treasures of the deep are not so precious
As are the conceal'd comforts of a man
Lock'd up in woman's love. I scent the air
Of blessings, when I come but near the house.
What a delicious breath marriage sends forth,
The violet bed's not sweeter!

MIDDLETON.

I have often had occasion to remark the fortitude with which women
sustain the most overwhelming reverses of fortune. Those disasters which
break down the spirits of a man, and prostrate him in the dust, seem
to call forth all the energies of the softer sex, and give such intrepidity
and elevation to their character, that at times it approaches to sublimity.
Nothing can be more touching than to behold a soft and tender female,
who had been all weakness and dependence, and alive to every trivial
roughness while treading the prosperous paths of life, suddenly rising in
mental force, to be the comforter and supporter of her husband under
misfortune, and abiding, with unshrinking firmness, the bitterest blasts
of adversity.

As the vine which has long twined its graceful foliage about the
oak, and been lifted by it into sunshine, will, when the hardy plant
is rifted by the thunderbolt, cling round it with its carressing tendrils
and bind up its shattered boughs; so is it beautifully ordered by
providence, that woman, who is the mere dependent and ornament of
man in his happier hours, should be his stay and solace when smitten
with sudden calamity, winding herself into the rugged recesses of
his nature; tenderly supporting the drooping head, and binding up the
broken heart.

I was once congratulating a friend, who had around him a blooming
family knit together in the strongest affection. "I can wish you no better
lot," said he, with enthusiasm, "than to have a wife and children. If
you are prosperous, there they are to share your prosperity; and if
otherwise, there they are to comfort you.—" And indeed I have observed
that a married man falling into misfortune, is more apt to retrieve his
situation in the world than a single one; partly because he is more
stimulated to exertion by the necessities of the helpless and beloved
beings who depend upon him for subsistence; but chiefly because his
spirits are soothed and relieved by domestic endearments, and his self
respect kept alive by finding, that though all abroad is darkness and
humiliation, yet there is still a little world of love at home, of which

he is the monarch. Whereas a single man is apt to run to waste and self neglect; to fancy himself lonely and abandoned, and his heart to fall to ruin like some deserted mansion for want of an inhabitant.

These observations call to mind a little domestic story, of which I was once a witness. My intimate friend Leslie had married a beautiful and accomplished girl, who had been brought up in the midst of fashionable life. She had, it is true, no fortune, but that of my friend was ample and he delighted in the anticipation of indulging her in every elegant pursuit; and administering to those delicate tastes and fancies, that spread a kind of witchery about the sex—"her life," said he, "shall be like a fairy tale."

The very difference in their characters produced an harmonious combination. He was of a romantic and somewhat serious cast; she was all life and gladness. I have often noticed the mute rapture with which he would gaze upon her in company, of which her sprightly powers made her the delight; and how in the midst of applause, her eye would still turn to him, as if there alone she sought favour and acceptance. When leaning on his arm her slender form contrasted finely with his tall, manly person. The fond confiding air with which she looked up to him, seemed to call forth a flush of triumphant pride and cherishing tenderness; as if he doted on his lovely burthen, for its very helplessness.—Never did a couple set forward on the flowery path of early and well suited marriage, with a fairer prospect of felicity.

It was the misfortune of my friend, however, to have embarked his property in large speculations, and he had not been married many months, when, by a succession of sudden disasters, it was swept from him, and he found himself reduced almost to penury. For a time he kept his situation to himself and went about with a haggard countenance and a breaking heart. His life was but a protracted agony, and what rendered it more insupportable was the necessity of keeping up a smile in the presence of his wife; for he could not bring himself to overwhelm her with the news. She saw, however, with the quick eyes of affection, that all was not well with him. She marked his altered looks and stifled sighs, and was not to be deceived by his sickly and vapid attempts at cheerfulness. She tasked all her sprightly powers and tender blandishments to win him back to happiness; but she only drove the arrow deeper into his soul—the more he saw cause to love her the more torturing was the thought that he was soon to make her wretched. A little while, thought he, and the smile will vanish from that cheek— the song will die away from those lips—the lustre of those eyes will be quenched with sorrow; and the happy heart which now beats lightly in that bosom, will be weighed down like mine by the cares and miseries of the world.

At length he came to me, one day, and related his whole situation in a tone of the deepest despair. When I had heard him through I enquired, "Does your wife know all this?"—at the question he burst into an agony of tears—"For God's sake!" cried he, "if you have any pity on me don't mention my wife—it is the thought of her that drives me almost to madness!"

"And why not?" said I, "she must know it sooner or later: you cannot keep it long from her, and the intelligence may break upon her in a more startling manner than if imparted by yourself; for the accents of those we love soften the harshest tidings. Besides you are depriving yourself of the comforts of her sympathy and not merely that, but also endangering the only bond that can keep hearts together, an unreserved community of thought and feeling. She will soon perceive that something is secretly preying upon your mind, and true love will not brook reserve: it feels undervalued and outraged when even the sorrows of those it loves are concealed from it."

"Oh but my friend! to think what a blow I am to give to all her future prospects—how I am to strike her very soul to the earth, by telling her that her husband is a beggar!—That she is to forego all the elegancies of life—all the pleasures of society—to shrink with me into indigence and obscurity!—To tell her that I have dragged her down from the sphere in which she might have continued to move in constant brightness—the light of every eye—the admiration of every heart!——How can she bear poverty!—she has been brought up in all the refinements of opulence.—How can she bear neglect!—she has been the idol of society—oh, it will break her heart!—it will break her heart!—"

I saw his grief was eloquent and I let it have its flow, for sorrow relieves itself by words. When his paroxysm had subsided and he had relapsed into moody silence, I resumed the subject gently, and urged him to break his situation at once to his wife. He shook his head mournfully, but positively.

"But how are you to keep it from her? It is necessary she should know it, that you may take the steps proper to the alteration of your circumstances. You must change your style of living——nay," observing a pang to pass across his countenance—"don't let that afflict you. I am sure you have never placed your happiness in outward shew—you have yet friends, warm friends, who will not think the worse of you for being less splendidly lodged;—and surely it does not require a palace to be happy with Mary—"

"I could be happy with her," cried he convulsively, "in a hovel!—I could go down with her into poverty and the dust!—I could—I could ——God bless her!—God bless her!—" cried he, bursting into a transport of grief and tenderness.

"And believe me my friend," said I stepping up and grasping him warmly by the hand—"believe me, she can be the same with you. Aye, more—it will be a source of pride and triumph to her—it will call forth all the latent energies and fervent sympathies of her nature; for she will rejoice to prove that she loves you for yourself. There is in every true woman's heart a spark of heavenly fire which lies dormant in the broad daylight of prosperity; but which kindles up, and beams and blazes in the dark hour of adversity. No man knows what the wife of his bosom is—no man knows what a ministering angel she is—until he has gone with her through the fiery trials of this world."

There was something in the earnestness of my manner, and the figurative style of my language that caught the excited imagination of Leslie. I knew the auditor I had to deal with; and following up the impression I had made, I finished by persuading him to go home and unburthen his sad heart to his wife.

I must confess, notwithstanding all I had said, I felt some little solicitude for the result. Who can calculate on the fortitude of one whose whole life has been a round of pleasures?—Her gay spirits might revolt at the dark downward path of low humility suddenly pointed out before her, and might cling to the sunny regions in which they had hitherto revelled. Besides, ruin in fashionable life is accompanied by so many galling mortifications to which in other ranks it is a stranger—in short, I could not meet Leslie the next morning without trepidation. He had made the disclosure.

—"And how did she bear it?"

"Like an angel! It seemed rather to be a relief to her mind, for she threw her arms round my neck, and asked if this was all that had lately made me unhappy—but, poor girl,"—added he, "she cannot realize the change we must undergo. She has no idea of poverty but in the abstract—she has only read of it in poetry, where it is allied to love. She feels as yet no privation—she suffers no loss of accustomed conveniences nor elegancies. When we come practically to experience its sordid cares, its paltry wants, its petty humiliations—then will be the real trial."

"But," said I, "now that you have got over the severest task, that of breaking it to her, the sooner you let the world into the secret the better. The disclosure may be mortifying, but then it is a single misery and soon over, whereas you otherwise suffer it in anticipation, every hour in the day. It is not poverty so much as pretence, that harrasses a ruined man. The struggle between a proud mind and an empty purse—the keeping up a hollow shew that must soon come to an end. Have the courage to appear poor and you disarm poverty of its sharpest sting."— On this point I found Leslie perfectly prepared. He had no false pride himself, and as to his wife she was only anxious to conform to their altered fortunes.

Some days afterwards he called upon me in the evening. He had disposed of his dwelling house and taken a small cottage in the country, a few miles from town. He had been busied all day in sending out furniture. The new establishment required few articles, and those of the simplest kind. All the splendid furniture of his late residence had been sold excepting his wife's Harp. That, he said, was too closely associated with the idea of herself—it belonged to the little story of their loves— for some of the sweetest moments of their courtship were those when he had leant over that instrument and listened to the melting tones of her voice.—I could not but smile at this instance of romantic gallantry in a doting husband.

He was now going out to the cottage, where his wife had been all day, superintending its arrangement. My feelings had become strongly interested in the progress of this family story and as it was a fine evening I offered to accompany him.

He was wearied with the fatigues of the day, and as we walked out, fell into a fit of gloomy musing.

"Poor Mary!" at length broke with a heavy sigh from his lips.

"And what of her," asked I, "has any thing happened to her?"

"What," said he, darting an impatient glance, "is it nothing to be reduced to this paltry situation—to be caged in a miserable cottage—to be obliged to toil almost in the menial concerns of her wretched habitation?"

"Has she then repined at the change?"

"Repined!—she has been nothing but sweetness and good humour. Indeed she seems in better spirits than I have ever known her—she has been to me all love and tenderness and comfort!"

"Admirable girl!" exclaimed I. "You call yourself poor my friend; you never were so rich—you never knew the boundless treasures of excellence you possessed in that woman."

"Oh, but my friend—if this first meeting at the cottage were over— I think I could then be comfortable. But this is her first day of real experience. She has been introduced into our humble dwelling. She has been employed all day in arranging its miserable equipments. She has for the first time known the fatigues of domestic employment—She has for the first time looked around her on a home destitute of every thing elegant,—almost of every thing convenient, and may now be sitting down exhausted and spiritless, brooding over a prospect of future poverty."

There was a degree of probability in this picture that I could not gainsay—so we walked on in silence.

After turning from the main road up a narrow lane so thickly shaded by forest trees as to give it a complete air of seclusion, we came in sight of the cottage. It was humble enough in its appearance for the most pastoral poet; and yet it had a pleasing rural look. A wild vine had over run one end with a profusion of foliage—a few trees threw their branches gracefully over it, and I observed several pots of flowers tastefully disposed about the door and on the grass plot in front. A small wicket gate opened upon a foot path that wound through some shrubbery to the door. Just as we approached we heard the sound of music.—Leslie grasped my arm—we paused and listened. It was Mary's voice singing, in a style of the most touching simplicity, a little air of which her husband was peculiarly fond.

I felt Leslie's hand tremble on my arm. He stepped forward to hear more distinctly—His step made a noise on the gravel walk—a bright beautiful face glanced out at the window and vanished—a light footstep was heard, and Mary came tripping forth to meet us. She was in a pretty, rural dress of white; a few wild flowers were twisted in her fine hair; a fresh bloom was on her cheek; her whole countenance beamed with smiles—I had never seen her look so lovely.

"My dear George," cried she, "I am so glad you are come—I've been watching and watching for you; and running down the lane, and looking out for you. I've set out a table under a beautiful tree behind the cottage —and I've been gathering some of the most delicious strawberries, for I know you are fond of them—and we have such excellent cream—and every thing is so sweet and still here—Oh!" said she, putting her arm within his, and looking up brightly in his face—"oh, we shall be so happy!"

Poor Leslie was overcome—He caught her to his bosom—he folded his arms round her—he kissed her again and again—he could not speak, but the tears gushed into his eyes—And he has often assured me that though the world has since gone prosperously with him, and his life has, indeed, been a happy one; yet never has he experienced a moment of more exquisite felicity.

RIP VAN WINKLE

The following Tale was found among the papers of the late Diedrich Knickerbocker, an old gentleman of New York, who was very curious in the Dutch history of the province, and the manners of the descendants from its primitive settlers. His historical researches, however, did not lie so much among books, as among men; for the former are lamentably scanty on his favourite topics; whereas he found the old burghers, and still more, their wives, rich in that legendary lore so invaluable to true history. Whenever, therefore, he happened upon a genuine Dutch family, snugly shut up in its low roofed farm house, under a spreading sycamore, he looked upon it as a little clasped volume of black letter, and studied it with the zeal of a bookworm.

The result of all these researches was a history of the province, during the reign of the Dutch governors, which he published some years since. There have been various opinions as to the literary character of his work and, to tell the truth, it is not a whit better than it should be. Its chief merit is its scrupulous accuracy, which indeed was a little questioned on its first appearance, but has since been completely established; and it is now admitted into all historical collections as a book of unquestionable authority.

The old gentleman died shortly after the publication of his work, and now that he is dead and gone, it cannot do much harm to his memory to say that his time might have been much better employed in weightier labours. He, however, was apt to ride his hobby his own way; and though it did now and then kick up the dust a little in the eyes of his neighbours, and grieve the spirit of some friends for whom he felt the truest deference and affection; yet his errors and follies are remembered "more in sorrow than in anger," and it begins to be suspected that he never intended to injure or offend. But however his memory may be appreciated by criticks, it is still held dear by many folk whose good opinion is well worth having; particularly by certain biscuit bakers, who have gone so far as to imprint his likeness on their new year cakes, and have thus given him a chance for immortality, almost equal to being stamped on a Waterloo medal, or a Queen Anne's farthing.

RIP VAN WINKLE

A Posthumous Writing of Diedrich Knickerbocker

By Woden, God of Saxons,
From whence comes Wensday, that is Wodensday,
Truth is a thing that ever I will keep
Unto thylke day in which I creep into
My sepulchre—

CARTWRIGHT.

Whoever has made a voyage up the Hudson must remember the Kaatskill mountains. They are a dismembered branch of the great Appalachian family, and are seen away to the west of the river swelling up to noble height and lording it over the surrounding country. Every change of season, every change of weather, indeed every hour of the day, produces some change in the magical hues and shapes of these mountains, and they are regarded by all the good wives far and near as perfect barometers. When the weather is fair and settled they are clothed in blue and purple, and print their bold outlines on the clear evening sky; but sometimes, when the rest of the landscape is cloudless, they will gather a hood of grey vapours about their summits, which, in the last rays of the setting sun, will glow and light up like a crown of glory.

At the foot of these fairy mountains the voyager may have descried the light smoke curling up from a village, whose shingle roofs gleam among the trees, just where the blue tints of the upland melt away into the fresh green of the nearer landscape. It is a little village of great antiquity, having been founded by some of the Dutch colonists in the early times of the province, just about the beginning of the government of the good Peter Stuyvesant, (may he rest in peace!) and there were some of the houses of the original settlers standing within a few years; built of small yellow bricks brought from Holland, having latticed windows and gable fronts, surmounted with weathercocks.

In that same village, and in one of these very houses (which to tell the precise truth was sadly time worn and weather beaten) there lived many years since, while the country was yet a province of Great Britain, a simple good natured fellow of the name of Rip Van Winkle. He was a descendant of the Van Winkles who figured so gallantly in the chivalrous days of Peter Stuyvesant, and accompanied him to the siege of Fort Christina. He inherited, however, but little of the martial character of his ancestors. I have observed that he was a simple good natured man; he was moreover a kind neighbour, and an obedient, henpecked husband. Indeed to the latter circumstance might be owing that meekness of spirit which gained him such universal popularity; for those men are most apt to be obsequious and conciliating abroad, who are under the discipline of shrews at home. Their tempers doubtless are rendered pliant and malleable in the fiery furnace of domestic tribulation, and a curtain lecture is worth all the sermons in the world for teaching the virtues of patience and long suffering. A termagant wife may therefore in some respects be considered a tolerable blessing—and if so, Rip Van Winkle was thrice blessed.

Certain it is that he was a great favourite among all the good wives of the village, who as usual with the amiable sex, took his part in all family squabbles, and never failed, whenever they talked those matters over in their evening gossippings, to lay all the blame on Dame Van Winkle. The children of the village too would shout with joy whenever he approached. He assisted at their sports, made their play things, taught them to fly kites and shoot marbles, and told them long stories of ghosts, witches and Indians. Whenever he went dodging about the village he was surrounded by a troop of them hanging on his skirts, clambering on his back and playing a thousand tricks on him with impunity; and not a dog would bark at him throughout the neighbourhood.

The great error in Rip's composition was an insuperable aversion to all kinds of profitable labour. It could not be from the want of assiduity or perseverance; for he would sit on a wet rock, with a rod as long and heavy as a Tartar's lance, and fish all day without a murmur, even though he should not be encouraged by a single nibble. He would carry a fowling piece on his shoulder for hours together, trudging through woods, and swamps and up hill and down dale, to shoot a few squirrels or wild pigeons; he would never refuse to assist a neighbour even in the roughest toil, and was a foremost man at all country frolicks for husking Indian corn, or building stone fences; the women of the village too used to employ him to run their errands and to do such little odd jobs as their less obliging husbands would not do for them— in a word Rip was ready to attend to any body's business but his own; but as to doing family duty, and keeping his farm in order, he found it impossible.

In fact he declared it was of no use to work on his farm; it was the most pestilent little piece of ground in the whole country; every thing about it went wrong and would go wrong in spite of him. His fences were continually falling to pieces; his cow would either go astray or get among the cabbages, weeds were sure to grow quicker in his fields than any where else; the rain always made a point of setting in just as he had some outdoor work to do. So that though his patrimonial estate had dwindled away under his management, acre by acre until there was little more left than a mere patch of Indian corn and potatoes, yet it was the worst conditioned farm in the neighbourhood.

His children too were as ragged and wild as if they belonged to nobody. His son Rip, an urchin begotten in his own likeness, promised to inherit the habits with the old clothes of his father. He was generally seen trooping like a colt at his mother's heels, equipped in a pair of his father's cast off galligaskins, which he had much ado to hold up with one hand, as a fine lady does her train in bad weather.

Rip Van Winkle, however, was one of those happy mortals of foolish, well oiled dispositions, who take the world easy, eat white bread or brown, whichever can be got with least thought or trouble, and would rather starve on a penny than work for a pound. If left to himself, he would have whistled life away in perfect contentment, but his wife kept continually dinning in his ears about his idleness, his carelessness and the ruin he was bringing on his family. Morning noon and night her tongue was incessantly going, and every thing he said or did was sure to produce a torrent of household eloquence. Rip had but one way of replying to all lectures of the kind, and that by frequent use had grown into a habit. He shrugged his shoulders, shook his head, cast up his eyes, but said nothing. This, however, always provoked a fresh volley from his wife, so that he was fain to draw off his forces and take to the outside of the house—the only side which in truth belongs to a henpecked husband.

Rip's sole domestic adherent was his dog Wolf who was as much henpecked as his master, for Dame Van Winkle regarded them as companions in idleness, and even looked upon Wolf with an evil eye as the cause of his master's going so often astray. True it is, in all points of spirit befitting an honourable dog, he was as courageous an animal as ever scoured the woods—but what courage can withstand the ever during and all besetting terrors of a woman's tongue? The moment Wolf entered the house his crest fell, his tail drooped to the ground or curled between his legs, he sneaked about with a gallows air, casting many a sidelong glance at Dame Van Winkle, and at the least flourish of a broomstick or ladle he would fly to the door with yelping precipitation.

Times grew worse and worse with Rip Van Winkle as years of matrimony rolled on; a tart temper never mellows with age, and a sharp tongue is the only edged tool that grows keener with constant use. For a long while he used to console himself when driven from home, by frequenting a kind of perpetual club of the sages, philosophers and other idle personages of the village which held its sessions on a bench before a small inn, designated by a rubicund portrait of his majesty George the Third. Here they used to sit in the shade, through a long lazy summer's day, talking listlessly over village gossip, or telling endless sleepy stories about nothing. But it would have been worth any statesman's money to have heard the profound discussions that sometimes took place, when by chance an old newspaper fell into their hands from some passing traveller. How solemnly they would listen to the contents as drawled out by Derrick Van Bummel the schoolmaster, a dapper, learned little man, who was not to be daunted by the most gigantic word in the dictionary; and how sagely they would deliberate upon public events some months after they had taken place.

The opinions of this junto were completely controlled by Nicholaus Vedder, a patriarch of the village, and landlord of the inn, at the door of which he took his seat from morning till night, just moving sufficiently to avoid the sun and keep in the shade of a large tree; so that the neighbours could tell the hour by his movements as accurately as by a sun dial. It is true he was rarely heard to speak, but smoked his pipe incessantly. His adherents, however (for every great man has his adherents), perfectly understood him and knew how to gather his opinions. When any thing that was read or related displeased him, he was observed to smoke his pipe vehemently and to send forth short, frequent and angry puffs; but when pleased he would inhale the smoke slowly and tranquilly and emit it in light and placid clouds, and sometimes taking the pipe from his mouth and letting the fragrant vapour curl about his nose, would gravely nod his head in token of perfect approbation.

From even this strong hold the unlucky Rip was at length routed by his termagant wife who would suddenly break in upon the tranquility of the assemblage and call the members all to naught; nor was that august personage Nicholaus Vedder himself sacred from the daring tongue of this terrible virago, who charged him outright with encouraging her husband in habits of idleness.

Poor Rip was at last reduced almost to despair; and his only alternative to escape from the labour of the farm and the clamour of his wife, was to take gun in hand and stroll away into the woods. Here he would sometimes seat himself at the foot of a tree and share the contents of his wallet with Wolf, with whom he sympathised as a fellow sufferer in persecution. "Poor Wolf," he would say, "thy mistress leads thee a dog's life of it, but never mind my lad, whilst I live thou shalt never want a friend to stand by thee!" Wolf would wag his tail, look wistfully in his master's face, and if dogs can feel pity I verily believe he reciprocated the sentiment with all his heart.

In a long ramble of the kind on a fine autumnal day, Rip had unconsciously scrambled to one of the highest parts of the Kaatskill mountains. He was after his favourite sport of squirrel shooting and the still solitudes had echoed and re-echoed with the reports of his gun. Panting and fatigued he threw himself, late in the afternoon, on a green knoll, covered with mountain herbage, that crowned the brow of a precipice. From an opening between the trees he could overlook all the lower country for many a mile of rich woodland. He saw at a distance the lordly Hudson, far, far below him, moving on its silent but majestic course, with the reflection of a purple cloud, or the sail of a lagging bark here and there sleeping on its glassy bosom, and at last losing itself in the blue highlands.

On the other side he looked down into a deep mountain glen, wild, lonely and shagged, the bottom filled with fragments from the impending cliffs and scarcely lighted by the reflected rays of the setting sun. For some time Rip lay musing on this scene, evening was gradually advancing, the mountains began to throw their long blue shadows over the valleys, he saw that it would be dark, long before he could reach the village, and he heaved a heavy sigh when he thought of encountering the terrors of Dame Van Winkle.

As he was about to descend he heard a voice from a distance hallooing "Rip Van Winkle! Rip Van Winkle!" He looked around, but could see nothing but a crow winging its solitary flight across the mountain. He thought his fancy must have deceived him and turned again to descend, when he heard the same cry ring through the still evening air: "Rip Van Winkle! Rip Van Winkle!"—at the same time Wolf bristled up his back and giving a low growl, skulked to his master's side, looking fearfully down into the glen. Rip now felt a vague apprehension stealing over him; he looked anxiously in the same direction and perceived a strange figure slowly toiling up the rocks and bending under the weight of something he carried on his back. He was surprised to see any human being in this lonely and unfrequented place, but supposing it to be some one of the neighbourhood in need of his assistance he hastened down to yield it.

On nearer approach he was still more surprised at the singularity of the stranger's appearance. He was a short, square built old fellow, with thick bushy hair and a grizzled beard. His dress was of the antique Dutch fashion, a cloth jerkin strapped round the waist, several pair of breeches, the outer one of ample volume decorated with rows of buttons down the sides and bunches at the knees. He bore on his shoulder a stout keg that seemed full of liquor, and made signs for Rip to approach and assist him with the load. Though rather shy and distrustful of this new acquaintance Rip complied with his usual alacrity, and mutually relieving each other they clambered up a narrow gully apparently the dry bed of a mountain torrent. As they ascended Rip every now and then heard long rolling peals like distant thunder, that seemed to issue out of a deep ravine or rather cleft between lofty rocks, toward which their rugged path conducted. He paused for an instant, but supposing it to be the muttering of one of those transient thunder showers which often take place in mountain heights, he proceeded. Passing through the ravine they came to a hollow like a small amphitheatre, surrounded by perpendicular precipices, over the brinks of which impending trees shot their branches, so that you only caught glimpses of the azure sky and the bright evening cloud. During the whole time Rip and his companion had laboured on in silence, for though the former marvelled greatly what could be the object of carrying a keg of liquor up this wild mountain, yet there was something strange and incomprehensible about the unknown, that inspired awe and checked familiarity.

On entering the amphitheatre new objects of wonder presented themselves. On a level spot in the centre was a company of odd looking personages playing at ninepins. They were dressed in a quaint outlandish fashion—some wore short doublets, others jerkins with long knives in their belts and most of them had enormous breeches of similar style with that of the guide's. Their visages too were peculiar. One had a large head, broad face and small piggish eyes. The face of another seemed to consist entirely of nose, and was surmounted by a white sugarloaf hat, set off with a little red cock's tail. They all had beards of various shapes and colours. There was one who seemed to be the Commander. He was a stout old gentleman, with a weatherbeaten countenance. He wore a laced doublet, broad belt and hanger, high crowned hat and feather, red stockings and high heel'd shoes with roses in them. The whole group reminded Rip of the figures in an old Flemish painting, in the parlour of Dominie Van Schaick the village parson, and which had been brought over from Holland at the time of the settlement.

What seemed particularly odd to Rip was, that though these folks were evidently amusing themselves, yet they maintained the gravest faces, the most mysterious silence, and were, withal, the most melancholy party of pleasure he had ever witnessed. Nothing interrupted the stillness of the scene, but the noise of the balls, which, whenever they were rolled, echoed along the mountains like rumbling peals of thunder.

As Rip and his companion approached them they suddenly desisted from their play and stared at him with such fixed statue like gaze, and such strange uncouth, lack lustre countenances, that his heart turned within him, and his knees smote together. His companion now emptied the contents of the keg into large flagons and made signs to him to wait upon the company. He obeyed with fear and trembling; they quaffed the liquor in profound silence and then returned to their game.

By degrees Rip's awe and apprehension subsided. He even ventured, when no eye was fixed upon him, to taste the beverage, which he found had much of the flavour of excellent hollands. He was naturally a

thirsty soul and was soon tempted to repeat the draught. One taste provoked another, and he reiterated his visits to the flagon so often that
at length his senses were overpowered, his eyes swam in his head—
his head gradually declined and he fell into a deep sleep.

On awaking he found himself on the green knoll from whence he
had first seen the old man of the glen. He rubbed his eyes—it was a
bright, sunny morning. The birds were hopping and twittering among the
bushes, and the eagle was wheeling aloft and breasting the pure
mountain breeze. "Surely," thought Rip, "I have not slept here all
night." He recalled the occurrences before he fell asleep. The strange
man with a keg of liquor—the mountain ravine—the wild retreat among
the rocks—the woe begone party at ninepins—the flagon—"ah! that flagon!
that wicked flagon!" thought Rip—"what excuse shall I make to Dame
Van Winkle?"

He looked round for his gun, but in place of the clean well oiled
fowling piece he found an old firelock lying by him, the barrel encrusted
with rust; the lock falling off and the stock worm eaten. He now suspected that the grave roysters of the mountain had put a trick upon
him, and having dosed him with liquor, had robbed him of his gun.
Wolf too had disappeared, but he might have strayed away after a
squirrel or partridge. He whistled after him and shouted his name—
but all in vain; the echoes repeated his whistle and shout, but no dog
was to be seen.

He determined to revisit the scene of the last evening's gambol, and if
he met with any of the party, to demand his dog and gun. As he
arose to walk he found himself stiff in the joints and wanting in his usual
activity. "These mountain beds do not agree with me," thought Rip, "and
if this frolick should lay me up with a fit of the rheumatism, I shall
have a blessed time with Dame Van Winkle." With some difficulty he
got down into the glen; he found the gully up which he and his companion had ascended the preceding evening, but to his astonishment a
mountain stream was now foaming down it; leaping from rock to rock,
and filling the glen with babbling murmurs. He, however, made shift
to scramble up its sides working his toilsome way through thickets of
birch, sassafras and witch hazel, and sometimes tripped up or entangled
by the wild grape vines that twisted their coils and tendrils from tree
to tree, and spread a kind of net work in his path.

At length he reached to where the ravine had opened through the
cliffs, to the amphitheatre—but no traces of such opening remained. The
rocks presented a high impenetrable wall over which the torrent came
tumbling in a sheet of feathery foam, and fell into a broad deep basin
black from the shadows of the surrounding forest. Here then poor Rip
was brought to a stand. He again called and whistled after his dog—

he was only answered by the cawing of a flock of idle crows, sporting high in air about a dry tree that overhung a sunny precipice; and who, secure in their elevation seemed to look down and scoff at the poor man's perplexities.

What was to be done? The morning was passing away and Rip felt famished for want of his breakfast. He grieved to give up his dog and gun; he dreaded to meet his wife; but it would not do to starve among the mountains. He shook his head, shouldered the rusty fire lock and with a heart full of trouble and anxiety, turned his steps homeward.

As he approached the village he met a number of people, but none whom he knew, which somewhat surprised him, for he had thought himself acquainted with every one in the country round. Their dress too was of a different fashion from that to which he was accustomed. They all stared at him with equal marks of surprise, and whenever they cast their eyes upon him, invariably stroked their chins. The constant recurrence of this gesture induced Rip involuntarily to do the same, when to his astonishment he found his beard had grown a foot long!

He had now entered the skirts of the village. A troop of strange children ran at his heels, hooting after him and pointing at his grey beard. The dogs too, not one of which he recognized for an old acquaintance, barked at him as he passed. The very village was altered —it was larger and more populous. There were rows of houses which he had never seen before, and those which had been his familiar haunts had disappeared. Strange names were over the doors—strange faces at the windows—every thing was strange. His mind now misgave him; he began to doubt whether both he and the world around him were not bewitched. Surely this was his native village which he had left but the day before. There stood the Kaatskill mountains—there ran the silver Hudson at a distance—there was every hill and dale precisely as it had always been—Rip was sorely perplexed—"That flagon last night," thought he, "has addled my poor head sadly!"

It was with some difficulty that he found the way to his own house, which he approached with silent awe, expecting every moment to hear the shrill voice of Dame Van Winkle. He found the house gone to decay—the roof fallen in, the windows shattered and the doors off the hinges. A half starved dog that looked like Wolf was skulking about it. Rip called him by name but the cur snarled, shewed his teeth and passed on. This was an unkind cut indeed—"My very dog," sighed poor Rip, "has forgotten me!"

He entered the house, which, to tell the truth, Dame Van Winkle had always kept in neat order. It was empty, forlorn and apparently abandoned. This desolateness overcame all his connubial fears—he called loudly for his wife and children—the lonely chambers rung for a moment with his voice, and then all again was silence.

He now hurried forth and hastened to his old resort, the village inn—but it too was gone. A large, ricketty wooden building stood in its place, with great gaping windows, some of them broken, and mended with old hats and petticoats, and over the door was printed "The Union Hotel, by Jonathan Doolittle." Instead of the great tree, that used to shelter the quiet little Dutch inn of yore, there now was reared a tall naked pole with something on top that looked like a red night cap, and from it was fluttering a flag on which was a singular assemblage of stars and stripes—all this was strange and incomprehensible. He recognized on the sign, however, the ruby face of King George under which he had smoked so many a peaceful pipe, but even this was singularly metamorphosed. The red coat was changed for one of blue and buff; a sword was held in the hand instead of a sceptre; the head was decorated with a cocked hat, and underneath was printed in large characters GENERAL WASHINGTON.

There was as usual a crowd of folk about the door; but none that Rip recollected. The very character of the people seemed changed. There was a busy, bustling disputatious tone about it, instead of the accustomed phlegm and drowsy tranquility. He looked in vain for the sage Nicholaus Vedder with his broad face, double chin and fair long pipe, uttering clouds of tobacco smoke instead of idle speeches. Or Van Bummel the schoolmaster doling forth the contents of an ancient newspaper. In place of these a lean bilious looking fellow with his pockets full of hand bills, was haranguing vehemently about rights of citizens—elections—members of Congress—liberty—Bunker's hill—heroes of seventy six—and other words which were a perfect babylonish jargon to the bewildered Van Winkle.

The appearance of Rip with his long grizzled beard, his rusty fowling piece his uncouth dress and an army of women and children at his heels soon attracted the attention of the tavern politicians. They crowded around him eying him from head to foot, with great curiosity. The orator bustled up to him, and drawing him partly aside, enquired "on which side he voted?"—Rip stared in vacant stupidity. Another short but busy little fellow, pulled him by the arm and rising on tiptoe, enquired in his ear "whether he was Federal or Democrat?"—Rip was equally at a loss to comprehend the question—when a knowing, self important old gentleman, in a sharp cocked hat, made his way through the crowd, putting them to the right and left with his elbows as he passed, and planting himself before Van Winkle, with one arm akimbo, the other resting on his cane, his keen eyes and sharp hat penetrating as it were into his very soul, demanded in an austere tone—"what brought him to the election with a gun on his shoulder and a mob at his heels, and whether he meant to breed a riot in the village?"—"Alas gentlemen," cried Rip, somewhat dismayed, "I am a poor quiet man, a native of the place, and a loyal subject of the King—God bless him!"

Here a general shout burst from the byestanders—"A tory! a tory! a spy! a Refugee! hustle him! away with him!"—It was with great difficulty that the self important man in the cocked hat restored order; and having assumed a ten fold austerity of brow demanded again of the unknown culprit, what he came there for and whom he was seeking. The poor man humbly assured him that he meant no harm; but merely came there in search of some of his neighbours, who used to keep about the tavern.

"—Well—who are they?—name them."

Rip bethought himself a moment and enquired, "Where's Nicholaus Vedder?"

There was a silence for a little while, when an old man replied, in a thin, piping voice, "Nicholaus Vedder? why he is dead and gone these eighteen years! There was a wooden tombstone in the church yard that used to tell all about him, but that's rotted and gone too."

"Where's Brom Dutcher?"

"Oh he went off to the army in the beginning of the war; some say he was killed at the storming of Stoney Point—others say he was drowned in a squall at the foot of Antony's Nose—I don't know—he never came back again."

"Where's Van Bummel the schoolmaster?"

"He went off to the wars too—was a great militia general, and is now in Congress."

Rip's heart died away at hearing of these sad changes in his home and friends, and finding himself thus alone in the world—every answer puzzled him too by treating of such enormous lapses of time and of matters which he could not understand—war—Congress, Stoney Point— he had no courage to ask after any more friends, but cried out in despair, "Does nobody here know Rip Van Winkle?"

"Oh. Rip Van Winkle?" exclaimed two or three—"oh to be sure!— that's Rip Van Winkle—yonder—leaning against the tree."

Rip looked and beheld a precise counterpart of himself, as he went up the mountain: apparently as lazy and certainly as ragged! The poor fellow was now completely confounded. He doubted his own identity, and whether he was himself or another man. In the midst of his bewilderment the man in the cocked hat demanded who he was,— what was his name?

"God knows," exclaimed he, at his wit's end, "I'm not myself.—I'm somebody else—that's me yonder—no—that's somebody else got into

my shoes—I was myself last night; but I fell asleep on the mountain—
and they've changed my gun—and every thing's changed—and I'm
changed—and I can't tell what's my name, or who I am!"

The byestanders began now to look at each other, nod, wink signifi-
cantly and tap their fingers against their foreheads. There was a
whisper also about securing the gun, and keeping the old fellow from
doing mischief—at the very suggestion of which, the self important man
in the cocked hat retired with some precipitation. At this critical
moment a fresh likely looking woman pressed through the throng to get
a peep at the greybearded man. She had a chubby child in her arms,
which frightened at his looks began to cry. "Hush Rip," cried she, "hush
you little fool, the old man won't hurt you." The name of the child, the
air of the mother, the tone of her voice all awakened a train of
recollections in his mind. "What is your name my good woman?"
asked he.

"Judith Gardenier."

"And your father's name?"

"Ah, poor man, Rip Van Winkle was his name, but it's twenty years
since he went away from home with his gun and never has been
heard of since—his dog came home without him—but whether he shot
himself, or was carried away by the Indians no body can tell. I was
then but a little girl."

Rip had but one question more to ask, but he put it with a faltering
voice—

"Where's your mother?"—

Oh she too had died but a short time since—she broke a blood vessel
in a fit of passion at a New England pedlar.—

There was a drop of comfort at least in this intelligence. The honest
man could contain himself no longer—he caught his daughter and her
child in his arms.—"I am your father!" cried he—"Young Rip Van Winkle
once—old Rip Van Winkle now!—does nobody know poor Rip Van
Winkle!"

All stood amazed, until an old woman tottering out from among the
crowd put her hand to her brow and peering under it in his face for
a moment exclaimed—"Sure enough!—it is Rip Van Winkle—it is himself—welcome home again old neighbour—why, where have you been
these twenty long years?"

Rip's story was soon told, for the whole twenty years had been to him
but as one night. The neighbours stared when they heard it; some were
seen to wink at each other and put their tongues in their cheeks, and
the self important man in the cocked hat, who when the alarm was
over had returned to the field, screwed down the corners of his mouth

and shook his head—upon which there was a general shaking of the head throughout the assemblage.

It was determined, however, to take the opinion of old Peter Vanderdonk, who was seen slowly advancing up the road. He was a descendant of the historian of that name, who wrote one of the earliest accounts of the province. Peter was the most ancient inhabitant of the village and well versed in all the wonderful events and traditions of the neighbourhood. He recollected Rip at once, and corroborated his story in the most satisfactory manner. He assured the company that it was a fact handed down from his ancestor the historian, that the Kaatskill mountains had always been haunted by strange beings. That it was affirmed that the great Hendrick Hudson, the first discoverer of the river and country, kept a kind of vigil there every twenty years, with his crew of the Half Moon—being permitted in this way to revisit the scenes of his enterprize and keep a guardian eye upon the river and the great city called by his name. That his father had once seen them in their old Dutch dresses playing at nine pins in a hollow of the mountain; and that he himself had heard one summer afternoon the sound of their balls, like distant peals of thunder.

To make a long story short—the company broke up, and returned to the more important concerns of the election. Rip's daughter took him home to live with her; she had a snug well furnished house, and a stout cheery farmer for a husband whom Rip recollected for one of the urchins that used to climb upon his back. As to Rip's son and heir, who was the ditto of himself seen leaning against the tree; he was employed to work on the farm; but evinced an hereditary disposition to attend to any thing else but his business.

Rip now resumed his old walks and habits; he soon found many of his former cronies, though all rather the worse for the wear and tear of time; and preferred making friends among the rising generation, with whom he soon grew into great favour. Having nothing to do at home, and being arrived at that happy age when a man can be idle, with impunity, he took his place once more on the bench at the inn door and was reverenced as one of the patriarchs of the village and a chronicle of the old times "before the war." It was some time before he could get into the regular track of gossip, or could be made to comprehend the strange events that had taken place during his torpor. How that there had been a revolutionary war—that the country had thrown off the yoke of Old England and that instead of being a subject of his majesty George the Third, he was now a free citizen of the United States. Rip in fact was no politician; the changes of states and empires made but little impression on him; but there was one species of despotism under which he had long groaned and that was petticoat government. Happily that was at an end—he had got his neck out of the yoke of matrimony, and could go in and out whenever he pleased without dreading the tyranny of Dame Van Winkle. Whenever her name was mentioned, however, he shook his head, shrugged his shoulders and cast up his eyes; which might pass either for an expression of resignation to his fate or joy at his deliverance.

He used to tell his story to every stranger that arrived at Mr. Doolittle's Hotel. He was observed at first to vary on some points, every time he told it, which was doubtless owing to his having so recently awaked. It at last settled down precisely to the tale I have related and not a man woman or child in the neighbourhood but knew it by heart. Some always pretended to doubt the reality of it, and insisted that Rip had been out of his head, and that this was one point on which he always remained flighty. The old Dutch inhabitants, however, almost universally gave it full credit—Even to this day they never hear a thunder storm of a summer afternoon about the Kaatskill, but they say Hendrick Hudson and his crew are at their game of nine pins; and it is a common wish of all henpecked husbands in the neighbourhood, when life hangs heavy on their hands, that they might have a quieting draught out of Rip Van Winkle's flagon.

NOTE

The foregoing tale one would suspect had been suggested to Mr. Knickerbocker by a little German superstition about the emperor Frederick *der Rothbart* and the Kypphauser Mountain; the subjoined note, however, which he had appended to the tale, shews that it is an absolute fact, narrated with his usual fidelity.—

"The story of Rip Van Winkle may seem incredible to many, but nevertheless I give it my full belief, for I know the vicinity of our old Dutch settlements to have been very subject to marvellous events and appearances. Indeed I have heard many stranger stories than this, in the villages along the Hudson; all of which were too well authenticated to admit of a doubt. I have even talked with Rip Van Winkle myself, who when last I saw him was a very venerable old man and so perfectly rational and consistent on every other point, that I think no conscientious person could refuse to take this into the bargain—nay I have seen a certificate on the subject taken before a country justice and signed with a cross in the justice's own hand writing. The story therefore is beyond the possibility of doubt. D.K."

POSTSCRIPT

The following are travelling notes from a memorandum book of Mr. Knickerbocker.

The Kaatsberg or Catskill mountains have always been a region full of fable. The Indians considered them the abode of spirits who influenced the weather, spreading sunshine or clouds over the landscape and sending good or bad hunting seasons. They were ruled by an old squaw spirit, said to be their mother. She dwelt on the highest peak of the Catskills and had charge of the doors of day and night to open and shut them at the proper hour. She hung up the new moons in the skies and cut up the old ones into stars. In times of drought, if properly propitiated, she would spin light summer clouds out of cobwebs and morning dew, and send them off, from the crest of the mountain, flake after flake, like flakes of carded cotton to float in the air: until, dissolved by the heat of the sun, they would fall in gentle showers, causing the grass to spring, the fruits to ripen and the corn to grow an inch an hour. If displeased, however, she would brew up clouds black as ink, sitting in the midst of them like a bottle bellied spider in the midst of its web; and when these clouds broke—woe betide the valleys!

In old times say the Indian traditions, there was a kind of Manitou or Spirit, who kept about the wildest recesses of the Catskill mountains, and took a mischievous pleasure in wreaking all kinds of evils and vexations upon the red men. Sometimes he would assume the form of a bear a panther or a deer, lead the bewildered hunter a weary chace through tangled forests and among rugged rocks; and then spring off with a loud ho! ho! leaving him aghast on the brink of a beetling precipice or raging torrent.

The favorite abode of this Manitou is still shewn. It is a great rock or cliff in the loneliest part of the mountains, and, from the flowering vines which clamber about it, and the wild flowers which abound in its neighborhood, is known by the name of the Garden Rock. Near the foot of it is a small lake the haunt of the solitary bittern, with water snakes basking in the sun on the leaves of the pond lillies which lie on the surface. This place was held in great awe by the Indians, insomuch that the boldest hunter would not pursue his game within its precincts. Once upon a time, however, a hunter who had lost his way, penetrated to the garden rock where he beheld a number of gourds placed in the crotches of trees. One of these he seized and made off with it, but in the hurry of his retreat he let it fall among the rocks, when a great stream gushed forth which washed him away and swept him down precipices where he was dashed to pieces, and the stream made its way to the Hudson and continues to flow to the present day; being the identical stream known by the name of the Kaaters-kill.

ENGLISH WRITERS ON AMERICA

Methinks I see in my mind a noble and puissant nation rousing herself, like a strong man after sleep, and shaking her invincible locks:
methinks I see her as an eagle mewing her mighty youth, and kindling
her endazzled eyes at the full midday beam.

MILTON, ON THE LIBERTY OF THE PRESS.

It is with feelings of deep regret that I observe the literary animosity
daily growing up between England and America. Great curiosity has
been awakened of late with respect to the United States, and the London
press has teemed with volumes of travels through the republic; but they
seem intended to diffuse error rather than knowledge; and so successful
have they been, that, notwithstanding the constant intercourse between
the nations, there is no people concerning whom the great mass of the
British public have less pure information, or entertain more numerous
prejudices.

English travellers are the best, and the worst in the world. Where no
motives of pride or interest intervene, none can equal them for profound
and philosophical views of society, or faithful, and graphical descriptions of external objects; but when either the interest or reputation of
their own country comes in collision with that of another, they go to
the opposite extreme, and forget their usual probity and candour in the
indulgence of splenetic remark and an illiberal spirit of ridicule.

Hence their travels are more honest and accurate the more remote
the country described. I would place implicit confidence in an Englishman's description of the regions beyond the cataracts of the Nile; of
unknown islands in the Yellow Sea; of the interior of India, or of any
other tract which other travellers might be apt to picture out with the
illusions of their fancies; but I would cautiously receive his account of
his immediate neighbours, and of those nations with which he is in
habits of most frequent intercourse. However I might be disposed to
trust his probity I dare not trust his prejudices.

It has also been the peculiar lot of our country to be visited by the
worst kind of English travellers. While men of philosophical spirit and
cultivated minds have been sent from England to ransack the poles, to
penetrate the deserts, and to study the manners and customs of
barbarous nations, with which she can have no permanent intercourse
of profit or pleasure; it has been left to the broken down tradesman,
the scheming adventurer, the wandering mechanic, the Manchester and
Birmingham agent, to be her oracles respecting America. From such
sources she is content to receive her information respecting a country

in a singular state of moral and physical development; a country in which one of the greatest political experiments in the history of the world is now performing, and which presents the most profound and momentous studies to the statesman and the philosopher.

That such men should give prejudiced accounts of America is not a matter of surprize. The themes it offers for contemplation are too vast and elevated for their capacities. The national character is yet in a state of fermentation: it may have its frothings and sediment, but its ingredients are sound and wholesome; it has already given proofs of powerful and generous qualities, and the whole promises to settle down into something substantially excellent. But the causes which are operating to strengthen and ennoble it, and its daily indications of admirable properties, are all lost upon these pur-blind observers; who are only affected by the little asperities incident to its present situation. They are capable of judging only of the surface of things; of those matters which come in contact with their private interests and personal gratifications. They miss some of the snug conveniences and petty comforts which belong to an old, highly finished, and overpopulous state of society, where the ranks of useful labour are crowded, and many earn a painful and servile subsistence, by studying the very caprices of appetite and self indulgence. These minor comforts, however, are all important in the estimation of narrow minds, which either do not perceive, or will not acknowledge, that they are more than counterbalanced among us, by great and generally diffused blessings.

They may, perhaps, have been disappointed in some unreasonable expectation of sudden gain. They may have pictured America to themselves, an El Dorado, where gold and silver abounded, and the natives were lacking in sagacity; and where they were to become strangely and suddenly rich, in some unforeseen, but easy manner. The same weakness of mind that indulges absurd expectations, produces petulance in disappointment. Such persons become embittered against the country on finding that there, as every where else, a man must sow before he can reap; must win wealth by industry and talent; and must contend with the common difficulties of nature, and the shrewdness of an intelligent and enterprizing people.

Perhaps, through mistaken, or ill directed hospitality, or from the prompt disposition to cheer and countenance the stranger, prevalent among my countrymen, they may have been treated with unwonted respect in America; and having been accustomed all their lives to consider themselves below the surface of good society; and brought up in a servile feeling of inferiority; they become arrogant on the common boon of civility; they attribute to the lowliness of others, their own elevation; and under rate a society, where there are no artificial distinctions, and where, by any chance, such individuals as themselves can rise to consequence.

One would suppose, however, that information coming from such sources, on a subject where the truth is so desirable, would be received with caution by the censors of the press. That the motives of these men, their veracity, their opportunities of enquiry and observation and their capacities for judging correctly would be rigorously scrutinized, before their evidence was admitted in such sweeping extent, against a kindred nation. The very reverse, however, is the case, and it furnishes a striking instance of human inconsistency. Nothing can surpass the vigilance with which English critics will examine the credibility of the traveller, who publishes an account of some distant, and comparatively unimportant, country. How warily will they compare the measurements of a pyramid, or the descriptions of a ruin, and how sternly will they censure any inaccuracy in these contributions of merely curious knowledge; while they will receive, with eagerness and unhesitating faith, the gross misrepresentations of coarse and obscure writers, concerning a country with which their own is placed in the most important and delicate relations. Nay, they will even make these apocryphal volumes text books, on which to enlarge, with a zeal and an ability worthy of a more generous cause.

I shall not, however, dwell on this irksome and hackney'd topic; nor should I have adverted to it but for the undue interest apparently taken in it by my countrymen, and certain injurious effects, which I apprehended it might produce upon the national feeling. We attach too much consequence to these attacks. They cannot do us any essential injury. The tissue of misrepresentations attempted to be woven round us are like cobwebs, woven round the limbs of an infant giant. Our country continually outgrows them. One falsehood after another falls off of itself. We have but to live on, and every day we live a whole volume of refutation. All the writers of England united, if we could for a moment suppose their great minds stooping to so unworthy a combination, could not conceal our rapidly growing importance and matchless prosperity. They could not conceal that these are owing, not merely to physical and local, but also to moral causes. To the political liberty, the general diffusion of knowledge, the prevalence of sound moral and religious principles, which give force and sustained energy to the character of a people; and which, in fact have been the acknowledged and wonderful supporters of their own national power and glory.

But why are we so exquisitely alive to the aspersions of England? Why do we suffer ourselves to be so affected by the contumely she has endeavoured to cast upon us? It is not in the opinion of England alone that honor lives and reputation has its being. The world at large is the arbiter of a nation's fame; with its thousand eyes it witnesses a nation's deeds, and from their collective testimony is national glory or national disgrace established.

For ourselves, therefore, it is comparatively of but little importance whether England does us justice or not—it is perhaps of far more importance to herself. She is instilling anger and resentment into the bosom of a youthful nation, to grow with its growth and strengthen with its strength. If in America, as some of her writers are labouring to convince her, she is hereafter to find an invidious rival and a gigantic foe, she may thank those very writers, for having provoked rivalship, and irritated hostility. Every one knows the all pervading influence of literature at the present day, and how much the opinions and passions of mankind are under its control. The mere contests of the sword are temporary; their wounds are but in the flesh, and it is the pride of the generous to forgive and forget them: but the slanders of the pen pierce to the heart; they rankle longest in the noblest spirits; they dwell ever present in the mind; and render it morbidly sensitive to the most trifling collision. It is but seldom that any one overt act produces hostilities between two nations; there exists, most commonly, a previous jealousy and ill will; a predisposition to take offence. Trace these to their cause, and how often will they be found to originate in the mischievous effusions of mercenary writers, who, secure in their closets, and for ignominious bread, concoct and circulate the venom, that is to inflame the generous and the brave.

I am not laying too much stress upon this point; for it applies most emphatically to our particular case. Over no nation does the press hold a more absolute control than over the people of America; for the universal education of the poorest classes, makes every individual a reader. There is nothing published in England on the subject of our country that does not circulate through every part of it. There is not a calumny dropt from an English pen, nor an unworthy sarcasm uttered by an English statesman, that does not go to blight good will and add to the mass of latent resentment. Possessing then as England does, the fountain head from whence the literature of the language flows, how completely is it in her power, and how truly is it her duty, to make it the medium of amiable and magnanimous feeling—a stream where the two nations might meet together and drink in peace and kindness. Should she, however, persist in turning it to waters of bitterness, the time may come when she may repent her folly. The present friendship of America may be of but little moment to her; but the future destinies of that country do not admit of a doubt; over those of England there lower some shadows of uncertainty. Should then a day of gloom arrive; should those reverses overtake her, from which the proudest empires have not been exempt, she may look back with regret at her infatuation, in repulsing from her side a nation she might have grappled to her bosom, and thus destroying her only chance for real friendship beyond the boundaries of her own dominions.

There is a general impression in England that the people of the United States are inimical to the parent country. It is one of the errors which has been diligently propagated by designing writers. There is doubtless considerable political hostility, and a general soreness at the illiberality of the English press, but, generally speaking, the prepossessions of the people are strongly in favour of England. Indeed at one time they amounted, in many parts of the union, to an absurd degree of bigotry. The bare name of Englishman was a passport to the confidence and hospitality of every family, and too often gave a transient currency to the worthless and the ungrateful. Throughout the country there was something of enthusiasm connected with the idea of England. We looked to it with a hallowed feeling of tenderness and veneration as the land of our forefathers—the august repository of the monuments and antiquities of our race—the birth place and mausoleum of the sages and heroes of our paternal history. After our own country there was none in whose glory we more delighted—none whose good opinion we were more anxious to possess—none towards which our hearts yearned with such throbbings of warm consanguinity. Even during the late war, whenever there was the least opportunity for kind feelings to spring forth it was the delight of the generous spirits of our country to shew that in the midst of hostilities they still kept alive the sparks of future friendship.

Is all this to be at an end? Is this golden band of kindred sympathies, so rare between nations, to be broken forever?—Perhaps it is for the best —It may dispel an illusion which might have kept us in mental vassallage; which might have interfered occasionally with our true interests, and prevented the growth of proper national pride. But it is hard to give up the kindred tie!—and there are feelings dearer than interest—closer to the heart than pride—that will still make us cast back a look of regret, as we wander farther and farther from the paternal roof, and lament the waywardness of the parent, that would repel the affections of the child.

Short sighted and injudicious, however, as the conduct of England may be in this system of aspersion, recrimination on our part would be equally ill judged. I speak not of prompt and spirited vindication of our country, nor the keenest castigation of her slanderers—but I allude to a disposition to retaliate in kind; to retort sarcasm and inspire prejudice, which seems to be spreading widely among our writers. Let us guard particularly against such a temper, for it would double the evil instead of redressing the wrong. Nothing is so easy and inviting as the retort of abuse and sarcasm; but it is a paltry and an unprofitable contest. It is the alternative of a morbid mind fretted into petulance rather than warmed into indignation. If England is willing to permit the mean jealousies of trade or the rancorous animosities of politics to deprave the integrity of her press, and poison the fountain of public opinion, let us beware of her example. She may deem it her interest to diffuse error and engender antipathy, for the purpose of checking emigration; we have no purpose of the kind to serve. Neither have we any spirit of national jealousy to gratify, for as yet, in all our rivalships with England we are the rising and the gaining party. There can be no end to answer, therefore, but the gratification of resentment; a mere spirit of retaliation, and even that is impotent. Our retorts are never republished in England; they fall short, therefore, of their aim—but they foster a querulous and peevish temper among our writers—they sour the sweet flow of our early literature, and sow thorns and brambles among its blossoms. What is still worse they circulate through our own country, and, as far as they have effect, excite virulent national prejudices. This last is the evil most especially to be deprecated. Governed as we are entirely by public opinion, the utmost care should be taken to preserve the purity of the public mind. Knowledge is power, and truth is knowledge; whoever therefore knowingly propagates a prejudice, wilfully saps the foundation of his country's strength.

The members of a republic, above all other men, should be candid and dispassionate. They are individually portions of the sovereign mind and sovereign will, and should be enabled to come to all questions of national concern with calm and unbiassed judgements. From the peculiar nature of our relations with England, we must have more frequent questions of a difficult and delicate character with her, than with any other nation; questions that affect the most acute and excitable feelings; and as in the adjusting of these, our national measures must ultimately be determined by popular sentiment, we cannot be too anxiously attentive to purify it from all latent passion or prepossession.

Opening too, as we do, an asylum for strangers from every portion of the earth, we should receive all with impartiality. It should be our pride to exhibit an example of one nation at least, destitute of national antipathies, and exercising, not merely the overt acts of hospitality but those more rare and noble courtesies which spring from liberality of opinion.

What have we to do with national prejudices? They are the inveterate diseases of old countries, contracted in rude and ignorant ages, when nations knew but little of each other, and looked beyond their own boundaries with distrust and hostility. We, on the contrary, have sprung into national existence in an enlightened and philosophic age; when the different parts of the habitable world, and the various branches of the human family, have been indefatigably studied and made known to each other; and we forego the advantages of our birth, if we do not shake off the national prejudices, as we would the local superstitions, of the old world.

But above all, let us not be influenced by any angry feelings so far as to shut our eyes to the perception of what is really excellent and amiable in the English character. We are a young people, necessarily an imitative one, and must take our examples and models, in a great degree, from the existing nations of Europe. There is no country more worthy of our study than England. The spirit of her constitution is most analogous to ours. The manners of her people,—their intellectual activity —their freedom of opinion—their habits of thinking on those subjects which concern the dearest interests and most sacred charities of private life, are all congenial to the American character; and in fact are all intrinsically excellent: for it is in the moral feeling of the people that the deep foundations of British prosperity are laid; and however the superstructure may be time worn, or over run by abuses, there must be something solid in the basis, admirable in the materials, and stable in the structure of an edifice that so long has towered unshaken amidst the tempests of the world.

Let it be the pride of our writers, therefore, discarding all feelings of irritation and disdaining to retaliate the illiberality of British authors, to speak of the English nation without prejudice, and with determined candour. While they rebuke the undiscriminating bigotry with which some of our countrymen admire and imitate every thing english, merely because it is english, let them frankly point out what is really worthy of approbation. We may thus place England before us as a perpetual volume of reference, wherein are recorded sound deductions from ages of experience; and while we avoid the errors and absurdities which may have crept into the page, we may draw from thence golden maxims of practical wisdom, wherewith to strengthen and to embellish our national character.

RURAL LIFE IN ENGLAND

Oh! friendly to the best pursuits of man,
Friendly to thought, to virtue and to peace,
Domestic life in rural pleasure pass'd!

COWPER.

The stranger who would form a correct opinion of the English character must not confine his observations to the metropolis. He must go forth into the country; he must sojourn in villages and hamlets; he must visit castles, villas, farm houses, cottages; he must wander through parks and gardens; along hedges and green lanes; he must loiter about country churches, attend wakes and fairs and other rural festivals, and cope with the people in all their conditions, and all their habits and humours.

In some countries the large cities absorb the wealth and fashion of the nation; they are the only fixed abodes of elegant and intelligent society and the country is inhabited almost entirely by boorish peasantry. In England, on the contrary, the metropolis is a mere gathering place, or general rendezvous of the polite circles, where they devote a small portion of the year to a hurry of gaiety and dissipation, and having indulged this kind of carnival, return again to the apparently more congenial habits of rural life. The various orders of society are therefore diffused over the whole surface of the kingdom, and the most retired neighbourhoods afford specimens of the different ranks.

The English, in fact, are strongly gifted with the rural feeling. They possess a quick sensibility to the beauties of nature, and a keen relish for the pleasures and employments of the country. This passion seems inherent in them. Even the inhabitants of cities born and brought up among brick walls and bustling streets, enter with facility into rural habits and evince a tact for rural occupation. The merchant has his snug retreat in the vicinity of the metropolis, where he often displays as much pride and zeal in the cultivation of his flower garden and the maturing of his fruits as he does in the conduct of his business and the success of a commercial enterprise. Even those less fortunate individuals, who are doomed to pass their lives in the midst of din and traffic, contrive to have something that shall remind them of the green aspect of nature. In the most dark and dingy quarters of the city, the drawing room window resembles frequently a bank of flowers; every spot capable of vegetation, has its grass plot and flower bed; and every square its mimic park, laid out with picturesque taste, and gleaming with refreshing verdure.

Those who see the Englishman only in town are apt to form an unfavourable opinion of his social character. He is either absorbed in business, or distracted by the thousand engagements that dissipate time, thought and feeling, in this huge metropolis. He has therefore too commonly a look of hurry and abstraction. Wherever he happens to be, he is on the point of going somewhere else; at the moment he is talking on one subject his mind is wandering to another; and while paying a friendly visit, he is calculating how he shall economize time so as to pay the other visits allotted in the morning. An immense metropolis like London is calculated to make men selfish and uninteresting. In their casual and transient meetings they can but deal briefly in commonplaces. They present but the cold superficies of character—its rich and genial qualities have no time to be warmed into a flow.

It is in the country that the Englishman gives scope to his natural feelings. He breaks loose gladly from the cold formalities and negative civilities of town; throws off his habits of shy reserve, and becomes joyous and freehearted. He manages to collect around him all the conveniencies and elegancies of polite life, and to banish its restraints. His country seat abounds with every requisite either for studious retirement, tasteful gratification or rural exercise. Books, paintings, music, horses, dogs, and sporting implements of all kinds are at hand. He puts no constraint either upon his guests or himself, but in the true spirit of hospitality, provides the means of enjoyment, and leaves every one to partake according to his inclination.

The taste of the English in the cultivation of land and in what is called landscape gardening is unrivalled. They have studied nature intently and discover an exquisite sense of her beautiful forms and harmonious combinations. Those charms which in other countries she lavishes in wild solitudes are here assembled round the haunts of domestic life. They seem to have caught her coy and furtive graces, and spread them, like witchery, about their rural abodes.

Nothing can be more imposing than the magnificence of English park scenery. Vast lawns that extend like sheets of vivid green, with here and there clumps of gigantic trees heaping up rich piles of foliage. The solemn pomp of groves and woodland glades, with the deer trooping in silent herds across them, the hare bounding away to the covert or the pheasant suddenly bursting upon the wing. The brook, taught to wind in natural meanderings or expand into a glassy lake—The sequestered pool reflecting the quivering trees, with the yellow leaf sleeping on its bosom, and the trout roaming fearlessly about its limpid waters, while some rustic temple, or sylvan statue grown green and dank with age, gives an air of classic sanctity to the seclusion.

These are but a few of the features of park scenery; but what most

delights me is the creative talent with which the English decorate the
unostentatious abodes of middle life. The rudest habitation; the most un-
promising and scanty portion of land, in the hands of an Englishman of
taste, becomes a little paradise. With a nicely discriminating eye he
seizes at once upon its capabilities, and pictures in his mind the future
landscape. The sterile spot grows into loveliness under his hand; and
yet the operations of art which produce the effect are scarcely to be
perceived. The cherishing and training of some trees; the cautious
pruning of others; the nice distribution of flowers and plants of
tender and graceful foliage; the introduction of a green slope of velvet
turf; the partial opening to a peep of blue distance or silver gleam of
water—all these are managed with a delicate tact, a pervading yet quiet
assiduity, like the magic touchings with which a painter finishes up a
favourite picture.

The residence of people of fortune and refinement in the country has
diffused a degree of taste and elegance in rural economy, that descends
to the lowest class. The very labourer, with his thatched cottage and narrow slip of ground, attends to their embellishment. The trim hedge, the
grass plot before the door, the little flower bed bordered with snug box;
the woodbine trained up against the wall and hanging its blossoms about
the lattice; the pot of flowers in the window; the holly providently
planted about the house to cheat winter of its dreariness, and to throw in a
semblance of green summer to cheer the fire side—all these bespeak the
influence of taste, flowing down from high sources, and pervading the
lowest levels of the public mind. If ever love, as poets sing, delights to
visit a cottage, it must be the cottage of an English peasant.

The fondness for rural life among the higher classes of the English has
had a great and salutary effect upon the national character. I do not
know a finer race of men than the English gentlemen. Instead of the
softness and effeminacy which characterize the men of rank in most
countries, they exhibit a union of elegance and strength, a robustness of
frame and freshness of complexion, which I am inclined to attribute to
their living so much in the open air, and pursuing so eagerly the invigorating recreations of the country. These hardy exercises produce
also a healthful tone of mind and spirits, a manliness and simplicity
of manners, which even the follies and dissipations of the town cannot
easily pervert, and can never entirely destroy. In the country too, the
different orders of society seem to approach more freely, to be more
disposed to blend and operate favourably upon each other. The distinctions between them do not appear to be so marked and impassable as in
the cities. The manner in which property has been distributed into small
estates and farms has established a regular gradation from the nobleman,
through the classes of gentry, small landed proprietors, and substantial

farmers, down to the labouring peasantry; and while it has thus banded the extremes of society together, has infused in each intermediate rank a spirit of independence. This, it must be confessed, is not so universally the case at present as it was formerly; the larger estates having in late years of distress, absorbed the smaller, and in some parts of the country almost annihilated the sturdy race of small farmers. These, however, I believe, are but casual breaks in the general system I have mentioned.

In rural occupation there is nothing mean and debasing. It leads a man forth among scenes of natural grandeur and beauty; it leaves him to the workings of his own mind operated upon by the purest and most elevating of external influences. Such a man may be simple and rough, but he cannot be vulgar. The man of refinement, therefore, finds nothing revolting in an intercourse with the lower orders in rural life, as he does when he casually mingles with the lower orders of cities. He lays aside his distance and reserve, and is glad to wave the distinctions of rank, and to enter into the honest heartfelt enjoyments of common life. Indeed the very amusements of the country bring men more and more together; and the sound of hound and horn blend all feelings into harmony. I believe this is one great reason why the nobility and gentry are more popular among the inferior orders in England than they are in any other country; and why the latter have endured so many excessive pressures and extremities, without repining more generally at the unequal distribution of fortune and privilege.

To this mingling of cultivated and rustic society may also be attributed the rural feeling that runs through British literature: the frequent use of illustrations from rural life: those incomparable descriptions of nature that abound in the British poets; that have continued down from "The Flower and the Leaf" of Chaucer, and have brought into our closets all the freshness and fragrance of the dewy landscape. The pastoral writers of other countries appear as if they had paid nature an occasional visit, and become acquainted with her general charms; but the British poets have lived and revelled with her—they have wooed her in her most secret haunts, they have watched her minutest caprices. A spray could not tremble in the breeze; a leaf could not rustle to the ground; a diamond drop could not patter in the stream; a fragrance could not exhale from the humble violet, nor a daisy unfold its crimson tints to the morning, but it has been noticed by these impassioned and delicate observers, and wrought up into some beautiful morality.

The effect of this devotion of elegant minds to rural occupations has been wonderful on the face of the country. A great part of the island is rather level, and would be monotonous were it not for the charms of culture, but it is studded and gemmed, as it were, with castles and palaces, and embroidered with parks and gardens. It does not abound in grand and sublime prospects, but rather in little, home scenes of rural repose and sheltered quiet. Every antique farm house and moss grown cottage is a picture, and as the roads are continually winding, and the view shut in by groves and hedges, the eye is delighted by a continual succession of small landscapes of captivating loveliness.

The great charm, however, of English scenery is the moral feeling that seems to pervade it. It is associated in the mind with ideas of order, of quiet, of sober well established principles, of hoary usage and reverend custom. Every thing seems to be the growth of ages of regular, and peaceful existence. The old church of remote architecture, with its low massive portal; its gothic tower; its windows rich with tracery and painted glass in scrupulous preservation; its stately monuments of warriors and worthies of the olden time, ancestors of the present lords of the soil; its tombstones recording successive generations of sturdy yeomanry, whose progeny still plow the same fields and kneel at the same altar. The parsonage, a quaint irregular pile, partly antiquated, but repaired and altered in the tastes of various ages and occupants. The style and footpath leading from the church yard, across pleasant fields and along shady hedge rows, according to an immemorial right of way. The neighbouring village, with its venerable cottages, its public green sheltered by trees under which the forefathers of the present race have sported. The antique family mansion, standing apart in some little rural domain, but looking down with a protecting air on the surrounding scene. —All these common features of English landscape evince a calm and settled security, and hereditary transmission of home bred virtues and local attachments, that speak deeply and touchingly for the moral character of the nation.

It is a pleasing sight of a Sunday morning, when the bell is sending its sober melody across the quiet fields, to behold the peasantry in their best finery, with ruddy faces and modest cheerfulness, thronging tranquilly along the green lanes to church: but it is still more pleasing to see them in the evenings, gathering about their cottage doors, and appearing to exult in the humble comforts and embellishments, which their own hands have spread around them.

It is this sweet home feeling; this settled repose of affection in the domestic scene, that is, after all, the parent of the steadiest virtues and purest enjoyments, and I cannot close these desultory remarks better, than by quoting the words of a modern English poet, who has depicted it with remarkable felicity.

> Through each gradation, from the castled hall,
> The city dome, the villa crown'd with shade,
> But chief from modest mansions numberless,

In town or hamlet shelt'ring middle life,
Down to the cottag'd vale and straw-roof'd shed,
This western isle hath long been fam'd for scenes
Where bliss domestic finds a dwelling place:
Domestic bliss, that, like a harmless dove,
(Honour and sweet endearment keeping guard)
Can centre in a little quiet nest
All that desire would fly for through the earth;
That can, the world eluding, be itself
A world enjoy'd; that wants no witnesses
But its own sharers, and approving heaven.
That, like a flower deep hid in rocky cleft,
Smiles, though 'tis looking only at the sky.°

°From a poem on the death of the Princess Charlotte, by the Reverend Rann Kennedy, A. M.

THE BROKEN HEART

I never heard
Of any true affection but 'twas nipt
With care, that, like the caterpillar, eats
The leaves of the spring's sweetest book, the rose.
MIDDLETON.

It is a common practice with those who have outlived the susceptibility of early feeling, or have been brought up in the gay heartlessness of dissipated life, to laugh at all love stories, and to treat the tales of romantic passion as mere fictions of novelists and poets. My observations on human nature have induced me to think otherwise. They have convinced me, that however the surface of the character may be chilled and frozen by the cares of the world, or cultivated into mere smiles by the arts of society, still there are dormant fires lurking in the depths of the coldest bosom, which, when once enkindled, become impetuous and are sometimes desolating in their effects. Indeed, I am a true believer in the blind deity, and go to the full extent of his doctrines—Shall I confess it?— I believe in broken hearts and the possibility of dying of disappointed love!—I do not, however, consider it a malady often fatal to my own sex; but I firmly believe that it withers down many a lovely woman into an early grave.

Man is the creature of interest and ambition. His nature leads him forth into the struggle and bustle of the world. Love is but the embellishment of his early life, or a song piped in the intervals of the acts. He seeks for fame, for fortune, for space in the world's thought, and dominion over his fellow men. But a woman's whole life is a history of the affections. The heart is her world: it is there her ambition strives for empire: it is there her avarice seeks for hidden treasures. She sends forth her sympathies on adventure; she embarks her whole soul in the traffic of affection, and if shipwrecked her case is hopeless, for it is a bankruptcy of the heart.

To a man the disappointment of love may occasion some bitter pangs— it wounds some feelings of tenderness—it blasts some prospects of felicity; but he is an active being—he may dissipate his thoughts in the whirl of varied occupation; or may plunge into the tide of pleasure. Or if the scene of disappointment be too full of painful associations, he can shift his abode at will, and, taking as it were the wings of the morning, can "fly to the uttermost parts of the earth and be at rest."

But woman's is comparatively a fixed, a secluded, and a meditative life. She is more the companion of her own thoughts and feelings; and if

they are turned to ministers of sorrow, where shall she look for consolation! Her lot is to be wooed and won; and if unhappy in her love, her
heart is like some fortress that has been captured, and sacked, and
abandoned and left desolate.

How many bright eyes grow dim—how many soft cheeks grow pale—
how many lovely forms fade away into the tomb, and none can tell the
cause that blighted their loveliness. As the dove will clasp its wings to
its side, and cover and conceal the arrow that is preying on its vitals;
so is it the nature of woman to hide from the world the pangs of
wounded affection. The love of a delicate female is always shy and
silent. Even when fortunate, she scarcely breathes it to herself; but when
otherwise, she buries it in the recesses of her bosom, and there lets it
cower and brood among the ruins of her peace. With her the desire of the
heart has failed. The great charm of existence is at an end. She neglects
all the cheerful exercises which gladden the spirits, quicken the pulses and
send the tide of life in healthful currents through the veins. Her rest is
broken—the sweet refreshment of sleep is poisoned by melancholy dreams
—"dry sorrow drinks her blood," until her enfeebled frame sinks under
the slightest external injury. Look for her, after a little while, and you
find friendship weeping over her untimely grave, and wondering that one,
who but lately glowed with all the radiance of health and beauty,
should so speedily be brought down to "darkness and the worm." You
will be told of some wintry chill, some casual indisposition that laid her
low—but no one knows of the mental malady which previously sapped
her strength and made her so easy a prey to the spoiler.

She is like some tender tree, the pride and beauty of the grove; graceful in its form; bright in its foliage, but with the worm preying at its
heart. We find it suddenly withering when it should be most fresh and
luxuriant. We see it drooping its branches to the earth and shedding
leaf by leaf; until wasted and perished away, it falls even in the stillness
of the forest; and as we muse over the beautiful ruin, we strive in vain to
recollect the blast or thunderbolt that could have smitten it with decay.

I have seen many instances of women running to waste and self neglect,
and disappearing gradually from the earth, almost as if they had been
exhaled to heaven; and have repeatedly fancied that I could trace their
deaths through the various declensions of consumption, cold, debility,
languor, melancholy, until I reached the first symptom of disappointed
love. But an instance of the kind was lately told to me; the circumstances
are well known in the country where they happened, and I shall but
give them in the manner in which they were related.

Every one must recollect the tragical story of young E——— the
Irish patriot; it was too touching to be soon forgotten. During the
troubles in Ireland he was tried, condemned and executed on a charge of

treason. His fate made a deep impression on public sympathy. He was so young—so intelligent—so generous—so brave—so every thing that we are apt to like in a young man. His conduct under trial too was so lofty and intrepid. The noble indignation with which he repelled the charge of treason against his country—the eloquent vindication of his name, his pathetic appeal to posterity in the hopeless hour of condemnation— all these entered deeply into every generous bosom, and even his enemies lamented the stern policy that dictated his execution.

But there was one heart, whose anguish it would be impossible to describe. In happier days and fairer fortunes he had won the affections of a beautiful and interesting girl, the daughter of a late celebrated Irish Barrister. She loved him with the disinterested fervour of a woman's first and early love. When every worldly maxim arrayed itself against him; when blasted in fortune, and disgrace and danger darkened around his name, she loved him the more ardently for his very sufferings. If then his fate could awaken the sympathy even of his foes, what must have been the agony of her whose whole soul was occupied by his image! Let those tell who have had the portals of the tomb suddenly closed between them, and the being they most loved on earth—who have sat at its threshold, as one shut out in a cold and lonely world, from whence all that was most lovely and loving had departed.

But then the horrors of such a grave! so frightful—so dishonoured!— There was nothing for memory to dwell on that could soothe the pang of separation—none of those tender though melancholy circumstances which endear the parting scene—nothing to melt sorrow into those blessed tears, sent like the dews of heaven, to revive the heart in the parching hour of anguish.

To render her widowed situation more desolate, she had incurred her father's displeasure by her unfortunate attachment, and was an exile from the paternal roof. But could the sympathy and kind offices of friends have reached a spirit so shocked and driven in by horror, she would have experienced no want of consolation, for the Irish are a people of quick and generous sensibilities. The most delicate and cherishing attentions were paid her by families of wealth and distinction. She was led into society; and they tried by all kinds of occupations and amusements to dissipate her grief and wean her from the tragical story of her loves. But it was all in vain. There are some strokes of calamity which scathe and scorch the soul; which penetrate to the vital seat of happiness, and blast it, never again to put forth bud or blossom. She never objected to frequent the haunts of pleasure, but was as much alone there, as in the depths of solitude; walking about in a sad reverie, apparently unconscious of the world around her. She carried with her an inward woe that mocked at all the blandishments of friendship, and "heeded not the song of the charmer, charm he never so wisely."

The person who told me her story had seen her at a masquerade. There can be no exhibition of far gone wretchedness more striking and painful than to meet it in such a scene. To find it wandering like a spectre, lonely and joyless, where all around is gay—To see it dressed out in the trappings of mirth, and looking so wan and woe begone, as if it had tried in vain to cheat the poor heart into a momentary forgetfulness of sorrow. After strolling through the splendid rooms and giddy crowd with an air of utter abstraction, she sat herself down on the steps of an orchestra, and looking about for some time with a vacant air that shewed her insensibility to the garish scene, she began, with the capriciousness of a sickly heart, to warble a little plaintive air. She had an exquisite voice; but on this occasion it was so simple, so touching, it breathed forth such a soul of wretchedness, that she drew a crowd mute and silent around her, and melted every one into tears.

The story of one so true and tender could not but excite great interest in a country remarkable for enthusiasm. It completely won the heart of a brave officer, who paid his addresses to her, and thought that one so true to the dead, could not but prove affectionate to the living. She declined his attentions, for her thoughts were irrevocably engrossed by the memory of her former lover. He, however, persisted in his suit. He solicited not her tenderness, but her esteem. He was assisted by her conviction of his worth, and her sense of her own destitute and dependent situation, for she was existing on the kindness of friends—In a word he at length succeeded in gaining her hand, though with the solemn assurance that her heart was unalterably another's.

He took her with him to Sicily, hoping that a change of scene might wear out the remembrance of early woes. She was an amiable and exemplary wife, and made an effort to be a happy one; but nothing could cure the silent and devouring melancholy that had entered into her very soul. She wasted away in a slow but hopeless decline, and at length sunk into the grave, the victim of a broken heart.

It was on her that Moore the distinguished Irish poet composed the following lines.

> She is far from the land where her young hero sleeps,
>   And lovers around her are sighing;
> But coldly she turns from their gaze and weeps,
>   For her heart in his grave is lying.

> She sings the wild song of her dear native plains,
>   Every note which he lov'd awaking—

Ah! little they think, who delight in her strains,
    How the heart of the minstrel is breaking!

He had liv'd for his love, for his country he died;
    They were all that to life had entwin'd him—
Nor soon shall the tears of his country be dried,
    Nor long will his love stay behind him!

Oh! make her a grave where the sunbeams rest,
    When they promise a glorious morrow;
They'll shine o'er her sleep, like a smile from the west,
    From her own lov'd island of sorrow!

THE ART OF BOOK MAKING

If that severe doom of Synesius be true, "it is a greater offence to steal dead
men's labors, than their clothes," what shall become of most writers?

BURTON'S ANATOMY OF MELANCHOLY.

I have often wondered at the extreme fecundity of the press, and how
it comes to pass that so many heads, on which nature seemed to have
inflicted the curse of barrenness, should teem with voluminous productions. As a man travels on, however, in the journey of life his objects of
wonder daily diminish, and he is continually finding out some very
simple cause, for some great matter of marvel. Thus have I chanced, in
my peregrinations about this great metropolis, to blunder upon a scene
which unfolded to me some of the mysteries of the bookmaking craft,
and at once put an end to my astonishment.

I was one summer's day loitering through the great saloons of the
British Museum, with that listlessness with which one is apt to saunter
about a museum in warm weather; sometimes lolling over the glass cases
of minerals, sometimes studying the hieroglyphics on an Egyptian
Mummy, and sometimes trying, with nearly equal success, to comprehend
the allegorical paintings on the lofty ceilings. Whilst I was gazing about
in this idle way my attention was attracted to a distant door, at the
end of a suite of apartments. It was closed, but every now and then it
would open and some strange favoured being, generally clothed in
black, would steal forth and glide through the rooms without noticing
any of the surrounding objects. There was an air of mystery about this
that piqued my languid curiosity, and I determined to attempt the
passage of that strait and to explore the unknown regions beyond. The
door yielded to my hand, with that facility with which the portals of
enchanted castles yield to the adventurous Knight errant. I found myself
in a spacious chamber, surrounded with great cases of venerable books.
Above the cases, and just under the cornice, were arranged a great
number of black looking portraits of ancient authors. About the room
were placed long tables, with stands for reading and writing, at which
sat many pale, studious personages, poring intently over dusty volumes,
rummaging among mouldy manuscripts, and taking copious notes of
their contents. A hushed stillness reigned through this mysterious
apartment, excepting that you might hear the racing of pens over sheets
of paper; or occasionally the deep sigh of one of these sages as he
shifted his position to turn over the page of an old folio; doubtless arising
from that hollowness and flatulency incident to learned research.

Now and then one of these personages would write something on a small slip of paper and ring a bell, whereupon a familiar would appear, take the paper in profound silence, glide out of the room and return shortly loaded with ponderous tomes, upon which the other would fall, tooth and nail, with famished voracity. I had no longer a doubt that I had happened upon a body of Magi, deeply engaged in the study of occult sciences. The scene reminded me of an old Arabian tale, of a philosopher shut up in an enchanted library, in the bosom of a mountain, which opened only once a year; where he made the spirits of the place bring him books of all kinds of dark knowledge, so that at the end of the year, when the magic portal once more swung open on its hinges, he issued forth so versed in forbidden lore, as to be able to soar above the heads of the multitude, and to control the powers of nature.

My curiosity being now fully aroused I whispered to one of the familiars, as he was about to leave the room, and begged an interpretation of the strange scene before me. A few words were sufficient for the purpose. I found that these mysterious personages whom I had mistaken for Magi, were principally authors and in the very act of manufacturing books. I was, in fact, in the reading room of the great British library, an immense collection of volumes of all ages and languages, many of which are now forgotten, and most of which are seldom read: one of these sequestered pools of obsolete literature, to which modern authors repair, and draw buckets full of classic lore, or "pure English undefiled" wherewith to swell their own scanty rills of thought.

Being now in possession of the secret, I sat down in a corner and watched the process of this book manufactory. I noticed one lean, bilious looking wight, who sought none but the most worm eaten volumes, printed in black letter. He was evidently constructing some work of profound erudition, that would be purchased by every man who wished to be thought learned, placed upon a conspicuous shelf of his library, or laid open upon his table—but never read. I observed him now and then draw a large fragment of biscuit out of his pocket, and gnaw; whether it was his dinner, or whether he was endeavouring to keep off that exhaustion of the stomach, produced by much pondering over dry works, I leave to harder students than myself to determine.

There was one dapper little gentleman in bright coloured clothes, with a chirping, gossipping expression of countenance, who had all the appearance of an author on good terms with his bookseller. After considering him attentively, I recognized in him a diligent getter up of miscellaneous works, which bustled off well with the trade. I was curious to see how he manufactured his wares. He made more stir and shew of business than any of the others; dipping into various books, fluttering over the leaves of manuscripts, taking a morsel out of one, a morsel out of another, line upon line, precept upon precept, here a little and there a little. The contents of his book seemed to be as heterogeneous as those of the witches' cauldron in Macbeth. It was, here a finger and there a thumb; toe of frog and blind worm's sting, with his own gossip poured in like "baboon's blood," to make the medley "slab and good."

After all, thought I, may not this pilfering disposition be implanted in authors for wise purposes; may it not be the way in which providence has taken care that the seeds of knowledge and wisdom shall be preserved from age to age, in spite of the inevitable decay of the works in which they were first produced. We see that nature has wisely, though whimsically, provided for the conveyance of seeds from clime to clime in the maws of certain birds; so that animals which in themselves are little better than carrion, and apparently the lawless plunderers of the orchard and the corn field, are in fact nature's carriers to disperse and perpetuate her blessings. In like manner the beauties and fine thoughts of ancient and obsolete writers, are caught up by these flights of predatory authors, and cast forth again to flourish and bear fruit in a remote and distant tract of time. Many of their works, also, undergo a kind of metempsychosis and spring up under new forms. What was formerly a ponderous history, revives in the shape of a romance—an old legend changes into a modern play, and a sober philosophical treatise, furnishes the body for a whole series of bouncing and sparkling essays. Thus it is in the clearing of our American woodlands; where we burn down a forest of stately pines, a progeny of dwarf oaks start up in their place; and we never see the prostrate trunk of a tree, mouldering into soil, but it gives birth to a whole tribe of fungi.

Let us not then lament over the decay and oblivion into which ancient writers descend; they do but submit to the great law of nature, which declares that all sublunary shapes of matter shall be limited in their duration, but which decrees also that their elements shall never perish. Generation after generation, both in animal and vegetable life, passes away, but the vital principle is transmitted to posterity, and the species continues to flourish. Thus also do authors beget authors, and having produced a numerous progeny, in a good old age they sleep with their fathers; that is to say, with the authors who preceded them— and from whom they had stolen.

Whilst I was indulging in these rambling fancies I had leaned my head against a pile of reverend folios. Whether it was owing to the soporific emanations from these works, or to the profound quiet of the room; or to the lassitude arising from much wandering, or to an unlucky habit of napping at improper times and places, with which I am grievously afflicted, so it was that I fell into a doze. Still however my imagination continued busy, and indeed the same scene remained before my mind's eye, only a little changed in some of the details. I dreamt that the chamber was still decorated with the portraits of ancient authors, but that the number was encreased. The long tables had disappeared and in place of the sage Magi I beheld a ragged, thread bare throng, such as may be seen plying about the great repository of cast off clothes Monmouth Street. Whenever they seized upon a book, by one of those incongruities common to dreams, methought it turned into a garment of foreign or antique fashion, with which they proceeded to equip themselves. I noticed, however, that no one pretended to clothe himself from any particular suit, but took a sleeve from one, a cape from another, a skirt from a third, thus decking himself out piece meal, while some of his original rags would peep out from among his borrowed finery.

There was a portly, rosy, well fed parson whom I observed ogling several mouldy polemical writers through an eye glass. He soon contrived to slip on the voluminous mantle of one of the old fathers, and having purloined the grey beard of another, endeavoured to look exceeding wise, but the smirking commonplace of his countenance set at naught all the trappings of wisdom. One sickly looking gentleman was busied embroidering a very flimsy garment with gold thread drawn out of several old court dresses of the reign of Queen Elizabeth. Another had trimmed himself magnificently from an illuminated manuscript, had stuck a nose-gay in his bosom, culled from "The Paradise of dainty Devices," and having put Sir Philip Sidney's hat on one side of his head, strutted off with an exquisite air of vulgar elegance. A third, who was but of puny dimensions, had bolstered himself out bravely with the spoils from several obscure tracts of philosophy, so that he had a very imposing front, but he was lamentably tattered in rear, and I perceived that he had patched his small clothes with scraps of parchment from a Latin author.

There were some well dressed gentlemen, it is true, who only helped themselves to a gem or so, which sparkled among their own ornaments, without eclipsing them. Some too, seemed to contemplate the costumes of the old writers merely to imbibe their principles of taste, and catch their air and spirit; but I grieve to say that too many were apt to array themselves from top to toe, in the patch work manner I have mentioned. I should not omit to speak of one genius in drab breeches and gaiters, and an arcadian hat, who had a violent propensity to the pastoral, but whose rural wanderings had been confined to the classic haunts of Primrose hill and the solitudes of the Regent's Park. He had decked himself in wreaths and ribbands from all the old pastoral poets, and hanging his head on one side, went about with a fantastical, lack-a-daisical air, "babbling about green fields." But the personage that most struck my attention was a pragmatical old gentleman in clerical robes, with a remarkably large and square, but bald head. He entered the room wheezing and puffing, elbowed his way through the throng with a look of sturdy self confidence, and having laid hands upon a thick Greek quarto, clapped it upon his head, and swept majestically away in a formidable frizzled wig.

In the height of this literary masquerade a cry suddenly resounded from every side of "Thieves! Thieves!" I looked, and lo the portraits about the walls became animated! The old authors thrust out first a head, then a shoulder from the canvass, looked down curiously for an instant upon the motley throng, and then descended, with fury in their eyes, to claim their rifled property. The scene of scampering and hubbub that ensued baffles all description. The unhappy culprits endeavoured in vain to escape with their plunder. On one side might be seen half a dozen old monks stripping a modern professor—on another there was sad devastation carried into the ranks of modern dramatic writers. Beaumont and Fletcher side by side, raged round the field like Castor and Pollux, and sturdy Ben Jonson enacted more wonders than when a volunteer with the army in Flanders. As to the dapper little compiler of farragoes mentioned sometime since, he had arrayed himself in as many patches and colours as harlequin, and there was as fierce a contention of claimants about him, as about the dead body of Patroclus. I was grieved to see many men, to whom I had been accustomed to look up with awe and reverence, fain to steal off with scarce a rag to cover their nakedness. Just then my eye was caught by the pragmatical old gentleman in the Greek grizzled wig, who was scrambling away in sore affright with half a score of authors in full cry after him. They were close upon his haunches; in a twinkling off went his wig; at every turn some strip of raiment was peeled away, until in a few moments, from his domineering pomp, he shrunk into a little, pursy "chopped bald shot," and made his exit with only a few tags and rags fluttering at his back.

There was something so ludicrous in the catastrophe of this learned Theban that I burst into an immoderate fit of laughter, which broke the whole illusion. The tumult and the scuffle were at an end. The chamber resumed its usual appearance. The old authors shrunk back into their picture frames and hung in shadowy solemnity along the walls. In short, I found myself wide awake in my corner, with the whole assemblage of Bookworms gazing at me with astonishment. Nothing of the dream had been real but my burst of laughter, a sound never before heard in that grave sanctuary, and so abhorrent to the ears of wisdom as to electrify the fraternity.

The librarian now stepped up to me and demanded whether I had a card of admission. At first I did not comprehend him, but I soon found that the library was a kind of literary "preserve," subject to game laws, and that no one must presume to hunt there without special licence and permission. In a word, I stood convicted of being an arrant poacher, and was glad to make a precipitate retreat, lest I should have a whole pack of authors let loose upon me.

A ROYAL POET

Though your body be confin'd,
  And soft love a prisoner bound,
Yet the beauty of your mind,
  Neither check nor chain hath found.
  Look out nobly, then, and dare
  Even the fetters that you wear.
                                        FLETCHER.

On a soft sunny morning in the genial month of May, I made an excursion to Windsor castle. It is a place full of storied and poetical associations. The very external aspect of the proud old pile is enough to inspire high thought. It rears its irregular walls and massive towers, like a mural crown, round the brow of a lofty ridge, waves its royal banner in the clouds, and looks down, with a lordly air, upon the surrounding world.

On this morning the weather was of that voluptuous vernal kind, which calls forth all the latent romance of a man's temperament, filling his mind with musick, and disposing him to quote poetry and dream of beauty. In wandering through the magnificent saloons, and long echoing galleries of the castle, I passed with indifference by whole rows of portraits of warriors and statesmen, but lingered in the chamber, where hang the likenesses of the beauties that graced the gay court of Charles the Second; and as I gazed upon them, depicted with amorous, half dishevelled tresses, and the sleepy eye of love, I blessed the pencil of Sir Peter Lely which had thus enabled me to bask in the reflected rays of beauty. In traversing also the "large green courts," with sunshine beaming on the gray walls, and glancing along the velvet turf, my mind was engrossed with the image of the tender, the gallant, but hapless Surrey, and his account of his loiterings about them in his stripling days when enamoured of the Lady Geraldine—

"With eyes cast up unto the maiden's tower,
With easie sighs, such as men draw in love."

In this mood of mere poetical susceptibility, I visited the ancient Keep of the Castle, where James the First of Scotland, the pride and theme of Scottish poets and historians, was for many years of his youth detained a prisoner of state. It is a large gray tower, that has stood the brunt of ages, and is still in good preservation. It stands on a mound, which elevates it above the other parts of the castle, and a great flight of steps leads to the interior. In the armoury, which is a gothic hall furnished with weapons of various kinds and ages, I was shewn a coat of armour hanging against the wall, which had once belonged to James. From hence I was conducted up a staircase to a suite of apartments of faded magnificence, hung with storied tapestry, which formed his prison, and the scene of that passionate and fanciful amour, which has woven into the web of his story the magical hues of poetry and fiction.

The whole history of this amiable but unfortunate prince is highly romantic. At the tender age of eleven he was sent from home by his father, Robert III. and destined for the French court, to be reared under the eye of the French monarch, secure from the treachery and danger that surrounded the royal house of Scotland. It was his mishap in the course of his voyage to fall into the hands of the English, and he was detained prisoner by Henry IV., notwithstanding that a truce existed between the two countries.

The intelligence of his capture, coming in the train of many sorrows and disasters, proved fatal to his unhappy father. "The news," we are told, "was brought to him while at supper, and did so overwhelm him with grief, that he was almost ready to give up the ghost into the hands of the servants that attended him. But being carried to his bed chamber, he abstained from all food, and in three days died of hunger and grief, at Rothesay."*

James was detained in captivity above eighteen years; but, though deprived of personal liberty, he was treated with the respect due to his rank. Care was taken to instruct him in all the branches of useful knowledge cultivated at that period, and to give him those mental and personal accomplishments deemed proper for a prince. Perhaps, in this respect, his imprisonment was an advantage, as it enabled him to apply himself the more exclusively to his improvement, and quietly to imbibe that rich fund of knowledge, and to cherish those elegant tastes, which have given such a lustre to his memory. The picture drawn of him in early life, by the Scottish historians, is highly captivating, and seems rather the description of a hero of romance, than of a character in real history. He was well learnt, we are told, "to fight with the sword, to joust, to tournay, to wrestle, to sing and dance; he was an expert mediciner, right crafty in playing both of lute and harp and sundry other instruments of musick, and was expert in grammar, oratory, and poetry."†

With this combination of manly and delicate accomplishments, fitting him to shine both in active and elegant life, and calculated to give him

*Buchanan.
†Ballenden's Translation of Hector Boyce.

an intense relish for joyous existence, it must have been a severe trial, in an age of bustle and chivalry, to pass the spring time of his years in monotonous captivity. It was the good fortune of James, however, to be gifted with a powerfully poetic fancy, and to be visited in his prison by the choicest inspirations of the muse. Some minds corrode and grow inactive, under the loss of personal liberty; others grow morbid and irritable; but it is the nature of the poet to become tender and imaginative in the loneliness of confinement. He banquets upon the honey of his own thoughts, and, like the captive bird, pours forth his soul in melody.

> Have you not seen the nightingale
> A pilgrim coop'd into a cage,
> How doth she chant her wonted tale,
> In that her lonely hermitage!
> Even there her charming melody doth prove
> That all her boughs are trees, her cage a grove.*

Indeed, it is the divine attribute of the imagination, that it is irrepressible, unconfinable. That when the real world is shut out, it can create a world for itself, and with a necromantic power, can conjure up glorious shapes and forms, and brilliant visions, to make solitude populous, and irradiate the gloom of the dungeon. Such was the world of pomp and pageant that lived round Tasso in his dismal cell at Ferrara, when he conceived the splendid scenes of his Jerusalem; and we may consider the "King's Quair," composed by James during his captivity at Windsor, as another of those beautiful breakings forth of the soul from the restraint and gloom of the prison house.

The subject of the poem is his love for the Lady Jane Beaufort, daughter of the Earl of Somerset, and a princess of the blood royal of England, of whom he became enamoured in the course of his captivity. What gives it peculiar value is, that it may be considered a transcript of the royal bard's true feelings, and the story of his real loves and fortunes. It is not often that sovereigns write poetry, or that poets deal in fact. It is gratifying to the pride of a common man, to find a monarch thus suing, as it were, for admission into his closet, and seeking to win his favour by administering to his pleasures. It is a proof of the honest equality of intellectual competition, which strips off all the trappings of factitious dignity, brings the candidate down to a level with his fellow men, and obliges him to depend on his own native powers for distinction. It is curious, too, to get at the history of a monarch's heart, and to

*Roger l'Estrange.

find the simple affections of human nature throbbing under the ermine. But James had learnt to be a poet before he was a king: he was schooled in adversity, and reared in the company of his own thoughts. Monarchs have seldom time to parley with their hearts, or meditate their minds into poetry; and had James been brought up amidst the adulation and gaiety of a court, we should never, in all probability, have had such a poem as the Quair.

I have been particularly interested by those parts of the poem which breathe his immediate thoughts concerning his situation, or which are connected with the apartment in the tower. They have thus a personal and local charm, and are given with such circumstantial truth, as to make the reader present with the captive in his prison, and the companion of his meditations.

Such is the account which he gives of his weariness of spirit, and of the incident which first suggested the idea of writing the poem. It was the still mid-watch of a clear moonlight night; the stars, he says, were twinkling as fire in the high vault of heaven; and "Cynthia rinsing her golden locks in Aquarius." He lay in bed, wakeful and restless, and took a book to beguile the tedious hours. The book he chose was Boetius' Consolations of Philosophy, a work popular among the writers of that day, and which had been translated by his great prototype Chaucer. From the high eulogium in which he indulges, it is evident this was one of his favourite volumes while in prison; and indeed it is an admirable text book for meditation under adversity. It is the legacy of a noble and enduring spirit, purified by sorrow and suffering, bequeathing to its successors in calamity, the maxims of sweet morality, and the trains of eloquent but simple reasoning, by which it was enabled to bear up against the various ills of life. It is a talisman, which the unfortunate may treasure up in his bosom, or like the good King James, lay upon his nightly pillow.

After closing the volume, he turns its contents over in his mind, and gradually falls into a fit of musing on the fickleness of fortune, the vicissitudes of his own life, and the evils that had overtaken him even in his tender youth. Suddenly he hears the bell ringing to matins; but its sound chiming in with his melancholy fancies, seems to him like a voice exhorting him to write his story. In the spirit of poetic errantry he determines to comply with this intimation; he therefore takes pen in hand, makes with it a sign of the cross to implore a benediction, and sallies forth into the fairy land of poetry. There is something extremely fanciful in all this, and it is interesting as furnishing a striking and beautiful instance of the simple manner in which whole trains of poetical thought are sometimes awakened, and literary enterprises suggested to the mind.

In the course of his poem he more than once bewails the peculiar
hardness of his fate; thus doomed to lonely and inactive life, and
shut up from the freedom and pleasure of the world, in which the meanest
animal indulges unrestrained. There is a sweetness however in his very
complaints; they are the lamentations of an amiable and social spirit
at being denied the indulgence of its kind and generous propensities;
there is nothing in them harsh nor exaggerated; they flow with a natural and touching pathos, and are perhaps rendered more touching by
their simple brevity. They contrast finely with those elaborate and
iterated repinings, which we sometimes meet with, in poetry;—the
effusions of morbid minds, sickening under miseries of their own
creating, and venting their bitterness upon an unoffending world. James
speaks of his privations with acute sensibility, but having mentioned
them passes on, as if his manly mind disdained to brood over unavoid-
able calamities. When such a spirit breaks forth into complaint, however brief, we are aware how great must be the suffering that extorts
the murmur. We sympathize with James, a romantic, active, and accomplished prince, cut off in the lustihood of youth from all the
enterprise, the noble uses, and vigorous delights of life; as we do with
Milton, alive to all the beauties of nature and glories of art, when he
breathes forth brief, but deep toned lamentations, over his perpetual
blindness.

Had not James evinced a deficiency of poetic artifice, we might
almost have suspected that these lourings of gloomy reflection were
meant as preparative to the brightest scene of his story; and to contrast
with that refulgence of light and loveliness, that exhilarating ac-
companiment of bird and song, and foliage and flower, and all the
revel of the year, with which he ushers in the lady of his heart. It is this
scene in particular, which throws all the magic of romance about the
old castle keep. He had risen, he says, at day break, according to custom,
to escape from the dreary meditations of a sleepless pillow. "Bewailing
in his chamber thus alone," despairing of all joy and remedy, "fortired
of thought and wo begone," he had wandered to the window, to indulge
the captive's miserable solace of gazing wistfully upon the world from
which he is excluded. The window looked forth upon a small garden
which lay at the foot of the tower. It was a quiet, sheltered spot, adorned
with arbours and green alleys, and protected from the passing gaze by
trees and hawthorn hedges.

> Now was there made fast by the tower's wall,
>   A garden faire, and in the corners set,
> An arbour green with wandis long and small
>   Railed about, and so with leaves beset

Was all the place and hawthorn hedges knet,
  That lyf* was none, walkyng there forbye,
  That might within scarce any wight espye.

So thick the branches and the leves grene,
  Beshaded all the alleys that there were,
And midst of every arbour might be seen
  The sharpe, grene, sweet juniper,
Growing so fair, with branches here and there,
  That as it seemed to a lyf without,
  The boughs did spread the arbour all about.

And on the small grene twistis† set
  The lytel swete nightingales and sung
So loud and clere, the hymnis consecrate
  Of lovis use, now soft, now loud among,
That all the garden and the wallis rung
  Right of their song——

It was the month of May, when every thing was in bloom; and he interprets the song of the nightingale into the language of his enamoured feeling:

Worship all ye that lovers be this May,
  For of your bliss the kalends are begun,
And sing with us, away, winter away,
  Come, summer come, the sweet season and sun.

As he gazes on the scene, and listens to the notes of the birds, he gradually lapses into one of those tender and undefinable reveries, which fill the youthful bosom in this delicious season. He wonders what this love may be, of which he has so often read, and which thus seems breathed forth in the quickening breath of May, and melting all nature into ecstacy and song. If it really be so great a felicity, and if it be a boon thus generally dispensed to the most insignificant beings, why is he alone cut off from its enjoyments?

Oft would I think, O Lord, what, may this be
  That love is of such noble myght and kynde?

---

*Lyf, person.
†Twistis, small boughs or twigs.
Note.—The language of the quotations is generally modernized.

Loving his folk, and such prosperitee
Is it of him, as we in books do find:
  May he oure hertes setten° and unbynd:
Hath he upon our hertes such maistrye?
Or is all this but feynit fantasye?

For giff he be of so grete excellence,
  That he of every wight hath care and charge,
What have I gilt† to him, or done offense?
  That I am thral'd, and birdis go at large.

In the midst of his musing, as he casts his eye downward, he beholds "the fairest and the freshest young floure," that ever he had seen. It is the lovely lady Jane walking in the garden to enjoy the beauty of that "fresh May morrowe." Breaking thus suddenly upon his sight in the moment of loneliness and excited susceptibility, she at once captivates the fancy of the romantic prince, and becomes the object of his wandering wishes, the sovereign of his ideal world.

There is, in this charming scene, an evident resemblance to the early part of Chaucer's Knight's Tale; where Palamon and Arcite fall in love with Emilia, whom they see walking in the garden of their prison. Perhaps the similarity of the actual fact to the incident which he had read in Chaucer, may have induced James to dwell on it in his poem. His description of the Lady Jane is given in the picturesque and minute manner of his master; and being doubtless taken from the life, is a perfect portrait of a beauty of that day. He dwells, with the fondness of a lover, on every article of her apparel, from the net of pearl, splendent with emeralds and sapphires, that confined her golden hair, even to the "goodly chaine of small orfeverye‡" about her neck, whereby there hung a ruby in shape of a heart, that seemed, he says, like a spark of fire burning upon her white bosom. Her dress of white tissue was looped up to enable her to walk with more freedom. She was accompanied by two female attendants, and about her sported a little hound decorated with bells; probably the small Italian hound of exquisite symmetry, which was a parlour favourite and pet among the fashionable dames of ancient times. James closes his description by a burst of general eulogium.

In her was youth, beauty, with humble port,
  Bountee, richesse, and womanly feature;

°*Setten*, incline.
†*Gilt*, what injury have I done, &c.
‡Wrought gold.

God better knows than my pen can report,
 Wisdom, largesse,° estate,† and cunning‡ sure,
In every point so guided her mesure,
 In word, in deed, in shape, in countenance,
 That nature might no more her child advance.

The departure of the lady Jane from the garden, puts an end to this transient riot of the heart. With her departs the amorous illusion that had shed a temporary charm over the scene of his captivity, and he relapses into loneliness, now rendered tenfold more intolerable by this passing beam of unattainable beauty. Through the long and weary day he repines at his unhappy lot, and when evening approaches, and Phœbus, as he beautifully expresses it, had "bad farewell to every leaf and flower," he still lingers at the window, and laying his head upon the cold stone, gives vent to a mingled flow of love and sorrow, until gradually lulled by the mute melancholy of the twilight hour, he lapses "half sleeping, half swoon," into a vision which occupies the remainder of the poem, and in which is allegorically shadowed out the history of his passion.

When he wakes from his trance, he rises from his stony pillow, and, pacing his apartment, full of dreary reflections, questions his spirit whither it has been wandering; whether, indeed, all that has passed before his dreaming fancy, has been conjured up by preceding circumstances; or whether it is a vision, intended to comfort and assure him in his despondency. If the latter, he prays that some token may be sent to confirm the promise of happier days, given him in his slumbers. Suddenly a turtle dove, of the purest whiteness, comes flying in at the window and alights upon his hand, bearing in her bill a branch of red gilliflower, on the leaves of which is written, in letters of gold, the following sentence:

Awake! awake! I bring, lover, I bring
 The newis glad that blissful is, and sure
Of thy comfort; now laugh, and play, and sing,
 For in the heaven decretit is thy cure.

He receives the branch with mingled hope and dread; reads it with rapture: and this, he says, was the first token of his succeeding happiness. Whether this is a mere poetic fiction, or whether the Lady Jane did actually send him a token of her favour in this romantic way, remains

° *Largesse*, bounty.
† *Estate*, dignity.
‡ *Cunning*, discretion.

to be determined according to the faith or fancy of the reader. He concludes his poem, by intimating that the promise conveyed in the vision and by the flower, is fulfilled, by his being restored to liberty, and made happy in the possession of the sovereign of his heart.

Such is the poetical account given by James of his love adventures in Windsor Castle. How much of it is absolute fact, and how much the embellishment of fancy, it is fruitless to conjecture: let us not, however, reject every romantic incident as incompatible with real life; but let us sometimes take a poet at his word. I have noticed merely those parts of the poem immediately connected with the Tower, and have passed over a large part, written in the allegorical vein, so much cultivated at that day. The language, of course, is quaint and antiquated, so that the beauty of many of its golden phrases will scarcely be perceived at the present day; but it is impossible not to be charmed with the genuine sentiment, the delightful artlessness and urbanity, which prevail throughout it. The descriptions of nature, too, with which it is embellished, are given with a truth, a discrimination, and a freshness, worthy of the most cultivated periods of the art.

As an amatory poem it is edifying, in these days of coarser thinking, to notice the nature, refinement, and exquisite delicacy which pervade it; banishing every gross thought or immodest expression, and presenting female loveliness, clothed in all its chivalrous attributes of almost supernatural purity and grace.

James flourished nearly about the time of Chaucer and Gower, and was evidently an admirer and studier of their writings. Indeed in one of his stanzas he acknowledges them as his masters; and in some parts of his poem we find traces of similarity to their productions, more especially to those of Chaucer. There are always, however, general features of resemblance in the works of contemporary authors, which are not so much borrowed from each other as from the times. Writers, like bees, toll their sweets in the wide world; they incorporate with their own conceptions the anecdotes and thoughts current in society; and thus each generation has some features in common, characteristic of the age in which it lives.

James belongs to one of the most brilliant eras of our literary history, and establishes the claims of his country to a participation in its primitive honours. Whilst a small cluster of English writers are constantly cited as the fathers of our verse, the name of their great Scottish compeer is apt to be passed over in silence; but he is evidently worthy of being enrolled in that little constellation of remote but never failing luminaries, who shine in the highest firmament of literature, and who, like morning stars, sang together at the bright dawning of British poesy.

Such of my readers as may not be familiar with Scottish history (though the manner in which it has of late been woven with captivating fiction, has made it a universal study), may be curious to learn something of the subsequent history of James, and the fortunes of his love. His passion for the Lady Jane, as it was the solace of his captivity, so it facilitated his release, it being imagined by the court that a connection with the blood royal of England would attach him to its interests. He was ultimately restored to his liberty and crown, having previously espoused the Lady Jane, who accompanied him to Scotland, and made him a most tender and devoted wife.

He found his kingdom in great confusion, the feudal chieftains having taken advantage of the troubles and irregularities of a long interregnum to strengthen themselves in their possessions, and place themselves above the power of the laws. James sought to found the basis of his power in the affections of his people. He attached the lower orders to him by the reformation of abuses, the temperate and equable administration of justice, the encouragement of the arts of peace, and the promotion of every thing that could diffuse comfort, competency, and innocent enjoyment through the humblest ranks of society. He mingled occasionally among the common people in disguise; visited their fire sides; entered into their cares, their pursuits, and their amusements; informed himself of the mechanical arts, and how they could best be patronized and improved; and was thus an all pervading spirit, watching with a benevolent eye over the meanest of his subjects. Having in this generous manner, made himself strong in the hearts of the common people, he turned himself to curb the power of the factious nobility; to strip them of those dangerous immunities which they had usurped; to punish such as had been guilty of flagrant offences; and to bring the whole into proper obedience to the crown. For some time they bore this with outward submission, but secret impatience and brooding resentment. A conspiracy was at length formed against his life, at the head of which was his own uncle, Robert Stewart Earl of Athol, who, being too old himself for the perpetration of the deed of blood, instigated his grandson Sir Robert Stewart, together with Sir Robert Graham, and others of less note, to commit the deed. They broke into his bed chamber at the Dominican Convent near Perth, where he was residing, and barbarously murdered him by oft repeated wounds. His faithful queen rushing to throw her tender body between him and the sword, was twice wounded in the ineffectual attempt to shield him from the assassin, and it was not until she had been forcibly torn from his person, that the murder was accomplished.

It was the recollection of this romantic tale of former times, and of the golden little poem which had its birth place in this tower, that made me visit the old pile with more than common interest. The suit of armour hanging up in the hall, richly gilt and embellished as if to figure in the tournay, brought the image of the gallant and romantic prince vividly before my imagination. I paced the deserted chambers where he had composed his poem; I leaned upon the window and endeavoured to persuade myself it was the very one where he had been visited by his vision; I looked out upon the spot where he had first seen the Lady Jane. It was the same genial and joyous month; the birds were again vying with each other in strains of liquid melody; every thing was bursting into vegetation, and budding forth the tender promise of the year. Time, which delights to obliterate the sterner memorials of human pride, seems to have passed lightly over this little scene of poetry and love, and to have withheld his desolating hand. Several centuries have gone by, yet the garden still flourishes at the foot of the tower. It occupies what was once the moat of the keep; and though some parts have been separated by dividing walls, yet others have still their arbours and shaded walks, as in the days of James, and the whole is sheltered, blooming, and retired. There is a charm about a spot that has been printed by the footsteps of departed beauty, and consecrated by the inspirations of the poet, which is heightened, rather than impaired, by the lapse of ages. It is, indeed, the gift of poetry to hallow every place in which it moves; to breathe round nature an odour more exquisite than the perfume of the rose, and to shed over it a tint more magical than the blush of morning.

Others may dwell on the illustrious deeds of James as a warrior and a legislator; but I have delighted to view him merely as the companion of his fellow man, the benefactor of the human heart, stooping from his high estate to sow the sweet flowers of poetry and song in the paths of common life. He was the first to cultivate the vigorous and hardy plant of Scottish genius, which has since become so prolific of the most wholesome and highly flavoured fruit. He carried with him into the sterner regions of the north, all the fertilizing arts of southern refinement. He did every thing in his power to win his countrymen to the gay, the elegant, and gentle arts, which soften and refine the character of a people, and wreathe a grace round the loftiness of a proud and warlike spirit. He wrote many poems, which, unfortunately for the fullness of his fame, are now lost to the world; one which is still preserved, called "Christ's Kirk of the Green," shews how diligently he had made himself acquainted with the rustic sports and pastimes, which constitute such a source of kind and social feeling among the Scottish peasantry; and with what simple and happy humour he could enter into their enjoyments. He contributed greatly to improve the national music; and traces of his tender sentiment, and elegant taste, are said to exist in those witching airs, still piped among the wild mountains and lonely glens of Scotland. He has thus connected his image with whatever is most gracious and endearing in the national character; he has embalmed his memory in song, and floated his name to after ages in the rich stream of Scottish melody. The recollection of these things was kindling at my heart, as I paced the silent scene of his imprisonment. I have visited Vaucluse with as much enthusiasm as a pilgrim would visit the shrine at Loretto; but I have never felt more poetical devotion than when contemplating the old tower and the little garden at Windsor, and musing over the romantic loves of the Lady Jane and the Royal Poet of Scotland.

THE COUNTRY CHURCH

A gentleman?
What, o'the woolpack? or the sugar chest?
Or lists of velvet? which is't pound, or yard,
You vend your gentry by?

BEGGAR'S BUSH.

There are few places more favourable to the study of character than an English country church. I was once passing a few weeks at the seat of a friend who resided in the vicinity of one the appearance of which particularly struck my fancy. It was one of those rich morsels of quaint antiquity which give such a peculiar charm to English landscape. It stood in the midst of a county filled with ancient families, and contained within its cold and silent aisles, the congregated dust of many noble generations. The interior walls were encrusted with monuments of every age and style. The light streamed through windows dimmed with armorial bearings, richly emblazoned in stained glass. In various parts of the church were tombs of knights and high born dames of gorgeous workmanship, with their effigies in coloured marble. On every side the eye was struck with some instance of aspiring mortality; some haughty memorial which human pride had erected over its kindred dust, in this temple of the most humble of all religions.

The congregation was composed of the neighbouring people of rank, who sat in pews sumptuously lined and cushioned, furnished with richly gilded prayer books, and decorated with their arms upon the pew doors; —the villagers and peasantry, who filled the back seats, and a small gallery beside the organ, and the poor of the parish, who were ranged on benches in the aisles.

The service was performed by a snuffling well fed vicar, who had a snug dwelling near the church. He was a privileged guest at all the tables of the neighbourhood and had been the keenest foxhunter in the county, until age and good living had disabled him from doing any thing more than ride to see the hounds throw off, and make one at the hunting dinner.

Under the ministry of such a pastor I found it impossible to get into the train of thought suitable to the time and place, so having, like many other feeble christians, compromised with my conscience by laying the sin of my own delinquency at another person's threshold, I occupied myself by making observations of my neighbours.

I was as yet a stranger in England, and curious to notice the manners of its fashionable classes. I found, as usual, that there was the least pretension where there was the most acknowledged title to respect. I was particularly struck for instance, with the family of a nobleman of high rank, consisting of several sons and daughters. Nothing could be more simple and unassuming than their appearance. They generally came to church in the plainest equipage, and often on foot. The young ladies would stop and converse in the kindest manner with the peasantry, caress the children, and listen to the stories of the humble cottagers. Their countenances were open, beautifully fair, with an expression of high refinement, but at the same time a frank cheerfulness and an engaging affability. Their brothers were tall and elegantly formed. They were dressed fashionably but simply; with strict neatness and propriety, but without any mannerism or foppishness. Their whole demeanour was easy and natural, with that lofty grace and noble frankness, which bespeak free born souls that have never been checked in their growth by feelings of inferiority. There is a healthful hardiness about real dignity, that never dreads contact and communion with others, however humble. It is only spurious pride that is morbid and sensitive and shrinks from every touch. I was pleased to see the manner in which they would converse with the peasantry about those rural concerns and field sports, in which the gentlemen of this country so much delight. In these conversations there was neither haughtiness on the one part, nor servility on the other; and you were only reminded of the difference of rank by the habitual respect of the peasant.

In contrast to these was the family of a wealthy citizen, who had amassed a vast fortune, and having purchased the estate and mansion of a ruined nobleman in the neighbourhood, was endeavouring to assume all the style and dignity of an hereditary lord of the soil. The family always came to church *en prince*. They were rolled majestically along in a carriage emblazoned with arms. The crest glittered in silver radiance from every part of the harness where a crest could possibly be placed. A fat coachman in a three cornered hat, richly laced, and a flaxen wig, curling close around his rosy face, was seated on the box, with a sleek Danish dog beside him. Two footmen in gorgeous liveries, with huge boquets and gold headed canes lolled behind. The carriage rose and sunk on its long springs with peculiar stateliness of motion. The very horses champed their bits, arched their necks and glanced their eyes more proudly than common horses, either because they had caught a little of the family feeling, or were reined up more tightly than ordinary.

I could not but admire the style with which this splendid pageant was brought up to the gate of the church yard. There was a vast effect produced at the turning of an angle of the wall. A great cracking of the whip—straining and scrambling of the horses—glistering of harness and flashing of wheels through gravel. This was the moment of triumph and vain glory to the Coachman. The horses were urged and checked until they were fretted into a foam. They threw out their feet in a prancing trot, dashing about pebbles at every step. The crowd of villagers sauntering quietly to church opened precipitately to the right and left, gaping in vacant admiration—On reaching the gate the horses were pulled up with a suddenness that produced an immediate stop and almost threw them on their haunches.

There was an extraordinary hurry of the footmen to alight, open the door, pull down the steps and prepare every thing for the descent on earth of this august family. The old citizen first emerged his round red face from out the door, looking about him with the pompous air of a man accustomed to rule on change and shake the stock market with a nod. His consort, a fine, fleshy, comfortable dame followed him. There seemed, I must confess, but little pride in her composition. She was the picture of broad, honest, vulgar enjoyment. The world went well with her—and she liked the world. She had fine clothes, a fine house, a fine carriage, fine children, every thing was fine about her: it was nothing but driving about, and visiting, and feasting. Life was to her a perpetual revel; it was one long, lord mayor's day.

Two daughters succeeded to this goodly couple. They certainly were handsome but had a supercilious air, that chilled admiration and disposed the spectator to be critical. They were ultra-fashionables in dress, and though no one could deny the richness of their decorations, yet their appropriateness might be questioned amidst the simplicity of a country church. They descended loftily from the carriage and moved up the line of peasantry, with a step that seemed dainty of the soil it trod on. They cast an excursive glance around that passed coldly over the burly faces of the peasantry, until they met the eyes of the nobleman's family, when their countenances immediately brightened into smiles and they made the most profound and elegant courtsies; which were returned in a manner that shewed they were but slight acquaintances.

I must not forget the two sons of this aspiring citizen, who came to church in a dashing curricle with outriders. They were arrayed in the extremity of the mode, with all that pedantry of dress, which marks the man of questionable pretensions to style. They kept entirely by themselves, eying every one askance that came near them; as if measuring his claims to respectability; yet they were without conversation, except the exchange of an occasional cant phrase. They even moved artificially, for their bodies, in compliance with the caprice of the day, had been disciplined into the absence of all ease and freedom. Art had done every thing to accomplish them as men of fashion, but nature had denied the nameless grace. They were vulgarly shaped, like men formed for the common purposes of life and had that air of supercilious assumption which is never seen in the true gentleman.

I have been rather minute in drawing the pictures of these two families, because I considered them specimens of what is often to be met with in this country—the unpretending great and the arrogant little. I have no respect for titled rank, unless it be accompanied by true nobility of soul; but I have remarked, in all countries where artificial distinctions exist, the very highest classes are always the most courteous and unassuming—Those who are well assured of their own standing are least apt to trespass on that of others; whereas nothing is so offensive as the aspirings of vulgarity, which thinks to elevate itself by humiliating its neighbour.

As I have brought these families into contrast I must notice their behaviour in church. That of the nobleman's family was quiet, serious and attentive. Not that they appeared to have any fervour of devotion but rather a respect for sacred things and sacred places, inseparable from good breeding. The others on the contrary were in a perpetual flutter and whisper; they betrayed a continual consciousness of finery, and a sorry ambition of being the wonders of a rural congregation.

The old gentleman was the only one really attentive to the service. He took the whole burthen of family devotion upon himself; standing bolt upright and uttering the responses with a loud voice that might be heard all over the church. It was evident that he was one of those thorough Church and King men who connect the idea of devotion and loyalty; who consider the deity somehow or other, of the government party, and religion "a very excellent sort of thing that ought to be countenanced and kept up."

When he joined so loudly in the service it seemed more by way of example to the lower orders, to shew them, that though so great and wealthy, he was not above being religious, as I have seen a turtle fed alderman swallow publicly a basin of charity soup, smacking his lips at every mouthful and pronouncing it "excellent food for the poor."

When the service was at an end I was curious to witness the several exits of my groups. The young noblemen and their sisters as the day was fine preferred strolling home across the fields, chatting with the country people as they went. The others departed as they came, in grand parade. Again were the equipages wheeled up to the gate. There was again the smacking of whips, the clattering of hoofs and the glittering of harness. The horses started off almost at a bound; the villagers again hurried to right and left; the wheels threw up a cloud of dust, and the aspiring family was rapt out of sight in a whirlwind.

THE WIDOW AND HER SON

Pittie olde age, within whose silver haires
Honour and reverence ever more have raign'd.
                    MARLOWE'S TAMBURLAINE.

Those who are in the habit of remarking such matters must have
noticed the pensive quiet of an English landscape on Sunday. The
clacking of the mill, the regularly recurring stroke of the flail; the din
of the blacksmith's hammer; the whistling of the plowman; the rattling
of the cart, and all other sounds of rural labor are suspended. The very
farm dogs bark less frequently, being less disturbed by passing travellers.
At such times I have almost fancied the winds sunk into quiet and that
the sunny landscape, with its fresh green tints melting into blue haze,
enjoyed the hallowed calm.

> Sweet day, so pure, so calm, so bright,
> The bridal of the earth and sky.

Well was it ordained that the day of devotion should be a day of rest.
The holy repose which reigns over the face of nature, has its moral
influence; every restless passion is charmed down, and we feel the
natural religion of the soul gently springing up within us. For my part
there are feelings that visit me, in a country church, amid the beautiful
serenity of nature, which I experience no where else; and if not a more
religious, I think I am a better man on Sunday than on any other day
of the seven.

During my recent residence in the country I used frequently to attend
at the old village church. Its shadowy aisles; its mouldering monuments;
its dark oaken panelling, all reverend with the gloom of departed years,
seemed to fit it for the haunt of solemn meditation; but being in a
wealthy aristocratic neighborhood, the glitter of fashion penetrated even
into the sanctuary; and I felt myself continually thrown back upon the
world by the frigidity and pomp of the poor worms around me. The
only being in the whole congregation who appeared thoroughly to feel
the humble and prostrate piety of a true christian, was a poor, decrepid
old woman, bending under the weight of years and infirmities. She bore
the traces of something better than abject poverty. The lingerings of
decent pride were visible in her appearance. Her dress, though humble
in the extreme, was scrupulously clean. Some trivial respect too had
been awarded her, for she did not take her seat among the village poor,

but sat alone on the steps of the altar. She seemed to have survived all love, all friendship, all society, and to have nothing left her but the hopes of heaven. When I saw her feebly rising and bending her aged form in prayer; habitually conning her prayer book, which her palsied hand and failing eyes would not permit her to read, but which she evidently knew by heart—I felt persuaded that the faltering voice of that poor woman arose to heaven far before the responses of the clerk, the swell of the organ or the chaunting of the choir.

I am fond of loitering about country churches, and this was so delightfully situated that it frequently attracted me. It stood on a knoll, round which a small stream made a beautiful bend and then wound its way through a long reach of soft meadow scenery. The church was surrounded by yew trees, which seemed almost coeval with itself. Its tall gothic spire shot up lightly from among them, with rooks and crows generally wheeling about it. I was seated there one still sunny morning watching two labourers who were digging a grave. They had chosen one of the most remote and neglected corners of the church yard, where, from the number of nameless graves around, it would appear that the indigent and friendless were huddled into the earth. I was told that the new made grave was for the only son of a poor widow. While I was meditating on the distinctions of worldly rank, which extend thus down into the very dust, the toll of the bell announced the approach of the funeral. They were the obsequies of poverty, with which pride had nothing to do. A coffin of the plainest materials, without pall or other covering, was borne by some of the villagers. The sexton walked before with an air of cold indifference. There were no mock mourners in the trappings of affected woe, but there was one real mourner who feebly tottered after the corpse. It was the aged mother of the deceased—the poor old woman whom I had seen seated on the steps of the altar. She was supported by a humble friend, who was endeavouring to comfort her. A few of the neighbouring poor had joined the train, and some children of the village were running, hand in hand, now shouting with unthinking mirth, and now pausing to gaze with childish curiosity on the grief of the mourner.

As the funeral train approached the grave the parson issued from the church porch arrayed in the surplice, with prayer book in hand and attended by the clerk. The service, however, was a mere act of charity. The deceased had been destitute and the survivor was penniless. It was shuffled through, therefore, in form, but coldly and unfeelingly. The well fed priest moved but a few steps from the church door—his voice could scarcely be heard at the grave, and never did I hear the funeral service, that sublime and touching ceremony, turned into such a frigid mummery of words.

I approached the grave. The coffin was placed on the ground. On it were inscribed the name and age of the deceased. "George Somers, aged 26 Years." The poor mother had been assisted to kneel down at the head of it. Her withered hands were clasped as if in prayer, but I could perceive by a feeble rocking of the body, and a convulsive motion of the lips, that she was gazing on the last reliques of her son with the yearnings of a mother's heart.

Preparations were made to deposit the coffin in the earth. There was that bustling stir, which breaks so harshly on the feelings of grief and affection—directions given in the cold tones of business—the striking of spades into sand and gravel, which, at the grave of those we love, is of all sounds the most withering. The bustle around seemed to awaken the mother from a wretched reverie. She raised her glazed eyes, and looked about, with a faint wildness. As the men approached with cords to lower the coffin into the grave she wrung her hands and broke into an agony of grief. The poor woman who attended her took her by the arm, endeavouring to raise her from the earth and to whisper something like consolation—"Nay now—nay now—don't take it so sorely to heart—" She could only shake her head and wring her hands, as one not to be comforted.

As they lowered the body into the earth the creaking of the cords seemed to agonize her; but when, on some accidental obstruction there was a justling of the coffin, all the tenderness of the mother burst forth; as if any harm could come to him, who was far beyond the reach of worldly suffering.

I could see no more—my heart swelled into my throat—my eyes filled with tears—I felt as if I were acting a barbarous part in standing by and gazing idly on this scene of maternal anguish. I wandered to another part of the church yard where I remained until the funeral train had dispersed.

When I saw the mother slowly and painfully quitting the grave, leaving behind her the remains of all that was dear to her on earth, and returning to silence and destitution, my heart ached for her—What, thought I, are the distresses of the rich!—they have friends to soothe; pleasures to beguile; a world to divert and dissipate their griefs—What are the sorrows of the young! Their growing minds soon close above the wound—their elastic spirits soon rise beneath the pressure—their green and ductile affections soon twine around new objects—But the sorrows of the poor, who have no outward appliances to soothe—the sorrows of the aged with whom life at best is but a wintry day, and who can look for no aftergrowth of joy—the sorrows of a widow, aged, solitary, destitute, mourning over an only son the last solace of her years—these are indeed sorrows which make us feel the impotency of consolation.

It was some time before I left the church yard—on my way homeward I met with the woman who had acted as comforter: she was just returning from accompanying the mother to her lonely habitation, and I drew from her some particulars connected with the affecting scene I had witnessed.

The parents of the deceased had resided in the village from childhood. They had inhabited one of the neatest cottages, and by various rural occupations and the assistance of a small garden, had supported themselves creditably and comfortably, and led a happy and a blameless life. They had one son who had grown up to be the staff and pride of their age—"Oh sir!" said the good woman, "he was such a likely lad; so sweet tempered; so kind to every one round him; so dutiful to his parents! It did one's heart good to see him of a Sunday, drest out in his best, so tall, so straight, so cheery—supporting his old mother to church—for she was always fonder of leaning on George's arm than on her good man's—and, poor soul, she might well be proud of him, for a finer lad, there was not in the country round."

Unfortunately the son was tempted during a year of scarcity and agricultural hardship, to enter into the service of one of the small craft that plied on a neighbouring river. He had not been long in this employ when he was entrapped by a press gang and carried off to sea. His parents received tidings of his seizure, but beyond that they could learn nothing. It was the loss of their main prop. The father who was already infirm, grew heartless and melancholy and sunk into his grave. The widow left lonely in her age and feebleness could no longer support herself, and came upon the parish. Still there was a kind feeling towards her throughout the village and a certain respect as being one of the oldest inhabitants. As no one applied for the cottage in which she had passed so many happy days, she was permitted to remain in it, where she lived solitary and almost helpless—The few wants of nature were chiefly supplied from the scanty productions of her little garden, which the neighbours would now and then cultivate for her. It was but a few days before the time at which these circumstances were told me, that she was gathering some vegetables for her repast, when she heard the cottage door which faced the garden suddenly opened. A stranger came out and seemed to be looking eagerly and wildly around. He was dressed in seaman's clothes, was emaciated and ghastly pale, and bore the air of one broken by sickness and hardships. He saw her and hastened towards her, but his steps were faint and faltering—he sank on his knees before her and sobbed like a child. The poor woman gazed upon him with a vacant and wondering eye—"Oh my dear-dear mother! don't you know your son!—your poor boy George!" It was indeed the wreck of her once noble lad; who, shattered by wounds, by sickness and foreign imprisonment, had at length dragged his wasted limbs homeward to repose among the scenes of his childhood.

I will not attempt to detail the particulars of such a meeting, where joy and sorrow were so completely blended—Still he was alive!—he was come home!—he might yet live to comfort and cherish her old age!— Nature, however, was exhausted in him, and if any thing had been wanting to finish the work of fate, the desolation of his native cottage would have been sufficient. He stretched himself on the pallet on which his widowed mother had passed many a sleepless night, and he never rose from it again.

The villagers, when they heard that George Somers had returned, crowded to see him, offering every comfort and assistance that their humble means afforded. He was too weak, however, to talk—he could only look his thanks. His mother was his constant attendant; and he seemed unwilling to be helped by any other hand.

There is something in sickness that breaks down the pride of manhood; that softens the heart and brings it back to the feelings of infancy. Who that has languished, even in advanced life, in sickness and despondency— who that has pined on a weary bed in the neglect and loneliness of a foreign land—but has thought on the mother "that looked on his child-hood," that smoothed his pillow and administered to his helplessness.— Oh! there is an enduring tenderness in the love of a mother to her son that transcends all other affections of the heart. It is neither to be chilled by selfishness—nor daunted by danger—nor weakened by worthlessness— nor stifled by ingratitude. She will sacrifice every comfort to his con-venience—she will surrender every pleasure to his enjoyment—she will glory in his fame and exult in his prosperity. And if misfortune overtake him he will be the dearer to her from misfortune—and if dis-grace settle upon his name, she will still love and cherish him in spite of his disgrace—and if all the world beside cast him off, she will be all the world to him—

Poor George Somers had known what it was to be in sickness and none to soothe, lonely and in prison and none to visit him. He could not endure his mother from his sight—if she moved away, his eye would follow her. She would sit for hours by his bed watching him as he slept. Sometimes he would start from a feverish dream, and look anxiously up until he saw her bending over him, when he would take her hand, lay it on his bosom and fall asleep with the tranquility of a child—In this way he died.

My first impulse on hearing this humble tale of affliction, was to visit the cottage of the mourner and administer pecuniary assistance, and, if possible comfort. I found, however, on enquiry, that the good feelings of the villagers had prompted them to do every thing that the case admitted: and as the poor know best how to console each other's sorrows, I did not venture to intrude.

The next Sunday I was at the village church; when to my surprize, I saw the poor old woman tottering down the aisle to her accustomed seat on the steps of the altar.

She had made an effort to put on something like mourning for her son; and nothing could be more touching than this struggle between pious affection and utter poverty—A black ribband, or so—a faded black handkerchief—and one or two more such humble attempts to express by outward signs that grief which passes shew—When I looked round upon the storied monuments—the stately hatchments—the cold marble pomp, with which grandeur mourned magnificently over departed pride; and turned to this poor widow bowed down by age and sorrow at the altar of her god, and offering up the prayers and praises of a pious, though a broken heart, I felt that this living monument of real grief was worth them all.

I related her story to some of the wealthy members of the congregation and they were moved by it. They exerted themselves to render her situation more comfortable, and to lighten her afflictions. It was, however, but smoothing a few steps to the grave. In the course of a Sunday or two after she was missed from her usual seat at church, and before I left the neighbourhood I heard with a feeling of satisfaction that she had quietly breathed her last, and had gone to rejoin those she loved, in that world where sorrow is never known, and friends are never parted.

A SUNDAY IN LONDON*

In a preceding paper I have spoken of an English Sunday in the country and its tranquilizing effect upon the landscape; but where is its sacred influence more strikingly apparent than in the very heart of that great Babel, London? On this sacred day the gigantic monster is charmed into repose. The intolerable din and struggle of the week are at an end. The shops are shut. The fires of forges and manufactories are extinguished; and the sun, no longer obscured by murky clouds of smoke, pours down a sober yellow radiance into the quiet streets. The few pedestrians we meet, instead of hurrying forward with anxious countenances, move leisurely along; their brows are smoothed from the wrinkles of business and care; they have put on their Sunday looks, and Sunday manners, with their Sunday clothes, and are cleansed in mind as well as in person.

And now the melodious clangor of bells from church towers summons their several flocks to the fold. Forth issues from his mansion the family of the decent tradesman; the small children in the advance; then the citizen and his comely spouse, followed by the grown up daughters, with small morocco bound prayerbooks laid in the folds of their pocket-handkerchiefs. The housemaid looks after them from the window, admiring the finery of the family, and receiving, perhaps, a nod and smile from her young mistresses, at whose toilette she has assisted.

Now rumbles along the carriage of some magnate of the city; peradventure an Alderman or a Sheriff; and now the patter of many feet announces a procession of charity scholars in uniforms of antique cut, and each with a prayerbook under his arm.

The ringing of bells is at an end; the rumbling of the carriage has ceased; the pattering of feet is heard no more: the flocks are folded in ancient churches cramped up in bye lanes and corners of the crowded city; where the vigilant beadle keeps watch, like the shepherd's dog, round the threshhold of the sanctuary. For a time every thing is hushed; but soon is heard the deep pervading sound of the organ, rolling and vibrating through the empty lanes and courts; and the sweet chaunting of the choir making them resound with melody and praise. Never have I been more sensible of the sanctifying effect of church music than when I have heard it thus poured forth, like a river of joy through the inmost recesses of this great metropolis, cleansing it, as it were, from all the sordid pollutions of the week; and bearing the poor world worn soul on a tide of triumphant harmony to heaven.

*Part of a sketch omitted in the preceding editions.

The morning service is at an end. The streets are again alive with the congregations returning to their homes, but soon again relapse into silence. Now comes on the Sunday dinner, which to the city tradesman, is a meal of some importance. There is more leisure for social enjoyment at the board. Members of the family can now gather together, who are separated by the laborious occupations of the week. A school boy may be permitted on that day to come to the paternal home; an old friend of the family takes his accustomed Sunday seat at the board, tells over his well known stories and rejoices young and old with his well known jokes.

On Sunday afternoon the city pours forth its legions to breathe the fresh air and enjoy the sunshine of the parks and rural environs. Satyrists may say what they please about the rural enjoyments of a London citizen on Sunday, but to me there is something delightful in beholding the poor prisoner of the crowded and dusty city enabled thus to come forth once a week and throw himself upon the green bosom of nature. He is like a child restored to the mother's breast; and they who first spread out these noble parks and magnificent pleasure grounds which surround this huge metropolis, have done at least as much for its health and morality as if they had expended the amount of cost in hospitals, prisons and penitentiaries.

THE BOAR'S HEAD TAVERN, EAST CHEAP
A Shakespearian Research

A tavern is the rendezvous, the Exchange, the staple of good fellows. I have heard my great grandfather tell, how his great, great grandfather should say, that it was an old proverb when his great grandfather was a child, that "it was a good wind that blew a man to the wine."

MOTHER BOMBIE.

It is a pious custom in some Catholic countries to honour the memory of saints, by votive lights burnt before their pictures. The popularity of a saint, therefore, may be known by the number of these offerings. One perhaps is left to moulder in the darkness of his little chapel; another may have a solitary lamp to throw its blinking rays athwart his effigy; while the whole blaze of adoration is lavished at the shrine of some beatified father of renown. The wealthy devotee brings his huge luminary of wax, the eager zealot his seven branched candlestick, and even the mendicant pilgrim is by no means satisfied that sufficient light is thrown upon the deceased, unless he hang up his little lamp of smoking oil. The consequence is, that in the eagerness to enlighten they are often apt to obscure; and I have occasionally seen an unlucky saint, almost smoked out of countenance by the officiousness of his followers.

In like manner has it fared with the immortal Shakespeare. Every writer considers it his bounden duty to light up some portion of his character or works, and to rescue some merit from oblivion. The commentator, opulent in words, produces vast tomes of dissertations; the common herd of editors send up mists of obscurity from their notes at the bottom of each page, and every casual scribbler brings his farthing rush light of eulogy or research, to swell the cloud of incense and of smoke.

As I honour all established usages of my brethren of the quill, I thought it but proper to contribute my mite of homage to the memory of the illustrious bard. I was for some time, however, sorely puzzled in what way I should discharge this duty. I found myself anticipated in every attempt at a new reading; every doubtful line had been explained a dozen different ways and perplexed beyond the reach of elucidation; and as to fine passages, they had all been amply praised by previous admirers; nay, so completely had the bard of late been overlarded with panegyrick by a great German critick, that it was difficult now to find even a fault that had not been argued into a beauty.

In this perplexity I was one morning turning over his pages, when

I casually opened upon the comic scenes of Henry the Fourth, and was in a moment completely lost in the mad cap revelry of the Boar's head Tavern. So vividly and naturally are these scenes of humour depicted, and with such force and consistency are the characters sustained, that they become mingled up in the mind with the facts and personages of real life. To few readers does it occur that these are all ideal creations of a poet's brain, and that, in sober truth, no such knot of merry roysters ever enlivened the dull neighbourhood of East cheap.

For my part I love to give myself up to the illusions of poetry. A Hero of fiction who never existed, is just as valuable to me as a hero of history who existed a thousand years since; and, if I may be excused such an insensibility to the common ties of human nature, I would not give up fat Jack, for half the great men of ancient chronicle. What have the heroes of yore done for me, or men like me?—They have conquered countries of which I do not enjoy an acre—or they have gained laurels of which I do not inherit a leaf—or they have furnished examples of hairbrained prowess, which I have neither the opportunity nor the inclination to follow. But old Jack Falstaff!—kind Jack Falstaff!—sweet Jack Falstaff!—has enlarged the boundaries of human enjoyment; he has added vast regions of wit and good humour, in which the poorest man may revel; and has bequeathed a never failing inheritance of jolly laughter to make mankind merrier and better to the latest posterity.

A thought suddenly struck me—"I will make a pilgrimage to East cheap," said I, closing the book, "and see if the old Boar's head Tavern still exists. Who knows but I may light upon some legendary traces of Dame Quickly and her guests; at any rate, there will be a kindred pleasure in treading the halls once vocal with their mirth, to that the toper enjoys, in smelling to the empty cask, once filled with generous wine."

The resolution was no sooner formed than put in execution. I forbear to treat of the various adventures and wonders I encountered in my travels—of the haunted regions of Cock-lane—of the faded glories of Little Britain and the parts adjacent; what perils I ran in Cateaton Street and Old Jewry; of the renowned Guildhall and its two stunted Giants, the pride and wonder of the city and the terror of all unlucky urchins—and how I visited London Stone and struck my staff upon it in imitation of that arch rebel Jack Cade.

Let it suffice to say, that I at length arrived in merry East cheap, that ancient region of wit and wassail, where the very names of the streets relished of good cheer, as Pudding Lane bears testimony even at the present day. For East cheap says old Stow, "was always famous for its convivial doings. The cookes cried hot ribbes of beef rosted, pies well baked and other victuals: there was clattering of pewter pots, harpe, pipe and sawtrie." Alas! how sadly is the scene changed since the roaring days of Falstaff and old Stow. The mad cap royster has given place to the plodding tradesman—the clattering of pots and the sound of "harp and sawtry" to the din of carts and the accursed dinging of the dustman's bell; and no song is heard save haply the strain of some syren from Billingsgate chaunting the eulogy of deceased mackrel.

I sought in vain for the ancient abode of Dame Quickly. The only relique of it is a boar's head carved in relief in stone, which formerly served as the sign, but at present is built into the parting line of two houses which stand on the scite of the renowned old Tavern.

For the history of this little empire of good fellowship I was referred to a Tallow chandler's widow opposite, who had been born and brought up on the spot, and was looked up to as the indisputable chronicler of the neighbourhood. I found her seated in a little back parlour, the window of which looked out upon a yard about eight feet square, laid out as a flower garden; while a glass door opposite afforded a distant peep of the street through a vista of soap and tallow candles: the two views which comprised in all probability her prospects of life, and the little world in which she had lived, and moved, and had her being, for the better part of a century.

To be versed in the history of East cheap, great and little, from London Stone even unto the Monument, was doubtless in her opinion to be acquainted with the history of the universe. Yet with all this she possessed the simplicity of true wisdom, and that liberal, communicative disposition, which I have generally remarked in intelligent old ladies, knowing in the concerns of their neighbourhood.

Her information, however, did not extend far back into antiquity. She could throw no light upon the history of the Boar's head from the time that Dame Quickly espoused the valiant Pistol, until the great fire of London, when it was unfortunately burnt down. It was soon rebuilt, and continued to flourish under the old name and sign, until a dying Landlord, struck with remorse for double scores, bad measures, and other iniquities which are incident to the sinful race of Publicans, endeavoured to make his peace with heaven by bequeathing the tavern to St. Michael's church, Crooked Lane, towards the supporting of a chaplain. For some time the vestry meetings were regularly held there, but it was observed that the old Boar never held up his head under church government. He gradually declined, and finally gave his last gasp about thirty years since. The tavern was then turned into shops, but she informed me that a picture of it was still preserved in St. Michael's church, which stood just in the rear. To get a sight of this picture was now my determination, so having informed myself of the abode of the sexton I took my leave of the venerable chronicler of East cheap, my visit having doubtless raised greatly her opinion of her legendary lore, and furnished an important incident in the history of her life.

It cost me some difficulty and much curious enquiry to ferret out the humble hanger on to the church. I had to explore Crooked Lane and divers little alleys and elbows and dark passages, with which this old city is perforated, like an ancient cheese, or a worm eaten chest of drawers. At length I traced him to a corner of a small court, surrounded by lofty houses, where the inhabitants enjoy about as much of the face of heaven, as a community of frogs at the bottom of a well. The sexton was a meek acquiescing little man, of a bowing lowly habit; yet he had a pleasant twinkle in his eye, and if encouraged would now and then hazard a small pleasantry, such as a man of his low estate might venture to make in the company of high church wardens, and other mighty men of the earth. I found him in company with the deputy organist, seated apart, like Milton's angels discoursing no doubt on high doctrinal points, and settling the affairs of the church over a friendly pot of ale—for the lower classes of English seldom deliberate on any weighty matter without the assistance of a cool tankard to clear their understandings. I arrived at the moment when they had finished their ale and their argument, and were about to repair to the church to put it in order, so having made known my wishes I received their gracious permission to accompany them.

The church of St. Michael, Crooked Lane, standing a short distance from Billingsgate, is enriched with the tombs of many Fishmongers of renown, and as every profession has its galaxy of glory and its constellation of great men, I presume the monument of a mighty Fishmonger of the olden time, is regarded with as much reverence by succeeding generations of the craft as poets feel on contemplating the tomb of Virgil, or soldiers the monument of a Marlborough or a Turenne.

I cannot but turn aside, while thus speaking of illustrious men, to observe that St. Michael's Crooked Lane contains also the ashes of that doughty champion William Walworth, knight, who so manfully clove down the sturdy wight Wat Tyler in Smithfield, a hero worthy of honorable blazon as almost the only Lord Mayor on record, famous for deeds of arms:—the Sovereigns of Cockney being generally renowned, as the most pacific of all potentates.*

Note

*The following was the ancient inscription on the monument of this worthy—which unhappily was destroyed in the great conflagration—

> Hereunder lyth a man of Fame
> William Walworth callyd by name:
> Fishmonger he was in Lyfftime here

Adjoining the church, in a small cemetery, immediately under the back windows of what was once the Boar's head stands the tomb stone of Robert Preston, whilom drawer at the Tavern. It is now nearly a century since this trusty drawer of good liquor closed his bustling career, and was thus quietly deposited within call of his customers. As I was clearing away the weeds from his epitaph the little sexton drew me on one side with a mysterious air, and informed me in a low voice, that once upon a time on a dark wintry night, when the wind was unruly, howling and whistling, banging about doors and windows and twirling weather cocks so that the living were frightened out of their beds and even the dead could not sleep quietly in their graves, the ghost of honest Preston, which happened to be airing itself in the church yard, was attracted by the well known call of "waiter" from the Boar's head, and made its sudden appearance in the midst of a roaring club, just as the parish clerk was singing a stave from the "mirrie garland of captain Death"—to the discomfiture of sundry train-band captains and the conversion of an infidel attorney, who became a zealous christian on the spot and was never known to twist the truth afterwards except in the way of business.

I beg it may be remembered that I do not pledge myself for the authenticity of this anecdote, though it is well known that the church yards and bye corners of this old metropolis are very much infested with perturbed spirits and every one must have heard of the Cock Lane Ghost, and the apparition that guards the regalia in the Tower, which has frightened so many bold sentinels almost out of their wits.

Be all this as it may, this Robert Preston seems to have been a worthy successor to the nimble tongued Francis who attended upon the revels of Prince Hal, to have been equally prompt with his "anon, anon, sir"

And twise Lord Maior, as in Books appere;
Who with courage stout and manly myght
Slew Jackstraw in King Richards syght.
For which act done and trew Entent
The Kyng made him Knyght incontinent;
And gave him armes, as here you see,
To declare his Fact and chivaldrie.
He left this Lyff the yere of our God
Thirteen hondred fourscore and three odd.

An error in the foregoing inscription has been corrected by the venerable Stow— "Whereas," saith he, "it hath been far spread abroad by vulgar opinion, that the rebel smitten down so manfully by Sir William Walworth, the then worthy Lord Maior was named Jack Straw and not Wat Tyler, I thought good to reconcile this rash conceived doubt by such testimony as I find in ancient and good records. The principal Leaders or captains of the commons were Wat Tyler as the first man; the second was John or Jack Straw &c &c." Stow's London.

and to have transcended his predecessor in honesty, for Falstaff, the veracity of whose taste no man will venture to impeach, flatly accuses Francis of putting lime in his sack: whereas honest Preston's epitaph lauds him for the sobriety of his conduct, the soundness of his wine and the fairness of his measure.° The worthy dignitaries of the church, however, did not appear much captivated by the sober virtues of the Tapster; the deputy organist, who had a moist look out of the eye, made some shrewd remark on the abstemiousness of a man brought up among full hogsheads, and the little sexton corroborated his opinion by a significant wink and a dubious shake of the head.

Thus far my researches, though they threw much light on the history of Tapsters, Fishmongers and Lord Mayors, yet disappointed me in the great object of my quest, the picture of the Boar's head Tavern. No such painting was to be found in the church of St. Michael. "Marry and amen!" said I, "here endeth my research!" So I was giving the matter up with the air of a baffled antiquary, when my friend the sexton, perceiving me to be curious in every thing relative to the old Tavern, offered to shew me the choice vessels of the vestry, which had been handed down from remote times, when the parish meetings were held at the Boar's head. These were deposited in the Parish club room, which had been transferred, on the decline of the ancient establishment, to a tavern in the neighbourhood.

A few steps brought us to the house which stands No. 12. Miles Lane, bearing the title of The Mason's arms, and is kept by Master Edward Honeyball, the "bully Rock" of the establishment. It is one of those little taverns which abound in the heart of the city and form the centre of gossip and intelligence of the neighbourhood.

We entered the bar room, which was narrow and darkling; for in these close lanes but few rays of reflected light are enabled to struggle down

Note.

°As this inscription is rife with excellent morality, I transcribe it for the admonition of delinquent Tapsters. It is no doubt the production of some choice spirit who once frequented the Boar's head.

> "Bacchus to give the toping world surprize
> Produced one sober son, and here he lies.
> Though rear'd among full hogsheads he defy'd
> The charms of wine, and every one beside.
> O reader if to justice thou'rt inclin'd
> Keep honest Preston daily in thy mind.
> He drew good wine, took care to fill his pots
> Had sundry virtues that excus'd his faults.
> You that on Bacchus have the like dependance,
> Pray copy Bob, in measure and attendance."

to the inhabitants, whose broad day is at best but a tolerable twilight. The room was partitioned into boxes, each containing a table spread with a clean white cloth ready for dinner. This shewed that the guests were of the good old stamp, and divided their day equally; for it was but just one O'clock. At the lower end of the room was a clear coal fire, before which a breast of lamb was roasting. A row of bright brass candlesticks and pewter mugs glistened along the mantle piece, and an old fashioned clock ticked in one corner. There was something primitive in this medley of Kitchen, Parlour and Hall, that carried me back to earlier times and pleased me. The place indeed was humble, but every thing had that look of order and neatness which bespeaks the superintendance of a notable English housewife. A group of amphibious looking beings, who might be either fishermen or sailors were regaling themselves in one of the boxes. As I was a visitor of rather higher pretensions I was ushered into a little misshapen back room having at least nine corners. It was lighted by a sky light, furnished with antiquated leathern chairs and ornamented with the portrait of a fat pig. It was evidently appropriated to particular customers, and I found a shabby gentleman, in a red nose and oil cloth hat, seated in one corner, meditating on a half empty pot of porter.

The old sexton had taken the landlady aside and with an air of profound importance imparted to her my errand. Dame Honeyball was a likely, plump, bustling little woman, and no bad substitute for that paragon of hostesses Dame Quickly. She seemed delighted with an opportunity to oblige, and hurrying up stairs to the archives of her house, where the precious vessels of the parish club were deposited, she returned smiling and curtseying with them in her hands.

The first she presented me was a japanned iron Tobacco box of gigantic size, out of which I was told the vestry had smoked at their stated meetings since time immemorial; and which was never suffered to be profaned by vulgar hands or used on common occasions. I received it with becoming reverence, but what was my delight on beholding on its cover the identical painting of which I was in quest. There was displayed the outside of the Boar's head Tavern, and before the door was to be seen the whole convivial group at table in full revel; pictured with that wonderful fidelity and force, with which the portraits of renowned generals and commodores are illustrated on Tobacco boxes, for the benefit of posterity. Lest, however, there should be any mistake, the cunning limner had warily inscribed the names of Prince Hal and Falstaff on the bottoms of their chairs.

On the inside of the cover was an inscription, nearly obliterated, recording that this box was the gift of Sir Richard Gore, for the use of the vestry meetings at the Boar's head Tavern, and that it was "repaired and beautified by his successor Mr. John Packard 1767." Such is a faithful description of this august and venerable relique, and I question whether the learned Scriblerius contemplated his Roman shield, or the Knights of the Round Table the long sought san-greal with more exultation.

While I was meditating on it with enraptured gaze, Dame Honeyball, who was highly gratified by the interest it excited, put in my hands a drinking cup or goblet, which also belonged to the vestry, and was descended from the old Boar's head. It bore the inscription of having been the gift of Francis Wythers, Knight, and was held, she told me, in exceeding great value, being considered very "antyke." This last opinion was strengthened by the shabby gentleman in the red nose and oil cloth hat, and whom I strongly suspected of being a lineal descendant from the valiant Bardolph. He suddenly aroused from his meditation on the pot of porter, and casting a knowing look at the goblet exclaimed— "Aye-aye, the head don't ache now, that made that there article."—

The great importance attached to this memento of ancient revelry by modern church wardens, at first puzzled me; but there is nothing sharpens the apprehension so much as antiquarian research; for I immediately perceived that this could be no other than the identical "parcel-gilt goblet" on which Falstaff made his loving but faithless vow to Dame Quickly; and which would of course be treasured up with care among the regalia of her domains, as a testimony of that solemn contract.*

Mine hostess indeed gave me a long history how the goblet had been handed down from generation to generation. She also entertained me with many particulars concerning the worthy vestrymen who have seated themselves thus quietly on the stools of the ancient roysters of East cheap, and, like so many commentators, utter clouds of smoke in honour of Shakespeare. These I forbear to relate, lest my readers should not be as curious in these matters as myself. Suffice it to say, the neighbours one and all about East cheap, believe that Falstaff and his merry crew actually lived and revelled there. Nay there are several legendary anecdotes concerning him still extant among the oldest frequenters of the Mason's arms; which they give, as transmitted down from their forefathers; and Mr. McKash, an Irish hair dresser, whose shop stands on

Note.

*Thou didst swear to me, upon a *parcel-gilt goblet*, sitting in my Dolphin chamber, at the round table, by a sea coal fire, on Wednesday in Whitsunweek, when the prince broke thy head for likening his father to a singing man of Windsor; thou didst swear to me then, as I was washing thy wound, to marry me, and make me my lady thy wife. Canst thou deny it? II⌀ Part. Henry IV.

the scite of the old Boar's head, has several dry jokes of Fat Jack's, not laid down in the books, with which he makes his customers ready to die of laughter.

I now turned to my friend the sexton to make some further enquiries, but I found him sunk in pensive meditation. His head had declined a little on one side—a deep sigh heaved from the very bottom of his stomach, and though I could not see a tear trembling in his eye, yet a moisture was evidently stealing from a corner of his mouth. I followed the direction of his eye through the door which stood open and found it fixed wistfully on the savoury breast of lamb, roasting in dripping richness before the fire.

I now called to mind, that in the eagerness of my recondite investigation I was keeping the poor man from his dinner. My bowels yearned with sympathy, and, putting in his hand a small token of my gratitude and good will, I departed with a hearty benediction on him, Dame Honeyball and the parish club of Crooked Lane—not forgetting my shabby, but sententious friend, in the oil cloth hat and copper nose.

Thus have I given a "tedious brief" account of this interesting research, for which, if it prove too short and unsatisfactory, I can only plead my inexperience in this branch of literature so deservedly popular at the present day. I am aware that a more skillful illustrator of the immortal bard would have swelled the materials I have but touched upon, to a good merchantable bulk—comprizing the biographies of William Walworth, Jack Straw and Robert Preston—some notice of the Eminent Fishmongers of St. Michael's—the history of East cheap, great and little— private anecdotes of Dame Honeyball and her pretty daughter, whom I have not even mentioned, to say nothing of a damsel tending the breast of lamb (and whom, by the way, I remarked to be a comely lass, with a neat foot and ancle)—the whole enlivened by the riots of Wat Tyler, and illuminated by the great fire of London.

All this I leave as a rich mine to be worked by future commentators; nor do I despair of seeing the Tobacco box and the "parcel-gilt goblet" which I have thus brought to light, the subjects of future engravings and almost as fruitful of voluminous dissertations and disputes as the shield of Achilles, or the far famed Portland vase.

THE
MUTABILITY OF LITERATURE
A COLLOQUY IN WESTMINSTER ABBEY

I know that all beneath the moon decays,
And what by mortals in this world is brought,
In time's great period shall return to nought.
I know that all the muses' heavenly layes,
With toil of sprite which are so dearly bought,
As idle sounds of few or none are sought,
That there is nothing lighter than mere praise.
DRUMMOND OF HAWTHORNDEN.

There are certain half dreaming moods of mind, in which we naturally steal away from noise and glare, and seek some quiet haunt, where we may indulge our reveries and build our air castles undisturbed. In such a mood I was loitering about the old gray cloisters of Westminster Abbey, enjoying that luxury of wandering thought which one is apt to dignify with the name of reflection, when suddenly an irruption of madcap boys from Westminster school playing at football broke in upon the monastic stillness of the place, making the vaulted passages and mouldering tombs echo with their merriment. I sought to take refuge from their noise by penetrating still deeper into the solitudes of the pile, and applied to one of the vergers for admission to the library. He conducted me through a portal rich with the crumbling sculpture of former ages, which opened upon a gloomy passage leading to the chapter house and the chamber in which doomsday book is deposited. Just within the passage is a small door on the left. To this the verger applied a key; it was double locked, and opened with some difficulty, as if seldom used. We now ascended a dark narrow staircase, and passing through a second door, entered the library.

I found myself in a lofty antique hall, the roof supported by massive joists of old English oak. It was soberly lighted by a row of Gothic windows at a considerable height from the floor, and which apparently opened upon the roofs of the cloisters. An ancient picture of some reverend dignitary of the church in his robes hung over the fire place. Around the hall and in a small gallery were the books, arranged in carved oaken cases. They consisted principally of old polemical writers, and were much more worn by time than use. In the centre of the library was a solitary table with two or three books on it; an inkstand without ink, and a few pens parched by long disuse. The place seemed fitted for quiet study and profound meditation. It was buried deep among the massive walls of the abbey, and shut up from the tumult of the world. I could only hear now and then the shouts of the schoolboys faintly swelling from the cloister, and the sound of a bell tolling for prayers, echoing soberly along the roofs of the abbey. By degrees the shouts of merriment grew fainter and fainter, and at length died away. The bell ceased to toll, and a profound silence reigned through the dusky hall.

I had taken down a little thick quarto, curiously bound in parchment, with brass clasps, and seated myself at the table in a venerable elbow chair. Instead of reading, however, I was beguiled by the solemn monastic air, and lifeless quiet of the place, into a train of musing. As I looked around upon the old volumes in their mouldering covers, thus ranged on the shelves, and apparently never disturbed in their repose, I could not but consider the library a kind of literary catacomb, where authors, like mummies, are piously entombed, and left to blacken and moulder in dusty oblivion.

How much, thought I, has each of these volumes, now thrust aside with such indifference, cost some aching head; how many weary days— how many sleepless nights. How have their authors buried themselves in the solitude of cells and cloisters; shut themselves up from the face of man, and the still more blessed face of nature, and devoted themselves to painful research and intense reflection. And all for what! to occupy an inch of dusty shelf—to have the title of their works read now and then in a future age, by some drowsy churchman, or casual straggler like myself; and in another age to be lost, even to remembrance. Such is the amount of this boasted immortality.—A mere temporary rumour, a local sound, like the tone of that bell which has just tolled among these towers, filling the ear for a moment—lingering transiently in echo—and then passing away, like a thing that was not!

While I sat half murmuring, half meditating these unprofitable speculations, with my head resting on my hand, I was thrumming with the other hand upon the quarto, until I accidentally loosened the clasps, when, to my utter astonishment, the little book gave two or three yawns, like one awakening from a deep sleep; then a husky hem, and at length began to talk. At first its voice was very hoarse and broken, being much troubled by a cobweb which some studious spider had woven across it; and having probably contracted a cold from long exposure to the chills and damps of the abbey. In a short time, however, it became more distinct, and I soon found it an exceedingly fluent conversable little tome. Its language, to be sure, was rather quaint and obsolete, and its pronunciation, what, in the present day, would be deemed barbarous; but I shall endeavour, as far as I am able, to render it in modern parlance.

It began with railings about the neglect of the world—about merit being suffered to languish in obscurity, and other such common place topics of literary repining, and complained bitterly that it had not been opened for more than two centuries. That the Dean only looked now and then into the library, sometimes took down a volume or two, trifled with them for a few moments, and then returned them to their shelves. "What a plague do they mean," said the little quarto, which I began to perceive was somewhat choleric, "what a plague do they mean by keeping several thousand volumes of us shut up here, and watched by a set of old vergers like so many beauties in a harem, merely to be looked at now and then by the Dean? Books were written to give pleasure and to be enjoyed; and I would have a rule passed that the Dean should pay each of us a visit at least once a year; or if he is not equal to the task, let them once in a while turn loose the whole school of Westminster among us, that at any rate we may now and then have an airing."

"Softly, my worthy friend," replied I, "you are not aware how much better you are off than most books of your generation. By being stored away in this ancient library, you are like the treasured remains of those saints and monarchs which lie enshrined in the adjoining chapels, while the remains of your contemporary mortals, left to the ordinary course of nature, have long since returned to dust."

"Sir," said the little tome, ruffling his leaves and looking big, "I was written for all the world, not for the bookworms of an abbey. I was intended to circulate from hand to hand, like other great contemporary works; but here have I been clasped up for more than two centuries, and might have silently fallen a prey to these worms that are playing the very vengeance with my intestines, if you had not by chance given me an opportunity of uttering a few last words before I go to pieces."

"My good friend," rejoined I, "had you been left to the circulation of which you speak, you would long ere this have been no more. To judge from your physiognomy, you are now well stricken in years: very few of your contemporaries can be at present in existence; and those few owe their longevity to being immured like yourself in old libraries; which, suffer me to add, instead of likening to harems, you might more properly and gratefully have compared to those infirmaries attached to religious establishments, for the benefit of the old and decrepid, and where, by quiet fostering and no employment, they often endure to an amazingly good for nothing old age. You talk of your contemporaries as if in circulation—where do we meet with their works? what do we hear of Robert Grosteste of Lincoln? No one could have toiled harder than he for immortality. He is said to have written nearly two hundred volumes. He built, as it were, a pyramid of books to perpetuate his name: but, alas! the pyramid has long since fallen, and only a few fragments are scattered in various libraries, where they are scarcely disturbed even by the antiquarian. What do we hear of Gyraldus Cambrensis, the historian, antiquary, philosopher, theologian, and poet? He declined two bishoprics that he might shut himself up and write for posterity; but posterity never inquires after his labours. What of Henry of Huntingdon, who, beside a learned history of England, wrote a treatise on the contempt of the world, which the world has revenged by forgetting him. What is quoted of Joseph of Exeter, styled the miracle of his age in classical composition? Of his three great heroic poems one is lost forever, excepting a mere fragment; the others are known only to a few of the curious in literature, and as to his love verses and epigrams, they have entirely disappeared. What is in current use of John Wallis, the Franciscan, who acquired the name of the tree of life? Of William of Malmsbury;—of Simeon of Durham; of Benedict of Peterborough; of John Hanvill of St. Albans; of———"

"Prithee, friend," cried the quarto in a testy tone, "how old do you think me? You are talking of authors that lived long before my time, and wrote either in Latin or French, so that they in a manner expatriated themselves, and deserved to be forgotten;* but I, sir, was ushered into the world from the press of the renowned Wynkyn de Worde. I was written in my own native tongue at a time when the language had become fixed, and indeed I was considered a model of pure and elegant English."

(I should observe that these remarks were couched in such intolerably antiquated terms, that I have had infinite difficulty in rendering them into modern phraseology.)

"I cry you mercy," said I, "for mistaking your age; but it matters little; almost all the writers of your time have likewise passed into forgetfulness; and De Worde's publications are mere literary rarities among book collectors. The purity and stability of language, too, on which you found your claims to perpetuity, have been the fallacious dependence of authors of every age, even back to the times of the worthy Robert of Gloucester, who wrote his history in rhymes of mongrel Saxon.† Even now, many talk

---

*In Latin and French hath many soueraine wittes had great delyte to endite, and have many noble thinges fulfilde, but certes there ben some that speaken their poisye in French, of which speche the French men have as good a fantasye as we have in heryng of Frenchemen's Englishe. *Chaucer's Testament of Love.*

†Holinshed, in his Chronicle, observes, "afterward, also, by diligent travell of Geffray Chaucer and John Gowre, in the time of Richard the second, and after them of John Scogan and John Lydgate, monke of Berrie, our said toong was brought to an excellent passe, notwithstanding that it never came unto the type of perfection until the time of Queen Elizabeth, wherein John Jewell, Bishop of Sarum, John Fox, and sundrie learned and excellent writers, have fully accomplished the ornature of the same, to their great praise and immortal commendation."

of Spenser's 'well of pure English undefiled,' as if the language ever sprang from a well or fountain head, and was not rather a mere confluence of various tongues, perpetually subject to changes and intermixtures. It is this which has made English literature so extremely mutable, and the reputation built upon it so fleeting. Unless thought can be committed to something more permanent and unchangeable than such a medium, even thought must share the fate of every thing else, and fall into decay. This should serve as a check upon the vanity and exultation of the most popular writer. He finds the language in which he has embarked his fame gradually altering, and subject to the dilapidations of time and the caprice of fashion. He looks back and beholds the early authors of his country, once the favourites of their day, supplanted by modern writers. A few short ages have covered them with obscurity, and their merits can only be relished by the quaint taste of the bookworm. And such, he anticipates, will be the fate of his own work, which, however it may be admired in its day, and held up as a model of purity, will in the course of years grow antiquated and obsolete, until it shall become almost as unintelligible in its native land as an Egyptian obelisk, or one of those Runic inscriptions said to exist in the deserts of Tartary. I declare," added I with some emotion, "when I contemplate a modern library, filled with new works in all the bravery of rich gilding and binding, I feel disposed to sit down and weep, like the good Xerxes when he surveyed his army, pranked out in all the splendour of military array, and reflected that in one hundred years not one of them would be in existence!"

"Ah," said the little quarto, with a heavy sigh, "I see how it is; these modern scribblers have superseded all the good old authors. I suppose nothing is read now-a-days but Sir Philip Sidney's Arcadia, Sackville's stately plays, and Mirror for Magistrates, or the fine spun euphuisms of the "unparalelled John Lyly."

"There you are again mistaken," said I, "the writers whom you suppose in vogue, because they happened to be so when you were last in circulation, have long since had their day. Sir Philip Sydney's Arcadia, the immortality of which was so fondly predicted by his admirers,° and which, in truth, is full of noble thoughts, delicate images, and graceful turns of language, is now scarcely ever mentioned. Sackville has strutted into obscurity; and even Lyly, though his writings were once the

°Live ever sweete booke; the silver image of his gentle witt, and the golden pillar of his noble courage; and ever notify unto the world that thy writer was the secretary of eloquence, the breath of the muses, the honey bee of the dayntiest flowers of witt and arte, the pith of morale and intellectual virtues, the arme of Bellona in the field, the tongue of Suada in the chamber, the spirite of Practise in esse, and the paragon of excellency in print. *Harvey's Pierce's Supererogation.*

delight of a court, and apparently perpetuated by a proverb, is now scarcely known even by name. A whole crowd of authors who wrote and wrangled at the time, have likewise gone down with all their writings and their controversies. Wave after wave of succeeding literature has rolled over them, until they are buried so deep, that it is only now and then that some industrious diver after the fragments of antiquity brings up a specimen for the gratification of the curious.

"For my part," I continued, "I consider this mutability of language a wise precaution of Providence for the benefit of the world at large, and of authors in particular. To reason from analogy, we daily behold the varied and beautiful tribes of vegetables springing up, flourishing, adorning the fields for a short time, and then fading into dust, to make way for their successors. Were not this the case, the fecundity of nature would be a grievance instead of a blessing. The earth would groan with rank and excessive vegetation, and its surface become a tangled wilderness. In like manner, the works of genius and learning decline and make way for subsequent productions. Language gradually varies, and with it fade away the writings of authors who have flourished their allotted time; otherwise the creative powers of genius would overstock the world, and the mind would be completely bewildered in the endless mazes of literature. Formerly there were some restraints on this excessive multiplication. Works had to be transcribed by hand, which was a slow and laborious operation; they were written either on parchment, which was expensive, so that one work was often erased to make way for another; or on papyrus, which was fragile and extremely perishable. Authorship was a limited and unprofitable craft, and pursued chiefly by monks in the leisure and solitude of their cloisters. The accumulation of manuscripts was slow and costly, and confined almost entirely to monasteries. To these circumstances it may in some measure be owing that we have not been inundated by the intellect of antiquity; that the fountains of thought have not been broken up, and modern genius drowned in the deluge. But the inventions of paper and the press have put an end to all these restraints. They have made every one a writer, and enabled every mind to pour itself into print, and diffuse itself over the whole intellectual world. The consequences are alarming. The stream of literature has swoln into a torrent—augmented into a river—expanded into a sea. A few centuries since, five or six hundred manuscripts constituted a great library; but what would you say to libraries, such as actually exist, containing three and four hundred thousand volumes; legions of authors at the same time busy, and the press going on with fearfully increasing activity, to double and quadruple the number? Unless some unforeseen mortality should break out among the progeny of the muse, now that she has become so prolific, I tremble for posterity.

I fear the mere fluctuation of language will not be sufficient. Criticism may do much; it increases with the increase of literature, and resembles one of those salutary checks on population spoken of by economists. All possible encouragement, therefore, should be given to the growth of critics, good or bad. But I fear all will be in vain; let criticism do what it may, writers will write, printers will print, and the world will inevitably be overstocked with good books. It will soon be the employment of a life time merely to learn their names. Many a man of passable information at the present day reads scarce any thing but reviews, and before long a man of erudition will be little better than a mere walking catalogue."

"My very good sir," said the little quarto, yawning most drearily in my face, "excuse my interrupting you, but I perceive you are rather given to prose. I would ask the fate of an author who was making some noise just as I left the world. His reputation, however, was considered quite temporary. The learned shook their heads at him, for he was a poor half educated varlet, that knew little of Latin, and nothing of Greek, and had been obliged to run the country for deer stealing. I think his name was Shakspeare. I presume he soon sunk into oblivion."

"On the contrary," said I, "it is owing to that very man that the literature of his period has experienced a duration beyond the ordinary term of English literature. There arise authors now and then, who seem proof against the mutability of language, because they have rooted themselves in the unchanging principles of human nature. They are like gigantic trees that we sometimes see on the banks of a stream; which, by their vast and deep roots, penetrating through the mere surface, and laying hold on the very foundations of the earth, preserve the soil around them from being swept away by the everflowing current, and hold up many a neighbouring plant, and, perhaps, worthless weed, to perpetuity. Such is the case with Shakspeare, whom we behold, defying the encroachments of time, retaining in modern use the language and literature of his day, and giving duration to many an indifferent author, merely from having flourished in his vicinity. But even he, I grieve to say, is gradually assuming the tint of age, and his whole form is overrun by a profusion of commentators, who, like clambering vines and creepers, almost bury the noble plant that upholds them."

Here the little quarto began to heave his sides and chuckle, until at length he broke out into a short plethoric fit of laughter that had well nigh choked him, by reason of his excessive corpulency. "Mighty well!" cried he, as soon as he could recover breath, "mighty well! and so you would persuade me that the literature of an age is to be perpetuated by a vagabond deer stealer! by a man without learning! by a poet, forsooth—a poet!" And here he wheezed forth another fit of laughter.

I confess I felt somewhat nettled at this rudeness, which, however, I pardoned on account of his having flourished in a less polished age. I determined, nevertheless, not to give up my point.

"Yes," resumed I positively, "a poet; for of all writers he has the best chance for immortality. Others may write from the head, but he writes from the heart, and the heart will always understand him. He is the faithful portrayer of nature, whose features are always the same, and always interesting. Prose writers are voluminous and unwieldy; their pages are crowded with common places, and their thoughts expanded into tediousness. But with the true poet every thing is terse, touching, or brilliant. He gives the choicest thoughts in the choicest language. He illustrates them by every thing that he sees most striking in nature and art. He enriches them by pictures of human life, such as it is passing before him. His writings, therefore, contain the spirit, the aroma, if I may use the phrase, of the age in which he lives. They are caskets which inclose within a small compass the wealth of the language—its family jewels, which are thus transmitted in a portable form to posterity. The setting may occasionally be antiquated, and require now and then to be renewed, as in the case of Chaucer; but the brilliancy and intrinsic value of the gems continue unaltered. Cast a look back over the long reach of literary history. What vast valleys of dulness, filled with monkish legends and academical controversies. What bogs of theological speculations; what dreary wastes of metaphysics. Here and there only do we behold the heaven illumined bards, elevated like beacons on their widely separated heights, to transmit the pure light of poetical intelligence from age to age."*

I was just about to launch forth into eulogiums upon the poets of the day, when the sudden opening of the door caused me to turn my head. It was the verger, who came to inform me that it was time to close the library. I sought to have a parting word with the quarto, but the worthy little tome was silent; the clasps were closed, and it

*Thorow earth, and waters deepe,
　The pen by skill doth passe:
And featly nyps the worldes abuse,
　And shoes us in a glasse,
The vertu and the vice
　Of every wight alyve;
The honey combe that bee doth make,
　Is not so sweete in hyve,
As are the golden leves
　That drop from poets head:
Which doth surmount our common talke
　As farre as dros doth lead.
　　　　　　　　　　CHURCHYARD.

looked perfectly unconscious of all that had passed. I have been to the library two or three times since, and have endeavoured to draw it into farther conversation, but in vain. And whether all this rambling colloquy actually took place, or whether it was another of those odd day dreams to which I am subject, I have never, to this moment, been able to discover.

RURAL FUNERALS

Here's a few flowers; but about midnight more:
The herbs that have on them cold dew o' the night
Are strewings fitt'st for graves.———
You were as flowers now wither'd: even so
These herb'lets shall, which we upon you strow.

CYMBELINE.

Among the beautiful and simple hearted customs of rural life which
still linger in some parts of England, are those of strewing flowers before the funerals, and planting them at the graves, of departed friends.
These, it is said, are the remains of some of the rites of the primitive
church; but they are of still higher antiquity, having been observed
among the Greeks and Romans, and frequently mentioned by their
writers, and were no doubt the spontaneous tributes of unlettered
affection, originating long before art had tasked itself to modulate sorrow into song, or story it on the monument. They are now only to be
met with in the most distant and retired places of the kingdom, where
fashion and innovation have not been able to throng in, and trample out
all the curious and interesting traces of the olden time.

In Glamorganshire, we are told, the bed whereon the corpse lies,
is covered with flowers, a custom alluded to in one of the wild and
plaintive ditties of Ophelia:

> White his shroud as the mountain snow
> Larded all with sweet flowers;
> Which be-wept to the grave did go,
> With true-love showers.

There is also a most delicate and beautiful rite observed in some of
the remote villages of the south, at the funeral of a female who has
did young and unmarried. A chaplet of white flowers is borne before
the corpse by a young girl nearest in age, size, and resemblance, and
is afterwards hung up in the church over the accustomed seat of the
deceased. These chaplets are sometimes made of white paper, in
imitation of flowers, and inside of them is generally a pair of white
gloves. They are intended as emblems of the purity of the deceased, and
the crown of glory which she has received in heaven.

In some parts of the country, also, the dead are carried to the grave
with the singing of psalms and hymns: a kind of triumph, "to show,"

says Bourne, "that they have finished their course with joy, and are become conquerors." This, I am informed, is observed in some of the northern counties, particularly in Northumberland, and it has a pleasing, though melancholy effect, to hear, of a still evening, in some lonely country scene, the mournful melody of a funeral dirge swelling from a distance, and to see the train slowly moving along the landscape.

> Thus, thus, and thus, we compass round
> Thy harmlesse and unhaunted ground,
> And as we sing thy dirge, we will
>   The Daffodill,
> And other flowers lay upon
> The altar of our love, thy stone.°

There is also a solemn respect paid by the traveller to the passing funeral in these sequestered places, for such spectacles, occurring among the quiet abodes of nature, sink deep into the soul. As the mourning train approaches, he pauses, uncovered, to let it go by; he then follows silently in the rear; sometimes quite to the grave, at other times for a few hundred yards, and having paid this tribute of respect to the deceased, turns and resumes his journey.

The rich vein of melancholy which runs through the English character, and gives it some of its most touching and ennobling graces, is finely evidenced in these pathetic customs, and in the solicitude shown by the common people for an honoured and a peaceful grave. The humblest peasant, whatever may be his lowly lot while living, is anxious that some little respect may be paid to his remains. Sir Thomas Overbury, describing the "faire and happy milkmaid," observes, "thus lives she, and all her care is, that she may die in the spring time, to have store of flowers stucke upon her winding sheet." The poets, too, who always breathe the feeling of a nation, continually advert to this fond solicitude about the grave. In "The Maid's Tragedy," by Beaumont and Fletcher, there is a beautiful instance of the kind, describing the capricious melancholy of a broken hearted girl:

> When she sees a bank
> Stuck full of flowers, she, with a sigh, will tell
> Her servants, what a pretty place it were
> To bury lovers in; and make her maids
> Pluck 'em, and strew her over like a corse.

°Herrick

The custom of decorating graves was once universally prevalent: osiers were carefully bent over them to keep the turf uninjured, and about them were planted evergreens and flowers. "We adorn their graves," says Evelyn, in his Sylva, "with flowers and redolent plants, just emblems of the life of man, which has been compared in holy scriptures to those fading beauties, whose roots being buried in dishonour, rise again in glory." This usage has now become extremely rare in England; but it may still be met with in the church yards of retired villages, among the Welsh mountains; and I recollect an instance of it at the small town of Ruthen, which lies at the head of the beautiful vale of Clewyd. I have been told also by a friend, who was present at the funeral of a young girl in Glamorganshire, that the female attendants had their aprons full of flowers, which, as soon as the body was interred, they stuck about the grave. He noticed several graves which had been decorated in the same manner. As the flowers had been merely stuck in the ground, and not planted, they had soon withered, and might be seen in various states of decay; some drooping others quite perished. They were afterwards to be supplanted by holly, rosemary, and other evergreens; which on some graves had grown to great luxuriance, and overshadowed the tomb stones.

There was formerly a melancholy fancifulness in the arrangement of these rustic offerings that had something in it truly poetical. The rose was sometimes blended with the lily, to form a general emblem of frail mortality. "This sweet flower," says Evelyn, "borne on a branch set with thorns, and accompanied with the lily, are natural hieroglyphics of our fugitive, umbratile, anxious, and transitory life, which, making so fair a shew for a time, is not yet without its thorns and crosses." The nature and colour of the flowers, and of the ribbands with which they were tied, had often a particular reference to the qualities or story of the deceased, or were expressive of the feelings of the mourner. In an old poem, entitled "Corydon's Doleful Knell," a lover specifies the decorations he intends to use:

> A garland shall be framed
>   By art and nature's skill,
> Of sundry-coloured flowers,
>   In token of good will.
>
> And sundry-coloured ribbands
>   On it I will bestow;
> But chiefly blacke and yellowe
>   With her to grave shall go.

> I'll deck her tomb with flowers
>   The rarest ever seen;
> And with my tears as showers
>   I'll keepe them fresh and green.

The white rose, we are told, was planted at the grave of a virgin; her chaplet was tied with white ribbands, in token of her spotless innocence, though sometimes black ribbands were intermingled, to bespeak the grief of the survivors. The red rose was occasionally used in remembrance of such as had been remarkable for benevolence; but roses in general were appropriated to the graves of lovers. Evelyn tells us that the custom was not altogether extinct in his time, near his dwelling in the county of Surrey, "where the maidens yearly planted and decked the graves of their defunct sweethearts with rose-bushes." And Camden, likewise, remarks in his Britannia: "Here is also a certain custom, observed time out of mind, of planting rose trees upon the graves, especially by the young men and maids who have lost their loves; so that this church yard is now full of them."

When the deceased had been unhappy in their loves, emblems of a more gloomy character were used, such as the yew and cypress; and if flowers were strewn they were of the most melancholy colours. Thus, in poems by Thomas Stanley, Esq. (published in 1651) is the following stanza:

> Yet strew
> Upon my dismall grave
> Such offerings as you have,
>   Forsaken cypresse and sad yewe;
> For kinder flowers can take no birth
> Or growth from such unhappy earth.

In "The Maid's Tragedy," a pathetic little air is introduced, illustrative of this mode of decorating the funerals of females who had been disappointed in love:

> Lay a garland on my hearse
>   Of the dismall yew,
> Maidens willow branches wear,
>   Say I died true.

> My love was false, but I was firm
>   From my hour of birth,
> Upon my buried body lie
>   Lightly, gentle earth.

The natural effect of sorrow over the dead is to refine and elevate
the mind, and we have a proof of it in the purity of sentiment and
the unaffected elegance of thought which pervaded the whole of these
funereal observances. Thus, it was an especial precaution, that none
but sweet scented evergreens and flowers should be employed. The
intention seems to have been to soften the horrors of the tomb, to
beguile the mind from brooding over the disgraces of perishing mortality, and to associate the memory of the deceased with the most
delicate and beautiful objects in nature. There is a dismal process
going on in the grave, ere dust can return to its kindred dust, which
the imagination shrinks from contemplating; and we seek still to think
of the form we have loved, with those refined associations which it
awakened when blooming before us in youth and beauty. "Lay her
i'the earth," says Laertes of his virgin sister,

> And from her fair and unpolluted flesh
> May violets spring!

Herrick, also, in his "Dirge of Jeptha," pours forth a fragrant flow
of poetical thought and image, which in a manner embalms the dead
in the recollections of the living.

> Sleep in thy peace, thy bed of spice,
> And make this place all Paradise:
> May sweets grow here! and smoke from hence,
> > Fat frankinscence.
> Let balme and cassia send their scent
> From out thy maiden monument.
>
>   ✿   ✿   ✿   ✿   ✿
>
> May all shie maids at wonted hours
> Come forth to strew thy tombe with flowers;
> May virgins when they come to mourn,
> > Male incense burn
> Upon thine altar! then return
> And leave thee sleeping in thine urn.

I might crowd my pages with extracts from the older British poets,
who wrote when these rites were more prevalent, and delighted frequently to allude to them; but I have already quoted more than is
necessary. I cannot however refrain from giving a passage from
Shakspeare, even though it should appear trite, which illustrates the
emblematical meaning often conveyed in these floral tributes, and at

the same time possesses that magic of language and appositeness of
imagery for which he stands pre-eminent:

> With fairest flowers,
> Whilst summer lasts, and I live here, Fidele,
> I'll sweeten thy sad grave; thou shalt not lack
> The flower that's like thy face, pale primrose; nor
> The azur'd harebell like thy veins; no, nor
> The leaf of eglantine; whom not to slander,
> Outsweetened not thy breath.

There is certainly something more affecting in these prompt and
spontaneous offerings of nature, than in the most costly monuments
of art; the hand strews the flower while the heart is warm, and the
tear falls on the grave as affection is binding the osier around the sod;
but pathos expires under the slow labour of the chisel, and is chilled
among the cold conceits of sculptured marble.

It is greatly to be regretted, that a custom so truly elegant and
touching has disappeared from general use, and exists only in the
most remote and insignificant villages. But it seems as if poetical
custom always shuns the walks of cultivated society. In proportion as
people grow polite they cease to be poetical. They talk of poetry, but
they have learnt to check its free impulses, to distrust its sallying
emotions, and to supply its most affecting and picturesque usages, by
studied form and pompous ceremonial. Few pageants can be more
stately and frigid than an English funeral in town. It is made up of
show and gloomy parade: mourning carriages, mourning horses, mourning plumes, and hireling mourners, who make a mockery of grief. "There
is a grave digged," says Jeremy Taylor, "and a solemn mourning, and
a great talk in the neighbourhood, and when the daies are finished, they
shall be, and they shall be remembered no more." The associate in the
gay and crowded city is soon forgotten; the hurrying succession of
new intimates and new pleasures effaces him from our minds, and
the very scenes and circles in which he moved are incessantly fluctuating.
But funerals in the country are solemnly impressive. The stroke of
death makes a wider space in the village circle, and is an awful event
in the tranquil uniformity of rural life. The passing bell tolls its knell
in every ear; it steals with its pervading melancholy over hill and
vale, and saddens all the landscape.

The fixed and unchanging features of the country also, perpetuate
the memory of the friend with whom we once enjoyed them, who was
the companion of our most retired walks, and gave animation to every

lonely scene. His idea is associated with every charm of nature; we hear his voice in the echo which he once delighted to awaken; his spirit haunts the grove which he once frequented; we think of him in the wild upland solitude, or amidst the pensive beauty of the valley. In the freshness of joyous morning, we remember his beaming smiles and bounding gayety; and when sober evening returns with its gathering shadows and subduing quiet, we call to mind many a twilight hour of gentle talk and sweet souled melancholy.

> Each lonely place shall him restore,
> For him the tear be duly shed,
> Belov'd till life can charm no more,
> And mourn'd, till pity's self be dead.

Another cause that perpetuates the memory of the deceased in the country, is, that the grave is more immediately in sight of the survivors. They pass it on their way to prayer; it meets their eyes when their hearts are softened by the exercises of devotion; they linger about it on the sabbath, when the mind is disengaged from worldly cares, and most disposed to turn aside from present pleasures and present loves, and to sit down among the solemn mementos of the past. In North Wales the peasantry kneel and pray over the graves of their deceased friends for several Sundays after the interment; and where the tender rite of strewing and planting flowers is still practised, it is always renewed on Easter, Whitsuntide, and other festivals, when the season brings the companion of former festivity more vividly to mind. It is also invariably performed by the nearest relatives and friends; no menials nor hirelings are employed, and if a neighbour yields assistance, it would be deemed an insult to offer compensation.

I have dwelt upon this beautiful rural custom, because, as it is one of the last, so is it one of the holiest offices of love. The grave is the ordeal of true affection. It is there that the divine passion of the soul manifests its superiority to the instinctive impulse of mere animal attachment. The latter must be continually refreshed and kept alive by the presence of its object, but the love that is seated in the soul can live on long remembrance. The mere inclinations of sense languish and decline with the charms which excited them, and turn with shuddering disgust from the dismal precincts of the tomb; but it is thence that truly spiritual affection rises purified from every sensual desire, and returns, like a holy flame, to illumine and sanctify the heart of the survivor.

The sorrow for the dead is the only sorrow from which we refuse

to be divorced. Every other wound we seek to heal—every other affliction to forget; but this wound we consider it a duty to keep open—
this affliction we cherish and brood over in solitude. Where is the
mother who would willingly forget the infant that perished like a
blossom from her arms, though every recollection is a pang? Where
is the child that would willingly forget the most tender of parents,
though to remember be but to lament? Who, even in the hour of
agony, would forget the friend over whom he mourns? Who, even
when the tomb is closing upon the remains of her he most loved, when
he feels his heart, as it were, crushed in the closing of its portal, would
accept of consolation that must be bought by forgetfulness?—No, the
love which survives the tomb is one of the noblest attributes of the
soul. If it has its woes, it has likewise its delights; and when the
overwhelming burst of grief is calmed into the gentle tear of recollection; when the sudden anguish and the convulsive agony over the
present ruins of all that we most loved, is softened away into pensive
meditation on all that it was in the days of its loveliness—who would
root out such a sorrow from the heart? Though it may sometimes
throw a passing cloud over the bright hour of gayety; or spread a
deeper sadness over the hour of gloom; yet who would exchange it
even for the song of pleasure, or the burst of revelry? No, there is a
voice from the tomb sweeter than song. There is a remembrance of
the dead to which we turn even from the charms of the living. Oh
the grave!—the grave!—It buries every error—covers every defect—ex-
tinguishes every resentment. From its peaceful bosom spring none but
fond regrets and tender recollections. Who can look down upon the
grave even of an enemy, and not feel a compunctious throb, that he
should ever have warred with the poor handful of earth that lies
mouldering before him!

But the grave of those we loved—what a place for meditation! There
it is that we call up in long review the whole history of virtue and
gentleness, and the thousand endearments lavished upon us almost
unheeded in the daily intercourse of intimacy;—there it is that we
dwell upon the tenderness, the solemn, awful tenderness of the parting
scene—the bed of death, with all its stifled griefs, its noiseless attendance, its mute, watchful assiduities—the last testimonies of expiring
love—the feeble, fluttering, thrilling, oh! how thrilling! pressure of the
hand—the faint, faltering accents struggling in death to give one more
assurance of affection—the last fond look of the glazing eye, turning
upon us even from the threshold of existence!

Aye, go to the grave of buried love, and meditate! There settle the
account with thy conscience for every past benefit unrequited—every

past endearment unregarded, of that departed being, who can never—never—never return to be soothed by thy contrition!

If thou art a child, and hast ever added a sorrow to the soul, or a furrow to the silvered brow of an affectionate parent—if thou art a husband, and hast ever caused the fond bosom that ventured its whole happiness in thy arms, to doubt one moment of thy kindness or thy truth—if thou art a friend, and hast ever wronged, in thought, or word, or deed, the spirit that generously confided in thee—if thou art a lover, and hast ever given one unmerited pang to that true heart which now lies cold and still beneath thy feet;—then be sure that every unkind look, every ungracious word, every ungentle action, will come thronging back upon thy memory, and knocking dolefully at thy soul—then be sure that thou wilt lie down sorrowing and repentant on the grave, and utter the unheard groan, and pour the unavailing tear, more deep, more bitter, because unheard and unavailing.

Then weave thy chaplet of flowers, and strew the beauties of nature about the grave; console thy broken spirit, if thou canst, with these tender, yet futile tributes of regret;—but take warning by the bitterness of this thy contrite affliction over the dead, and henceforth be more faithful and affectionate in the discharge of thy duties to the living.

In writing the preceding article, it was not intended to give a full detail of the funeral customs of the English peasantry, but merely to furnish a few hints and quotations illustrative of particular rites; to be appended, by way of note, to another paper, which has been withheld. The article swelled insensibly into its present form, and this is mentioned as an apology for so brief and casual a notice of these usages, after they have been amply and learnedly investigated in other works.

I must observe, also, that I am well aware that this custom of adorning graves with flowers prevails in other countries besides England. Indeed, in some it is much more general, and is observed even by the rich and fashionable, but it is then apt to lose its simplicity, and to degenerate into affectation. Bright, in his travels in Lower Hungary, tells of monuments of marble, with recesses formed for retirement, with seats placed among bowers of green house plants; and that the graves generally are covered with the gayest flowers of the season. He gives a casual picture of filial piety, which I cannot but transcribe; for I trust it is as useful as it is delightful to illustrate the amiable virtues of the sex. "When I was at Berlin," says he, "I followed the celebrated Iffland to the grave. Mingled with some pomp, you might trace much real feeling. In the midst of the ceremony, my attention was attracted by a young woman who stood on a mound of earth, newly covered with turf, which she anxiously protected from the feet of the passing crowd. It was the tomb of her parent; and the figure of this affectionate daughter presented a monument more striking than the most costly work of art."

I will barely add an instance of sepulchral decoration that I once met with among the mountains of Switzerland. It was at the village of Gersau, which stands on the borders of the lake of Lucerne, at the foot of Mount Rigi. It was once the capital of a miniature republic, shut up between the Alps and the lake, and accessible on the land side only by foot paths. The whole force of the republic did not exceed six hundred fighting men; and a few miles of circumference, scooped out as it were from the bosom of the mountains, comprised its territory. The village of Gersau seemed separated from the rest of the world, and retained the golden simplicity of a purer age. It had a small church, with a burying ground adjoining. At the heads of the graves were placed crosses of wood or iron. On some were affixed miniatures, rudely executed, but evidently attempts at likenesses of the deceased. On the crosses were hung chaplets of flowers, some withering, others fresh, as if occasionally renewed. I paused with interest at this scene; I felt that I was at the source of poetical description, for these were the beautiful but unaffected offerings of the heart which poets are fain to record. In a gayer and more populous place, I should have suspected them to have been suggested by factitious sentiment, derived from books; but the good people of Gersau knew little of books; there was not a novel nor a love poem in the village; and I question whether any peasant of the place dreamt, while he was twining a fresh chaplet for the grave of his mistress, that he was fulfilling one of the most fanciful rites of poetical devotion, and that he was practically a poet.

THE INN KITCHEN

Shall I not take mine ease in mine inn?
FALSTAFF.

During a journey that I once made through the Netherlands, I had
arrived one evening at the *Pomme d'Or*, the principal inn of a small
Flemish village. It was after the hour of the *table d'hote*, so that I
was obliged to make a solitary supper from the reliques of its ampler
board. The weather was chilly; I was seated alone in one end of a
great gloomy dining room, and my repast being over, I had the
prospect before me of a long dull evening, without any visible means
of enlivening it. I summoned mine host, and requested something to
read; he brought me the whole literary stock of his household, a
Dutch family bible, an almanack in the same language, and a number
of old Paris newspapers. As I sat dozing over one of the latter, reading
old news and stale criticisms, my ear was now and then struck with
bursts of laughter which seemed to proceed from the kitchen. Every
one that has travelled on the continent, must know how favourite a
resort the kitchen of a country inn is to the middle and inferior order
of travellers, particularly in that equivocal kind of weather, when a
fire becomes agreeable toward evening. I threw aside the newspaper,
and explored my way to the kitchen, to take a peep at the group
that appeared to be so merry. It was composed partly of travellers
who had arrived some hours before in a diligence, and partly of the
usual attendants and hangers on of inns. They were seated around a
great burnished stove, that might have been mistaken for an altar,
at which they were worshipping. It was covered with various kitchen
vessels of resplendent brightness; among which steamed and hissed a
huge copper tea kettle. A large lamp threw a strong mass of light
upon the group, bringing out many odd features in strong relief. Its
yellow rays partially illumined the spacious kitchen, dying duskily
away into remote corners, except where they settled in mellow radiance
on the broad side of a flitch of bacon, or were reflected back from well
scoured utensils, that gleamed from the midst of obscurity. A strapping
Flemish lass, with long golden pendants in her ears, and a necklace
with a golden heart suspended to it, was the presiding priestess of
the temple.

Many of the company were furnished with pipes, and most of them
with some kind of evening potation. I found their mirth was occasioned

by anecdotes which a little swarthy Frenchman, with a dry weazen face and large whiskers, was giving of his love adventures; at the end of each of which there was one of those bursts of honest unceremonious laughter, in which a man indulges in that temple of true liberty, an Inn.

As I had no better mode of getting through a tedious blustering evening, I took my seat near the stove, and listened to a variety of travellers' tales, some very extravagant, and most very dull. All of them, however, have faded from my treacherous memory except one, which I will endeavour to relate. I fear, however, it derived its chief zest from the manner in which it was told, and the peculiar air and appearance of the narrator. He was a corpulent old Swiss, who had the look of a veteran traveller. He was dressed in a tarnished green travelling jacket, with a broad belt round his waist, and a pair of overalls, with buttons from the hips to the ankles. He was of a full, rubicund countenance, with a double chin, aquiline nose, and a pleasant twinkling eye. His hair was light, and curled from under an old green velvet travelling cap stuck on one side of his head. He was interrupted more than once by the arrival of guests, or the remarks of his auditors; and paused now and then to replenish his pipe; at which times he had generally a roguish leer, and a sly joke for the buxom kitchen maid.

I wish my readers could imagine the old fellow lolling in a huge arm chair, one arm akimbo, the other holding a curiously twisted tobacco pipe, formed of genuine *écume de mer*, decorated with silver chain and silken tassel—his head cocked on one side, and a whimsical cut of the eye occasionally, as he related the following story.

THE
SPECTRE BRIDEGROOM
A Traveller's Tale*

He that supper for is dight,
He lyes full cold, I trow, this night!
Yestreen to chamber I him led,
This night Gray-steel has made his bed!
      Sir Eger, Sir Grahame, and Sir Gray-steel.

On the summit of one of the heights of the Odenwald, a wild and romantic tract of upper Germany, that lies not far from the confluence of the Main and the Rhine, there stood, many, many years since, the Castle of the Baron Von Landshort. It is now quite fallen to decay, and almost buried among beech trees and dark firs, above which, however, its old watch tower may still be seen struggling, like the former possessor I have mentioned, to carry a high head, and look down upon the neighbouring country.

The Baron was a dry branch of the great family of Katzenellenbogen,† and inherited the reliques of the property, and all the pride of his ancestors. Though the warlike disposition of his predecessors had much impaired the family possessions, yet the Baron still endeavoured to keep up some show of former state. The times were peaceable, and the German nobles, in general, had abandoned their inconvenient old castles, perched like eagles' nests among the mountains, and had built more convenient residences in the valleys: still the Baron remained proudly drawn up in his little fortress, cherishing with hereditary inveteracy, all the old family feuds; so that he was on ill terms with some of his nearest neighbours, on account of disputes that had happened between their great great grandfathers.

The Baron had but one child, a daughter; but nature, when she grants but one child, always compensates by making it a prodigy; and so it was with the daughter of the Baron. All the nurses, gossips, and country cousins, assured her father that she had not her equal for

---

*The erudite reader, well versed in good for nothing lore, will perceive that the above tale must have been suggested to the old Swiss by a little French anecdote, of a circumstance said to have taken place at Paris.

†*i.e.* Catselbow. The name of a family of those parts very powerful in former times. The appellation, we are told, was given in compliment to a peerless dame of the family, celebrated for a fine arm.

beauty in all Germany; and who should know better than they. She had, moreover, been brought up with great care under the superintendance of two maiden aunts, who had spent some years of their early life at one of the little German courts, and were skilled in all the branches of knowledge necessary to the education of a fine lady. Under their instructions, she became a miracle of accomplishments. By the time she was eighteen she could embroider to admiration, and had worked whole histories of the saints in tapestry, with such strength of expression in their countenances, that they looked like so many souls in purgatory. She could read without great difficulty, and had spelled her way through several church legends, and almost all the chivalric wonders of the Heldenbuch. She had even made considerable proficiency in writing, could sign her own name without missing a letter, and so legibly, that her aunts could read it without spectacles. She excelled in making little elegant good for nothing lady like nick-nacks of all kinds; was versed in the most abstruse dancing of the day; played a number of airs on the harp and guitar; and knew all the tender ballads of the Minne-lieders by heart.

Her aunts, too, having been great flirts and coquettes in their younger days, were admirably calculated to be vigilant guardians and strict censors of the conduct of their niece; for there is no duenna so rigidly prudent, and inexorably decorous, as a superannuated coquette. She was rarely suffered out of their sight; never went beyond the domains of the castle, unless well attended, or rather, well watched; had continual lectures read to her about strict decorum and implicit obedience; and, as to the men—pah!—she was taught to hold them at such distance and in such absolute distrust, that, unless properly authorized, she would not have cast a glance upon the handsomest cavalier in the world—no, not if he were even dying at her feet!

The good effects of this system were wonderfully apparent. The young lady was a pattern of docility and correctness. While others were wasting their sweetness in the glare of the world, and liable to be plucked and thrown aside by every hand, she was coyly blooming into fresh and lovely womanhood under the protection of those immaculate spinsters, like a rose bud blushing forth among guardian thorns. Her aunts looked upon her with pride and exultation, and vaunted that though all the other young ladies in the world might go astray, yet thank heaven, nothing of the kind could happen to the heiress of Katzenellenbogen.

But, however scantily the Baron Von Landshort might be provided with children, his household was by no means a small one, for providence had enriched him with abundance of poor relations. They, one and all, possessed the affectionate disposition common to humble relatives: were wonderfully attached to the Baron, and took every possible occasion to come in swarms and enliven the castle. All family festivals were commemorated by these good people at the Baron's expense; and when they were filled with good cheer, they would declare that there was nothing on earth so delightful as these family meetings, these jubilees of the heart.

The Baron, though a small man, had a large soul, and it swelled with satisfaction at the consciousness of being the greatest man in the little world about him. He loved to tell long stories about the stark old warriors whose portraits looked grimly down from the walls around, and he found no listeners equal to those who fed at his expense. He was much given to the marvellous, and a firm believer in all those supernatural tales with which every mountain and valley in Germany abounds. The faith of his guests exceeded even his own: they listened to every tale of wonder with open eyes and mouth, and never failed to be astonished, even though repeated for the hundredth time. Thus lived the Baron Von Landshort, the oracle of his table, the absolute monarch of his little territory, and happy above all things, in the persuasion that he was the wisest man of the age.

At the time of which my story treats, there was a great family gathering at the Castle, on an affair of the utmost importance. It was to receive the destined bridegroom of the Baron's daughter. A negotiation had been carried on between the father, and an old nobleman of Bavaria, to unite the dignity of their houses by the marriage of their children. The preliminaries had been conducted with proper punctilio. The young people were betrothed without seeing each other, and the time was appointed for the marriage ceremony. The young Count Von Altenburg had been recalled from the army for the purpose, and was actually on his way to the Baron's to receive his bride. Missives had even been received from him, from Wurtzburg, where he was accidentally detained, mentioning the day and hour when he might be expected to arrive.

The castle was in a tumult of preparation to give him a suitable welcome. The fair bride had been decked out with uncommon care. The two aunts had superintended her toilet, and quarrelled the whole morning about every article of her dress. The young lady had taken advantage of their contest to follow the bent of her own taste; and fortunately it was a good one. She looked as lovely as youthful bridegroom could desire; and the flutter of expectation heightened the lustre of her charms.

The suffusions that mantled her face and neck, the gentle heaving of the bosom, the eye now and then lost in reverie, all betrayed the soft tumult that was going on in her little heart. The aunts were continually hovering around her; for maiden aunts are apt to take great interest in affairs of this nature. They were giving her a world of staid counsel how to deport herself, what to say, and in what manner to receive the expected lover.

The Baron was no less busied in preparations. He had, in truth, nothing exactly to do; but he was naturally a fuming, bustling little man, and could not remain passive when all the world was in a hurry. He worried from top to bottom of the castle, with an air of infinite anxiety; he continually called the servants from their work to exhort them to be diligent, and buzzed about every hall and chamber, as idly restless and importunate as a blue bottle fly of a warm summer's day.

In the mean time, the fatted calf had been killed; the forests had rung with the clamour of the huntsmen; the kitchen was crowded with good cheer; the cellars had yielded up whole oceans of *Rhein-wein* and *Ferne-wein,* and even the great Heidelberg tun had been laid under contribution. Every thing was ready to receive the distinguished guest with *Saus und Braus* in the true spirit of German hospitality—but the guest delayed to make his appearance. Hour rolled after hour. The sun that had poured his downward rays upon the rich forests of the Odenwald, now just gleamed along the summits of the mountains. The Baron mounted the highest tower, and strained his eyes in hopes of catching a distant sight of the Count and his attendants. Once he thought he beheld them; the sound of horns came floating from the valley, prolonged by the mountain echoes. A number of horsemen were seen far below, slowly advancing along the road; but when they had nearly reached the foot of the mountain, they suddenly struck off in a different direction. The last ray of sunshine departed— the bats began to flit by in the twilight—the road grew dimmer and dimmer to the view; and nothing appeared stirring in it, but now and then a peasant lagging homeward from his labour.

While the old castle of Landshort was in this state of perplexity, a very interesting scene was transacting in a different part of the Odenwald.

The young Count Von Altenburg was tranquilly pursuing his route in that sober jog trot way in which a man travels towards matrimony, when his friends have taken all the trouble and uncertainty of courtship off his hands, and a bride is waiting for him, as—certainly as a dinner, at the end of his journey. He had encountered, at Wurtzburg, a youthful companion in arms, with whom he had seen some service on the frontiers; Herman Von Starkenfaust, one of the stoutest hands, and worthiest hearts, of German chivalry, who was now returning from

the army. His father's castle was not far distant from the old fortress
of Landshort, although an hereditary feud rendered the families hostile,
and strangers to each other.

In the warm hearted moment of recognition, the young friends related
all their past adventures and fortunes, and the count gave the whole
history of his intended nuptials with a young lady whom he had
never seen, but of whose charms he had received the most en-
rapturing descriptions.

As the route of the friends lay in the same direction, they agreed
to perform the rest of their journey together; and that they might do
it the more leisurely, set off from Wurtzburg at an early hour, the count
having given directions for his retinue to follow and overtake him.

They beguiled their wayfaring with recollections of their military
scenes and adventures; but the count was apt to be a little tedious,
now and then, about the reputed charms of his bride, and the felicity
that awaited him.

In this way they had entered among the mountains of the Odenwald,
and were traversing one of its most lonely and thickly wooded passes.
It is well known that the forests of Germany have always been as
much infested by robbers as its castles by spectres; and, at this time,
the former were particularly numerous from the hordes of disbanded
soldiers wandering about the country. It will not appear extraordinary,
therefore, that the cavaliers were attacked by a gang of these stragglers,
in the midst of the forest. They defended themselves with bravery,
but were nearly overpowered, when the count's retinue arrived to
their assistance. At sight of them the robbers fled, but not until the
count had received a mortal wound. He was slowly and carefully
conveyed back to the city of Wurtzburg, and a friar summoned from
a neighbouring convent, who was famous for his skill in administering
to both soul and body. But half of his skill was superfluous; the
moments of the unfortunate count were numbered.

With his dying breath he entreated his friend to repair instantly
to the castle of Landshort, and explain the fatal cause of his not
keeping his appointment with his bride. Though not the most ardent
of lovers, he was one of the most punctilious of men; and appeared
earnestly solicitous that this mission should be speedily and courteously
executed. "Unless this is done," said he, "I shall not sleep quietly in
my grave!" He repeated these last words with peculiar solemnity. A
request, at a moment so impressive, admitted no hesitation. Starkenfaust endeavoured to soothe him to calmness, promised faithfully to
execute his wish, and gave him his hand in solemn pledge. The dying
man pressed it in acknowledgment, but soon lapsed into delirium—

raved about his bride—his engagement—his plighted word; ordered his horse, that he might ride to the castle of Landshort, and expired in the fancied act of vaulting into the saddle.

Starkenfaust bestowed a sigh, and a soldier's tear, on the untimely fate of his comrade; and then pondered on the awkward mission he had undertaken. His heart was heavy, and his head perplexed; for he was to present himself an unbidden guest among hostile people, and to damp their festivity with tidings fatal to their hopes. Still there were certain whisperings of curiosity in his bosom to see this far famed beauty of Katzenellenbogen, so cautiously shut up from the world; for he was a passionate admirer of the sex, and there was a dash of eccentricity and enterprize in his character that made him fond of all singular adventure.

Previous to his departure, he made all due arrangements with the holy fraternity of the convent for the funeral solemnities of his friend, who was to be buried in the cathedral of Wurtzburg, near some of his illustrious relatives; and the mourning retinue of the count took charge of his remains.

It is now high time that we should return to the ancient family of Katzenellenbogen, who were impatient for their guest, and still more for their dinner; and to the worthy little Baron, whom we left airing himself on the watch tower.

Night closed in, but still no guest arrived. The Baron descended from the tower in despair. The banquet, which had been delayed from hour to hour could no longer be postponed. The meats were already overdone; the cook in an agony; and the whole household had the look of a garrison that had been reduced by famine. The Baron was obliged reluctantly to give orders for the feast without the presence of the guest. All were seated at table, and just on the point of commencing, when the sound of a horn from without the gate gave notice of the approach of a stranger. Another long blast filled the old courts of the castle with its echoes, and was answered by the warder from the walls. The Baron hastened to receive his future son in law.

The drawbridge had been let down, and the stranger was before the gate. He was a tall gallant cavalier, mounted on a black steed. His countenance was pale, but he had a beaming, romantic eye, and an air of stately melancholy. The Baron was a little mortified that he should have come in this simple, solitary style. His dignity for a moment was ruffled, and he felt disposed to consider it a want of proper respect for the important occasion, and the important family with which he was to be connected. He, however, pacified himself

with the conclusion that it must have been youthful impatience which
had induced him thus to spur on sooner than his attendants.

"I am sorry," said the stranger, "to break in upon you thus un-
seasonably—"

Here the Baron interrupted him with a world of compliments and
greetings; for, to tell the truth, he prided himself upon his courtesy
and his eloquence. The stranger attempted, once or twice, to stem
the torrent of words, but in vain, so he bowed his head and suffered
it to flow on. By the time the Baron had come to a pause, they had
reached the inner court of the castle; and the stranger was again
about to speak, when he was once more interrupted by the appearance
of the female part of the family, leading forth the shrinking and
blushing bride. He gazed on her for a moment as one entranced; it
seemed as if his whole soul beamed forth in the gaze, and rested upon
that lovely form. One of the maiden aunts whispered something in
her ear; she made an effort to speak; her moist blue eye was timidly
raised, gave a shy glance of inquiry on the stranger, and was cast
again to the ground. The words died away; but there was a sweet
smile playing about her lips, and a soft dimpling of the cheek, that
showed her glance had not been unsatisfactory. It was impossible for
a girl of the fond age of eighteen, highly predisposed for love and
matrimony, not to be pleased with so gallant a cavalier.

The late hour at which the guest had arrived, left no time for parley.
The Baron was peremptory, and deferred all particular conversation
until the morning, and led the way to the untasted banquet.

It was served up in the great hall of the castle. Around the walls
hung the hard favoured portraits of the heroes of the house of
Katzenellenbogen, and the trophies which they had gained in the
field and in the chase. Hacked corslets; splintered jousting spears, and
tattered banners, were mingled with the spoils of sylvan warfare: the
jaws of the wolf, and the tusks of the boar, grinned horribly among
cross bows and battle axes, and a huge pair of antlers branched
immediately over the head of the youthful bridegroom.

The cavalier took but little notice of the company, or the entertainment. He scarce tasted the banquet, but seemed absorbed in
admiration of his bride. He conversed in a low tone that could not
be overheard—for the language of love is never loud; but where is
the female ear so dull that it cannot catch the softest whisper of the
lover? There was a mingled tenderness and gravity in his manner,
that appeared to have a powerful effect upon the young lady. Her
colour came and went as she listened with deep attention. Now and
then she made some blushing reply, and when his eye was turned

away, she would steal a side long glance at his romantic countenance, and heave a gentle sigh of tender happiness. It was evident that the young couple were completely enamoured. The aunts, who were deeply versed in the mysteries of the heart, declared that they had fallen in love with each other at first sight.

The feast went on merrily, or at least noisily, for the guests were all blessed with those keen appetites that attend upon light purses and mountain air. The Baron told his best and longest stories, and never had he told them so well, or with such great effect. If there was any thing marvellous, his auditors were lost in astonishment; and if any thing facetious, they were sure to laugh exactly in the right place. The Baron, it is true, like most great men, was too dignified to utter any joke but a dull one; it was always enforced, however, by a bumper of excellent Hoch-heimer; and even a dull joke at one's own table, served up with jolly old wine, is irresistible. Many good things were said by poorer and keener wits, that would not bear repeating, except on similar occasions; many sly speeches whispered in ladies' ears, that almost convulsed them with suppressed laughter; and a song or two roared out by a poor, but merry and broad faced cousin of the Baron, that absolutely made the maiden aunts hold up their fans.

Amidst all this revelry, the stranger guest maintained a most singular and unseasonable gravity. His countenance assumed a deeper cast of dejection as the evening advanced, and, strange as it may appear, even the Baron's jokes seemed only to render him the more melancholy. At times he was lost in thought, and at times there was a perturbed and restless wandering of the eye that bespoke a mind but ill at ease. His conversations with the bride became more and more earnest and mysterious. Lowering clouds began to steal over the fair serenity of her brow, and tremors to run through her tender frame.

All this could not escape the notice of the company. Their gayety was chilled by the unaccountable gloom of the bridegroom; their spirits were infected; whispers and glances were interchanged, accompanied by shrugs and dubious shakes of the head. The song and the laugh grew less and less frequent; there were dreary pauses in the conversation, which were at length succeeded by wild tales, and supernatural legends. One dismal story produced another still more dismal, and the Baron nearly frightened some of the ladies into hysterics with the history of the goblin horseman that carried away the fair Leonora; a dreadful, but true story, which has since been put into excellent verse, and is read and believed by all the world.

The bridegroom listened to this tale with profound attention. He kept his eyes steadily fixed on the Baron, and as the story drew to a close, began gradually to rise from his seat, growing taller and taller, until, in the Baron's entranced eye, he seemed almost to tower into a giant. The moment the tale was finished, he heaved a deep sigh, and took a solemn farewell of the company. They were all amazement. The Baron was perfectly thunderstruck.

"What! going to leave the castle at midnight? why, every thing was prepared for his reception: a chamber was ready for him if he wished to retire."

The stranger shook his head mournfully, and mysteriously; "I must lay my head in a different chamber tonight!"

There was something in this reply, and the tone in which it was uttered, that made the Baron's heart misgive him; but he rallied his forces and repeated his hospitable entreaties.

The stranger shook his head silently, but positively, at every offer, and waving his farewell to the company, stalked slowly out of the hall. The maiden aunts were absolutely petrified—the bride hung her head, and a tear stole to her eye.

The Baron followed the stranger to the great court of the castle, where the black charger stood pawing the earth, and snorting with impatience. When they had reached the portal, whose deep archway was dimly lighted by a cresset, the stranger paused, and addressed the Baron in a hollow tone of voice, which the vaulted roof rendered still more sepulchral.

"Now that we are alone," said he, "I will impart to you the reason of my going. I have a solemn, an indispensable engagement—"

"Why," said the Baron, "cannot you send some one in your place?"

"It admits of no substitute—I must attend it in person—I must away to Wurtzburg cathedral—"

"Aye," said the Baron, plucking up spirit, "but not until tomorrow—tomorrow you shall take your bride there."

"No! no!" replied the stranger, with tenfold solemnity, "my engagement is with no bride—the worms! the worms expect me! I am a dead man—I have been slain by robbers—my body lies at Wurtzburg—at midnight I am to be buried—the grave is waiting for me—I must keep my appointment!"

He sprang on his black charger, dashed over the drawbridge, and the clattering of his horse's hoofs was lost in the whistling of the night blast.

The Baron returned to the hall in the utmost consternation, and related what had passed. Two ladies fainted outright, others sickened at the idea of having banquetted with a spectre. It was the opinion of some, that this might be the wild huntsman famous in German legend.

Some talked of mountain sprites, of wood demons, and of other super-natural beings, with which the good people of Germany have been so grievously harassed since time immemorial. One of the poor relations ventured to suggest that it might be some sportive evasion of the young cavalier, and that the very gloominess of the caprice seemed to accord with so melancholy a personage. This, however, drew on him the indignation of the whole company, and especially of the Baron, who looked upon him as little better than an infidel; so that he was fain to abjure his heresy as speedily as possible, and come into the faith of the true believers.

But, whatever may have been the doubts entertained, they were completely put to an end by the arrival, next day, of regular missives, confirming the intelligence of the young Count's murder, and his interment in Wurtzburg cathedral.

The dismay at the castle may well be imagined. The Baron shut himself up in his chamber. The guests who had come to rejoice with him, could not think of abandoning him in his distress. They wandered about the courts, or collected in groups in the hall, shaking their heads and shrugging their shoulders, at the troubles of so good a man; and sat longer than ever at table, and ate and drank more stoutly than ever, by way of keeping up their spirits. But the situation of the widowed bride was the most pitiable. To have lost a husband before she had even embraced him—and such a husband! if the very spectre could be so gracious and noble, what must have been the living man! She filled the house with lamentations.

On the night of the second day of her widowhood she had retired to her chamber, accompanied by one of her aunts, who insisted on sleeping with her. The aunt, who was one of the best tellers of ghost stories in all Germany, had just been recounting one of her longest, and had fallen asleep in the very midst of it. The chamber was remote, and overlooked a small garden. The niece lay pensively gazing at the beams of the rising moon, as they trembled on the leaves of an aspen tree before the lattice. The castle clock had just tolled midnight, when a soft strain of music stole up from the garden. She rose hastily from her bed, and stepped lightly to the window. A tall figure stood among the shadows of the trees. As it raised its head, a beam of moonlight fell upon the countenance. Heaven and earth! she beheld the Spectre Bridegroom! A loud shriek at that moment burst upon her ear, and her aunt, who had been awakened by the music, and had followed her silently to the window, fell into her arms. When she looked again, the spectre had disappeared.

Of the two females, the aunt now required the most soothing, for she was perfectly beside herself with terror. As to the young lady, there was something, even in the spectre of her lover, that seemed endearing. There was still the semblance of manly beauty; and though the shadow of a man is but little calculated to satisfy the affections of a love sick girl, yet, where the substance is not to be had, even that is consoling. The aunt declared she would never sleep in that chamber again; the niece, for once, was refractory, and declared as strongly that she would sleep in no other in the castle: the consequence was, that she had to sleep in it alone; but she drew a promise from her aunt not to relate the story of the spectre, lest she should be denied the only melancholy pleasure left her on earth—that of inhabiting the chamber over which the guardian shade of her lover kept its nightly vigils.

How long the good old lady would have observed this promise is uncertain, for she dearly loved to talk of the marvellous, and there is a triumph in being the first to tell a frightful story; it is, however, still quoted in the neighbourhood, as a memorable instance of female secrecy, that she kept it to herself for a whole week, when she was suddenly absolved from all further restraint, by intelligence brought to the breakfast table one morning, that the young lady was not to be found. Her room was empty—the bed had not been slept in—the window was open, and the bird had flown!

The astonishment and concern with which the intelligence was received, can only be imagined by those who have witnessed the agitation which the mishaps of a great man cause among his friends. Even the poor relations paused for a moment from the indefatigable labours of the trencher; when the aunt, who had at first been struck speechless, wrung her hands, and shrieked out, "the goblin! the goblin! she's carried away by the goblin!"

In a few words, she related the fearful scene of the garden, and concluded that the spectre must have carried off his bride. Two of the domestics corroborated the opinion, for they had heard the clattering of a horse's hoofs down the mountain about midnight, and had no doubt that it was the spectre on his black charger, bearing her away to the tomb. All present were struck with the direful probability; for events of the kind are extremely common in Germany, as many well authenticated histories bear witness.

What a lamentable situation was that of the poor Baron! What a heartrending dilemma for a fond father, and a member of the great family of Katzenellenbogen! His only daughter had either been rapt away to the grave, or he was to have some wood demon for a son in law, and, perchance, a troop of goblin grand children. As usual, he was completely bewildered, and all the castle in an uproar. The men were ordered to take horse, and to scour every road, and path, and glen of the Odenwald. The Baron himself had just drawn on his jack boots, girded on his sword, and was about to mount his steed to sally forth on the doubtful quest, when he was brought to a pause by a new apparition. A lady was seen approaching the castle, mounted on a palfrey, attended by a cavalier on horseback. She galloped up to the gate, sprang from her horse, and falling at the Baron's feet, embraced his knees. It was his lost daughter, and her companion—the Spectre Bridegroom! The Baron was astounded. He looked at his daughter, then at the Spectre, and almost doubted the evidence of his senses. The latter, too, was wonderfully improved in his appearance, since his visit to the world of spirits. His dress was splendid, and set off a noble figure of manly symmetry. He was no longer pale and melancholy. His fine countenance was flushed with the glow of youth, and joy rioted in his large dark eye.

The mystery was soon cleared up. The cavalier (for in truth, as you must have known all the while, he was no goblin) announced himself as Sir Herman Von Starkenfaust. He related his adventure with the young Count. He told how he had hastened to the castle to deliver the unwelcome tidings, but that the eloquence of the Baron had interrupted him in every attempt to tell his tale. How the sight of the bride had completely captivated him, and that to pass a few hours near her, he had tacitly suffered the mistake to continue. How he had been sorely perplexed in what way to make a decent retreat, until the Baron's goblin stories had suggested his eccentric exit. How, fearing the feudal hostility of the family, he had repeated his visits by stealth—had haunted the garden beneath the young lady's window—had wooed—had won—had borne away in triumph—and, in a word, had wedded the fair.

Under any other circumstances, the Baron would have been inflexible, for he was tenacious of paternal authority, and devoutly obstinate in all family feuds; but he loved his daughter; he had lamented her lost; he rejoiced to find her still alive; and, though her husband was of a hostile house, yet, thank heaven, he was not a goblin. There was something, it must be acknowledged, that did not exactly accord with his notions of strict veracity, in the joke the knight had passed upon him of his being a dead man; but several old friends present, who had served in the wars, assured him that every stratagem was excusable in love, and that the cavalier was entitled to especial privilege, having lately served as a trooper.

Matters, therefore, were happily arranged. The Baron pardoned the young couple on the spot. The revels at the castle were resumed. The poor relations overwhelmed this new member of the family with loving kindness; he was so gallant, so generous, and so rich. The aunts, it is true, were somewhat scandalized that their system of strict seclusion, and passive obedience, should be so badly exemplified, but attributed it all to their negligence in not having the windows grated. One of them was particularly mortified at having her marvellous story marred, and that the only spectre she had ever seen should turn out a counterfeit; but the niece seemed perfectly happy at having found him substantial flesh and blood—and so the story ends.

WESTMINSTER ABBEY

When I behold, with deepe astonishment,
To famous Westminster how there resorte,
Living in brasse or stoney monyment,
The princes and the worthies of all sorte:
Doe not I see reformde nobilitie,
Without contempt, or pride, or ostentation,
And looke upon offenselesse majesty,
Naked of pompe or earthly domination?
And how a play-game of a painted stone,
Contents the quiet now and silent sprites,
Whome all the world which late they stood upon,
Could not content nor quench their appetites.
    Life is a froste of cold felicitie
    And death the thaw of all our vanitie.
      CHRISTOLERO'S EPIGRAMS, BY T. B. 1598.

On one of those sober and rather melancholy days, in the latter part of Autumn, when the shadows of morning and evening almost mingle together, and throw a gloom over the decline of the year, I passed several hours in rambling about Westminster Abbey. There was something congenial to the season in the mournful magnificence of the old pile; and as I passed its threshold, it seemed like stepping back into the regions of antiquity, and losing myself among the shades of former ages.

I entered from the inner court of Westminster School, through a long, low, vaulted passage, that had an almost subterranean look, being dimly lighted in one part by circular perforations in the massy walls. Through this dark avenue I had a distant view of the cloisters, with the figure of an old verger, in his black gown, moving along their shadowy vaults, and seeming like a spectre from one of the neighbouring tombs. The approach to the abbey through these gloomy monastic remains prepares the mind for its solemn contemplation. The cloisters still retain something of the quiet and seclusion of former days. The grey walls are discoloured by damps, and crumbling with age; a coat of hoary moss has gathered over the inscriptions of the mural monuments, and obscured the death's heads, and other funereal emblems. The sharp touches of the chisel are gone from the rich tracery of the arches; the roses which adorned the key stones have lost their leafy beauty; every thing bears marks of the gradual dilapidations of time, which yet has something touching and pleasing in its very decay.

The sun was pouring down a yellow autumnal ray into the square of the cloisters; beaming upon a scanty plot of grass in the centre, and lighting up an angle of the vaulted passage with a kind of dusty splendour. From between the arcades the eye glanced up to a bit of blue sky or a passing cloud; and beheld the sun gilt pinnacles of the abbey towering into the azure heaven.

As I paced the cloisters, sometimes contemplating this mingled picture of glory and decay, and sometimes endeavouring to decipher the inscriptions on the tombstones, which formed the pavement beneath my feet, my eye was attracted to three figures, rudely carved in relief, but nearly worn away by the footsteps of many generations. They were the effigies of three of the early abbots; the epitaphs were entirely effaced; the names alone remained, having no doubt been renewed in later times; (Vitalis. Abbas. 1082, and Gislebertus Crispinus. Abbas. 1114, and Laurentius. Abbas. 1176). I remained some little while, musing over these casual reliques of antiquity, thus left like wrecks upon this distant shore of time, telling no tale but that such beings had been, and had perished; teaching no moral but the futility of that pride which hopes still to exact homage in its ashes, and to live in an inscription. A little longer and even these faint records will be obliterated, and the monument will cease to be a memorial. Whilst I was yet looking down upon these gravestones, I was roused by the sound of the abbey clock, reverberating from buttress to buttress, and echoing among the cloisters. It is almost startling to hear this warning of departed time sounding among the tombs, and telling the lapse of the hour, which like a billow has rolled us onward towards the grave.

I pursued my walk to an arched door opening to the interior of the abbey. On entering here, the magnitude of the building breaks fully upon the mind, contrasted with the vaults of the cloisters. The eye gazes with wonder at clustered columns of gigantic dimensions, with arches springing from them to such an amazing height; and man wandering about their bases, shrunk into insignificance in comparison with his own handywork. The spaciousness and gloom of this vast edifice produce a profound and mysterious awe. We step cautiously and softly about, as if fearful of disturbing the hallowed silence of the tomb; while every footfall whispers along the walls, and chatters among the sepulchres, making us more sensible of the quiet we have interrupted.

It seems as if the awful nature of the place presses down upon the soul, and hushes the beholder into noiseless reverence. We feel that we are surrounded by the congregated bones of the great men of past times; who have filled history with their deeds, and the earth with their renown. And yet it almost provokes a smile at the vanity of human ambition, to see how they are crowded together and justled in the dust: what parsimony is observed in doling out a scanty nook; a gloomy corner; a little portion of earth, to those, whom, when alive, kingdoms could not satisfy: and how many shapes, and forms and artifices, are devised to catch the casual notice of the passenger, and save from forgetfulness, for a few short years, a name which once aspired to occupy ages of the world's thought and admiration.

I passed some time in Poets' Corner, which occupies an end of one of the transepts or cross aisles of the Abbey. The monuments are generally simple; for the lives of literary men afford no striking themes for the sculptor. Shakespeare and Addison have statues erected to their memories; but the greater part have busts, medallions, and sometimes mere inscriptions. Notwithstanding the simplicity of these memorials, I have always observed that the visitors to the abbey remain longest about them. A kinder and fonder feeling takes place of that cold curiosity or vague admiration with which they gaze on the splendid monuments of the great and the heroic. They linger about these as about the tombs of friends and companions; for indeed there is something of companionship between the author and the reader. Other men are known to posterity only through the medium of history, which is continually growing faint and obscure; but the intercourse between the author and his fellow men is ever new, active and immediate. He has lived for them more than for himself; he has sacrificed surrounding enjoyments, and shut himself up from the delights of social life, that he might the more intimately commune with distant minds and distant ages. Well may the world cherish his renown; for it has been purchased, not by deeds of violence and blood, but by the diligent dispensation of pleasure. Well may posterity be grateful to his memory; for he has left it an inheritance, not of empty names and sounding actions, but whole treasures of wisdom, bright gems of thought, and golden veins of language.

From Poets' Corner I continued my stroll towards that part of the abbey which contains the sepulchres of the kings. I wandered among what once were chapels, but which are now occupied by the tombs and monuments of the great. At every turn I met with some illustrious name; or the cognizance of some powerful house renowned in history. As the eye darts into these dusky chambers of death, it catches glimpses of quaint effigies; some kneeling in niches, as if in devotion; others stretched upon the tombs, with hands piously pressed together; warriors in armour, as if reposing after battle; prelates with croziers and mitres; and nobles in robes and coronets, lying as it were in state. In glancing over this scene, so strangely populous, yet where every

form is so still and silent, it seems almost as if we were treading a
mansion of that fabled city, where every being had been suddenly
transmuted into stone.

I paused to contemplate a tomb on which lay the effigy of a knight
in complete armour. A large buckler was on one arm; the hands were
pressed together in supplication upon the breast; the face was almost
covered by the morion; the legs were crossed in token of the warrior's
having been engaged in the holy war. It was the tomb of a crusader;
of one of those military enthusiasts, who so strangely mingled religion
and romance, and whose exploits form the connecting link between
fact and fiction; between the history and the fairy tale. There is something extremely picturesque in the tombs of these adventurers, decorated as they are with rude armorial bearings and gothic sculpture.
They comport with the antiquated chapels in which they are generally
found; and in considering them, the imagination is apt to kindle
with the legendary associations, the romantic fictions, the chivalrous
pomp and pageantry which poetry has spread over the wars for the
Sepulchre of Christ. They are the reliques of times utterly gone by;
of beings passed from recollection; of customs and manners with which
ours have no affinity. They are like objects from some strange and
distant land, of which we have no certain knowledge, and about
which all our conceptions are vague and visionary. There is something
extremely solemn and awful in those effigies on gothic tombs, extended
as if in the sleep of death, or in the supplication of the dying hour.
They have an effect infinitely more impressive on my feelings than
the fanciful attitudes, the overwrought conceits, and allegorical groups,
which abound on modern monuments. I have been struck, also, with
the superiority of many of the old sepulchral inscriptions. There was
a noble way, in former times, of saying things simply, and yet saying
them proudly; and I do not know an epitaph that breathes a loftier
consciousness of family worth and honourable lineage, than one which
affirms, of a noble house, that "all the brothers were brave, and all
the sisters virtuous."

In the opposite transept to Poets' Corner stands a monument which
is among the most renowned achievements of modern art; but which,
to me, appears horrible rather than sublime. It is the tomb of Mrs.
Nightingale, by Roubillac. The bottom of the monument is represented
as throwing open its marble doors, and a sheeted skeleton is starting
forth. The shroud is falling from his fleshless frame as he launches his
dart at his victim. She is sinking into her affrighted husband's arms,
who strives, with vain and frantic effort, to avert the blow. The whole
is executed with terrible truth and spirit; we almost fancy we hear

the gibbering yell of triumph, bursting from the distended jaws of the spectre.—But why should we thus seek to clothe death with unnecessary terrors, and to spread horrors round the tomb of those we love? The grave should be surrounded by every thing that might inspire tenderness and veneration for the dead; or that might win the living to virtue. It is the place, not of disgust and dismay, but of sorrow and meditation.

While wandering about these gloomy vaults and silent aisles, studying the records of the dead, the sound of busy existence from without occasionally reaches the ear;—the rumbling of the passing equipage; the murmur of the multitude; or perhaps the light laugh of pleasure. The contrast is striking with the deathlike repose around: and it has a strange effect upon the feelings, thus to hear the surges of active life hurrying along and beating against the very walls of the sepulchre.

I continued in this way to move from tomb to tomb, and from chapel to chapel. The day was gradually wearing away; the distant tread of loiterers about the abbey grew less and less frequent; the sweet tongued bell was summoning to evening prayers; and I saw at a distance the choristers, in their white surplices, crossing the aisle and entering the choir. I stood before the entrance to Henry the Seventh's chapel. A flight of steps leads up to it, through a deep and gloomy, but magnificent arch. Great gates of brass, richly and delicately wrought, turn heavily upon their hinges, as if proudly reluctant to admit the feet of common mortals into this most gorgeous of sepulchres.

On entering, the eye is astonished by the pomp of architecture, and the elaborate beauty of sculptured detail. The very walls are wrought into universal ornament, encrusted with tracery, and scooped into niches, crowded with the statues of saints and martyrs. Stone seems, by the cunning labour of the chisel, to have been robbed of its weight and density, suspended aloft, as if by magic, and the fretted roof achieved with the wonderful minuteness and airy security of a cobweb.

Along the sides of the chapel are the lofty stalls of the Knights of the Bath, richly carved of oak, though with the grotesque decorations of gothic architecture. On the pinnacles of the stalls are affixed the helmets and crests of the knights, with their scarfs and swords; and above them are suspended their banners, emblazoned with armorial bearings, and contrasting the splendour of gold and purple and crimson, with the cold grey fretwork of the roof. In the midst of this grand mausoleum stands the sepulchre of its founder,—his effigy, with that of his queen, extended on a sumptuous tomb, and the whole surrounded by a superbly wrought brazen railing.

There is a sad dreariness in this magnificence; this strange mixture of tombs and trophies; these emblems of living and aspiring ambition, close beside mementos which show the dust and oblivion in which all must sooner or later terminate. Nothing impresses the mind with a deeper feeling of loneliness, than to tread the silent and deserted scene of former throng and pageant. On looking round on the vacant stalls of the knights and their esquires; and on the rows of dusty but gorgeous banners that were once borne before them, my imagination conjured up the scene when this hall was bright with the valour and beauty of the land; glittering with the splendour of jewelled rank and military array; alive with the tread of many feet and the hum of an admiring multitude. All had passed away: the silence of death had settled again upon the place; interrupted only by the casual chirping of birds, which had found their way into the chapel, and built their nests among its friezes and pendants—sure signs of solitariness and desertion.

When I read the names inscribed on the banners, they were those of men scattered far and wide about the world; some tossing upon distant seas; some under arms in distant lands; some mingling in the busy intrigues of courts and cabinets: all seeking to deserve one more distinction in this mansion of shadowy honours; the melancholy reward of a monument.

Two small aisles on each side of this chapel present a touching instance of the equality of the grave; which brings down the oppressor to a level with the oppressed, and mingles the dust of the bitterest enemies together. In one is the sepulchre of the haughty Elizabeth, in the other is that of her victim, the lovely and unfortunate Mary. Not an hour in the day but some ejaculation of pity is uttered over the fate of the latter, mingled with indignation at her oppressor. The walls of Elizabeth's sepulchre continually echo with the sighs of sympathy heaved at the grave of her rival.

A peculiar melancholy reigns over the aisle where Mary lies buried. The light struggles dimly through windows darkened by dust. The greater part of the place is in deep shadow, and the walls are stained and tinted by time and weather. A marble figure of Mary is stretched upon the tomb, round which is an iron railing, much corroded, bearing her national emblem the thistle. I was weary with wandering, and sat down to rest myself by the monument, revolving in my mind the chequered and disastrous story of poor Mary.

The sound of casual footsteps had ceased from the abbey. I could only hear, now and then, the distant voice of the priest repeating the evening service, and the faint responses of the choir; these paused for a time, and all was hushed. The stillness, the desertion and obscurity that were gradually prevailing around, gave a deeper and more solemn interest to the place:

> For in the silent grave no conversation,
> No joyful tread of friends, no voice of lovers,
> No careful father's counsel—nothing's heard,
> For nothing is, but all oblivion,
> Dust and an endless darkness.

Suddenly the notes of the deep labouring organ burst upon the ear, falling with doubled and redoubled intensity, and rolling, as it were, huge billows of sound. How well do their volume and grandeur accord with this mighty building! With what pomp do they swell through its vast vaults, and breathe their awful harmony through these caves of death, and make the silent sepulchre vocal!—And now they rise in triumphant acclamation, heaving higher and higher their accordant notes, and piling sound on sound.—And now they pause, and the soft voices of the choir break out into sweet gushes of melody; they soar aloft, and warble along the roof, and seem to play about these lofty vaults like the pure airs of heaven. Again the pealing organ heaves its thrilling thunders, compressing air into music, and rolling it forth upon the soul. What long drawn cadences! What solemn sweeping concords! It grows more and more dense and powerful—it fills the vast pile, and seems to jar the very walls—the ear is stunned—the senses are overwhelmed. And now it is winding up in full jubilee—it is rising from the earth to heaven—the very soul seems rapt away and floated upwards on this swelling tide of harmony!

I sat for some time lost in that kind of reverie which a strain of music is apt sometimes to inspire: the shadows of evening were gradually thickening around me; the monuments began to cast deeper and deeper gloom; and the distant clock again gave token of the slowly waning day.

I rose and prepared to leave the abbey. As I descended the flight of steps which lead into the body of the building, my eye was caught by the shrine of Edward the Confessor, and I ascended the small staircase that conducts to it, to take from thence a general survey of this wilderness of tombs. The shrine is elevated upon a kind of platform, and close around it are the sepulchres of various kings and queens. From this eminence the eye looks down between pillars and funeral trophies to the chapels and chambers below, crowded with tombs; where warriors, prelates, courtiers and statesmen lie mouldering in their "beds of darkness." Close by me stood the great chair of coronation, rudely carved of oak, in the barbarous taste of a remote and gothic age. The scene seemed almost as if contrived, with theatrical artifice, to produce an effect upon the beholder. Here was a type of the beginning and the end of human pomp and power; here it was literally but a step from the throne to the sepulchre. Would not one think that these incongruous mementos had been gathered together as a lesson to living greatness?—to show it, even in the moment of its proudest exaltation, the neglect and dishonour to which it must soon arrive; how soon that crown which encircles its brow must pass away; and it must lie down in the dust and disgraces of the tomb, and be trampled upon by the feet of the meanest of the multitude. For, strange to tell, even the grave is here no longer a sanctuary. There is a shocking levity in some natures, which leads them to sport with awful and hallowed things; and there are base minds, which delight to revenge on the illustrious dead the abject homage and grovelling servility which they pay to the living. The coffin of Edward the Confessor has been broken open, and his remains despoiled of their funeral ornaments; the sceptre has been stolen from the hand of the imperious Elizabeth, and the effigy of Henry the Fifth lies headless. Not a royal monument but bears some proof how false and fugitive is the homage of mankind. Some are plundered; some mutilated; some covered with ribaldry and insult—all more or less outraged and dishonoured!

The last beams of day were now faintly streaming through the painted windows in the high vaults above me: the lower parts of the abbey were already wrapped in the obscurity of twilight. The chapels and aisles grew darker and darker. The effigies of the kings faded into shadows; the marble figures of the monuments assumed strange shapes in the uncertain light; the evening breeze crept through the aisles like the cold breath of the grave; and even the distant footfall of a verger, traversing the Poets' Corner, had something strange and dreary in its sound. I slowly retraced my morning's walk, and as I passed out at the portal of the cloisters, the door, closing with a jarring noise behind me, filled the whole building with echoes.

I endeavoured to form some arrangement in my mind of the objects I had been contemplating, but found they were already falling into indistinctness and confusion. Names, inscriptions, trophies, had all become confounded in my recollection, though I had scarcely taken my foot from off the threshold. What, thought I, is this vast assemblage of sepulchres but a treasury of humiliation; a huge pile of reiterated homilies on the emptiness of renown, and the certainty of oblivion! It is, indeed, the empire of death; his great shadowy palace; where he sits in state, mocking at the reliques of human glory, and spreading dust and forgetfulness on the monuments of princes. How idle a boast, after all, is the immortality of a name! Time is ever silently turning over his pages; we are too much engrossed by the story of the present, to think of the characters and anecdotes that gave interest to the past; and each age is a volume thrown aside to be speedily forgotten. The idol of today pushes the hero of yesterday out of our recollection; and will, in turn, be supplanted by his successor of tomorrow. "Our fathers," says Sir Thomas Brown, "find their graves in our short memories, and sadly tell us how we may be buried in our survivors." History fades into fable; fact becomes clouded with doubt and controversy; the inscription moulders from the tablet; the statue falls from the pedestal. Columns, arches, pyramids, what are they but heaps of sand; and their epitaphs, but characters written in the dust? What is the security of a tomb, or the perpetuity of an embalmment? The remains of Alexander the Great have been scattered to the wind, and his empty sarcophagus is now the mere curiosity of a museum. "The Egyptian mummies, which Cambyses or time hath spared, avarice now consumeth; Mizraim cures wounds, and Pharaoh is sold for balsams."°

What then is to insure this pile which now towers above me from sharing the fate of mightier mausoleums? The time must come when its gilded vaults, which now spring so loftily, shall lie in rubbish beneath the feet; when, instead of the sound of melody and praise, the wind shall whistle through the broken arches, and the owl hoot from the shattered tower—when the garish sun beam shall break into those gloomy mansions of death; and the ivy twine round the fallen column; and the fox glove hang its blossoms about the nameless urn, as if in mockery of the dead. Thus man passes away; his name perishes from record and recollection; his history is as a tale that is told, and his very monument becomes a ruin.

NOTES CONCERNING
WESTMINSTER ABBEY

Toward the end of the sixth century when Britain, under the dominion of the Saxons, was in a state of barbarism and idolatry Pope Gregory the Great, struck with the beauty of some Anglo Saxon youths, exposed for sale in the Market place at Rome, conceived a fancy for the race and determined to send missionaries to preach the Gospel among these comely but benighted islanders. He was encouraged to this by

°Sir T. Brown.

learning that Ethelbert King of Kent and the most potent of the Anglo Saxon princes, had married Bertha a christian princess, only daughter of the King of Paris, and that she was allowed by stipulation, the full exercise of her religion.

The shrewd Pontiff knew the influence of the sex in matters of religious faith. He forthwith dispatched Augustine a Roman Monk with forty associates to the Court of Ethelbert at Canterbury, to effect the conversion of the King and to obtain through him a foothold in the island.

Ethelbert received them warily and held a conference in the open air; being distrustful of foreign priest craft, and fearful of spells and magic. They ultimately succeeded in making him as good a christian as his wife; the conversion of the King of course produced the conversion of his loyal subjects. The zeal and success of Augustine were rewarded by his being made archbishop of Canterbury and being endowed with authority over all the British churches.

One of the most prominent converts was Segebert or Sebert, King of the East Saxons a nephew of Ethelbert. He reigned at London, of which Mellitus, one of the Roman Monks who had come over with Augustine was made bishop.

Sebert, in 605, in his religious zeal founded a monastery by the river side to the west of the city on the ruins of a temple of Apollo, being in fact the origin of the present pile of Westminster Abbey. Great preparations were made for the consecration of the church which was to be dedicated to St. Peter. On the morning of the appointed day Mellitus the bishop proceeded with great pomp and solemnity to perform the ceremony. On approaching the edifice he was met by a fisherman who informed him that it was needless to proceed as the ceremony was over. The bishop stared with surprise when the fisherman went on to relate that the night before, as he was in his boat on the Thames St. Peter appeared to him and told him that he intended to consecrate the church himself that very night. The Apostle accordingly went into the church which suddenly became illuminated. The ceremony was performed in sumptuous style accompanied by strains of heavenly music and clouds of fragrant incense. After this the Apostle came onto the boat and ordered the fisherman to cast his net. He did so and had a miraculous draft of fishes; one of which he was commanded to present to the Bishop, and to signify to him that the Apostle had relieved him from the necessity of consecrating the church.

Mellitus was a wary man, slow of belief, and required confirmation of the fisherman's tale. He opened the church doors and beheld wax candles, crosses, holy water; oil sprinkled in various places and various other traces of a grand ceremonial. If he had still any lingering doubts they were completely removed on the fisherman's producing the identical fish which he had been ordered by the Apostle to present to him. To resist this would have been to resist ocular demonstration. The good bishop accordingly was convinced that the church had actually been consecrated by St. Peter in person; so he reverently abstained from proceeding further in the business.

The foregoing tradition is said to be the reason why King Edward the Confessor chose this place as the scite of a religious house which he meant to endow. He pulled down the old church and built another in its place in 1045. In this his remains were deposited in a magnificent shrine.

The sacred edifice again underwent modifications if not a reconstruction by Henry III in 1220 and began to assume its present appearance.

Under Henry VIII it lost its conventual character, that monarch turning the monks away and seizing upon the revenues.

Reliques of Edward the Confessor

A curious narrative was printed in 1688 by one of the choiristers of the Cathedral, who appears to have been the Paul Pry of the sacred edifice, giving an account of his rummaging among the bones of Edward the Confessor, after they had quietly reposed in their sepulchre upwards of six hundred years, and of his drawing forth the crucifix and golden chain of the deceased monarch. During eighteen years that he had officiated in the choir it had been a common tradition, he says, among his brother choiristers and the grey headed servants of the abbey that the body of King Edward was deposited in a kind of chest or coffin which was indistinctly seen in the upper part of the shrine erected to his memory. None of the abbey gossips, however, had ventured upon a nearer inspection, until the worthy narrator to gratify his curiosity mounted to the coffin by the aid of a ladder and found it to be made of wood, apparently very strong and firm, being secured by bands of iron.

Subsequently, in 1685, on taking down the scaffolding used in the coronation of James II, the coffin was found to be broken, a hole appearing in the lid, probably made through accident, by the workmen. No one ventured, however, to meddle with the sacred depository of royal rest, until, several weeks afterwards, the circumstance came to the knowledge of the aforesaid choirister. He forthwith repaired to the abbey in company with two friends of congenial tastes who were desirous of inspecting the tombs. Procuring a ladder he again mounted to the coffin and found, as had been represented, a hole in the lid about six inches long and four inches broad, just in front of the left breast. Thrusting in his hand and groping among the bones he drew from underneath the shoulder a crucifix, richly adorned and enamelled affixed to a gold chain twenty four inches long. These he shewed to his inquisitive friends, who were equally surprized with himself.

"At the time," says he, "when I took the cross and chain out of the coffin, *I drew the head to the hole and viewed it*, being very sound and firm with the upper and nether jaws whole and full of teeth, and a list of gold above an inch broad, in the nature of a coronet, surrounding the temples. There was also in the coffin, white linen and gold coloured flowered silk, that looked indifferent fresh but the least stress put thereto shewed it was well nigh perished. There were all his bones and much dust likewise which I left as I found." It is difficult to conceive a more grotesque lesson to human pride than the scull of Edward the Confessor thus irreverently pulled about in its coffin by a prying choirister, and brought to grin face to face with him through a hole in the lid!

Having satisfied his curiosity the choirister put the crucifix and chain back again into the coffin and sought the Dean, to apprize him of his discovery. The Dean not being accessible at the time; and fearing that the "holy treasure" might be taken away by other hands, he got a brother choirister to accompany him to the shrine about two or three hours afterwards and in his presence again drew forth the reliques. These he afterwards delivered on his knees to King James. The King subsequently had the old coffin enclosed in a new one of great strength: "each plank being two inches thick and cramped together with large iron wedges, where it now remains (1688) as a testimony of his pious care that no abuse might be offered to the sacred ashes therein reposited."

As the history of this shrine is full of moral I subjoin a description of it in modern times. "The solitary and forlorn shrine," says a British writer, "now stands a mere skeleton of what it was. A few faint traces of its sparkling decorations inlaid on solid mortar catch the rays of the sun, forever set on its splendor ○ ○ ○ ○ Only two of the spiral pillars remain. The wooden Ionic top is much broken and covered with dust. The mosaic is picked away in every part within reach, only the lozenges of about a foot square and five circular pieces of the rich marble remain."   Malcolm. Lond. Rediv.

Inscription on a monument alluded to in the Sketch.

Here lyes the Loyal Duke of Newcastle, and his Dutchess his second wife, by whom he had no issue. Her name was Margaret Lucas, youngest sister to the Lord Lucas of Colchester, a noble Family; for all the brothers were valiant and all the sisters virtuous. This Dutchess was a wise, witty, and learned Lady, which her many Bookes do well testify: she was a most virtuous, and loving and careful wife, and was with her lord all the time of his banishment and miseries, and when he came home, never parted from him in his solitary retirements.

In the winter time, when the days are short, the service in the afternoon is performed by the light of tapers. The effect is fine of the choir partially lighted up; while the main body of the cathedral and the transepts are in profound and cavernous darkness. The white dresses of the choiristers gleam amidst the deep brown of the oaken slatts and canopies; the partial illumination makes enormous shadows from columns and screens, and darting into the surrounding gloom catches here and there upon a sepulchral decoration, or monumental effigy. The swelling notes of the organ accord well with the scene.

When the service is over the Dean is lighted to his dwelling, in the old conventual part of the pile, by the boys of the choir in their white dresses, bearing tapers, and the procession passes through the abbey and along the shadowy cloisters, lighting up angles and arches and grim sepulchral monuments and leaving all behind in darkness.

On entering the cloisters at night from what is called the Dean's Yard the eye ranging through a dark vaulted passage catches a distant view of a white marble figure reclining on a tomb, on which a strong glare thrown by a gas light, has quite a spectral effect. It is a mural monument of one of the Pultneys.

The cloisters are well worth visiting by moonlight, when the moon is in the full.

Christmas

But is old, old, good old Christmas gone? Nothing but the hair of his good, gray old head and beard left? Well, I will have that, seeing I cannot have more of him.

HUE AND CRY AFTER CHRISTMAS.

CHRISTMAS

A man might then behold
  At Christmas, in each hall,
Good fires to curb the cold,
  And meat for great and small:
The neighbours were friendly bidden,
  And all had welcome true,
The poor from the gates were not chidden,
  When this old cap was new.
OLD SONG.

Nothing in England exercises a more delightful spell over my imagination, than the lingerings of the holyday customs and rural games of former times. They recall the pictures my fancy used to draw in the May morning of life, when as yet I only knew the world through books, and believed it to be all that poets had painted it; and they bring with them the flavour of those honest days of yore, in which, perhaps with equal fallacy, I am apt to think the world was more homebred, social, and joyous, than at present. I regret to say that they are daily growing more and more faint, being gradually worn away by time, but still more obliterated by modern fashion. They resemble those picturesque morsels of Gothic architecture, which we see crumbling in various parts of the country, partly dilapidated by the waste of ages, and partly lost in the additions and alterations of latter days. Poetry, however, clings with cherishing fondness about the rural game and holyday revel, from which it has derived so many of its themes—as the ivy winds its rich foliage about the gothic arch and mouldering tower, gratefully repaying their support, by clasping together their tottering remains, and, as it were, embalming them in verdure.

Of all the old festivals, however, that of Christmas awakens the strongest and most heartfelt associations. There is a tone of solemn and sacred feeling that blends with our conviviality, and lifts the spirit to a state of hallowed and elevated enjoyment. The services of the church about this season are extremely tender and inspiring. They dwell on the beautiful story of the origin of our faith, and the pastoral scenes that accompanied its announcement. They gradually increase in fervour and pathos during the season of Advent, until they break forth in full jubilee on the morning that brought peace and good will to men. I do not know a grander effect of music on the moral feelings, than to hear the full choir and the pealing organ performing a Christmas anthem in a cathedral, and filling every part of the vast pile with triumphant harmony.

It is a beautiful arrangement, also, derived from days of yore, that this festival, which commemorates the announcement of the religion of peace and love, has been made the season for gathering together of family connexions, and drawing closer again those bands of kindred hearts, which the cares and pleasures and sorrows of the world are continually operating to cast loose; of calling back the children of a family, who have launched forth in life, and wandered widely asunder, once more to assemble about the paternal hearth, that rallying place of the affections, there to grow young and loving again among the endearing mementos of childhood.

There is something in the very season of the year that gives a charm to the festivity of Christmas. At other times we derive a great portion of our pleasures from the mere beauties of nature. Our feelings sally forth and dissipate themselves over the sunny landscape, and we "live abroad and every where." The song of the bird, the murmur of the stream, the breathing fragrance of spring, the soft voluptuousness of summer, the golden pomp of autumn, earth with its mantle of refreshing green, and heaven with its deep delicious blue and its cloudy magnificence, all fill us with mute but exquisite delight, and we revel in the luxury of mere sensation. But in the depth of winter, when nature lies despoiled of every charm, and wrapped in her shroud of sheeted snow, we turn for our gratifications to moral sources. The dreariness and desolation of the landscape, the short gloomy days and darksome nights, while they circumscribe our wanderings, shut in our feelings also from rambling abroad, and make us more keenly disposed for the pleasures of the social circle. Our thoughts are more concentrated, our friendly sympathies more aroused. We feel more sensibly the charm of each other's society, and are brought more closely together by dependence on each other for enjoyment. Heart calleth unto heart, and we draw our pleasures from the deep wells of living kindness which lie in the quiet recesses of our bosoms, and which, when resorted to, furnish forth the pure element of domestic felicity.

The pitchy gloom without, makes the heart dilate on entering the room filled with the glow and warmth of the evening fire. The ruddy blaze diffuses an artificial summer and sunshine through the room, and lights up each countenance into a kindlier welcome. Where does the honest face of hospitality expand into a broader and more cordial smile—where is the shy glance of love more sweetly eloquent—than by the winter fireside;—and as the hollow blast of wintry wind rushes through the hall, claps the distant door, whistles about the casement, and rumbles down the chimney—what can be more grateful than that feeling of sober and sheltered security, with which we look round upon the comfortable chamber, and the scene of domestic hilarity?

The English, from the great prevalence of rural habits throughout every class of society, have always been fond of those festivals and holydays which agreeably interrupt the stillness of country life; and they were, in former days, particularly observant of the religious and social rites of Christmas. It is inspiring to read even the dry details which some antiquaries have given of the quaint humours, the burlesque pageants, the complete abandonment to mirth and good fellowship, with which this festival was celebrated. It seemed to throw open every door, and unlock every heart. It brought the peasant and the peer together, and blended all ranks in one warm generous flow of joy and kindness. The old halls of castles and manor houses resounded with the harp and the Christmas carol, and their ample boards groaned under the weight of hospitality. Even the poorest cottage welcomed the festive season with green decorations of bay and holly—the cheerful fire glanced its rays through the lattice, inviting the passenger to raise the latch, and join the gossip knot huddled round the hearth, beguiling the long evening with legendary jokes, and oft told Christmas tales.

One of the least pleasing effects of modern refinement is the havoc it has made among the hearty old holyday customs. It has completely taken off the sharp touchings and spirited reliefs of these embellishments of life, and has worn down society into a more smooth and polished, but certainly a less characteristic surface. Many of the games and ceremonials of Christmas have entirely disappeared, and, like the sherris sack of old Falstaff, are become matters of speculation and dispute among commentators. They flourished in times full of spirit and lustihood, when men enjoyed life roughly, but heartily and vigorously: times wild and picturesque, which have furnished poetry with its richest materials, and the drama with its most attractive variety of characters and manners. The world has become more worldly. There is more of dissipation, and less of enjoyment. Pleasure has expanded into a broader, but a shallower stream, and has forsaken many of those deep and quiet channels where it flowed sweetly through the calm bosom of domestic life. Society has acquired a more enlightened and elegant tone; but it has lost many of its strong local peculiarities, its homebred feelings, its honest fireside delights. The traditionary customs of golden hearted antiquity, its feudal hospitalities, and lordly was-sailings, have passed away with the baronial castles and stately manor houses in which they were celebrated. They comported with the shadowy hall, the great oaken gallery, and the tapestried parlour, but were unfitted to the light showy saloons and gay drawing rooms of the modern villa.

Shorn, however, as it is, of its ancient and festive honours, Christmas is still a period of delightful excitement in England. It is gratifying to see that home feeling completely aroused which holds so powerful a place in every English bosom. The preparations making on every side for the social board that is again to unite friends and kindred— the presents of good cheer passing and repassing, those tokens of regard and quickeners of kind feelings—the evergreens distributed about houses and churches, emblems of peace and gladness—all these have the most pleasing effect in producing fond associations, and kindling benevolent sympathies. Even the sound of the Waits, rude as may be their minstrelsy, breaks upon the midwatches of a winter night with the effect of perfect harmony. As I have been awakened by them in that still and solemn hour "when deep sleep falleth upon man," I have listened with a hushed delight, and connecting them with the sacred and joyous occasion, have almost fancied them into another celestial choir, announcing peace and good will to mankind.

How delightfully the imagination, when wrought upon by these moral influences, turns every thing to melody and beauty. The very crowing of the cock, heard sometimes in the profound repose of the country, "telling the night watches to his feathery dames," was thought by the common people to announce the approach of this sacred festival:

> Some say that ever 'gainst that season comes
> Wherein our Saviour's birth is celebrated,
> This bird of dawning singeth all night long:
> And then, they say, no spirit dares stir abroad;
> The nights are wholesome—then no planets strike,
> No fairy takes, no witch hath power to charm,
> So hallowed and so gracious is the time.

Amidst the general call to happiness, the bustle of the spirits, and stir of the affections, which prevail at this period, what bosom can remain insensible? It is, indeed, the season of regenerated feeling—the season for kindling not merely the fire of hospitality in the hall, but the genial flame of charity in the heart.

The scene of early love again rises green to memory beyond the sterile waste of years, and the idea of home, fraught with the fragrance of home dwelling joys, reanimates the drooping spirit—as the Arabian breeze will sometimes waft the freshness of the distant fields to the weary pilgrim of the desert.

Stranger and sojourner as I am in the land—though for me no social hearth may blaze, no hospitable roof throw open its doors, nor the warm grasp of friendship welcome me at the threshold—yet I feel the influence of the season beaming into my soul from the happy looks of those around me. Surely happiness is reflective, like the light of heaven; and every countenance bright with smiles, and glowing with innocent enjoyment, is a mirror transmitting to others the rays of a supreme and ever shining benevolence. He who can turn churlishly away from contemplating the felicity of his fellow beings, and can sit down darkling and repining in his loneliness when all around is joyful, may have his moments of strong excitement and selfish gratification, but he wants the genial and social sympathies which constitute the charm of a merry Christmas.

THE STAGE COACH

Omne benè
Sine poenâ
Tempus est ludendi.
Venit hora
Absque morâ
Libros deponendi.
OLD HOLYDAY SCHOOL SONG.

In the preceding paper I have made some general observations on the Christmas festivities of England, and am tempted to illustrate them by some anecdotes of a Christmas passed in the country: in perusing which, I would most courteously invite my reader to lay aside the austerity of wisdom, and to put on that genuine holyday spirit, which is tolerant of folly, and anxious only for amusement.

In the course of a December tour in Yorkshire, I rode for a long distance in one of the public coaches, on the day preceding Christmas. The coach was crowded, both inside and out, with passengers, who, by their talk, seemed principally bound to the mansions of relations or friends, to eat the Christmas dinner. It was loaded also with hampers of game, and baskets and boxes of delicacies; and hares hung dangling their long ears about the coachman's box, presents from distant friends for the impending feast. I had three fine rosy cheeked school boys for my fellow passengers inside, full of the buxom health and manly spirit which I have observed in the children in this country. They were returning home for the holydays, in high glee, and promising themselves a world of enjoyment. It was delightful to hear the gigantic plans of pleasure of the little rogues, and the impracticable feats they were to perform during their six weeks' emancipation from the abhorred thraldom of book, birch, and pedagogue. They were full of anticipations of the meeting with the family and household, down to the very cat and dog, and of the joy they were to give their little sisters by the presents with which their pockets were crammed; but the meeting to which they seemed to look forward with the greatest impatience was with Bantam, which I found to be a pony, and, according to their talk, possessed of more virtues than any steed since the days of Bucephalus. How he could trot! how he could run! and then such leaps as he would take—there was not a hedge in the whole country that he could not clear.

They were under the particular guardianship of the coachman, to whom, whenever an opportunity presented, they addressed a host of questions, and pronounced him one of the best fellows in the whole world. Indeed, I could not but notice the more than ordinary air of bustle and importance of the coachman, who wore his hat a little on one side, and had a large bunch of Christmas greens stuck in the button hole of his coat. He is always a personage full of mighty care and business, but he is particularly so during this season, having so many commissions to execute in consequence of the great interchange of presents. And here, perhaps, it may not be unacceptable to my untravelled readers, to have a sketch that may serve as a general representation of this very numerous and important class of functionaries, who have a dress, a manner, a language, an air, peculiar to themselves, and prevalent throughout the fraternity, so that, wherever an English stage coachman may be seen, he cannot be mistaken for one of any other craft or mystery.

He has commonly a broad full face, curiously mottled with red, as if the blood had been forced by hard feeding into every vessel of the skin; he is swelled into jolly dimensions by frequent potations of malt liquors, and his bulk is still further increased by a multiplicity of coats, in which he is buried like a cauliflower, the upper one reaching to his heels. He wears a broad brimmed low crowned hat, a huge roll of coloured handkerchief about his neck, knowingly knotted and tucked in at the bosom, and has in summer time a large boquet of flowers in his buttonhole, the present, most probably of some enamoured country lass. His waistcoat is commonly of some bright colour, striped, and his small clothes extend far below the knees, to meet a pair of jockey boots which reach about half way up his legs.

All this costume is maintained with much precision; he has a pride in having his clothes of excellent materials, and notwithstanding the seeming grossness of his appearance, there is still discernible that neatness and propriety of person, which is almost inherent in an Englishman. He enjoys great consequence and consideration along the road; has frequent conferences with the village housewives, who look upon him as a man of great trust and dependence; and he seems to have a good understanding with every bright eyed country lass. The moment he arrives where the horses are to be changed, he throws down the reins with something of an air, and abandons the cattle to the care of the hostler: his duty being merely to drive them from one stage to another. When off the box, his hands are thrust in the pockets of his great coat, and he rolls about the inn yard with an air of the most absolute lordliness. Here he is generally surrounded by an admiring throng of hostlers, stable boys, shoeblacks, and those nameless hangers on, that infest inns and taverns, and run errands, and do all kind of odd jobs, for the privilege of battening on the drippings of the kitchen and the leakage of the tap room. These all look up to him as to an oracle; treasure up his cant phrases; echo his opinions about horses and other topics of jockey lore; and above all, endeavour to imitate his air and carriage. Every ragamuffin that has a coat to his back, thrusts his hands in the pockets, rolls in his gait, talks slang, and is an embryo Coachey.

Perhaps it might be owing to the pleasing serenity that reigned in my own mind, that I fancied I saw cheerfulness in every countenance throughout the journey. A Stage Coach, however, carries animation always with it, and puts the world in motion as it whirls along. The horn, sounded at the entrance of a village, produces a general bustle. Some hasten forth to meet friends; some with bundles and bandboxes to secure places, and in the hurry of the moment can hardly take leave of the group that accompanies them. In the mean time, the coachman has a world of small commissions to execute; sometimes he delivers a hare or pheasant; sometimes jerks a small parcel or newspaper to the door of a public house, and sometimes, with knowing leer, and words of sly import, hands to some half blushing, half laughing house-maid, an odd shaped billet-doux from some rustic admirer. As the Coach rattles through the village, every one runs to the window, and you have glances on every side of fresh country faces, and blooming, giggling girls. At the corners are assembled juntos of village idlers and wise men, who take their stations there for the important purpose of seeing company pass: but the sagest knot is generally at the blacksmith's, to whom the passing of the coach is an event fruitful of much speculation. The smith, with the horse's heel in his lap, pauses as the vehicle whirls by; the cyclops round the anvil suspend their ringing hammers, and suffer the iron to grow cool; and the sooty spectre in brown paper cap, labouring at the bellows, leans on the handle for a moment, and permits the asthmatic engine to heave a long drawn sigh, while he glares through the murky smoke and sulphureous gleams of the smithy.

Perhaps the impending holyday might have given a more than usual animation to the country, for it seemed to me as if every body was in good looks and good spirits; game, poultry, and other luxuries of the table, were in brisk circulation in the villages; the grocer's, butcher's, and fruiterer's shops were thronged with customers. The housewives were stirring briskly about, putting their dwellings in order, and the glossy branches of holly, with their bright red berries, began to appear at the windows. The scene brought to mind an old writer's account of Christmas preparations. "Now capons and hens, besides turkeys, geese, and ducks, with beef and mutton—must all die—for in twelve days a multitude of people will not be fed with a little. Now plums and spice, sugar and honey, square it among pies and broath. Now or never must music be in tune, for the youth must dance and sing to get them a heat, while the aged sit by the fire. The country maid leaves half her market, and must be sent againe, if she forgets a pack of cards on Christmas even. Great is the contention of Holly and Ivy, whether master or dame wears the breeches. Dice and cards benefit the butler; and if the cook do not lack wit, he will sweetly lick his fingers."

I was roused from this fit of luxurious meditation, by a shout from my little travelling companions. They had been looking out of the coach windows for the last few miles, recognising every tree and cottage as they approached home, and now there was a general burst of joy. "There's John! and there's old Carlo! and there's Bantam!" cried the happy little rogues, clapping their hands.

At the head of a lane there was an old sober looking servant in livery, waiting for them; he was accompanied by a superannuated pointer, and by the redoubtable Bantam, a little old rat of a pony, with a shagged mane and long rusty tail, who stood dozing quietly by the road side, little dreaming of the bustling times that awaited him.

I was pleased to see the fondness with which the little fellows leaped about the steady old footman, and hugged the pointer, who wriggled his whole body for joy. But Bantam was the great object of interest; all wanted to mount at once, and it was with some difficulty that John arranged that they should ride by turns, and the eldest should ride first.

Off they set at last, one on the pony with the dog bounding and barking before him, and the others holding John's hands, both talking at once, and overpowering him with questions about home, and with school anecdotes. I looked after them with a feeling in which I do not know whether pleasure or melancholy predominated; for I was reminded of those days when, like them, I had neither known care nor sorrow, and a holyday was the summit of earthly felicity. We stopped a few moments afterwards to water the horses; and on resuming our route, a turn of the road brought us in sight of a neat country seat. I could just distinguish the forms of a lady and two young girls in the portico, and I saw my little comrades, with Bantam, Carlo, and old John, trooping along the carriage road. I leaned out of the coach window, in hopes of witnessing the happy meeting, but a grove of trees shut it from my sight.

In the evening we reached a village where I had determined to pass the night. As we drove into the great gateway of the inn, I saw on one side, the light of a rousing kitchen fire beaming through a window. I entered and admired, for the hundredth time, that picture of convenience, neatness, and broad honest enjoyment, the kitchen of an English inn. It was of spacious dimensions, hung round with copper and tin vessels highly polished, and decorated here and there with a Christmas green. Hams, tongues, and flitches of bacon, were suspended from the ceiling; a smoke jack made its ceaseless clanking beside the fire place, and a clock ticked in one corner. A well scoured deal table extended along one side of the kitchen, with a cold round of beef, and other hearty viands, upon it, over which two foaming tankards of ale seemed mounting guard. Travellers of inferior order were preparing to attack this stout repast, whilst others sat smoking and gossipping over their ale on two high backed oaken seats beside the fire. Trim housemaids were hurrying backwards and forwards under the directions of a fresh bustling landlady; but still seizing an occasional moment to exchange a flippant word, and have a rallying laugh, with the group around the fire. The scene completely realized Poor Robin's humble idea of the comforts of mid-winter:

> Now trees their leafy hats do bare
> To reverence Winter's silver hair;
> A handsome hostess, merry host,
> A pot of ale now and a toast,
> Tobacco and a good coal fire,
> Are things this season doth require.°

I had not been long at the inn when a post chaise drove up to the door. A young gentleman stepped out, and by the light of the lamps I caught a glimpse of a countenance which I thought I knew. I moved forward to get a nearer view, when his eye caught mine. I was not mistaken; it was Frank Bracebridge, a sprightly good humoured young fellow, with whom I had once travelled on the continent. Our meeting was extremely cordial, for the countenance of an old fellow traveller always brings up the recollection of a thousand pleasant scenes, odd adventures, and excellent jokes. To discuss all these in a transient interview at an inn was impossible, and finding that I was not pressed for time, and was merely making a tour of observation, he insisted that I should give him a day or two at his father's country seat, to which he was going to pass the Holydays, and which lay at a few

°Poor Robin's Almanack, 1684.

miles distance. "It is better than eating a solitary Christmas dinner at an inn," said he, "and I can assure you of a hearty welcome in something of the old fashioned style." His reasoning was cogent, and I must confess the preparation I had seen for universal festivity and social enjoyment, had made me feel a little impatient of my loneliness. I closed, therefore, at once with his invitation; the chaise drove up to the door, and in a few moments I was on my way to the family mansion of the Bracebridges.

CHRISTMAS EVE

Saint Francis and Saint Benedight
Blesse this house from wicked wight;
From the night-mare and the goblin,
That is hight good fellow Robin;
Keep it from all evil spirits,
Fairies, weezels, rats, and ferrets:
    From curfew-time
    To the next prime.

CARTWRIGHT.

It was a brilliant moonlight night, but extremely cold: our chaise whirled rapidly over the frozen ground; the post boy cracked his whip incessantly, and a part of the time his horses were upon a gallop. "He knows where he is going," said my companion, laughing, "and is eager to arrive in time for some of the merriment and good cheer of the servants' hall. My father, you must know, is a bigoted devotee of the old school, and prides himself upon keeping up something of old English hospitality. He is a tolerable specimen of what you will rarely meet with now-a-days in its purity, the old English country gentleman; for our men of fortune spend so much of their time in town, and fashion is carried so much into the country, that the strong rich peculiarities of ancient rural life are almost polished away. My father, however, from early years, took honest Peacham* for his text book, instead of Chesterfield; he determined in his own mind, that there was no condition more truly honourable and enviable than that of a country gentleman on his paternal lands, and, therefore, passes the whole of his time on his estate. He is a strenuous advocate for the revival of the old rural games and holyday observances, and is deeply read in the writers, ancient and modern, who have treated of the subject. Indeed, his favourite range of reading is among the authors who flourished at least two centuries since, who, he insists, wrote and thought more like true Englishmen than any of their successors. He even regrets sometimes that he had not been born a few centuries earlier, when England was itself, and had its peculiar manners and customs. As he lives at some distance from the main road, in rather a lonely part of the country, without any rival gentry near him, he has that most enviable of all blessings to an Englishman, an oppor-

*Peacham's Compleat Gentleman, 1622.

tunity of indulging the bent of his own humour, without molestation. Being representative of the oldest family in the neighbourhood, and a great part of the peasantry being his tenants, he is much looked up to, and, in general, is known simply by the appellation of 'The Squire;' a title which has been accorded to the head of the family since time immemorial. I think it best to give you these hints about my worthy old father, to prepare you for any little eccentricities that might otherwise appear absurd."

We had passed for some time along the wall of a park, and at length the chaise stopped at the gate. It was in a heavy magnificent old stile; of iron bars, fancifully wrought at top into flourishes and flowers. The huge square columns that supported the gate were surmounted by the family crest. Close adjoining was the porter's lodge, sheltered under dark fir trees, and almost buried in shrubbery.

The post boy rung a large porter's bell, which resounded through the still frosty air, and was answered by the distant barking of dogs, with which the mansion house seemed garrisoned. An old woman immediately appeared at the gate. As the moonlight fell strongly upon her, I had a full view of a little primitive dame, dressed very much in the antique taste, with a neat kerchief and stomacher, and her silver hair peeping from under a cap of snowy whiteness. She came curtseying forth, with many expressions of simple joy at seeing her young master. Her husband, it seemed, was up at the house keeping Christmas eve, in the servants' hall; they could not do without him, as he was the best hand at a song and story in the household.

My friend proposed that we should alight and walk through the park to the hall, which was at no great distance, while the chaise should follow on. Our road wound through a noble avenue of trees, among the naked branches of which the moon glittered as she rolled through the deep vault of a cloudless sky: the lawn beyond was sheeted with a slight covering of snow, which here and there sparkled as the moon beams caught a frosty chrystal; and at a distance might be seen a thin transparent vapour, stealing up from the low grounds, and threatening gradually to shroud the landscape.

My companion looked round him with transport:—"How often," said he, "have I scampered up this avenue, on returning home on school vacations. How often have I played under these trees when a boy. I feel a degree of filial reverence for them as we look up to those who have cherished us in childhood. My father was always scrupulous in exacting our holydays, and having us around him on family festivals. He used to direct and superintend our games with the strictness that some parents do the studies of their children. He was very particular that we should play the old English games according to their original form, and consulted old books for precedent and authority for every 'merrie disport.' Yet I assure you there never was pedantry so delightful. It was the policy of the good old gentleman to make his children feel that home was the happiest place in the world, and I value this delicious home feeling as one of the choicest gifts a parent could bestow."

We were interrupted by the clamour of a troop of dogs of all sorts and sizes, "mongrel, puppy, whelp and hound, and curs of low degree," that, disturbed by the ringing of the porter's bell, and the rattling of the chaise, came bounding open mouthed across the lawn.

> ——The little dogs and all,
> Tray, Blanch and Sweetheart, see, they bark at me!

cried Bracebridge, laughing. At the sound of his voice, the bark was changed into a yelp of delight, and in a moment he was surrounded and almost overpowered by the caresses of the faithful animals.

We had now come in full view of the old family mansion, partly thrown in deep shadow, and partly lit up by the cold moonshine. It was an irregular building of some magnitude, and seemed to be of the architecture of different periods. One wing was evidently very ancient, with heavy stone shafted bow windows jutting out and over run with ivy, from among the foliage of which the small diamond shaped panes of glass glittered with the moonbeams. The rest of the house was in the French taste of Charles the Second's time, having been repaired and altered, as my friend told me, by one of his ancestors, who returned with that monarch at the restoration. The grounds about the house were laid out in the old formal manner of artificial flower beds, clipped shrubberies, raised terraces, with heavy stone ballustrades, ornamented with urns, a leaden statue or two, and a jet of water. The old gentleman, I was told, was extremely careful to preserve this obsolete finery in all its original state. He admired this fashion in gardening; it had an air of magnificence, was courtly and noble, and befitting good old family style. The boasted imitation of nature in modern gardening had sprung up with modern republican notions, but did not suit a monarchical government; it smacked of the levelling system. I could not help smiling at this introduction of politics into gardening, though I expressed some apprehension that I should find the old gentleman rather intolerant in his creed. Frank assured me, however, that it was almost the only instance in which he had ever heard his father meddle with politics, and he believed that he had got this notion from a member of parliament who once passed a few weeks with him. The

Squire was glad of any argument to defend his clipped yew trees and formal terraces, which had been occasionally attacked by modern landscape gardeners.

As we approached the house, we heard the sound of music, and now and then a burst of laughter, from one end of the building. This, Bracebridge said, must proceed from the servants' hall, where a great deal of revelry was permitted, and even encouraged, by the Squire, throughout the twelve days of Christmas, provided every thing was done conformably to ancient usage. Here were kept up the old games of hoodman blind, shoe the wild mare, hot cockles, steal the white loaf, Bob apple, and snap dragon: the Yule clog, and Christmas candle, were regularly burnt, and the misletoe, with its white berries, hung up, to the imminent peril of all the pretty housemaids.°

So intent were the servants upon their sports, that we had to ring repeatedly before we could make ourselves heard. On our arrival being announced, the Squire came out to receive us, accompanied by his two other sons; one a young officer of the army, home on leave of absence, the other an Oxonian, just from the university. The Squire was a fine healthy looking old gentleman, with silver hair curling lightly round an open florid countenance, in which a physiognomist, with the advantage, like myself, of a previous hint or two, might discover a singular mixture of whim and benevolence.

The family meeting was warm and affectionate; as the evening was far advanced, the Squire would not permit us to change our travelling dresses, but ushered us at once to the company, which was assembled in a large old fashioned hall. It was composed of different branches of a numerous family connexion, where there were the usual proportions of old uncles and aunts, comfortable married dames, superannuated spinsters, blooming country cousins, half fledged striplings, and bright eyed boarding school hoydens. They were variously occupied: some at a round game of cards; others conversing around the fire place; at one end of the hall was a group of the young folks, some nearly grown up, others of a more tender and budding age, fully engrossed by a merry game; and a profusion of wooden horses, penny trumpets, and tattered dolls, about the floor, showed traces of a troop of little fairy beings, who, having frolicked through a happy day, had been carried off to slumber through a peaceful night.

While the mutual greetings were going on between young Bracebridge and his relatives, I had time to scan the apartment. I have

---

°The misletoe is still hung up in farm houses and kitchens at Christmas; and the young men have the privilege of kissing the girls under it, plucking each time a berry from the bush. When the berries are all plucked, the privilege ceases.

called it a hall, for so it had certainly been in old times, and the Squire had evidently endeavoured to restore it to something of its primitive state. Over the heavy projecting fire place was suspended a picture of a warrior in armour, standing by a white horse, and on the opposite wall hung a helmet, buckler and lance. At one end an enormous pair of antlers were inserted in the wall, the branches serving as hooks on which to suspend hats, whips and spurs; and in the corners of the apartment were fowling pieces, fishing rods, and other sporting implements. The furniture was of the cumbrous workmanship of former days, though some articles of modern convenience had been added, and the oaken floor had been carpeted, so that the whole presented an odd mixture of parlour and hall.

The grate had been removed from the wide overwhelming fire place, to make way for a fire of wood, in the midst of which was an enormous log glowing and blazing, and sending forth a vast volume of light and heat: this I understood was the Yule clog, which the Squire was particular in having brought in and illumined on a Christmas eve, according to ancient custom.°

It was really delightful to see the old Squire, seated in his hereditary elbow chair, by the hospitable fireside of his ancestors, and looking around him like the sun of a system, beaming warmth and gladness to every heart. Even the very dog that lay stretched at his feet, as he lazily shifted his position and yawned, would look fondly up in his master's face, wag his tail against the floor, and stretch himself again to sleep, confident of kindness and protection. There is an emanation

°The *Yule clog* is a great log of wood, sometimes the root of a tree, brought into the house with great ceremony, on Christmas eve, laid in the fire place, and lighted with the brand of the last year's clog. While it lasted, there was great drinking, singing, and telling of tales. Sometimes it was accompanied by Christmas candles; but in the cottages the only light was from the ruddy blaze of the great wood fire. The Yule clog was to burn all night; if it went out it was considered a sign of ill luck.

Herrick mentions it in one of his songs:

> Come bring with a noise,
> My merrie, merrie boyes,
> The Christmas Log to the firing;
> While my good dame, she
> Bids ye all be free,
> And drink to your hearts desiring.

The Yule clog is still burnt in many farm houses and kitchens in England, particularly in the north, and there are several superstitions connected with it among the peasantry. If a squinting person come to the house while it is burning, or a person bare footed, it is considered an ill omen. The brand remaining from the Yule clog is carefully put away to light the next year's Christmas fire.

from the heart in genuine hospitality, which cannot be described, but is immediately felt, and puts the stranger at once at his ease. I had not been seated many minutes by the comfortable hearth of the worthy old cavalier, before I found myself as much at home as if I had been one of the family.

Supper was announced shortly after our arrival. It was served up in a spacious oaken chamber, the pannels of which shone with wax, and around which were several family portraits decorated with holly and ivy. Besides the accustomed lights, two great wax tapers, called Christmas candles, wreathed with greens, were placed on a highly polished beaufet among the family plate. The table was abundantly spread with substantial fare; but the Squire made his supper of frumenty, a dish made of wheat cakes, boiled in milk with rich spices; being a standing dish in old times, for Christmas eve. I was happy to find my old friend, minced pie, in the retinue of the feast, and finding him to be perfectly orthodox, and that I need not be ashamed of my predilection, I greeted him with all the warmth wherewith we usually greet an old and very genteel acquaintance.

The mirth of the company was greatly promoted by the humours of an eccentric personage whom Mr. Bracebridge always addressed with the quaint appellation of Master Simon. He was a tight brisk little man, with the air of an arrant old Bachelor. His nose was shaped like the bill of a parrot; his face slightly pitted with the small pox, with a dry perpetual bloom on it, like a frost bitten leaf in autumn. He had an eye of great quickness and vivacity, with a drollery and lurking waggery of expression that was irresistible. He was evidently the wit of the family, dealing very much in sly jokes and innuendoes with the ladies, and making infinite merriment by harpings upon old themes, which, unfortunately, my ignorance of the family chronicles did not permit me to enjoy. It seemed to be his great delight during supper, to keep a young girl next him in a continual agony of stifled laughter, in spite of her awe of the reproving looks of her mother, who sat opposite. Indeed, he was the idol of the younger part of the company, who laughed at every thing he said or did, and at every turn of his countenance. I could not wonder at it; for he must have been a miracle of accomplishments in their eyes. He could imitate Punch and Judy; make an old woman of his hand, with the assistance of a burnt cork and pocket handkerchief; and cut an orange into such a ludicrous caricature, that the young folks were ready to die with laughing.

I was let briefly into his history by Frank Bracebridge. He was an old bachelor, of a small independent income, which, by careful management, was sufficient for all his wants. He revolved through the family system like a vagrant comet in its orbit, sometimes visiting one branch, and sometimes another quite remote, as is often the case with gentlemen of extensive connexions and small fortunes, in England. He had a chirping, buoyant disposition, always enjoying the present moment; and his frequent change of scene and company prevented his acquiring those rusty, unaccommodating habits, with which old bachelors are so uncharitably charged. He was a complete family chronicle, being versed in the genealogy, history, and intermarriages of the whole house of Bracebridge, which made him a great favourite with the old folks; he was a beau of all the elder ladies and super-annuated spinsters, among whom he was habitually considered rather a young fellow, and he was master of the revels among the children; so that there was not a more popular being in the sphere in which he moved, than Mr. Simon Bracebridge. Of late years, he had resided almost entirely with the Squire, to whom he had become a factotum, and whom he particularly delighted by jumping with his humour in respect to old times, and by having a scrap of an old song to suit every occasion. We had presently a specimen of his last mentioned talent; for no sooner was supper removed, and spiced wines and other beverages peculiar to the season introduced, than Master Simon was called on for a good old Christmas song. He bethought himself for a moment, and then, with a sparkle of the eye, and a voice that was by no means bad, excepting that it ran occasionally into a falsetto, like the notes of a split reed, he quavered forth a quaint old ditty.

> Now Christmas is come,
> Let us beat up the drum,
> And call all our neighbours together;
> And when they appear,
> Let us make them such cheer,
> As will keep out the wind and the weather. &c.

The supper had disposed every one to gayety, and an old harper was summoned from the servants' hall, where he had been strumming all the evening, and to all appearance comforting himself with some of the Squire's home brewed. He was a kind of hanger on, I was told, of the establishment, and though ostensibly a resident of the village, was oftener to be found in the Squire's kitchen than his own home; the old gentleman being fond of the sound of "Harp in hall."

The dance, like most dances after supper, was a merry one: some of the older folks joined in it, and the Squire himself figured down several couple with a partner with whom he affirmed he had danced at every Christmas for nearly half a century. Master Simon, who seemed to be a kind of connecting link between the old times and the new, and to be withal a little antiquated in the taste of his accomplishments, evidently piqued himself on his dancing, and was endeavouring to gain credit by the heel and toe, rigadoon, and other graces of the ancient school; but he had unluckily assorted himself with a little romping girl from boarding school, who, by her wild vivacity, kept him continually on the stretch, and defeated all his sober attempts at elegance:—such are the ill sorted matches to which antique gentlemen are unfortunately prone!

The young Oxonian, on the contrary, had led out one of his maiden aunts, on whom the rogue played a thousand little knaveries with impunity; he was full of practical jokes, and his delight was to tease his aunts and cousins; yet, like all mad cap youngsters, he was a universal favourite among the women. The most interesting couple in the dance was the young officer, and a ward of the Squire's, a beautiful blushing girl of seventeen. From several shy glances which I had noticed in the course of the evening, I suspected there was a little kindness growing up between them; and, indeed, the young soldier was just the hero to captivate a romantic girl. He was tall, slender, and handsome; and, like most young British officers of late years, had picked up various small accomplishments on the continent—he could talk French and Italian—draw landscapes—sing very tolerably—dance divinely; but, above all, he had been wounded at Waterloo:—what girl of seventeen, well read in poetry and romance, could resist such a mirror of chivalry and perfection!

The moment the dance was over, he caught up a guitar, and lolling against the old marble fire place, in an attitude which I am half inclined to suspect was studied, began the little French air of the Troubadour. The Squire, however, exclaimed against having any thing on Christmas eve but good old English; upon which the young minstrel, casting up his eye for a moment, as if in an effort of memory, struck into another strain, and with a charming air of gallantry, gave Herrick's "night piece to Julia."

> Her eyes the glow-worm lend thee,
> The shooting stars attend thee,
>   And the elves also,
>   Whose little eyes glow
> Like the sparks of fire, befriend thee.
>
> No Will o' th' Wisp mislight thee;
> Nor snake or slow worm bite thee;

But on, on thy way,
Not making a stay,
Since ghost there is none to affright thee.

Then let not the dark thee cumber;
What though the moon does slumber?
The stars of the night
Will lend thee their light,
Like tapers clear without number.

Then Julia, let me woo thee,
Thus, thus, to come unto me;
And when I shall meet
Thy silvery feet,
My soul I'll pour into thee.

The song might or might not have been intended in compliment to the fair Julia, for so I found his partner was called: she, however, was certainly unconscious of any such application; for she never looked at the singer, but kept her eyes cast upon the floor; her face was suffused, it is true, with a beautiful blush, and there was a gentle heaving of the bosom, but all that was doubtless caused by the exercise of the dance: indeed, so great was her indifference, that she was amusing herself with plucking to pieces a choice boquet of hot house flowers, and by the time the song was concluded, the nosegay lay in ruins on the floor.

The party now broke up for the night with the kind hearted old custom of shaking hands. As I passed through the hall, on my way to my chamber, the dying embers of the yule clog still sent forth a dusky glow, and had it not been the season when "no spirit dares stir abroad," I should have been half tempted to steal from my room at midnight, and peep, whether the fairies might not be at their revels about the hearth.

My chamber was in the old part of the mansion, the ponderous furniture of which might have been fabricated in the days of the giants. The room was pannelled, with cornices of heavy carved work, in which flowers and grotesque faces were strangely intermingled, and a row of black looking portraits stared mournfully at me from the walls. The bed was of rich, though faded damask, with a lofty tester, and stood in a niche opposite a bow window. I had scarcely got into bed when a strain of music seemed to break forth in the air just below the window. I listened, and found it proceeded from a band, which I concluded to be the waits from some neighbouring village. They went round the house, playing under the windows. I drew aside the curtains to hear them more distinctly. The moon beams fell through the upper part of the casement, partially lighting up the antiquated apartment. The sounds as they receded, became more soft and aerial, and seemed to accord with the quiet and moon light. I listened and listened—they became more and more tender and remote, and as they gradually died away, my head sunk upon the pillow, and I fell asleep.

CHRISTMAS DAY

Dark and dull night flie hence away,
And give the honour to this day
That sees December turn'd to May.

* * * *

Why does the chilling winter's morne
Smile like a field beset with corne?
Or smell like to a meade new-shorne,
Thus on the sudden?—Come and see
The cause why things thus fragrant be.
HERRICK.

When I awoke the next morning, it seemed as if all the events of the preceding evening had been a dream, and nothing but the identity of the ancient chamber convinced me of their reality. While I lay musing on my pillow, I heard the sound of little feet pattering outside of the door, and a whispering consultation. Presently a choir of small voices chaunted forth an old Christmas carol, the burden of which was

> Rejoice, our Saviour he was born
> On Christmas day in the morning.

I rose softly, slipt on my clothes, opened the door suddenly, and beheld one of the most beautiful little fairy groups that a painter could imagine. It consisted of a boy and two girls, the eldest not more than six, and lovely as seraphs. They were going the rounds of the house and singing at every chamber door, but my sudden appearance frightened them into mute bashfulness. They remained for a moment playing on their lips with their fingers, and now and then stealing a shy glance from under their eyebrows, until as if by one impulse, they scampered away, and as they turned an angle of the gallery, I heard them laughing in triumph at their escape.

Every thing conspired to produce kind and happy feelings in this strong hold of old fashioned hospitality. The window of my chamber looked out upon what in summer would have been a beautiful landscape. There was a sloping lawn, a fine stream winding at the foot of it, and a tract of park beyond, with noble clumps of trees, and herds of deer. At a distance was a neat hamlet, with the smoke from the cottage chimneys hanging over it; and a church with its dark spire in strong relief against the clear cold sky. The house was surrounded with evergreens, according to the English custom, which would have given almost an appearance of summer; but the morning was extremely frosty; the light vapour of the preceding evening had been precipitated by the cold, and covered all the trees and every blade of grass with its fine chrystalizations. The rays of a bright morning sun had a dazzling effect among the glittering foliage. A robin perched upon the top of a mountain ash that hung its clusters of red berries just before my window, was basking himself in the sunshine, and piping a few querulous notes, and a peacock was displaying all the glories of his train, and strutting with the pride and gravity of a Spanish grandee on the terrace walk below.

I had scarce dressed myself, when a servant appeared to invite me to family prayers. He showed me the way to a small chapel in the old wing of the house, where I found the principal part of the family already assembled in a kind of gallery, furnished with cushions, hassocks, and large prayer books; the servants were seated on benches below. The old gentleman read prayers from a desk in front of the gallery, and Master Simon acted as clerk and made the responses, and I must do him the justice to say that he acquitted himself with great gravity and decorum.

The service was followed by a Christmas carol, which Mr. Bracebridge himself had constructed from a poem of his favourite author, Herrick; and it had been adapted to an old church melody by Master Simon. As there were several good voices among the household, the effect was extremely pleasing; but I was particularly gratified by the exaltation of heart, and sudden sally of grateful feeling, with which the worthy Squire delivered one stanza, his eye glistening, and his voice rambling out of all the bounds of time and tune.

> 'Tis thou that crown'st my glittering hearth
> With guiltlesse mirth,
> And giv'st me Wassaile Bowles to drink
> Spic'd to the brink.
> Lord, 'tis thy plenty-dropping hand
> That soiles my land;
> And giv'st me, for my bushell sowne,
> Twice ten for one.

I afterwards understood that early morning service was read on every Sunday and saint's day throughout the year, either by Mr. Bracebridge or by some member of the family. It was once almost universally the case at the seats of the nobility and gentry of England, and it is much to be regretted that the custom is falling into neglect; for the dullest observer must be sensible of the order and serenity prevalent in those households, where the occasional exercise of a beautiful form of worship in the morning gives, as it were, the key note to every temper for the day, and attunes every spirit to harmony.

Our breakfast consisted of what the Squire denominated true old English fare. He indulged in some bitter lamentations over modern breakfasts of tea and toast, which he censured as among the causes of modern effeminacy and weak nerves, and the decline of old English heartiness: and though he admitted them to his table to suit the palates of his guests, yet there was a brave display of cold meats, wine, and ale, on the sideboard.

After breakfast, I walked about the grounds with Frank Bracebridge and Master Simon, or Mr. Simon, as he was called by every body but the Squire. We were escorted by a number of gentleman like dogs, that seemed loungers about the establishment, from the frisking spaniel to the steady old stag hound, the last of which was of a race that had been in the family time out of mind: they were all obedient to a dog whistle which hung at Master Simon's button hole, and in the midst of their gambols would glance an eye occasionally upon a small switch he carried in his hand.

The old mansion had a still more venerable look in the yellow sunshine than by pale moonlight; and I could not but feel the force of the Squire's idea, that the formal terraces, heavily moulded ballustrades, and clipped yew trees, carried with them an air of proud aristocracy. There appeared to be an unusual number of peacocks about the place, and I was making some remarks upon what I termed a flock of them that were basking under a sunny wall, when I was gently corrected in my phraseology by Master Simon, who told me that, according to the most ancient and approved treatise on hunting, I must say a *muster* of peacocks. "In the same way," added he, with a slight air of pedantry, "we say a flight of doves or swallows, a bevy of quails, a herd of deer, of wrens or cranes, a skulk of foxes, or a building of rooks." He went on to inform me that, according to Sir Anthony Fitzherbert, we ought to ascribe to this bird "both understanding and glory; for, being praised, he will presently set up his tail, chiefly against the sun, to the intent you may the better behold the beauty thereof. But at the fall of the leaf, when his tail falleth, he will mourn and hide himself in corners, till his tail come again as it was."

I could not help smiling at this display of small erudition on so whimsical a subject; but I found that the peacocks were birds of some consequence at the hall; for Frank Bracebridge informed me that they were great favourites with his father, who was extremely careful to keep up the breed, partly because they belonged to chivalry, and were in great request at the stately banquets of the olden time; and partly because they had a pomp and magnificence about them, highly becoming an old family mansion. Nothing, he was accustomed to say, had an air of greater state and dignity than a peacock perched upon an antique stone ballustrade.

Master Simon had now to hurry off, having an appointment at the parish church with the village choristers, who were to perform some music of his selection. There was something extremely agreeable in the cheerful flow of animal spirits of the little man; and I confess I had been somewhat surprised at his apt quotations from authors, who certainly were not in the range of every day reading. I mentioned this last circumstance to Frank Bracebridge, who told me with a smile that Master Simon's whole stock of erudition was confined to some half a dozen old authors, which the Squire had put into his hands, and which he read over and over, whenever he had a studious fit, as he some-times had of a rainy day, or a long winter evening. Sir Anthony Fitz-herbert's book of Husbandry; Markham's Country Contentments; the Tretyse of Hunting, by Sir Thomas Cockayne, Knight; Isaac Walton's Angler, and two or three more such ancient worthies of the pen, were his standard authorities; and, like all men who know but a few books, he looked up to them with a kind of idolatry, and quoted them on all occasions. As to his songs, they were chiefly picked out of old books in the Squire's library, and adapted to tunes that were popular among the choice spirits of the last century. His practical application of scraps of literature, however, had caused him to be looked upon as a prodigy of book knowledge by all the grooms, huntsmen, and small sportsmen of the neighbourhood.

While we were talking, we heard the distant toll of the village bell, and I was told that the Squire was a little particular in having his household at church on Christmas morning; considering it a day of pouring out of thanks and rejoicing, for, as old Tusser observed,

> At Christmas be merry, *and thankful withal*,
> And feast thy poor neighbours, the great with the small.

"If you are disposed to go to church," said Frank Bracebridge, "I can promise you a specimen of my cousin Simon's musical achieve-ments. As the church is destitute of an organ, he has formed a band from the village amateurs, and established a musical club for their improvement; he has also sorted a choir, as he sorted my father's pack of hounds, according to the directions of Jervaise Markham, in his Country Contentments; for the bass he has sought out all the 'deep, solemn mouths,' and for the tenor the 'loud ringing mouths' among the country bumpkins; and for 'sweete mouths,' he has culled with curious taste among the prettiest lasses in the neighbourhood, though these last, he affirms, are the most difficult to keep in tune, your pretty female singer being exceedingly wayward and capricious, and very liable to accident."

As the morning, though frosty, was remarkably fine and clear, the most of the family walked to the church, which was a very old building of grey stone, and stood near a village, about half a mile from the park gate. Adjoining it was a low snug parsonage, which seemed coeval with the church. The front of it was perfectly matted with a yew tree, that had been trained against its walls; through the dense foliage of which, apertures had been formed to admit light into the small antique lattices. As we passed this sheltered nest, the parson issued forth, and preceded us.

I had expected to see a sleek well conditioned pastor, such as is often found in a snug living in the vicinity of a rich patron's table, but I was disappointed. The parson was a little, meagre, black looking man, with a grizzled wig that was too wide, and stood off from each ear, so that his head seemed to have shrunk away within it, like a dried filbert in its shell. He wore a rusty coat with great skirts and pockets that would have held the church bible and prayer book; and his small legs seemed still smaller, from being planted in large shoes, decorated with enormous buckles.

I was informed by Frank Bracebridge, that the parson had been a chum of his father's at Oxford, and had received this living shortly after the latter had come to his estate. He was a complete black letter hunter, and would scarcely read a work printed in the Roman character. The editions of Caxton and Wynkin de Worde were his delight, and he was indefatigable in his researches after such old English writers as have fallen into oblivion from their worthlessness. In deference, perhaps, to the notions of Mr. Bracebridge, he had made diligent investigations into the festive rites and holyday customs of former times, and had been as zealous in the inquiry, as if he had been a boon companion; but it was merely with that plodding spirit, with which men of adust temperament follow up any track of study, merely because it is denominated learning, indifferent to its intrinsic nature, whether it be the illustration of the wisdom or of the ribaldry and obscenity of antiquity. He had pored over these old volumes so intensely, that they seemed to have been reflected into his countenance, which, if the face be, indeed, an index of the mind, might be compared to a title page of black letter.

On reaching the church porch, we found the parson rebuking the gray headed sexton for having used misletoe among the greens with which the church was decorated. It was, he observed, an unholy plant; profaned by having been used by the Druids in their mystic ceremonies, and though it might be innocently employed in the festive ornamenting of halls and kitchens, yet it had been deemed by the fathers of the church as unhallowed, and totally unfit for sacred purposes. So tenacious was he on this point, that the poor sexton was obliged to strip down a great part of the humble trophies of his taste, before the parson would consent to enter upon the service of the day.

The interior of the church was venerable, but simple: on the walls were several mural monuments of the Bracebridges; and just beside the altar was a tomb of ancient workmanship, on which lay the effigy of a warrior in armour, with his legs crossed, a sign of his having been a crusader. I was told it was one of the family who had signalized himself in the holy land, and the same whose picture hung over the fire place in the hall.

During service, Master Simon stood up in the pew, and repeated the responses very audibly; evincing that kind of ceremonious devotion punctually observed by a gentleman of the old school, and a man of old family connexions. I observed, too, that he turned over the leaves of a folio prayer book with something of a flourish, possibly to show off an enormous seal ring which enriched one of his fingers, and which had the look of a family relique. But he was evidently most solicitous about the musical part of the service, keeping his eye fixed intently on the choir, and beating time with much gesticulation and emphasis.

The orchestra was in a small gallery, and presented a most whimsical grouping of heads, piled one above the other, among which I particularly noticed that of the village taylor, a pale fellow with a retreating forehead and chin, who played on the clarinet, and seemed to have blown his face to a point; and there was another, a short pursy man, stooping and labouring at a bass viol, so as to show nothing but the top of a round bald head, like the egg of an ostrich. There were two or three pretty faces among the female singers, to which the keen air of a frosty morning had given a bright rosy tint; but the gentlemen choristers had evidently been chosen, like old Cremona fiddles, more for tone than looks; and as several had to sing from the same book, there were clusterings of odd physiognomies, not unlike those groups of cherubs we sometimes see on country tombstones.

The usual services of the choir were managed tolerably well, the vocal parts generally lagging a little behind the instrumental, and some loitering fiddler now and then making up for lost time by travelling over a passage with prodigious celerity, and clearing more bars than the keenest fox hunter, to be in at the death. But the great trial was an anthem that had been prepared and arranged by Master Simon, and on which he had founded great expectations. Unluckily, there was a blunder at the very outset; the musicians became flurried; Master Simon was in a fever; every thing went on lamely and irregularly until they came to a chorus beginning "Now let us sing with one accord," which seemed to be a signal for parting company: all became discord and confusion, each shifted for himself, and got to the end as well, or, rather, as soon as he could, excepting one old chorister in a pair of horn spectacles, bestriding and pinching a long sonorous nose, who, happening to stand a little apart, and being wrapped up in his own melody, kept on a quavering course, wriggling his head, ogling his book, and winding all up by a nasal solo of at least three bars duration.

The parson gave us a most erudite sermon on the rites and ceremonies of Christmas, and the propriety of observing it, not merely as a day of thanksgiving, but of rejoicing; supporting the correctness of his opinions by the earliest usages of the church, and enforcing them by the authorities of Theophilus of Cesarea, St. Cyprian, St. Chrysostom, St. Augustine, and a cloud more of saints and fathers, from whom he made copious quotations. I was a little at a loss to perceive the necessity of such a mighty array of forces to maintain a point which no one present seemed inclined to dispute; but I soon found that the good man had a legion of ideal adversaries to contend with, having, in the course of his researches on the subject of Christmas, got completely embroiled in the sectarian controversies of the revolution, when the Puritans made such a fierce assault upon the ceremonies of the church, and poor old Christmas was driven out of the land by proclamation of Parliament.* The worthy parson lived but with times past, and knew but little of the present.

Shut up among worm eaten tomes in the retirement of his antiquated little study, the pages of old times were to him as the gazettes of the

*From "The Flying Eagle," a small Gazette published December 24th, 1652.— "The House spent much time this day about the businesse of the Navy for settling the affairs at sea, and before they rose were presented with a terrible remonstrance against Christmas day, grounded upon divine Scriptures, 2 Cor. v. 16. 1 Cor. xv. 14.17; and in honour of the Lord's day, grounded upon these Scriptures, John, xx. 1.

day; while the era of the Revolution was mere modern history. He forgot that nearly two centuries had elapsed since the fiery persecution of poor Mince pie throughout the land; when plum porridge was denounced as "mere popery," and roast beef as antichristian; and that Christmas had been brought in again triumphantly with the merry court of King Charles at the restoration. He kindled into warmth with the ardour of his contest, and the host of imaginary foes with whom he had to combat; had a stubborn conflict with old Prynne and two or three other forgotten champions of the round heads, on the subject of Christmas festivity; and concluded by urging his hearers, in the most solemn and affecting manner, to stand to the traditionary customs of their fathers, and feast and make merry on this joyful anniversary of the church.

I have seldom known a sermon attended apparently with more immediate effects; for on leaving the church the congregation seemed one and all possessed with the gayety of spirit so earnestly enjoined by their pastor. The elder folks gathered in knots in the church yard, greeting and shaking hands, and the children ran about crying Ule! Ule! and repeating some uncouth rhymes,° which the parson, who had joined us, informed me had been handed down from days of yore. The villagers doffed their hats to the Squire as he passed, giving him the good wishes of the season with every appearance of heartfelt sincerity, and were invited by him to the hall, to take something to keep out the cold of the weather; and I heard blessings uttered by several of the poor, which convinced me that, in the midst of his enjoyments, the worthy old cavalier had not forgotten the true Christmas virtue of charity.

On our way homeward, his heart seemed overflowing with generous and happy feelings. As we passed over a rising ground which commanded something of a prospect, the sounds of rustic merriment now and then reached our ears; the Squire paused for a few moments, and looked around with an air of inexpressible benignity. The beauty of the day was, of itself, sufficient to inspire philanthropy. Notwithstanding the frostiness of the morning, the sun in his cloudless journey had

---

Rev. i. 10.   Psalms, cxviii. 24.   Lev. xxiii. 7.11.   Mark. xvi. 8.   Psalms, lxxxiv. 10. In which Christmas is called Antichrist's masse, and those Masse-mongers and Papists who observe it, &c. In consequence of which Parliament spent some time in consultation about the abolition of Christmas day, passed orders to that effect, and resolved to sit on the following day, which was commonly called Christmas day."

°"Ule! Ule!
Three puddings in a pule;
Crack nuts and cry ule!"

acquired sufficient power to melt away the thin covering of snow from every southern declivity, and to bring out the living green which adorns an English landscape even in mid winter. Large tracts of smiling verdure, contrasted with the dazzling whiteness of the shaded slopes and hollows. Every sheltered bank, on which the broad rays rested, yielded its silver rill of cold and limpid water, glittering through the dripping grass; and sent up slight exhalations to contribute to the thin haze that hung just above the surface of the earth. There was something truly cheering in this triumph of warmth and verdure over the frosty thraldom of winter: it was, as the Squire observed, an emblem of Christmas hospitality breaking through the chills of ceremony and selfishness, and thawing every heart into a flow. He pointed with pleasure to the indications of good cheer reeking from the chimneys of the comfortable farm houses, and low thatched cottages. "I love," said he, "to see this day well kept by rich and poor; it is a great thing to have one day in the year at least, when you are sure of being welcome wherever you go, and of having, as it were, the world all thrown open to you; and I am almost disposed to join with poor Robin, in his malediction on every churlish enemy to this honest festival."

> Those who at Christmas do repine
> And would fain hence despatch him,
> May they with old duke Humphry dine,
> Or else may Squire Ketch catch 'em.

The Squire went on to lament the deplorable decay of the games and amusements which were once prevalent at this season among the lower orders, and countenanced by the higher. When the old halls of castles and manor houses were thrown open at daylight; when the tables were covered with brawn, and beef, and humming ale; when the harp and the carol resounded all day long, and when rich and poor were alike welcome to enter and make merry.* "Our old games and local customs," said he, "had a great effect in making the peasant fond of his home, and the promotion of them by the gentry made him fond of his lord. They made the times merrier, and kinder, and better, and I can truly say with one of our old poets,

*"An English gentleman at the opening of the great day, i.e. on Christmas day in the morning, had all his tenants and neighbours enter his hall by day break. The strong beer was broached, and the black jacks went plentifully about with toast, sugar, nutmeg, and good Cheshire cheese. The Hackin (the great sausage) must be boiled by daybreak, or else two young men must take the maiden (i.e. the cook,) by the arms and run her round the market place till she is ashamed of her laziness." —*Round about our Sea-coal Fire.*

> I like them well—the curious preciseness
> And all pretended gravity of those
> That seek to banish hence these harmless sports,
> Have thrust away much ancient honesty.

"The nation," continued he, "is altered; we have almost lost our simple, true hearted peasantry. They have broken asunder from the higher classes, and seem to think their interests are separate. They have become too knowing, and begin to read newspapers, listen to ale house politicians, and talk of reform. I think one mode to keep them in good humour in these hard times, would be for the nobility and gentry to pass more time on their estates, mingle more among the country people, and set the merry old English games going again."

Such was the good Squire's project for mitigating public discontent: and, indeed, he had once attempted to put his doctrine in practice, and a few years before had kept open house during the holydays in the old style. The country people, however, did not understand how to play their parts in the scene of hospitality: many uncouth circumstances occurred; the manor was overrun by all the vagrants of the country, and more beggars drawn into the neighbourhood in one week than the parish officers could get rid of in a year. Since then, he had contented himself with inviting the decent part of the neighbouring peasantry to call at the hall on Christmas day, and with distributing beef, and bread, and ale, among the poor, that they might make merry in their own dwellings.

We had not been long home when the sound of music was heard from a distance. A band of country lads without coats, their shirt sleeves fancifully tied with ribands, their hats decorated with greens, and clubs in their hands, were seen advancing up the avenue, followed by a large number of villagers and peasantry. They stopped before the hall door, where the music struck up a peculiar air, and the lads performed a curious and intricate dance, advancing, retreating, and striking their clubs together, keeping exact time to the music; while one, whimsically crowned with a fox's skin, the tail of which flaunted down his back, kept capering round the skirts of the dance, and rattling a Christmas box with many antic gesticulations.

The Squire eyed this fanciful exhibition with great interest and delight, and gave me a full account of its origin, which he traced to the times when the Romans held possession of the island, plainly proving that this was a lineal descendant of the sword dance of the ancients. "It was now," he said, "nearly extinct, but he had accidentally met with traces of it in the neighbourhood, and had encouraged its revival, though, to tell the truth, it was too apt to be followed up by rough cudgel play, and broken heads, in the evening."

After the dance was concluded, the whole party was entertained with brawn and beef, and stout home brewed. The Squire himself mingled among the rustics, and was received with awkward demonstrations of deference and regard. It is true, I perceived two or three of the younger peasants, as they were raising their tankards to their mouths, when the Squire's back was turned, making something of a grimace, and giving each other the wink, but the moment they caught my eye they pulled grave faces, and were exceedingly demure. With Master Simon, however, they all seemed more at their ease. His varied occupations and amusements had made him well known throughout the neighbourhood. He was a visiter at every farm house and cottage, gossipped with the farmers and their wives, romped with their daughters, and like that type of a vagrant bachelor, the humble bee, tolled the sweets from all the rosy lips of the country round.

The bashfulness of the guests soon gave way before good cheer and affability. There is something genuine and affectionate in the gayety of the lower orders, when it is excited by the bounty and familiarity of those above them; the warm glow of gratitude enters into their mirth, and a kind word, and a small pleasantry frankly uttered by a patron, gladdens the heart of the dependant more than oil and wine. When the Squire had retired, the merriment increased, and there was much joking and laughter; particularly between Master Simon and a hale ruddy faced white headed farmer, who appeared to be the wit of the village, for I observed all his companions to wait with open mouths for his retorts, and burst into a gratuitous laugh before they could well understand them.

The whole house indeed seemed abandoned to merriment: as I passed to my room to dress for dinner, I heard the sound of music in a small court, and looking through a window that commanded it, I perceived a band of wandering musicians with pandean pipes and tambourine: a pretty coquettish housemaid was dancing a jig with a smart country lad, while several of the other servants were looking on. In the midst of her sport the girl caught a glimpse of my face at the window, and colouring up, ran off with an air of roguish affected confusion.

THE CHRISTMAS DINNER

Lo, now is come our joyful'st feast!
    Let every man be jolly,
Eache roome with yvie leaves is drest,
    And every post with holly.
Now all our neighbours' chimneys smoke
    And Christmas blocks are burning;
Their ovens they with bak't meats choke,
    And all their spits are turning.
      Without the door let sorrow lie,
      And if, for cold, it hap to die,
      Wee'le bury 't in a Christmas pye,
      And ever more be merry.
               WITHERS' JUVENILIA.

I had finished my toilet, and was loitering with Frank Bracebridge
in the library, when we heard a distant thwacking sound, which he
informed me was a signal for the serving up of the dinner. The Squire
kept up old customs in kitchen as well as hall, and the rolling pin
struck upon the dresser by the cook, summoned the servants to carry
in the meats.

    Just in this nick the cook knock'd thrice,
    And all the waiters in a trice
      His summons did obey;
    Each serving man, with dish in hand,
    March'd boldly up, like our train band,
      Presented, and away.°

The dinner was served up in the great hall, where the Squire always
held his Christmas banquet. A blazing, crackling fire of logs had been
heaped on to warm the spacious apartment, and the flame went sparkling
and wreathing up the wide mouthed chimney. The great picture of
the crusader and his white horse had been profusely decorated with
greens for the occasion, and holly and ivy had likewise been wreathed
round the helmet and weapons on the opposite wall, which I
understood were the arms of the same warrior. I must own, by the by,
I had strong doubts about the authenticity of the painting and armour
as having belonged to the crusader, they certainly having the stamp

°Sir John Suckling.

of more recent days; but I was told that the painting had been so considered time out of mind; and that, as to the armour, it had been found in a lumber room, and elevated to its present situation by the Squire, who at once determined it to be the armour of the family hero; and as he was absolute authority on all such subjects in his own household, the matter had passed into current acceptation. A sideboard was set out just under this chivalric trophy, on which was a display of plate that might have vied (at least in variety) with Belshazzar's parade of the vessels of the temple: "flagons, cans, cups, beakers, goblets, basins, and ewers;" the gorgeous utensils of good companionship, that had gradually accumulated through many generations of jovial housekeepers; before these stood the two yule candles beaming like two stars of the first magnitude; other lights were distributed in branches, and the whole array glittered like a firmament of silver.

We were ushered into this banqueting scene with the sound of minstrelsy; the old harper being seated on a stool beside the fireplace, and twanging his instrument, with a vast deal more power than melody. Never did Christmas board display a more goodly and gracious assemblage of countenances; those who were not handsome, were, at least, happy; and happiness is a rare improver of your hard favoured visage. I always consider an old English family as well worth studying as a collection of Holbein's portraits or Albert Durer's prints. There is much antiquarian lore to be acquired; much knowledge of the physiognomies of former times. Perhaps it may be from having continually before their eyes those rows of old family portraits, with which the mansions of this country are stocked; certain it is, that the quaint features of antiquity are often most faithfully perpetuated in these ancient lines; and I have traced an old family nose through a whole picture gallery, legitimately handed down from generation to generation, almost from the time of the conquest. Something of the kind was to be observed in the worthy company around me. Many of their faces had evidently originated in a gothic age, and been merely copied by succeeding generations; and there was one little girl in particular, of staid demeanour, with a high Roman nose, and an antique vinegar aspect, who was a great favourite of the Squire's, being, as he said, a Bracebridge all over, and the very counterpart of one of his ancestors who figured in the court of Henry VIII.

The parson said grace, which was not a short familiar one, such as is commonly addressed to the deity, in these unceremonious days; but a long, courtly, well worded one, of the ancient school. There was now a pause, as if something was expected, when suddenly the Butler entered the hall, with some degree of bustle: he was attended by a servant on each side with a large wax light, and bore a silver dish, on which was an enormous pig's head, decorated with rosemary, with a lemon in its mouth, which was placed with great formality at the head of the table. The moment this pageant made its appearance, the harper struck up a flourish; at the conclusion of which the young Oxonian, on receiving a hint from the Squire, gave, with an air of the most comic gravity; an old carol, the first verse of which was as follows:

> Caput apri defero
> Reddens laudes Domino.
> The boar's head in hand bring I,
> With garlands gay and rosemary.
> I pray you all synge merily
> Qui estis in convivio.

Though prepared to witness many of these little eccentricities, from being apprized of the peculiar hobby of mine host; yet, I confess, the parade with which so odd a dish was introduced, somewhat perplexed me, until I gathered from the conversation of the Squire and the parson, that it was meant to represent the bringing in of the boar's head, a dish formerly served up with much ceremony, and the sound of minstrelsy and song, at great tables on Christmas day. "I like the old custom," said the Squire, "not merely because it is stately and pleasing in itself, but because it was observed at the college at Oxford, at which I was educated. When I hear the old song chanted, it brings to mind the time when I was young and gamesome—and the noble old college hall—and my fellow students loitering about it in their black gowns, many of whom, poor lads, are now in their graves!"

The parson, however, whose mind was not haunted by such associations, and who was always more taken up with the text than the sentiment, objected to the Oxonian's version of the carol, which he affirmed was different from that sung at college. He went on with the dry perseverance of a commentator, to give the college reading, accompanied by sundry annotations, addressing himself at first to the company at large; but finding their attention gradually diverted to other talk and other objects, he lowered his tone as his number of auditors diminished, until he concluded his remarks in an under voice, to a fat headed old gentleman next him, who was silently engaged in the discussion of a huge plate full of turkey.°

°The old ceremony of serving up the boar's head on Christmas day is still observed in the hall of Queen's College Oxford. I was favoured by the parson with a copy of the carol as now sung, and as it may be acceptable to such of my readers as are curious in these grave and learned matters, I give it entire.

The table was literally loaded with good cheer, and presented an epitome of country abundance, in this season of overflowing larders. A distinguished post was allotted to "ancient sirloin," as mine host termed it, being, as he added, "the standard of old English hospitality, and a joint of goodly presence, and full of expectation." There were several dishes quaintly decorated, and which had evidently something traditionary in their embellishments, but about which, as I did not like to appear over curious, I asked no questions.

I could not, however, but notice a pie, magnificently decorated with peacock's feathers, in imitation of the tail of that bird, which overshadowed a considerable tract of the table. This the Squire confessed, with some little hesitation, was a pheasant pie, though a peacock pie was certainly the most authentical; but there had been such a mortality among the peacocks this season, that he could not prevail upon himself to have one killed.°

> The boar's head in hand bear I,
> Bedeck'd with bays and rosemary;
> And I pray you, my masters, be merry
>   Quot estis in convivio.
>   Caput apri defero
>   Reddens laudes Domino.
>
> The boar's head, as I understand,
> Is the rarest dish in all this land,
> Which thus bedeck'd with a gay garland
>   Let us servire cantico.
>   Caput apri defero, &c.
>
> Our steward hath provided this
> In honour of the King of bliss,
> Which on this day to be served is
>   In Reginensi Atrio.
>   Caput apri defero,
>   &c. &c. &c.

°The peacock was anciently in great demand for stately entertainments. Sometimes it was made into a pie, at one end of which the head appeared above the crust in all its plumage, with the beak richly gilt; at the other end the tail was displayed. Such pies were served up at the solemn banquets of chivalry, when Knights errant pledged themselves to undertake any perilous enterprize, whence came the ancient oath, used by Justice Shallow, "by cock and pye."

The peacock was also an important dish for the Christmas feast, and Massinger in his City Madam gives some idea of the extravagance with which this, as well as other dishes, was prepared for the gorgeous revels of the olden times:—

Men may talk of Country-Christmasses,
Their thirty pound butter'd eggs, their pies of carps' tongues;
Their pheasants drench'd with ambergris; *the carcasses of three fat
    wethers bruised for gravy to make sauce for a single peacock!*

It would be tedious, perhaps, to my wiser readers, who may not have that foolish fondness for odd and obsolete things to which I am a little given, were I to mention the other make shifts of this worthy old humourist, by which he was endeavouring to follow up, though at humble distance, the quaint customs of antiquity. I was pleased, however, to see the respect shown to his whims by his children and relatives, who, indeed, entered readily into the full spirit of them, and seemed all well versed in their parts, having doubtless been present at many a rehearsal. I was amused, too, at the air of profound gravity with which the butler and other servants executed the duties assigned them, however eccentric. They had an old fashioned look, having, for the most part, been brought up in the household, and grown into keeping with the antiquated mansion, and the humours of its lord, and most probably looked upon all his whimsical regulations, as the established laws of honourable housekeeping.

When the cloth was removed, the butler brought in a huge silver vessel of rare and curious workmanship, which he placed before the Squire. Its appearance was hailed with acclamation; being the Wassail Bowl, so renowned in Christmas festivity. The contents had been prepared by the Squire himself; for it was a beverage in the skilful mixture of which he particularly prided himself; alleging that it was too abstruse and complex for the comprehension of an ordinary servant. It was a potation, indeed, that might well make the heart of a toper leap within him; being composed of the richest and raciest wines, highly spiced and sweetened, with roasted apples bobbing about the surface.°

The old gentleman's whole countenance beamed with a serene look of indwelling delight, as he stirred this mighty bowl. Having raised it to his lips, with a hearty wish of a merry Christmas to all present, he sent it brimming round the board, for every one to follow his example, according to the primitive style; pronouncing it, "the ancient fountain of good feeling, where all hearts met together."†

°The Wassail Bowl was sometimes composed of ale instead of wine; with nutmeg, sugar, toast, ginger, and roasted crabs: in this way the nut brown beverage is still prepared in some old families, and round the hearths of substantial farmers at Christmas. It is also called Lamb's wool, and is celebrated by Herrick in his Twelfth Night:

Next crowne the bowle full
With gentle Lamb's wooll,
Add sugar, nutmeg, and ginger,
With store of ale too;
And thus ye must doe
To make the Wassaile a swinger.

†"The custom of drinking out of the same cup gave place to each having his cup. When the steward came to the doore with the Wassel, he was to cry three

There was much laughing and rallying as the honest emblem of Christmas joviality circulated, and was kissed rather coyly by the ladies. When it reached Master Simon he raised it in both hands, and with the air of a boon companion struck up an old Wassail chanson:

> The brown bowle,
> The merry brown bowle,
> As it goes round about-a,
>> Fill
>> Still
> Let the world say what it will
> And drink your fill all out-a.
>
> The deep canne,
> The merry deep canne,
> As thou dost freely quaff-a,
>> Sing
>> Fling
> Be as merry as a king,
> And sound a lusty laugh-a.°

Much of the conversation during dinner turned upon family topics, to which I was a stranger. There was, however, a great deal of rallying of Master Simon about some gay widow, with whom he was accused of having a flirtation. This attack was commenced by the ladies; but it was continued throughout the dinner by the fat headed old gentleman next the parson, with the persevering assiduity of a slow hound; being one of those long winded jokers, who, though rather dull at starting game, are unrivalled for their talents in hunting it down. At every pause in the general conversation, he renewed his bantering in pretty much the same terms; winking hard at me with both eyes, whenever he gave Master Simon what he considered a home thrust. The latter, indeed, seemed fond of being teased on the subject, as old bachelors are apt to be, and he took occasion to inform me, in an under tone, that the lady in question was a prodigiously fine woman, and drove her own curricle.

The dinner time passed away in this flow of innocent hilarity, and though the old hall may have resounded in its time with many a scene of broader rout and revel, yet I doubt whether it ever witnessed more

---

times *Wassel, Wassel, Wassel,* and then the chappel (chaplain) was to answer with a song." ARCHÆOLOGIA.

°From Poor Robin's Almanack.

honest and genuine enjoyment. How easy it is for one benevolent being to diffuse pleasure around him; and how truly is a kind heart a fountain of gladness, making every thing in its vicinity to freshen into smiles. The joyous disposition of the worthy Squire was perfectly contagious; he was happy himself, and disposed to make all the world happy; and the little eccentricities of his humour did but season, in a manner, the sweetness of his philanthropy.

When the ladies had retired, the conversation, as usual, became still more animated: many good things were broached which had been thought of during dinner, but which would not exactly do for a lady's ear; and though I cannot positively affirm that there was much wit uttered, yet I have certainly heard many contests of rare wit produce much less laughter. Wit, after all, is a mighty tart, pungent ingredient, and much too acid for some stomachs; but honest good humour is the oil and wine of a merry meeting, and there is no jovial companionship equal to that, where the jokes are rather small, and the laughter abundant.

The Squire told several long stories of early college pranks and adventures, in some of which the parson had been a sharer; though in looking at the latter, it required some effort of imagination to figure such a little dark anatomy of a man, into the perpetrator of a mad cap gambol. Indeed, the two college chums presented pictures of what men may be made by their different lots in life: the Squire had left the university to live lustily on his paternal domains, in the vigorous enjoyment of prosperity and sunshine, and had flourished on to a hearty and florid old age, whilst the poor parson, on the contrary, had dried and withered away, among dusty tomes, in the silence and shadows of his study. Still there seemed to be a spark of almost extinguished fire, feebly glimmering in the bottom of his soul; and as the Squire hinted at a sly story of the parson and a pretty milkmaid whom they once met on the banks of the Isis, the old gentleman made an "alphabet of faces," which, as far as I could decypher his physiognomy, I verily believe was indicative of laughter;—indeed, I have rarely met with an old gentleman that took absolute offence at the imputed gallantries of his youth.

I found the tide of wine and wassail fast gaining on the dry land of sober judgment. The company grew merrier and louder as their jokes grew duller. Master Simon was in as chirping a humour as a grasshopper filled with dew; his old songs grew of a warmer complexion, and he began to talk maudlin about the widow. He even gave a long song about the wooing of a widow, which he informed me he had gathered from an excellent black letter work entitled "Cupid's Solicitor

for Love;" containing store of good advice for Bachelors, and which he
promised to lend me; the first verse was to this effect:

> He that will woo a widow must not dally,
>   He must make hay while the sun doth shine;
> He must not stand with her, shall I, shall I,
>   But boldy say, Widow thou must be mine.

This song inspired the fat headed old gentleman, who made several
attempts to tell a rather broad story out of Joe Miller, that was pat
to the purpose; but he always stuck in the middle, every body recol-
lecting the latter part except himself. The parson, too, began to show
the effects of good cheer, having gradually settled down into a doze,
and his wig setting most suspiciously on one side. Just at this juncture
we were summoned to the drawing room, and I suspect, at the private
instigation of mine host, whose joviality seemed always tempered with
a proper love of decorum.

After the dinner table was removed, the hall was given up to the
younger members of the family, who, prompted to all kind of noisy
mirth, by the Oxonian and Master Simon, made its old walls ring
with their merriment, as they played at romping games. I delight in
witnessing the gambols of children, and particularly at this happy
holiday season, and could not help stealing out of the drawing room
on hearing one of their peals of laughter. I found them at the game of
blind-man's-buff. Master Simon, who was the leader of their revels,
and seemed on all occasions to fulfil the office of that ancient potentate,
the Lord of Misrule,° was blinded in the midst of the hall. The little
beings were as busy about him as the mock fairies about Falstaff,
pinching him, plucking at the skirts of his coat, and tickling him with
straws. One fine blue eyed girl of about thirteen, with her flaxen hair
all in beautiful confusion, her frolick face in a glow, her frock half
torn off her shoulders, a complete picture of a romp, was the chief
tormentor; and from the slyness with which Master Simon avoided
the smaller game, and hemmed this wild little nymph in corners, and
obliged her to jump shrieking over chairs, I suspected the rogue of
being not a whit more blinded than was convenient.

When I returned to the drawing room, I found the company seated
round the fire, listening to the parson, who was deeply ensconced in a
high backed oaken chair, the work of some cunning artificer of yore,

° At christmasse there was in the Kinges house, wheresoever hee was lodged, a
lorde of misrule, or mayster of merie disportes, and the like had ye in the house of
every nobleman of honor, or good worshippe, were he spirituall or temporall. STOW.

which had been brought from the library for his particular accommodation. From this venerable piece of furniture, with which his shadowy figure and dark weazen face so admirably accorded, he was dealing forth strange accounts of the popular superstitions, and legends of the surrounding country, with which he had become acquainted in the course of his antiquarian researches. I am half inclined to think that the old gentleman was himself somewhat tinctured with superstition, as men are very apt to be, who live a recluse and studious life in a sequestered part of the country, and pore over black letter tracts, so often filled with the marvellous and supernatural. He gave us several anecdotes of the fancies of the neighbouring peasantry, concerning the effigy of the crusader, which lay on the tomb by the church altar. As it was the only monument of the kind in that part of the country, it had always been regarded with feelings of superstition by the good wives of the village. It was said to get up from the tomb and walk the rounds of the church yard of stormy nights, particularly when it thundered; and one old woman whose cottage bordered on the church yard had seen it, through the windows of the church, when the moon shone, slowly pacing up and down the aisles. It was the belief that some wrong had been left unredressed by the deceased, or some treasure hidden, which kept the spirit in a state of trouble and restlessness. Some talked of gold and jewels buried in the tomb, over which the spectre kept watch; and there was a story current of a sexton in old times who endeavoured to break his way to the coffin at night; but just as he reached it, received a violent blow from the marble hand of the effigy, which stretched him senseless on the pavement. These tales were often laughed at by some of the sturdier among the rustics, yet when night came on, there were many of the stoutest unbelievers that were shy of venturing alone in the footpath that led across the church yard.

From these and other anecdotes that followed, the crusader appeared to be the favourite hero of ghost stories throughout the vicinity. His picture, which hung up in the hall, was thought by the servants to have something supernatural about it; for they remarked that, in whatever part of the hall you went, the eyes of the warrior were still fixed on you. The old porter's wife too, at the lodge, who had been born and brought up in the family, and was a great gossip among the maid servants, affirmed, that in her young days she had often heard say, that on midsummer eve, when it is well known all kinds of ghosts, goblins, and fairies, become visible and walk abroad, the crusader used to mount his horse, come down from his picture, ride about the house, down the avenue, and so to the church to visit the tomb; on which occasion the church door most civilly swung open of itself: not that he needed it; for he rode through closed gates and even stone walls, and had been seen by one of the dairy maids to pass between two bars of the great park gate, making himself as thin as a sheet of paper.

All these superstitions I found had been very much countenanced by the Squire, who, though not superstitious himself, was very fond of seeing others so. He listened to every goblin tale of the neighbouring gossips with infinite gravity, and held the porter's wife in high favour on account of her talent for the marvellous. He was himself a great reader of old legends and romances, and often lamented that he could not believe in them, for a superstitious person, he thought, must live in a kind of fairy land.

Whilst we were all attention to the parson's stories, our ears were suddenly assailed by a burst of heterogeneous sounds from the hall, in which were mingled something like the clang of rude minstrelsy, with the uproar of many small voices and girlish laughter. The door suddenly flew open, and a train came trooping into the room, that might almost have been mistaken for the breaking up of the court of Fairy. That indefatigable spirit, Master Simon, in the faithful discharge of his duties, as lord of misrule, had conceived the idea of a Christmas mummery, or masqueing; and having called in to his assistance the Oxonian and the young officer, who were equally ripe for any thing that should occasion romping and merriment, they had carried it into instant effect. The old housekeeper had been consulted; the antique clothes presses and wardrobes rummaged, and made to yield up the reliques of finery that had not seen the light for several generations; the younger part of the company had been privately convened from parlour and hall, and the whole had been bedizened out, into a burlesque imitation of an antique masque.°

Master Simon led the van, as "Ancient Christmas," quaintly apparelled in a ruff, a short cloak, which had very much the aspect of one of the old housekeeper's petticoats, and a hat that might have served for a village steeple, and must indubitably have figured in the days of the Covenanters. From under this his nose curved boldly forth, flushed with a frost bitten bloom, that seemed the very trophy of a December blast. He was accompanied by the blue eyed romp, dished up as "Dame Mince Pie," in the venerable magnificence of faded brocade, long stomacher, peaked hat, and high heeled shoes. The young officer ap-

°Masquings or mummeries were favourite sports at Christmas in old times; and the wardrobes at halls and manor houses were often laid under contribution to furnish dresses and fantastic disguisings. I strongly suspect Master Simon to have taken the idea of his from Ben Jonson's Masque of Christmas.

peared as Robin Hood, in a sporting dress of Kendal green, and a foraging cap with a gold tassel. The costume, to be sure, did not bear testimony to deep research, and there was an evident eye to the picturesque, natural to a young gallant in the presence of his mistress. The fair Julia hung on his arm in a pretty rustic dress, as "Maid Marian." The rest of the train had been metamorphosed in various ways; the girls trussed up in the finery of the ancient belles of the Bracebridge line, and the striplings bewhiskered with burnt cork, and gravely clad in broad skirts, hanging sleeves, and full bottomed wigs, to represent the characters of Roast Beef, Plum Pudding, and other worthies celebrated in ancient masquings. The whole was under the control of the Oxonian, in the appropriate character of Misrule; and I observed that he exercised rather a mischievous sway with his wand over the smaller personages of the pageant.

The irruption of this motley crew, with beat of drum, according to ancient custom, was the consummation of uproar and merriment. Master Simon covered himself with glory by the stateliness with which, as Ancient Christmas, he walked a minuet with the peerless, though giggling, Dame Mince Pie. It was followed by a dance of all the characters, which, from its medley of costumes, seemed as though the old family portraits had skipped down from their frames to join in the sport. Different centuries were figuring at cross hands and right and left; the dark ages were cutting pirouettes and rigadoons; and the days of Queen Bess jigging merrily down the middle, through a line of succeeding generations.

The worthy Squire contemplated these fantastic sports, and this resurrection of his old wardrobe, with the simple relish of childish delight. He stood chuckling and rubbing his hands, and scarcely hearing a word the parson said, notwithstanding that the latter was discoursing most authentically on the ancient and stately dance of the Paon, or peacock, from which he conceived the minuet to be derived.* For my part, I was in a continual excitement from the varied scenes of whim and innocent gayety passing before me. It was inspiring to see wild eyed frolick and warm hearted hospitality breaking out from among the chills and glooms of winter, and old age throwing off its apathy, and catching once more the freshness of youthful enjoyment. I felt also

---

*Sir John Hawkins, speaking of the dance called the Pavon, from pavo, a peacock, says, "It is a grave and majestic dance; the method of dancing it anciently was by gentlemen, dressed with caps and swords, by those of the long robe in their gowns, by the peers in their mantles, and by the ladies in gowns with long trains, the motion whereof, in dancing, resembled that of a peacock." HISTORY OF MUSIC.

an interest in the scene, from the consideration that these fleeting customs were posting fast into oblivion, and that this was, perhaps, the only family in England in which the whole of them was still punctiliously observed. There was a quaintness too, mingled with all this revelry that gave it a peculiar zest: it was suited to the time and place; and as the old manor house almost reeled with mirth and wassail, it seemed echoing back the joviality of long departed years.°

But enough of Christmas and its gambols: it is time for me to pause in this garrulity. Methinks I hear the question asked by my graver readers, "To what purpose is all this—how is the world to be made wiser by this talk?" Alas! is there not wisdom enough extant for the instruction of the world? And if not, are there not thousands of abler pens labouring for its improvement?—It is so much pleasanter to please than to instruct—to play the companion rather than the preceptor. What, after all, is the mite of wisdom that I could throw into the mass of knowledge; or how am I sure that my sagest deductions may be safe guides for the opinions of others? But in writing to amuse, if I fail, the only evil is my own disappointment. If, however, I can by any lucky chance, in these days of evil, rub out one wrinkle from the brow of care, or beguile the heavy heart of one moment of sorrow; if I can now and then penetrate through the gathering film of misanthropy, prompt a benevolent view of human nature, and make my reader more in good humour with his fellow beings and himself, surely, surely, I shall not then have written entirely in vain.

°At the time of the first publication of this paper, the picture of an old fashioned Christmas in the country was pronounced by some as out of date. The author had afterwards an opportunity of witnessing almost all the customs above described, existing in unexpected vigor on the skirts of Derbyshire and Yorkshire, where he passed the Christmas Holydays. The reader will find some notice of them in the author's account of his sojourn at Newstead Abbey.

LONDON ANTIQUES

> ――――I do walk
> Methinks like Guido Vaux, with my dark lanthorn,
> Stealing to set the town o' fire; i' th' country
> I should be taken for William o' the Wisp,
> Or Robin Goodfellow.
>
> FLETCHER.

I am somewhat of an antiquity hunter and am fond of exploring London in quest of the reliques of old times. These are principally to be found in the depths of the city, swallowed up and almost lost in a wilderness of brick and mortar; but deriving poetical and romantic interest from the commonplace prosaic world around them. I was struck with an instance of the kind in the course of a recent summer ramble into the city; for the city is only to be explored to advantage in summer time; when free from the smoke and fog, and rain and mud of winter. I had been buffeting for some time against the current of population setting through Fleet Street. The warm weather had unstrung my nerves and made me sensitive to every jar and jostle and discordant sound. The flesh was weary, the spirit faint and I was getting out of humor with the bustling busy throng through which I had to struggle, when in a fit of desperation I tore my way through the crowd, plunged into a bye lane, and after passing through several obscure nooks and angles emerged into a quaint and quiet court with a grass plot in the centre overhung by elms, and kept perpetually fresh and green by a fountain with its sparkling jet of water. A student with book in hand was seated on a stone bench, partly reading, partly meditating on the movements of two or three trim nursery maids with their infant charges.

I was like an Arab who had suddenly come upon an oasis amid the panting sterility of the desert. By degrees the quiet and coolness of the place soothed my nerves and refreshed my spirit. I pursued my walk and came, hard by, to a very ancient chapel with a low browed saxon portal of massive and rich architecture. The interior was circular and lofty, and lighted from above. Around were monumental tombs of ancient date, on which were extended the marble effigies of warriors in armour. Some had the hands devoutly crossed upon the breast; others grasped the pummel of the sword—menacing hostility even in the tomb!—while the crossed legs of several indicated soldiers of the Faith who had been on crusades to the Holy Land.

I was in fact, in the chapel of the Knights Templars, strangely situated in the very centre of sordid traffic; and I do not know a more impressive lesson for the man of the world than thus suddenly to turn aside from the high way of busy money seeking life, and sit down among these shadowy sepulchres, where all is twilight, dust and forgetfulness.

In a subsequent tour of observation I encountered another of these reliques of a "foregone world" locked up in the heart of the city. I had been wandering for some time through dull monotonous streets, destitute of any thing to strike the eye or excite the imagination, when I beheld before me a gothic gate way of mouldering antiquity. It opened into a spacious quadrangle forming the court yard of a stately gothic pile the portal of which stood "invitingly open."

It was apparently a public edifice, and as I was antiquity hunting I ventured in, though with dubious steps. Meeting no one either to oppose or rebuke my intrusion I continued on until I found myself in a great hall with a lofty arched roof and oaken gallery, all of gothic architecture. At one end of the hall was an enormous fireplace with wooden settles on each side; at the other end was a raised platform or dais, the seat of state, above which was the portrait of a man in antique garb, with a long robe, a ruff and a venerable grey beard.

The whole establishment had an air of monastic quiet and seclusion, and what gave it a mysterious charm was, that I had not met with a human being since I had passed the threshold.

Encouraged by this loneliness I seated myself in a recess of a large bow window which admitted a broad flood of yellow sunshine, chec-quered here and there by tints from panes of colored glass; while an open casement let in the soft summer air. Here leaning my head on my hand and my arm on an old oaken table I indulged in a sort of reverie about what might have been the ancient uses of this edifice. It had evidently been of monastic origin; perhaps one of those col-legiate establishments built of yore for the promotion of learning, where the patient monk, in the ample solitude of the cloister, added page to page and volume to volume, emulating in the productions of his brain the magnitude of the pile he inhabited.

As I was seated in this musing mood a small panneled door in an arch at the upper end of the hall was opened and a number of grey headed old men, clad in long black cloaks, came forth one by one; proceeding in that manner through the hall, without uttering a word, each turning a pale face on me as he passed, and disappearing through a door at the lower end.

I was singularly struck with their appearance; their black cloaks and antiquated air comported with the style of this most venerable and mysterious pile. It was as if the ghosts of the departed years about which I had been musing were passing in review before me. Pleasing myself with such fancies, I set out, in the spirit of Romance, to explore what I pictured to myself a realm of shadows, existing in the very centre of substantial realities.

My ramble led me through a labyrinth of interior courts and corridors and delapidated cloisters, for the main edifice had many additions and dependencies, built at various times and in various styles; in one open space a number of boys who evidently belonged to the establishment, were at their sports; but every where I observed those mysterious old grey men in black mantles, sometimes sauntering alone; sometimes conversing in groups: they appeared to be the pervading genii of the place. I now called to mind what I had read of certain colleges in old times where judicial astrology, geomancy, necromancy and other forbidden and magical sciences were taught. Was this an establishment of the kind—and were these black cloaked old men really professors of the black art?

These surmises were passing through my mind as my eye glanced into a chamber, hung round with all kinds of strange and uncouth objects: implements of savage warfare; strange idols and stuffed alligators; bottled serpents and monsters decorated the mantelpiece; while on the high tester of an old fashioned bed stead grinned a human scull, flanked on each side by a dried cat.

I approached to regard more narrowly this mystic chamber, which seemed a fitting laboratory for a necromancer, when I was startled at beholding a human countenance staring at me from a dusky corner. It was that of a small, shrivelled old man, with thin cheeks, bright eyes, and grey wiry projecting eyebrows. I at first doubted whether it were not a mummy curiously preserved, but it moved and I saw that it was alive. It was another of these black cloaked old men, and, as I regarded his quaint physiognomy, his obsolete garb, and the hideous and sinister objects by which he was surrounded, I began to persuade myself that I had come upon the Arch Mago, who ruled over this magical fraternity.

Seeing me pausing before the door he rose and invited me to enter. I obeyed, with singular hardihood, for how did I know whether a wave of his wand might not metamorphose me into some strange monster, or conjure me into one of the bottles on his mantel piece. He proved, however, to be any thing but a conjuror, and his simple garrulity soon dispelled all the magic and mystery with which I had enveloped this antiquated pile and its no less antiquated inhabitants.

It appeared that I had made my way into the centre of an ancient asylum for superannuated tradesmen and decayed householders, with which was connected a school for a limited number of boys. It was founded upwards of two centuries since on an old monastic establishment, and retained somewhat of the conventual air and character. The shadowy line of old men in black mantles who had passed before me in the hall, and whom I had elevated into magi, turned out to be the pensioners returning from morning service in the chapel.

John Hallum the little collector of curiosities whom I had made the arch magician, had been for six years a resident of the place, and had decorated this final nestling place of his old age with reliques and rarities picked up in the course of his life. According to his own account he had been somewhat of a traveller; having been once in France and very near making a visit to Holland. He regretted not having visited the latter country, "as then he might have said he had been there."—He was evidently a traveller of the simple kind.

He was aristocratical too in his notions; keeping aloof, as I found, from the ordinary run of pensioners. His chief associates were a blind man who spoke Latin and Greek, of both which languages Hallum was profoundly ignorant; and a broken down gentleman who had run through a fortune of forty thousand pounds left him by his father, and ten thousand pounds, the marriage portion of his wife. Little Hallum seemed to consider it an indubitable sign of gentle blood as well as of lofty spirit to be able to squander such enormous sums.

P.S. The picturesque remnant of old times into which I have thus beguiled the reader is what is called the Charter House, originally the Chartreuse. It was founded in 1611 on the remains of an ancient convent by Sir Thomas Sutton, being one of those noble charities set on foot by individual munificence, and kept up with the quaintness and sanctity of ancient times amidst the modern changes and innovations of London. Here eighty broken down men, who have seen better days, are provided, in their old age, with food, clothing, fuel and a yearly allowance for private expenses. They dine together as did the monks of old, in the hall which had been the refectory of the original convent. Attached to the establishment is a school for forty four boys.

Stow, whose work I have consulted on the subject; speaking of the obligations of the grey headed pensioners, says, "They are not to intermeddle with any business touching the affairs of the hospital; but to attend only to the service of God, and take thankfully what is provided for them, without muttering, murmuring or grudging. None to wear weapon, long hair, colored boots, spurs or colored shoes; feathers in their hats, or any ruffian like or unseemly apparel, but such as becomes hospital men to wear." "And in truth," adds Stow, "happy are they that are so taken from the cares and sorrows of the world, and fixed in so good a place as these old men are; having nothing to care for, but the good of their souls, to serve God and to live in brotherly love."

For the amusement of such as have been interested by the preceding sketch, taken down from my own observation, and who may wish to know a little more about the mysteries of London, I subjoin a modicum of local history, put into my hands by an odd looking old gentleman in a small brown wig and a snuff colored coat, with whom I became acquainted shortly after my visit to the Charter House. I confess I was a little dubious at first, whether it was not one of those apocryphal tales often passed off upon inquiring travellers like myself; and which have brought our general character for veracity into such unmerited reproach. On making proper inquiries, however, I have received the most satisfactory assurances of the author's probity; and, indeed, have been told that he is actually engaged in a full and particular account of the very interesting region in which he resides; of which the following may be considered merely as a foretaste.

LITTLE BRITAIN

What I write is most true. ° ° ° ° I have a whole booke of cases lying by me, which if I should sette foorth, some grave auntients (within the hearing of Bow bell) would bee out of charity with me.

NASHE.

In the centre of the great City of London lies a small neighbourhood, consisting of a cluster of narrow streets and courts, of very venerable and debilitated houses, which goes by the name of LITTLE BRITAIN. Christ Church School and St. Bartholomew's Hospital bound it on the west; Smith Field and Long Lane on the north; Aldersgate Street, like an arm of the sea, divides it from the eastern part of the city; whilst the yawning gulph of Bull and Mouth Street separates it from Butcher Lane, and the regions of New Gate. Over this little territory, thus bounded and designated, the great dome of St. Paul's, swelling above the intervening houses of Paternoster Row, Amen Corner, and Ave-Maria Lane, looks down with an air of motherly protection.

This quarter derives its appellation from having been, in ancient times, the residence of the Dukes of Britany. As London increased, however, rank and fashion rolled off to the west, and trade creeping on at their heels, took possession of their deserted abodes. For some time Little Britain became the great mart of learning, and was peopled by the busy and prolific race of booksellers: these also gradually deserted it, and emigrating beyond the great strait of New Gate Street, settled down in Paternoster Row and St. Paul's Church Yard; where they continue to increase and multiply even at the present day.

But though thus fallen into decline, Little Britain still bears traces of its former splendour. There are several houses, ready to tumble down, the fronts of which are magnificently enriched with old oaken carvings of hideous faces, unknown birds, beasts, and fishes; and fruits and flowers which it would perplex a naturalist to classify. There are also, in Aldersgate Street, certain remains of what were once spacious and lordly family mansions, but which have in latter days been sub-divided into several tenements. Here may often be found the family of a petty tradesman, with its trumpery furniture, burrowing among the relics of antiquated finery, in great rambling time stained apart-ments, with fretted ceilings, gilded cornices, and enormous marble fireplaces. The lanes and courts also contain many smaller houses, not on so grand a scale, but, like your small ancient gentry, sturdily main-taining their claims to equal antiquity. These have their gable ends to the street; great bow windows, with diamond panes set in lead; grotesque carvings; and low arched door ways.°

In this most venerable and sheltered little nest have I passed several quiet years of existence; comfortably lodged in the second floor of one of the smallest, but oldest edifices. My sitting room is an old wainscotted chamber, with small pannels, and set off with a miscellaneous array of furniture. 'I have a particular respect for three or four high backed claw footed chairs, covered with tarnished brocade; which bear the marks of having seen better days; and have doubtless figured in some of the old palaces of Little Britain. They seem to me to keep together, and to look down with sovereign contempt upon their leathern bottomed neighbours; as I have seen decayed gentry carry a high head among the plebeian society with which they were reduced to associate. The whole front of my sitting room is taken up with a bow window; on the panes of which are recorded the names of previous occupants for many generations; mingled with scraps of very indifferent, gentleman like poetry, written in characters which I can scarcely decipher; and which extol the charms of many a beauty of Little Britain, who has long, long since, bloomed, faded, and passed away. As I am an idle personage, with no apparent occupation, and pay my bill regularly every week, I am looked upon as the only independent gentleman of the neighbourhood; and being curious to learn the internal state of a community so apparently shut up within itself, I have managed to work my way into all the concerns and secrets of the place.

Little Britain may truly be called the heart's core of the city; the strong hold of true John Bullism. It is a fragment of London as it was in its better days, with its antiquated folks and fashions. Here flourish in great preservation many of the holyday games and customs of yore. The inhabitants most religiously eat pan cakes on Shrove Tuesday; hot cross buns on Good Friday, and roast goose at Michaelmas: they send love letters on Valentine's Day; burn the Pope on the Fifth of November, and kiss all the girls under the misletoe at Christmas. Roast beef and plum pudding are also held in superstitious veneration, and port and sherry maintain their grounds as the only true English wines; all others being considered vile outlandish beverages.

Little Britain has its long catalogue of city wonders, which its inhabitants consider the wonders of the world; such as the great bell of St. Paul's, which sours all the beer when it tolls; the figures that strike the hours at St. Dunstan's clock; the Monument; the lions in the

---

°It is evident that the author of this interesting communication has included in his general title of Little Britain, many of those little lanes and courts that belong immediately to Cloth Fair.

Tower; and the wooden giants in Guildhall. They still believe in dreams and fortune telling, and an old woman that lives in Bull and Mouth Street makes a tolerable subsistence by detecting stolen goods, and promising the girls good husbands. They are apt to be rendered uncomfortable by comets and eclipses; and if a dog howls dolefully at night, it is looked upon as a sure sign of a death in the place. There are even many ghost stories current, particularly concerning the old mansion houses; in several of which it is said strange sights are sometimes seen. Lords and ladies, the former in full bottomed wigs, hanging sleeves and swords, the latter in lappets, stays, hoops, and brocade, have been seen walking up and down the great waste chambers, on moonlight nights; and are supposed to be the shades of the ancient proprietors in their court dresses.

Little Britain has likewise its sages and great men. One of the most important of the former is a tall dry old gentleman, of the name of Skryme, who keeps a small apothecary's shop. He has a cadaverous countenance, full of cavities and projections; with a brown circle round each eye, like a pair of horn spectacles. He is much thought of by the old women, who consider him as a kind of conjuror, because he has two or three stuffed alligators hanging up in his shop, and several snakes in bottles. He is a great reader of almanacks and newspapers, and is much given to pore over alarming accounts of plots, conspiracies, fires, earthquakes, and volcanic eruptions; which last phenomena he considers as signs of the times. He has always some dismal tale of the kind to deal out to his customers, with their doses; and thus at the same time puts both soul and body into an uproar. He is a great believer in omens and predictions; and has the prophecies of Robert Nixon and Mother Shipton by heart. No man can make so much out of an eclipse, or even an unusually dark day; and he shook the tail of the last comet over the heads of his customers and disciples until they were nearly frightened out of their wits. He has lately got hold of a popular legend or prophecy, on which he has been unusually eloquent. There has been a saying current among the ancient Sybils, who treasure up these things, that when the grasshopper on the top of the Exchange shook hands with the dragon on the top of Bow Church steeple, fearful events would take place. This strange conjunction, it seems, has as strangely come to pass. The same architect has been engaged lately on the repairs of the cupola of the Exchange, and the steeple of Bow Church; and, fearful to relate, the dragon and the grasshopper actually lie, cheek by jole, in the yard of his workshop!

"Others," as Mr. Skryme is accustomed to say, "may go star gazing, and look for conjunctions in the heavens, but here is a conjunction on the earth, near at home, and under our own eyes, which surpasses all the signs and calculations of astrologers." Since these portentous weathercocks have thus laid their heads together, wonderful events had already occurred. The good old king, notwithstanding that he had lived eighty two years, had all at once given up the ghost; another king had mounted the throne; a royal duke had died suddenly—another, in France, had been murdered; there had been radical meetings in all parts of the kingdom; the bloody scenes at Manchester; the great plot in Cato Street;—and, above all, the Queen had returned to England! All these sinister events are recounted by Mr. Skryme with a mysterious look, and a dismal shake of the head; and, being taken with his drugs, and associated in the minds of his auditors with stuffed sea monsters, bottled serpents, and his own visage, which is a title page of tribulation, they have spread great gloom through the minds of the people in Little Britain. They shake their heads whenever they go by Bow Church, and observe, that they never expected any good to come of taking down that steeple, which in old times told nothing but glad tidings, as the history of Wittington and his Cat bears witness.

The rival oracle of Little Britain is a substantial cheesemonger, who lives in a fragment of one of the old family mansions, and is as magnificently lodged as a round bellied mite in the midst of one of his own Cheshires. Indeed he is a man of no little standing and importance; and his renown extends through Huggin Lane, and Lad Lane, and even unto Aldermanbury. His opinion is very much taken in affairs of state, having read the Sunday papers for the last half century, together with the Gentleman's Magazine, Rapin's History of England, and the Naval Chronicle. His head is stored with invaluable maxims which have borne the test of time and use for centuries. It is his firm opinion that "it is a moral impossible," so long as England is true to herself, that any thing can shake her: and he has much to say on the subject of the national debt; which, some how or other, he proves to be a great national bulwark and blessing. He passed the greater part of his life in the purlieus of Little Britain, until of late years, when, having become rich, and grown into the dignity of a Sunday cane, he begins to take his pleasure and see the world. He has therefore made several excursions to Hampstead, Highgate, and other neighbouring towns, where he has passed whole afternoons in looking back upon the metropolis through a telescope and endeavouring to descry the steeple of St. Bartholomew's. Not a stage coachman of Bull and Mouth Street, but touches his hat as he passes; and he is considered quite a patron at the coach office of the Goose and Gridiron, St. Paul's Church yard. His family have been very urgent for him to make an expedition to Margate, but he has great doubts of those new gim-cracks the steam boats, and indeed thinks himself too advanced in life to undertake sea voyages.

Little Britain has occasionally its factions and divisions, and party spirit ran very high at one time in consequence of two rival "Burial Societies" being set up in the place. One held its meeting at the Swan and Horse Shoe, and was patronized by the cheesemonger; the other at the Cock and Crown, under the auspices of the apothecary: it is needless to say that the latter was the most flourishing. I have passed an evening or two at each, and have acquired much valuable information as to the best mode of being buried; the comparative merits of church yards; together with diverse hints on the subject of patent iron coffins. I have heard the question discussed in all its bearings as to the legality of prohibiting the latter on account of their durability. The feuds occasioned by these societies have happily died of late; but they were for a long time prevailing themes of controversy, the people of Little Britain being extremely solicitous of funeral honours and of lying comfortably in their graves.

Besides these two funeral societies there is a third of quite a different cast, which tends to throw the sunshine of good humour over the whole neighbourhood. It meets once a week at a little old fashioned house, kept by a jolly publican of the name of Wagstaff, and bearing for insignia a resplendent half moon, with a most seductive bunch of grapes. The whole edifice is covered with inscriptions to catch the eye of the thirsty wayfarer; such as "Truman, Hanbury, and Co's. Entire," "Wine, Rum, and Brandy Vaults," "Old Tom, Rum and Compounds, &c." This indeed has been a temple of Bacchus and Momus from time immemorial. It has always been in the family of the Wagstaffs, so that its history is tolerably preserved by the present landlord. It was much frequented by the gallants and cavalieros of the reign of Elizabeth, and was looked into now and then by the wits of Charles the Second's day. But what Wagstaff principally prides himself upon, is, that Henry the Eighth, in one of his nocturnal rambles, broke the head of one of his ancestors with his famous walking staff. This however is considered as rather a dubious and vain glorious boast of the landlord.

The club which now holds its weekly sessions here, goes by the name of "the Roaring Lads of Little Britain." They abound in old catches, glees and choice stories, that are traditional in the place, and not to be met with in any other part of the metropolis. There is a mad cap undertaker who is inimitable at a merry song; but the life of the club, and indeed the prime wit of Little Britain, is bully Wagstaff himself. His ancestors were all wags before him, and he has inherited with the inn a large stock of songs and jokes, which go with it from generation to generation as heir looms. He is a dapper little fellow, with bandy legs and pot belly, a red face with a moist merry eye, and a little shock of grey hair behind. At the opening of every club night he is called in to sing his "Confession of Faith," which is the famous old drinking trowl from Gammer Gurton's Needle. He sings it, to be sure with many variations, as he received it from his father's lips; for it has been a standing favourite at the Half Moon and Bunch of Grapes ever since it was written; nay, he affirms that his predecessors have often had the honour of singing it before the nobility and gentry at Christmas mummeries, when Little Britain was in all its glory.°

°As mine host of the Half moon's Confession of Faith may not be familiar to the majority of readers, and as it is a specimen of the current songs of Little Britain, I subjoin it in its original orthography. I would observe that the whole club always join in the chorus with a fearful thumping on the table and clattering of pewter pots.

> I cannot eate but lytle meate,
>   My stomacke is not good,
> But sure I thinke that I can drinke
>   With him that weares a hood.
> Though I go bare take ye no care,
>   I nothing am a colde,
> I stuff my skyn so full within,
>   Of joly good ale and olde.

Chorus. Backe and syde go bare, go bare,
>   Booth foote and hand go colde,
> But belly, God send thee good ale ynoughe,
>   Whether it be new or olde.

> I love no rost, but a nut browne toste,
>   And a crab laid in the fyre;
> A little breade shall do me steade,
>   Much breade I not desyre.
> No frost nor snow, nor winde, I trowe,
>   Can hurte mee if I wolde,
> I am so wrapt and throwly lapt
>   Of joly good ale and olde.

Chorus. Back and syde go bare, go bare, &c.

> And Tyb my wife, that, as her lyfe,
>   Loveth well good ale to seeke,
> Full oft drynkes shee, tyll ye may see,
>   The teares run downe her cheeke.

It would do one's heart good to hear on a club night the shouts of merriment, the snatches of song, and now and then the choral bursts of half a dozen discordant voices, which issue from this jovial mansion. At such times the street is lined with listeners, who enjoy a delight equal to that of gazing into a confectioner's window, or snuffing up the steams of a cook shop.

There are two annual events which produce great stir and sensation in Little Britain; these are St. Bartholomew's Fair, and the Lord Mayor's day. During the time of the Fair, which is held in the adjoining regions of Smithfield, there is nothing going on but gossiping and gadding about. The late quiet streets of Little Britain are overrun with an irruption of strange figures and faces, every tavern is a scene of rout and revel. The fiddle and the song are heard from the tap room, morning, noon, and night; and at each window may be seen some group of boon companions, with half shut eyes, hats on one side, pipe in mouth and tankard in hand, fondling, and prozing, and singing maudlin songs over their liquor. Even the sober decorum of private families, which I must say is rigidly kept up at other times among my neighbours, is no proof against this saturnalia. There is no such thing as keeping maid servants within doors. Their brains are absolutely set madding with Punch and the Puppet Show; the Flying Horses; Signior Polito; the Fire Eater; the celebrated Mr. Paap; and the Irish Giant. The children too lavish all their holyday money in toys and gilt ginger bread, and fill the house with the Lilliputian din of drums, trumpets and penny whistles.

But the Lord Mayor's day is the great anniversary. The Lord Mayor is looked up to by the inhabitants of Little Britain as the greatest

---

> Then doth shee trowle to me the bowle,
>   Even as a mault-worme sholde,
> And sayth, sweete harte, I tooke my parte
>   Of this joly good ale and olde.
>
> *Chorus.*   Back and syde go bare, go bare, &c.
>
> Now let them drynke, tyll they nod and winke,
>   Even as goode fellowes should doe,
> They shall not mysse to have the blisse,
>   Good ale doth bring men to.
> And all poore soules that have scowred bowles,
>   Or have them lustily trolde,
> God save the lyves of them and their wives,
>   Whether they be yonge or olde.
>
> *Chorus.*   Back and syde go bare, go bare, &c.

potentate upon earth; his gilt coach with six horses as the summit of human splendour; and his procession, with all the Sheriffs and Aldermen in his train, as the grandest of earthly pageants. How they exult in the idea, that the King himself dare not enter the city, without first knocking at the gate of Temple Bar, and asking permission of the Lord Mayor: for if he did, heaven and earth! there is no knowing what might be the consequence. The man in armour who rides before the Lord Mayor, and is the city champion, has orders to cut down every body that offends against the dignity of the city; and then there is the little man with a velvet porringer on his head, who sits at the window of the state coach and holds the city sword, as long as a pike staff—Od's blood! if he once draws that sword, Majesty itself is not safe!

Under the protection of this mighty potentate, therefore, the good people of Little Britain sleep in peace. Temple Bar is an effectual barrier against all interior foes; and as to foreign invasion, the Lord Mayor has but to throw himself into the tower, call in the train bands, and put the standing army of Beef eaters under arms, and he may bid defiance to the world!

Thus wrapped up in its own concerns, its own habits, and its own opinions, Little Britain has long flourished as a sound heart to this great fungous metropolis. I have pleased myself with considering it as a chosen spot, where the principles of sturdy John Bullism were garnered up, like seed corn, to renew the national character, when it had run to waste and degeneracy. I have rejoiced also in the general spirit of harmony that prevailed throughout it; for though there might now and then be a few clashes of opinion between the adherents of the cheesemonger and the apothecary, and an occasional feud between the burial societies, yet these were but transient clouds, and soon passed away. The neighbours met with good will, parted with a shake of the hand, and never abused each other except behind their backs.

I could give rare descriptions of snug junketting parties at which I have been present; where we played at All-Fours, Pope-Joan, Tom-come-tickle-me, and other choice old games; and where we sometimes had a good old English country dance to the tune of Sir Roger de Coverly. Once a year also the neighbours would gather together and go on a gypsey party to Epping Forest. It would have done any man's heart good to see the merriment that took place here as we banqueted on the grass under the trees. How we made the woods ring with bursts of laughter at the songs of little Wagstaff and the merry undertaker! After dinner too, the young folks would play at blind-man's-buff

and hide and seek; and it was amusing to see them tangled among
the briars, and to hear a fine romping girl now and then squeak from
among the bushes. The elder folks would gather round the cheesemonger and the apothecary, to hear them talk politics; for they generally
brought out a newspaper in their pockets, to pass away time in the
country. They would now and then, to be sure, get a little warm
in argument; but their disputes were always adjusted by reference to
a worthy old umbrella maker in a double chin, who, never exactly
comprehending the subject, managed, some how or other, to decide
in favour of both parties.

All empires, however, says some philosopher or historian, are doomed
to changes and revolutions. Luxury and innovation creep in; factions
arise; and families now and then spring up, whose ambition and
intrigues throw the whole system into confusion. Thus in latter days
has the tranquillity of Little Britain been grievously disturbed, and
its golden simplicity of manners threatened with total subversion by
the aspiring family of a retired butcher.

The family of the Lambs had long been among the most thriving
and popular in the neighbourhood: the Miss Lambs were the belles
of Little Britain, and every body was pleased when Old Lamb had
made money enough to shut up shop, and put his name on a brass
plate on his door. In an evil hour, however, one of the Miss Lambs
had the honour of being a lady in attendance on the Lady Mayoress,
at her grand annual ball, on which occasion she wore three towering
ostrich feathers on her head. The family never got over it; they were
immediately smitten with a passion for high life; set up a one horse
carriage, put a bit of gold lace round the errand boy's hat, and have
been the talk and detestation of the whole neighbourhood ever since.
They could no longer be induced to play at Pope-Joan or blind-man's-
buff; they could endure no dances but quadrilles, which no body had
ever heard of in Little Britain; and they took to reading novels, talking
bad French, and playing upon the piano. Their brother too, who had
been articled to an attorney, set up for a dandy and a critic, characters
hitherto unknown in these parts; and he confounded the worthy folks
exceedingly by talking about Kean, the Opera and the Edinbro' Review.

What was still worse, the Lambs gave a grand ball, to which they
neglected to invite any of their old neighbours; but they had a great
deal of genteel company from Theobald's Road, Red lion Square, and
other parts towards the west. There were several beaux of their brother's
acquaintance from Grays inn Lane and Hatton Garden; and not less
than three Aldermen's ladies with their daughters. This was not to be
forgotten or forgiven. All Little Britain was in an uproar with the

smacking of whips, the lashing of miserable horses, and the rattling and jingling of hackney coaches. The gossips of the neighbourhood might be seen popping their night caps out at every window, watching the crazy vehicles rumble by; and there was a knot of virulent old crones, that kept a look out from a house just opposite the retired butcher's, and scanned and criticized every one that knocked at the door.

This dance was a cause of almost open war, and the whole neighbourhood declared they would have nothing more to say to the Lambs. It is true that Mrs. Lamb, when she had no engagements with her quality acquaintance, would give little hum drum tea junkettings to some of her old cronies, "quite," as she would say, "in a friendly way;" and it is equally true that her invitations were always accepted, in spite of all previous vows to the contrary. Nay the good ladies would sit and be delighted with the music of the Miss Lambs, who would condescend to strum an Irish melody for them on the piano; and they would listen with wonderful interest to Mrs. Lamb's anecdotes of Alderman Plunket's family of Portsoken ward, and the Miss Timberlakes, the rich heiresses of Crutched Friars; but then they relieved their consciences, and averted the reproaches of their confederates, by canvassing at the next gossiping convocation every thing that had passed, and pulling the Lambs and their rout all to pieces.

The only one of the family that could not be made fashionable was the retired butcher himself. Honest Lamb, in spite of the meekness of his name, was a rough hearty old fellow, with the voice of a lion, a head of black hair like a shoe brush, and a broad face mottled like his own beef. It was in vain that the daughters always spoke of him as "the old gentleman," addressed him as "papa," in tones of infinite softness, and endeavoured to coax him into a dressing gown and slippers, and other gentlemanly habits. Do what they might, there was no keeping down the butcher. His sturdy nature would break through all their glozings. He had a hearty vulgar good humour that was irrepressible. His very jokes made his sensitive daughters shudder; and he persisted in wearing his blue cotton coat of a morning, dining at two o'clock, and having a "bit of sausage with his tea."

He was doomed, however, to share the unpopularity of his family. He found his old comrades gradually growing cold and civil to him; no longer laughing at his jokes; and now and then throwing out a fling at "some people," and a hint about "quality binding." This both nettled and perplexed the honest butcher; and his wife and daughters, with the consummate policy of the shrewder sex, taking advantage of the circumstance, at length prevailed upon him to give up his afternoon's pipe and tankard at Wagstaff's; to sit after dinner by himself and take his pint of port—a liquor he detested—and to nod in his chair in solitary and dismal gentility.

The Miss Lambs might now be seen flaunting along the streets in French bonnets, with unknown beaux; and talking and laughing so loud that it distressed the nerves of every good lady within hearing. They even went so far as to attempt patronage, and actually induced a French dancing master to set up in the neighbourhood; but the worthy folks of Little Britain took fire at it, and did so persecute the poor Gaul, that he was fain to pack up fiddle and dancing pumps, and decamp with such precipitation, that he absolutely forgot to pay for his lodgings.

I had flattered myself, at first, with the idea that all this fiery indignation on the part of the community, was merely the overflowing of their zeal for good old English manners, and their horror of innovation; and I applauded the silent contempt they were so vociferous in expressing, for upstart pride, French fashions, and the Miss Lambs. But I grieve to say that I soon perceived the infection had taken hold; and that my neighbours, after condemning, were beginning to follow their example. I overheard my landlady importuning her husband to let their daughters have one quarter at French and music, and that they might take a few lessons in the quadrille. I even saw, in the course of a few Sundays, no less than five French bonnets, precisely like those of the Miss Lambs, parading about Little Britain.

I still had my hopes that all this folly would gradually die away; that the Lambs might move out of the neighbourhood; might die, or might run away with attornies' apprentices; and that quiet and simplicity might be again restored to the community. But unluckily a rival power arose. An opulent oil man died and left a widow with a large jointure and a family of buxom daughters. The young ladies had long been repining in secret at the parsimony of a prudent father which kept down all their elegant aspirings. Their ambition being now no longer restrained broke out into a blaze, and they openly took the field against the family of the butcher. It is true that the Lambs, having had the first start, had naturally an advantage of them in the fashionable career. They could speak a little bad French, play the piano, dance quadrilles, and had formed high acquaintances; but the Trotters were not to be distanced. When the Lambs appeared with two feathers in their hats, the Miss Trotters mounted four, and of twice as fine colours. If the Lambs gave a dance, the Trotters were sure not to be behind hand; and though they might not boast of as good company, yet they had double the number and were twice as merry.

The whole community has at length divided itself into fashionable factions, under the banners of these two families. The old games of Pope-Joan and Tom-come-tickle-me are entirely discarded; there is no such thing as getting up an honest country dance; and, on my attempting to kiss a young lady under the misletoe last Christmas, I was indignantly repulsed; the Miss Lambs having pronounced it "shocking vulgar." Bitter rivalry has also broken out as to the most fashionable part of Little Britain; the Lambs standing up for the dignity of Cross Keys Square, and the Trotters for the vicinity of St. Bartholomew's.

Thus is this little territory torn by factions and internal dissensions, like the great empire whose name it bears; and what will be the result would puzzle the apothecary himself, with all his talent at prognostics, to determine; though I apprehend that it will terminate in the total downfall of genuine John Bullism.

The immediate effects are extremely unpleasant to me. Being a single man, and, as I observed before, rather an idle good for nothing personage, I have been considered the only gentleman by profession in the place. I stand therefore in high favour with both parties, and have to hear all their cabinet counsels and mutual backbitings. As I am too civil not to agree with the ladies on all occasions, I have committed myself most horribly with both parties, by abusing their opponents. I might manage to reconcile this to my conscience, which is a truly accommodating one, but I cannot to my apprehension—if the Lambs and Trotters ever come to a reconciliation and compare notes, I am ruined!

I have determined, therefore, to beat a retreat in time, and am actually looking out for some other nest in this great city, where old English manners are still kept up; where French is neither eaten, drunk, danced nor spoken; and where there are no fashionable families of retired tradesmen. This found, I will, like a veteran rat, hasten away before I have an old house about my ears; bid a long, though a sorrowful adieu to my present abode, and leave the rival factions of the Lambs and the Trotters, to divide the distracted empire of LITTLE BRITAIN.

STRATFORD-ON-AVON

Thou soft flowing Avon, by thy silver stream,
Of things more than mortal sweet Shakespeare would dream;
The fairies by moonlight dance round his green bed,
For hallowed the turf is which pillowed his head.

GARRICK.

To a homeless man, who has no spot on this wide world which he can truly call his own, there is a momentary feeling of something like independence and territorial consequence, when, after a weary day's travel, he kicks off his boots, thrusts his feet into slippers, and stretches himself before an inn fire. Let the world without go as it may; let kingdoms rise or fall, so long as he has the wherewithal to pay his bill, he is, for the time being, the very monarch of all he surveys. The arm chair is his throne; the poker his sceptre, and the little parlour of some twelve feet square, his undisputed empire. It is a morsel of certainty, snatched from the midst of the uncertainties of life; it is a sunny moment gleaming out kindly on a cloudy day; and he who has advanced some way on the pilgrimage of existence, knows the importance of husbanding even morsels and moments of enjoyment. "Shall I not take mine ease in mine inn?" thought I, as I gave the fire a stir, lolled back in my elbow chair, and cast a complacent look about the little parlour of the Red Horse, at Stratford-on-Avon.

The words of sweet Shakespeare were just passing through my mind as the clock struck midnight from the tower of the church in which he lies buried. There was a gentle tap at the door, and a pretty chamber maid, putting in her smiling face, inquired, with a hesitating air, whether I had rung. I understood it as a modest hint that it was time to retire. My dream of absolute dominion was at an end; so abdicating my throne, like a prudent potentate, to avoid being deposed, and putting the Stratford Guide Book under my arm, as a pillow companion, I went to bed, and dreamt all night of Shakespeare, the Jubilee, and David Garrick.

The next morning was one of those quickening mornings which we sometimes have in early spring; for it was about the middle of March. The chills of a long winter had suddenly given way; the north wind had spent its last gasp; and a mild air came stealing from the west, breathing the breath of life into nature, and wooing every bud and flower to burst forth into fragrance and beauty.

I had come to Stratford on a poetical pilgrimage. My first visit was to the house where Shakespeare was born, and where, according to tradition, he was brought up to his father's craft of wool combing. It is a small mean looking edifice of wood and plaster, a true nestling place of genius, which seems to delight in hatching its offspring in bye corners. The walls of its squalid chambers are covered with names and inscriptions, in every language, by pilgrims of all nations, ranks, and conditions, from the prince to the peasant; and present a simple, but striking instance of the spontaneous and universal homage of mankind to the great poet of nature.

The house is shown by a garrulous old lady in a frosty red face, lighted up by a cold blue anxious eye, and garnished with artificial locks of flaxen hair, curling from under an exceedingly dirty cap. She was peculiarly assiduous in exhibiting the relics with which this, like all other celebrated shrines, abounds. There was the shattered stock of the very matchlock with which Shakespeare shot the deer, on his poaching exploit. There, too, was his tobacco box; which proves that he was a rival smoker of Sir Walter Raleigh; the sword also with which he played Hamlet; and the identical lanthorn with which Friar Laurence discovered Romeo and Juliet at the tomb! There was an ample supply also of Shakespeare's mulberry tree, which seems to have as extraordinary powers of self multiplication as the wood of the true cross; of which there is enough extant to build a ship of the line.

The most favourite object of curiosity, however, is Shakespeare's chair. It stands in the chimney nook of a small gloomy chamber, just behind what was his father's shop. Here he may many a time have sat when a boy, watching the slowly revolving spit with all the longing of an urchin; or of an evening, listening to the crones and gossips of Stratford, dealing forth church yard tales and legendary anecdotes of the troublesome times of England. In this chair it is the custom of every one that visits the house to sit: whether this be done with the hope of imbibing any of the inspiration of the bard I am at a loss to say, I merely mention the fact; and mine hostess privately assured me, that though built of solid oak, such was the fervent zeal of devotees, that the chair had to be new bottomed at least once in three years. It is worthy of notice also, in the history of this extraordinary chair, that it partakes something of the volatile nature of the Santa Casa of Loretto, or the flying chair of the Arabian enchanter, for though sold some few years since to a northern princess, yet, strange to tell, it has found its way back again to the old chimney corner.

I am always of easy faith in such matters, and am ever willing to be deceived, where the deceit is pleasant, and costs nothing. I am therefore a ready believer in relics, legends, and local anecdotes of goblins and great men; and would advise all travellers who travel for their gratification to be the same. What is it to us whether these stories be true or false, so long as we can persuade ourselves into the belief of them, and enjoy all the charm of the reality? There is nothing like resolute good humoured credulity in these matters; and on this occasion I went even so far as willingly to believe the claims of mine hostess to a lineal descent from the poet, when, unluckily for my faith, she put into my hands a play of her own composition, which set all belief in her consanguinity at defiance.

From the birth place of Shakespeare a few paces brought me to his grave. He lies buried in the chancel of the parish church, a large and venerable pile, mouldering with age, but richly ornamented. It stands on the banks of the Avon, on an embowered point, and separated by adjoining gardens from the suburbs of the town. Its situation is quiet and retired: the river runs murmuring at the foot of the church yard, and the elms which grow upon its banks droop their branches into its clear bosom. An avenue of limes, the boughs of which are curiously interlaced, so as to form in summer an arched way of foliage, leads up from the gate of the yard to the church porch. The graves are overgrown with grass; the grey tombstones, some of them nearly sunk into the earth, are half covered with moss, which has likewise tinted the reverend old building. Small birds have built their nests among the cornices and fissures of the walls, and keep up a continual flutter and chirping; and rooks are sailing and cawing about its lofty grey spire.

In the course of my rambles I met with the grey headed sexton, Edmonds, and accompanied him home to get the key of the church. He had lived in Stratford, man and boy, for eighty years, and seemed still to consider himself a vigorous man, with the trivial exception that he had nearly lost the use of his legs for a few years past. His dwelling was a cottage, looking out upon the Avon and its bordering meadows; and was a picture of that neatness, order, and comfort, which pervade the humblest dwellings in this country. A low white washed room, with a stone floor carefully scrubbed, served for parlour, kitchen, and hall. Rows of pewter and earthen dishes glittered along the dresser. On an old oaken table, well rubbed and polished, lay the family Bible and Prayer book, and the drawer contained the family library, composed of about half a score of well thumbed volumes. An ancient clock, that important article of cottage furniture, ticked on the opposite side of the room; with a bright warming pan hanging on one side of it, and the old man's horn handled Sunday cane on the other. The fireplace, as usual, was wide and deep enough to admit a gossip knot within its jambs. In one corner sat the old man's grand daughter sewing, a pretty blue eyed girl,—and in the opposite corner was a superannuated crony, whom he addressed by the name of John Ange, and who, I found, had been his companion from childhood. They had played together in infancy; they had worked together in manhood; they were now tottering about and gossiping away the evening of life; and in a short time they will probably be buried together in the neighbouring church yard. It is not often that we see two streams of existence running thus evenly and tranquilly side by side; it is only in such quiet "bosom scenes" of life that they are to be met with.

I had hoped to gather some traditionary anecdotes of the bard from these ancient chroniclers; but they had nothing new to impart. The long interval during which Shakespeare's writings lay in comparative neglect has spread its shadow over his history; and it is his good or evil lot that scarcely any thing remains to his biographers but a scanty handful of conjectures.

The sexton and his companion had been employed as carpenters on the preparations for the celebrated Stratford jubilee, and they remembered Garrick, the prime mover of the fête, who superintended the arrangements, and who, according to the sexton, was "a short punch man very lively and bustling." John Ange had assisted also in cutting down Shakespeare's mulberry tree, of which he had a morsel in his pocket for sale; no doubt a sovereign quickener of literary conception.

I was grieved to hear these two worthy wights speak very dubiously of the eloquent dame who shows the Shakespeare house. John Ange shook his head when I mentioned her valuable and inexhaustible collection of relics, particularly her remains of the mulberry tree; and the old sexton even expressed a doubt as to Shakespeare having been born in her house. I soon discovered that he looked upon her mansion with an evil eye, as a rival to the poet's tomb; the latter having comparatively but few visitors. Thus it is that historians differ at the very outset, and mere pebbles make the stream of truth diverge into different channels even at the fountain head.

We approached the church through the avenue of limes, and entered by a gothic porch, highly ornamented, with carved doors of massive oak. The interior is spacious, and the architecture and embellishments superior to those of most country churches. There are several ancient monuments of nobility and gentry, over some of which hang funeral escutcheons, and banners dropping piecemeal from the walls. The tomb of Shakespeare is in the chancel. The place is solemn and sepulchral. Tall elms wave before the pointed windows, and the Avon, which

runs at a short distance from the walls, keeps up a low perpetual murmur. A flat stone marks the spot where the bard is buried. There are
four lines inscribed on it, said to have been written by himself, and
which have in them something extremely awful. If they are indeed
his own, they show that solicitude about the quiet of the grave, which
seems natural to fine sensibilities and thoughtful minds:

> Good friend, for Jesus' sake, forbeare
> To dig the dust encloased here.
> Blessed be the man that spares these stones,
> And curst be he that moves my bones.

Just over the grave, in a niche of the wall, is a bust of Shakespeare,
put up shortly after his death, and considered as a resemblance. The
aspect is pleasant and serene, with a finely arched forehead; and I
thought I could read in it clear indications of that cheerful, social
disposition, by which he was as much characterized among his co-
temporaries as by the vastness of his genius. The inscription mentions
his age at the time of his decease—fifty three years; an untimely death
for the world: for what fruit might not have been expected from
the golden autumn of such a mind, sheltered as it was from the stormy
vicissitudes of life, and flourishing in the sunshine of popular and
royal favour.

The inscription on the tombstone has not been without its effect.
It has prevented the removal of his remains from the bosom of his
native place to Westminster Abbey, which was at one time contemplated.
A few years since also, as some labourers were digging to make an
adjoining vault, the earth caved in, so as to leave a vacant space
almost like an arch, through which one might have reached into his
grave. No one, however, presumed to meddle with his remains, so
awfully guarded by a malediction; and lest any of the idle or the
curious, or any collector of relics, should be tempted to commit
depredations, the old sexton kept watch over the place for two days,
until the vault was finished and the aperture closed again. He told
me that he had made bold to look in at the hole, but could see neither
coffin nor bones; nothing but dust. It was something, I thought, to
have seen the dust of Shakespeare.

Next to this grave are those of his wife, his favourite daughter Mrs.
Hall, and others of his family. On a tomb close by, also, is a full length
effigy of his old friend John Combe, of usurious memory; on whom
he is said to have written a ludicrous epitaph. There are other monuments around, but the mind refuses to dwell on any thing that is not

connected with Shakespeare. His idea pervades the place: the whole pile seems but as his mausoleum. The feelings, no longer checked and thwarted by doubt, here indulge in perfect confidence: other traces of him may be false or dubious, but here is palpable evidence and absolute certainty. As I trod the sounding pavement, there was something intense and thrilling in the idea, that, in very truth, the remains of Shakespeare were mouldering beneath my feet. It was a long time before I could prevail upon myself to leave the place; and as I passed through the church yard I plucked a branch from one of the yew trees, the only relic that I have brought from Stratford.

I had now visited the usual objects of a pilgrim's devotion, but I had a desire to see the old family seat of the Lucys at Charlecot, and to ramble through the park where Shakespeare, in company with some of the roysters of Stratford, committed his youthful offence of deer stealing. In this harebrained exploit we are told that he was taken prisoner, and carried to the keeper's lodge, where he remained all night in doleful captivity. When brought into the presence of Sir Thomas Lucy, his treatment must have been galling and humiliating; for it so wrought upon his spirit as to produce a rough pasquinade, which was affixed to the park gate at Charlecot.*

This flagitious attack upon the dignity of the Knight so incensed him, that he applied to a lawyer at Warwick to put the severity of the laws in force against the rhyming deer stalker. Shakespeare did not wait to brave the united puissance of a Knight of the Shire and a country attorney. He forthwith abandoned the pleasant banks of the Avon and his paternal trade; wandered away to London; became a hanger on to the theatres; then an actor; and, finally, wrote for the stage; and thus, through the persecution of Sir Thomas Lucy, Stratford lost an indifferent wool comber and the world gained an immortal poet. He retained, however, for a long time, a sense of the harsh treatment of the Lord of Charlecot, and revenged himself in his writings; but in the sportive way of a good natured mind. Sir Thomas is said to be the

---

*The following is the only stanza extant of this lampoon:—

> A parliament member, a justice of peace,
> At home a poor scarecrow, at London an asse,
> If lowsie is Lucy, as some volke miscalle it,
> Then Lucy is lowsie, whatever befall it.
> He thinks himself great;
> Yet an asse in his state,
> We allow, by his ears, but with asses to mate.
> If Lucy is lowsie, as some volke miscall it,
> Then sing lowsie Lucy whatever befall it.

original of Justice Shallow, and the satire is slyly fixed upon him by the Justice's armorial bearings, which, like those of the Knight, had white luces° in the quarterings.

Various attempts have been made by his biographers to soften and explain away this early transgression of the poet; but I look upon it as one of those thoughtless exploits natural to his situation and turn of mind. Shakespeare, when young, had doubtless all the wildness and irregularity of an ardent, undisciplined, and undirected genius. The poetic temperament has naturally something in it of the vagabond. When left to itself it runs loosely and wildly, and delights in every thing eccentric and licentious. It is often a turn up of a die, in the gambling freaks of fate, whether a natural genius shall turn out a great rogue or a great poet; and had not Shakespeare's mind fortunately taken a literary bias, he might have as daringly transcended all civil, as he has all dramatic laws.

I have little doubt that, in early life, when running, like an unbroken colt, about the neighbourhood of Stratford, he was to be found in the company of all kinds of odd anomalous characters; that he associated with all the mad caps of the place, and was one of those unlucky urchins, at mention of whom old men shake their heads, and predict that they will one day come to the gallows. To him the poaching in Sir Thomas Lucy's park was doubtless like a foray to a Scottish Knight, and struck his eager, and as yet untamed, imagination, as something delightfully adventurous.†

The old mansion of Charlecot and its surrounding park still remain in the possession of the Lucy family, and are peculiarly interesting from being connected with this whimsical but eventful circumstance in the scanty history of the bard. As the house stood at little more than three miles distance from Stratford, I resolved to pay it a pedestrian visit,

°The luce is a pike, or jack, and abounds in the Avon about Charlecot.

†A proof of Shakespeare's random habits and associates in his youthful days, may be found in a traditionary anecdote, picked up at Stratford by the elder Ireland, and mentioned in his "Picturesque Views on the Avon."
About seven miles from Stratford lies the thirsty little market town of Bedford, famous for its ale. Two societies of the village yeomanry used to meet, under the appellation of the Bedford topers, and to challenge the lovers of good ale of the neighbouring villages, to a contest of drinking. Among others, the people of Strat-ford were called out to prove the strength of their heads; and in the number of the champions was Shakespeare, who, in spite of the proverb, that "they who drink beer will think beer," was as true to his ale as Falstaff to his sack. The chivalry of Stratford was staggered at the first onset, and sounded a retreat while they had yet legs to carry them off the field. They had scarcely marched a mile, when, their legs failing them, they were forced to lie down under a crab tree,

that I might stroll leisurely through some of those scenes from which Shakespeare must have derived his earliest ideas of rural imagery.

The country was yet naked and leafless; but English scenery is always verdant, and the sudden change in the temperature of the weather was surprising in its quickening effects upon the landscape. It was inspiring and animating to witness this first awakening of spring. To feel its warm breath stealing over the senses; to see the moist mellow earth beginning to put forth the green sprout and the tender blade; and the trees and shrubs, in their reviving tints and bursting buds, giving the promise of returning foliage and flower. The cold snow drop, that little borderer on the skirts of winter, was to be seen with its chaste white blossoms in the small gardens before the cottages. The bleating of the new dropt lambs was faintly heard from the fields. The sparrow twittered about the thatched eaves and budding hedges; the robin threw a livelier note into his late querulous wintry strain; and the lark, springing up from the reeking bosom of the meadow, towered away into the bright fleecy cloud, pouring forth torrents of melody. As I watched the little songster, mounting up higher and higher, until his body was a mere speck on the white bosom of the cloud, while the ear was still filled with his music, it called to mind Shakespeare's exquisite little song in Cymbeline:

> Hark! hark! the lark at heav'n's gate sings,
>   And Phœbus 'gins arise,
> His steeds to water at those springs,
>   On chaliced flowers that lies.
>
> And winking mary-buds begin,
>   To ope their golden eyes;

---

where they passed the night. It is still standing, and goes by the name of Shakespeare's tree.

In the morning his companions awakened the bard, and proposed returning to Bedford, but he declined, saying he had had enough, having drank with

> Piping Pebworth, Dancing Marston,
> Haunted Hillbro', Hungry Grafton,
> Dudging Exhall, Papist Wicksford,
> Beggarly Broom, and Drunken Bedford.

"The villages here alluded to," says Ireland, "still bear the epithets thus given them; the people of Pebworth are still famed for their skill on the pipe and tabor: Hillborough is now called Haunted Hillborough: and Grafton is famous for the poverty of its soil."

> With every thing that pretty bin,
> My lady sweet arise!

Indeed the whole country about here is poetic ground: every thing is associated with the idea of Shakespeare. Every old cottage that I saw, I fancied into some resort of his boyhood, where he had acquired his intimate knowledge of rustic life and manners, and heard those legendary tales and wild superstitions which he has woven like witchcraft into his dramas. For in his time, we are told, it was a popular amusement in winter evenings "to sit round the fire, and tell merry tales of errant knights, queens, lovers, lords, ladies, giants, dwarfs, thieves, cheaters, witches, fairies, goblins, and friars."[*]

My route for a part of the way lay in sight of the Avon, which made a variety of the most fanciful doublings and windings through a wide and fertile valley; sometimes glittering from among willows, which fringed its borders; sometimes disappearing among groves, or beneath green banks; and sometimes rambling out into full view, and making an azure sweep round a slope of meadow land. This beautiful bosom of country is called the vale of the Red Horse. A distant line of undulating blue hills seems to be its boundary, whilst all the soft intervening landscape lies in a manner enchained in the silver links of the Avon.

After pursuing the road for about three miles, I turned off into a footpath, which led along the borders of fields and under hedge rows to a private gate of the park; there was a style, however, for the benefit of the pedestrian; there being a public right of way through the grounds. I delight in these hospitable estates, in which every one has a kind of property—at least as far as the footpath is concerned. It in some measure reconciles a poor man to his lot, and what is more, to the better lot of his neighbour, thus to have parks and pleasure grounds thrown open for his recreation. He breathes the pure air as freely, and lolls as luxuriously under the shade, as the lord of the soil; and if he has not the privilege of calling all that he sees his own, he has not, at the same time, the trouble of paying for it, and keeping it in order.

I now found myself among noble avenues of oaks and elms, whose vast size bespoke the growth of centuries. The wind sounded solemnly

---

[*]Scot, in his "Discoverie of Witchcraft," enumerates a host of these fireside fancies. "And they have so fraid us with bull-beggars, spirits, witches, urchins, elves, hags, fairies, satyrs, pans, faunes, syrens, kit with the can'sticke, tritons, centaurs, dwarfes, giantes, imps, calcars, conjurors, nymphes, changelings, incubus, Robin-good-fellow, the spoorne, the mare, the man in the oke, the hell-waine, the fier drake, the puckle, Tom Thombe, hobgoblins, Tom Tumbler, boneless, and such other bugs, that we were afraid of our own shadowes."

among their branches, and the rooks cawed from their hereditary nests in the tree tops. The eye ranged through a long lessening vista, with nothing to interrupt the view but a distant statue; and a vagrant deer stalking like a shadow across the opening.

There is something about these stately old avenues that has the effect of gothic architecture, not merely from the pretended similarity of form, but from their bearing the evidence of long duration, and of having had their origin in a period of time with which we associate ideas of romantic grandeur. They betoken also the long settled dignity, and proudly concentrated independence of an ancient family; and I have heard a worthy but aristocratic old friend observe, when speaking of the sumptuous palaces of modern gentry, that "money could do much with stone and mortar, but thank heaven there was no such thing as suddenly building up an avenue of oaks."

It was from wandering in early life among this rich scenery, and about the romantic solitudes of the adjoining park of Fulbroke, which then formed a part of the Lucy estate, that some of Shakespeare's commentators have supposed he derived his noble forest meditations of Jaques, and the enchanting woodland pictures in "As you like it." It is in lonely wanderings through such scenes, that the mind drinks deep but quiet draughts of inspiration, and becomes intensely sensible of the beauty and majesty of nature. The imagination kindles into reverie and rapture; vague but exquisite images and ideas keep breaking upon it; and we revel in a mute and almost incommunicable luxury of thought. It was in some such mood, and perhaps under one of those very trees before me, which threw their broad shades over the grassy banks and quivering waters of the Avon, that the poet's fancy may have sallied forth into that little song which breathes the very soul of a rural voluptuary:

> Under the green wood tree,
> Who loves to lie with me,
> And tune his merry throat
> Unto the sweet bird's note,
> Come hither, come hither, come hither,
>   Here shall he see
>   No enemy,
> But winter and rough weather.

I had now come in sight of the house. It is a large building of brick, with stone quoins, and is in the gothic style of Queen Elizabeth's day, having been built in the first year of her reign. The exterior remains very nearly in its original state, and may be considered a fair specimen of the residence of a wealthy country gentleman of those days. A great gateway opens from the park into a kind of court yard in front of the house, ornamented with a grass plot, shrubs, and flower beds. The gateway is in imitation of the ancient barbican; being a kind of outpost, and flanked by towers; though evidently for mere ornament, instead of defence. The front of the house is completely in the old style; with stone shafted casements, a great bow window of heavy stone work, and a portal with armorial bearings over it, carved in stone. At each corner of the building is an octagon tower, surmounted by a gilt ball and weathercock.

The Avon, which winds through the park, makes a bend just at the foot of a gently sloping bank, which sweeps down from the rear of the house. Large herds of deer were feeding or reposing upon its borders; and swans were sailing majestically upon its bosom. As I contemplated the venerable old mansion, I called to mind Falstaff's encomium on Justice Shallow's abode, and the affected indifference and real vanity of the latter:

"*Falstaff*. You have here a goodly dwelling and a rich.
   Shallow. Barren, barren, barren; beggars all, beggars all, Sir John:—marry, good air."

Whatever may have been the joviality of the old mansion in the days of Shakespeare, it had now an air of stillness and solitude. The great iron gateway that opened into the court yard was locked; there was no show of servants bustling about the place; the deer gazed quietly at me as I passed, being no longer harried by the moss troopers of Stratford. The only sign of domestic life that I met with, was a white cat stealing with wary look and stealthy pace towards the stables, as if on some nefarious expedition. I must not omit to mention the carcass of a scoundrel crow which I saw suspended against the barn wall, as it shows that the Lucys still inherit that lordly abhorrence of poachers, and maintain that rigorous exercise of territorial power which was so strenuously manifested in the case of the bard.

After prowling about for some time, I at length found my way to a lateral portal which was the every day entrance to the mansion. I was courteously received by a worthy old housekeeper, who, with the civility and communicativeness of her order, showed me the interior of the house. The greater part has undergone alterations, and been adapted to modern tastes and modes of living: there is a fine old oaken staircase; and the great hall, that noble feature in an ancient manor house, still retains much of the appearance it must have had in the days of

Shakespeare. The ceiling is arched and lofty; and at one end is a gallery, in which stands an organ. The weapons and trophies of the chace, which formerly adorned the hall of a country gentleman, have made way for family portraits. There is a wide hospitable fireplace, calculated for an ample old fashioned wood fire, formerly the rallying place of winter festivity. On the opposite side of the hall is the huge gothic bow window, with stone shafts, which looks out upon the court yard. Here are emblazoned in stained glass the armorial bearings of the Lucy family for many generations, some being dated in 1558. I was delighted to observe in the quarterings the three *white luces* by which the character of Sir Thomas was first identified with that of Justice Shallow. They are mentioned in the first scene of the Merry Wives of Windsor, where the Justice is in a rage with Falstaff for having "beaten his men, killed his deer, and broken into his lodge." The poet had no doubt the offences of himself and his comrades in mind at the time, and we may suppose the family pride and vindictive threats of the puissant Shallow to be a caricature of the pompous indignation of Sir Thomas.

"*Shallow*. Sir Hugh, persuade me not: I will make a Star-Chamber matter of it; if he were twenty Sir John Falstaffs, he shall not abuse Robert Shallow, Esq.

Slender. In the county of Gloster, justice of peace, and *coram*.

Shallow. Ay, cousin Slender, and *custalorum*.

Slender. Ay, and *ratalorum* too; and a gentleman born, master parson; who writes himself *Armigero* in any bill, warrant, quittance, or obligation, *Armigero*.

Shallow. Ay, that I do; and have done any time these three hundred years.

Slender. All his successors gone before him have done't, and all his ancestors that come after him may: they may give the dozen *white luces* in their coat. ° ° ° ° °

Shallow. The council shall hear it; it is a riot.

Evans. It is not meet the council hear of a riot; there is no fear of Got in a riot; the council, hear you, shall desire to hear the fear of Got, and not to hear a riot; take your vizaments in that.

Shallow. Ha! o' my life, if I were young again, the sword should end it!"

Near the window thus emblazoned, hung a portrait by Sir Peter Lely of one of the Lucy family, a great beauty of the time of Charles the Second; the old housekeeper shook her head as she pointed to the picture, and informed me that this lady had been sadly addicted to cards, and had gambled away a great portion of the family estate, among which was that part of the park where Shakespeare and his comrades had killed the deer. The lands thus lost had not been entirely regained by the family even at the present day. It is but justice to this recreant dame to confess that she had a surpassingly fine hand and arm.

The picture which most attracted my attention was a great painting over the fire place, containing likenesses of a Sir Thomas Lucy and his family who inhabited the hall in the latter part of Shakespeare's life time. I at first thought that it was the vindictive knight himself, but the housekeeper assured me that it was his son; the only likeness extant of the former being an effigy upon his tomb in the church of the neighbouring hamlet of Charlecot.° The picture gives a lively idea of the costume and manners of the time. Sir Thomas is dressed in ruff and doublet; white shoes with roses in them; and has a peaked yellow, or, as Master Slender would say, "a cane coloured beard." His lady is seated on the opposite side of the picture in wide ruff and long stomacher, and the children have a most venerable stiffness and formality of dress. Hounds and spaniels are mingled in the family group; a hawk is seated on his perch in the foreground, and one of the children holds a bow;—all intimating the knight's skill in hunting, hawking, and archery—so indispensable to an accomplished gentleman in those days.†

°This effigy is in white marble, and represents the Knight in complete armor. Near him lies the effigy of his wife, and on her tomb is the following inscription; which, if really composed by her husband, places him quite above the intellectual level of Master Shallow:

Here lyeth the Lady Joyce Lucy wife of Sr Thomas Lucy of Charlecot in ye county of Warwick, Knight, Daughter and heir of Thomas Acton of Sutton in ye county of Worcester Esquire who departed out of this wretched world to her heavenly kingdom ye 10 day of February in ye yeare of our Lord God 1595 and of her age 60 and three. All the time of her lyfe a true and faythful servant of her good God, never detected of any cryme or vice. In religion most sounde, in love to her husband most faythful and true. In friendship most constant; to what in trust was committed unto her most secret. In wisdom excelling. In governing of her house, bringing up of youth in ye fear of God that did converse with her moste rare and singular. A great maintayner of hospitality. Greatly esteemed of her betters; misliked of none unless of the envyous. When all is spoken that can be saide a woman so garnished with virtue as not to be bettered and hardly to be equalled by any. As shee lived most virtuously so shee died most Godly. Set downe by him yt best did knowe what hath byn written to be true. Thomas Lucye.

†Bishop Earle, speaking of the country gentleman of his time, observes, "his housekeeping is seen much in the different families of dogs, and serving men attendant on their kennels; and the deepness of their throats is the depth of his discourse. A hawk he esteems the true burden of nobility, and is exceedingly ambitious to seem delighted with the sport, and have his fist gloved with his

I regretted to find that the ancient furniture of the hall had disappeared; for I had hoped to meet with the stately elbow chair of carved oak, in which the country Squire of former days was wont to sway the sceptre of empire over his rural domains; and in which it might be presumed the redoubted Sir Thomas sat enthroned in awful state when the recreant Shakespeare was brought before him. As I like to deck out pictures for my entertainment, I pleased myself with the idea that this very hall had been the scene of the unlucky bard's examination on the morning after his captivity in the lodge. I fancied to myself the rural potentate, surrounded by his body guard of butler, pages, and blue coated serving men with their badges; while the luckless culprit was brought in, bedrooped and chapfallen; in the custody of game keepers, huntsmen and whippers in, and followed by a rabble rout of country clowns. I fancied bright faces of curious housemaids peeping from the half open doors, while from the gallery the fair daughters of the Knight leaned gracefully forward, eyeing the youthful prisoner with that pity "that dwells in womanhood."—Who would have thought that this poor varlet, thus trembling before the brief authority of a country Squire, and the sport of rustic boors, was soon to become the delight of princes; the theme of all tongues and ages; the dictator to the human mind; and was to confer immortality on his oppressor by a caricature and a lampoon!

I was now invited by the butler to walk into the garden, and I felt inclined to visit the orchard and arbour where the Justice treated Sir John Falstaff and Cousin Silence, "to a last year's pippen of his own graffing, with a dish of carraways;" but I had already spent so much of the day in my ramblings that I was obliged to give up any further investigations. When about to take my leave I was gratified by the civil entreaties of the housekeeper and butler, that I would take some refreshment: an instance of good old hospitality, which I grieve to say we castle hunters seldom meet with in modern days. I make no doubt it is a virtue which the present representative of the Lucys inherits from his ancestor; for Shakespeare, even in his caricature, makes Justice Shallow importunate in this respect, as witness his pressing instances to Falstaff:

---

jesses." And Gilpin, in his description of a Mr. Hastings remarks, "he kept all sorts of hounds that run buck, fox, hare, otter and badger; and had hawks of all kinds both long and short winged. His great hall was commonly strewed with marrow-bones, and full of hawk perches, hounds, spaniels and terriers. On a broad hearth paved with brick, lay some of the choicest terriers, hounds and spaniels."

"By cock and pye, Sir, you shall not away to night * * * *. I
will not excuse you; you shall not be excused; excuses shall not
be admitted; there is no excuse shall serve; you shall not be
excused * * * * * *. Some pigeons, Davy; a couple of shortlegged
hens; a joint of mutton; and any pretty little tiny kickshaws, tell
William Cook."

I now bade a reluctant farewell to the old hall. My mind had become so completely possessed by the imaginary scenes and characters
connected with it, that I seemed to be actually living among them.
Every thing brought them, as it were, before my eyes; and as the
door of the dining room opened, I almost expected to hear the feeble
voice of Master Silence quavering forth his favourite ditty:

> " 'Tis merry in hall, when beards wag all,
>   And welcome merry Shrove-tide!"

On returning to my inn, I could not but reflect on the singular gift
of the poet; to be able thus to spread the magic of his mind over the
very face of nature; to give to things and places a charm and character
not their own, and to turn this "working day world" into a perfect
fairy land. He is indeed the true enchanter, whose spell operates not
upon the senses, but upon the imagination and the heart. Under the
wizard influence of Shakespeare I had been walking all day in a
complete delusion. I had surveyed the landscape through the prism
of poetry, which tinged every object with the hues of the rainbow. I
had been surrounded with fancied beings; with mere airy nothings,
conjured up by poetic power; yet which, to me, had all the charm
of reality. I had heard Jaques soliloquize beneath his oak; had beheld
the fair Rosalind and her companion adventuring through the woodlands; and, above all, had been once more present in spirit with fat
Jack Falstaff, and his contemporaries, from the august Justice Shallow,
down to the gentle Master Slender, and the sweet Anne Page. Ten
thousand honours and blessings on the bard who has thus gilded
the dull realities of life with innocent illusions; who has spread exquisite and unbought pleasures in my chequered path; and beguiled
my spirit, in many a lonely hour, with all the cordial and cheerful
sympathies of social life!
As I crossed the bridge over the Avon on my return, I paused to
contemplate the distant church in which the poet lies buried, and
could not but exult in the malediction, which has kept his ashes
undisturbed in its quiet and hallowed vaults. What honour could his

name have derived from being mingled in dusty companionship with the epitaphs and escutcheons and venal eulogiums of a titled multitude. What would a crowded corner in Westminster Abbey have been, compared with this reverend pile, which seems to stand in beautiful loneliness as his sole mausoleum! The solicitude about the grave may be but the offspring of an overwrought sensibility; but human nature is made up of foibles and prejudices; and its best and tenderest affections are mingled with these factitious feelings. He who has sought renown about the world, and has reaped a full harvest of worldly favour, will find, after all, that there is no love, no admiration, no applause, so sweet to the soul as that which springs up in his native place. It is there that he seeks to be gathered in peace and honour among his kindred and his early friends. And when the weary heart and failing head begin to warn him that the evening of life is drawing on, he turns as fondly as does the infant to the mother's arms, to sink to sleep in the bosom of the scene of his childhood.

How would it have cheered the spirit of the youthful bard, when, wandering forth in disgrace upon a doubtful world, he cast back a heavy look upon his paternal home; could he have foreseen that, before many years, he should return to it covered with renown; that his name should become the boast and glory of his native place; that his ashes should be religiously guarded as its most precious treasure; and that its lessening spire, on which his eyes were fixed in tearful contemplation, should one day become the beacon, towering amidst the gentle landscape, to guide the literary pilgrim of every nation to his tomb.

TRAITS OF
INDIAN CHARACTER

"I appeal to any white man if ever he entered Logan's cabin hungry, and he gave him not to eat; if ever he came cold and naked, and he clothed him not."

SPEECH OF AN INDIAN CHIEF.

There is something in the character and habits of the North American savage, taken in connexion with the scenery over which he is accustomed to range, its vast lakes, boundless forests, majestic rivers and trackless plains, that is, to my mind, wonderfully striking and sublime. He is formed for the wilderness, as the Arab is for the desert. His nature is stern, simple and enduring; fitted to grapple with difficulties, and to support privations. There seems but little soil in his heart for the growth of the kindly virtues; and yet, if we would but take the trouble to penetrate through that proud stoicism and habitual taciturnity, which lock up his character from casual observation, we should find him linked to his fellow man of civilized life by more of those sympathies and affections than are usually ascribed to him.

It has been the lot of the unfortunate aborigines of America, in the early periods of colonization, to be doubly wronged by the white men. They have been dispossessed of their hereditary possessions by mercenary and frequently wanton warfare; and their characters have been traduced by bigoted and interested writers. The colonist has often treated them like beasts of the forest; and the author has endeavoured to justify him in his outrages. The former found it easier to exterminate than to civilize; the latter to vilify than to discriminate. The appellations of savage and pagan were deemed sufficient to sanction the hostilities of both; and thus the poor wanderers of the forest were persecuted and defamed, not because they were guilty, but because they were ignorant.

The rights of the savage have seldom been properly appreciated or respected by the white man. In peace he has too often been the dupe of artful traffic; in war he has been regarded as a ferocious animal, whose life or death was a question of mere precaution and convenience. Man is cruelly wasteful of life when his own safety is endangered, and he is sheltered by impunity; and little mercy is to be expected from him when he feels the sting of the reptile and is conscious of the power to destroy.

The same prejudices which were indulged thus early, exist in common circulation at the present day. Certain learned societies have, it is true, with laudable diligence, endeavoured to investigate and record the real characters and manners of the Indian tribes; the American government too, has wisely and humanely exerted itself to inculcate a friendly and forbearing spirit towards them, and to protect them from fraud and injustice.° The current opinion of the Indian character, however, is too apt to be formed from the miserable hordes which infest the frontiers, and hang on the skirts of the settlements. These are too commonly composed of degenerate beings, corrupted and enfeebled by the vices of society, without being benefited by its civilization. That proud independence, which formed the main pillar of savage virtue, has been shaken down, and the whole moral fabric lies in ruins. Their spirits are humiliated and debased by a sense of inferiority, and their native courage cowed and daunted by the superior knowledge and power of their enlightened neighbours. Society has advanced upon them like one of those withering airs that will sometimes breathe desolation over a whole region of fertility. It has enervated their strength, multiplied their diseases, and superinduced upon their original barbarity the low vices of artificial life. It has given them a thousand superfluous wants, whilst it has diminished their means of mere existence. It has driven before it the animals of the chase, who fly from the sound of the axe and the smoke of the settlement, and seek refuge in the depths of remoter forests and yet untrodden wilds. Thus do we too often find the Indians on our frontiers to be mere wrecks and remnants of once powerful tribes, who have lingered in the vicinity of the settlements, and sunk into precarious and vagabond existence. Poverty, repining and hopeless poverty, a canker of the mind unknown in savage life, corrodes their spirits and blights every free and noble quality of their natures. They become drunken, indolent, feeble, thievish and pusillanimous. They loiter like vagrants about the settlements, among spacious dwellings, replete with elaborate comforts, which only render them sensible of the comparative wretchedness of their own condition. Luxury spreads its ample board before their eyes, but they are excluded from the banquet. Plenty revels over the fields, but they are starving in the midst of its abundance; the whole

---

°The American government has been indefatigable in its exertions to ameliorate the situation of the Indians, and to introduce among them the arts of civilization, and civil and religious knowledge. To protect them from the frauds of the white traders, no purchase of land from them by individuals is permitted; nor is any person allowed to receive lands from them as a present, without the express sanction of government. These precautions are strictly enforced.

wilderness has blossomed into a garden; but they feel as reptiles that infest it.

How different was their state while yet the undisputed lords of the soil. Their wants were few, and the means of gratification within their reach. They saw every one round them sharing the same lot, enduring the same hardships, feeding on the same aliments, arrayed in the same rude garments. No roof then rose, but was open to the homeless stranger; no smoke curled among the trees, but he was welcome to sit down by its fire and join the hunter in his repast. "For," says an old historian of New England, "their life is so void of care, and they are so loving also, that they make use of those things they enjoy as common goods, and are therein so compassionate, that rather than one should starve through want, they would starve all; thus do they pass their time merrily, not regarding our pomp, but are better content with their own, which some men esteem so meanly of." Such were the Indians whilst in the pride and energy of their primitive natures; they resemble those wild plants which thrive best in the shades of the forest, but shrink from the hand of cultivation, and perish beneath the influence of the sun.

In discussing the savage character, writers have been too prone to indulge in vulgar prejudice and passionate exaggeration, instead of the candid temper of true philosophy. They have not sufficiently considered the peculiar circumstances in which the Indians have been placed, and the peculiar principles under which they have been educated. No being acts more rigidly from rule than the Indian. His whole conduct is regulated according to some general maxims early implanted in his mind. The moral laws that govern him are, to be sure, but few; but then he conforms to them all;—the white man abounds in laws of religion, morals and manners, but how many does he violate!

A frequent ground of accusation against the Indians is their disregard of treaties, and the treachery and wantonness with which, in time of apparent peace, they will suddenly fly to hostilities. The intercourse of the white men with the Indians, however, is too apt to be cold, distrustful, oppressive, and insulting. They seldom treat them with that confidence and frankness which are indispensable to real friendship; nor is sufficient caution observed not to offend against those feelings of pride or superstition, which often prompt the Indian to hostility quicker than mere considerations of interest. The solitary savage feels silently, but acutely. His sensibilities are not diffused over so wide a surface as those of the white man; but they run in steadier and deeper channels. His pride, his affections, his superstitions, are all directed towards fewer objects; but the wounds inflicted on them are proportionably severe, and furnish motives of hostility which we cannot sufficiently appreciate. Where a community is also limited in number, and forms one great patriarchal family, as in an Indian tribe, the injury of an individual is the injury of the whole; and the sentiment of vengeance is almost instantaneously diffused. One council fire is sufficient for the discussion and arrangement of a plan of hostilities. Here all the fighting men and sages assemble. Eloquence and superstition combine to inflame the minds of the warriors. The orator awakens their martial ardour, and they are wrought up to a kind of religious desperation, by the visions of the prophet and the dreamer.

An instance of one of those sudden exasperations, arising from a motive peculiar to the Indian character, is extant in an old record of the early settlement of Massachusetts. The planters of Plymouth had defaced the monuments of the dead at Passonagessit, and had plundered the grave of the Sachem's mother of some skins with which it had been decorated. The Indians are remarkable for the reverence which they entertain for the sepulchres of their kindred. Tribes, that have passed generations exiled from the abodes of their ancestors, when by chance they have been travelling in the vicinity, have been known to turn aside from the high way, and, guided by wonderfully accurate tradition, have crossed the country for miles to some tumulus, buried perhaps in woods, where the bones of their tribe were anciently deposited; and there have passed hours in silent meditation. Influenced by this sublime and holy feeling, the Sachem, whose mother's tomb had been violated, gathered his men together, and addressed them in the following beautifully simple and pathetic harangue; a curious specimen of Indian eloquence, and an affecting instance of filial piety in a savage.

"When last the glorious light of all the sky was underneath this globe, and birds grew silent, I began to settle, as my custom is, to take repose. Before mine eyes were fast closed, methought I saw a vision, at which my spirit was much troubled; and, trembling at that doleful sight, a spirit cried aloud, 'Behold, my son, whom I have cherished, see the breasts that gave thee suck, the hands that lapped thee warm, and fed thee oft! Canst thou forget to take revenge of those wild people, who have defaced my monument in a despiteful manner, disdaining our antiquities and honourable customs. See now, the Sachem's grave lies like the common people, defaced by an ignoble race. Thy mother doth complain, and implores thy aid against this thievish people, who have newly intruded on our land. If this be suffered, I shall not rest quiet in my everlasting habitation.' This said, the spirit vanished, and I, all in a sweat, not able scarce to speak, began to get some strength, and recollect my spirits that were fled, and determined to demand your counsel and assistance."

I have adduced this anecdote at some length, as it tends to show, how these sudden acts of hostility, which have been attributed to caprice and perfidy, may often arise from deep and generous motives, which our inattention to Indian character and customs prevents our properly appreciating.

Another ground of violent outcry against the Indians is their barbarity to the vanquished. This had its origin partly in policy and partly in superstition. The tribes, though sometimes called nations, were never so formidable in their numbers, but that the loss of several warriors was sensibly felt; this was particularly the case when they had been frequently engaged in warfare; and many an instance occurs in Indian history, where a tribe that had long been formidable to its neighbours, has been broken up and driven away, by the capture and massacre of its principal fighting men. There was a strong temptation, therefore, to the victor to be merciless; not so much to gratify any cruel revenge, as to provide for future security. The Indians had also the superstitious belief, frequent among barbarous nations, and prevalent also among the ancients, that the manes of their friends who had fallen in battle, were soothed by the blood of the captives. The prisoners, however, who are not thus sacrificed, are adopted into their families in place of the slain, and are treated with the confidence and affection of relatives and friends; nay, so hospitable and tender is their entertainment, that when the alternative is offered them they will often prefer to remain with their adopted brethren, rather than return to the home and the friends of their youth.

The cruelty of the Indians towards their prisoners has been heightened since the colonization of the whites. What was formerly a compliance with policy and superstition, has been exasperated into a gratification of vengeance. They cannot but be sensible that the white men are the usurpers of their ancient dominion, the cause of their degradation, and the gradual destroyers of their race. They go forth to battle, smarting with injuries and indignities which they have individually suffered, and they are driven to madness and despair by the wide spreading desolation, and the overwhelming ruin of European warfare. The whites have too frequently set them an example of violence, by burning their villages and laying waste their slender means of subsistence; and yet they wonder that savages do not show moderation and magnanimity towards those, who have left them nothing but mere existence and wretchedness.

We stigmatize the Indians, also, as cowardly and treacherous, because they use stratagem in warfare, in preference to open force; but in this they are fully justified by their rude code of honour. They are early taught that stratagem is praiseworthy: the bravest warrior thinks it no disgrace to lurk in silence, and take every advantage of his foe: he triumphs in the superior craft and sagacity by which he has been enabled to surprize and destroy an enemy. Indeed man is naturally more prone to subtilty than open valour, owing to his physical weakness in comparison with other animals. They are endowed with natural weapons of defence; with horns, with tusks, with hoofs and talons; but man has to depend on his superior sagacity. In all his encounters with these, his proper enemies, he resorts to stratagem; and when he perversely turns his hostility against his fellow man, he at first continues the same subtle mode of warfare.

The natural principle of war is to do the most harm to our enemy with the least harm to ourselves; and this of course is to be effected by stratagem. That chivalrous courage which induces us to despise the suggestions of prudence, and to rush in the face of certain danger, is the offspring of society, and produced by education. It is honourable, because it is in fact the triumph of lofty sentiment over an instinctive repugnance to pain, and over those yearnings after personal ease and security, which society has condemned as ignoble. It is kept alive by pride and the fear of shame; and thus the dread of real evil is overcome by the superior dread of an evil which exists but in the imagination. It has been cherished and stimulated also by various means. It has been the theme of spirit stirring song and chivalrous story. The poet and minstrel have delighted to shed round it the splendours of fiction; and even the historian has forgotten the sober gravity of narration, and broken forth into enthusiasm and rhapsody in its praise. Triumphs and gorgeous pageants have been its reward: monuments, on which art has exhausted its skill, and opulence its treasures, have been erected to perpetuate a nation's gratitude and admiration. Thus artificially excited, courage has arisen to an extraordinary and factitious degree of heroism; and, arrayed in all the glorious "pomp and circumstance of war," this turbulent quality has even been able to eclipse many of those quiet, but invaluable virtues, which silently ennoble the human character, and swell the tide of human happiness.

But if courage intrinsically consists in the defiance of danger and pain, the life of the Indian is a continual exhibition of it. He lives in a state of perpetual hostility and risk. Peril and adventure are congenial to his nature; or rather seem necessary to arouse his faculties and to give an interest to his existence. Surrounded by hostile tribes, whose mode of warfare is by ambush and surprisal, he is always prepared for fight, and lives with his weapons in his hands. As the ship careers in fearful singleness through the solitudes of ocean;—as the bird mingles among clouds, and storms, and wings its way, a mere speck, across the pathless fields of air;—so the Indian holds his course, silent, solitary, but undaunted, through the boundless bosom of the wilderness. His expeditions may vie in distance and danger with the pilgrimage of the devotee, or the crusade of the knight errant. He traverses vast forests, exposed to the hazards of lonely sickness, of lurking enemies and pining famine. Stormy lakes, those great inland seas, are no obstacles to his wanderings: in his light canoe of bark he sports, like a feather, on their waves, and darts, with the swiftness of an arrow, down the roaring rapids of the rivers. His very subsistence is snatched from the midst of toil and peril. He gains his food by the hardships and dangers of the chase; he wraps himself in the spoils of the bear, the panther, and the buffalo, and sleeps among the thunders of the cataract.

No hero of ancient or modern days can surpass the Indian in his lofty contempt of death, and the fortitude with which he sustains its cruelest infliction. Indeed we here behold him rising superior to the white man, in consequence of his peculiar education. The latter rushes to glorious death at the cannon's mouth; the former calmly contemplates its approach, and triumphantly endures it, amidst the varied torments of surrounding foes and the protracted agonies of fire. He even takes a pride in taunting his persecutors, and provoking their ingenuity of torture; and as the devouring flames prey on his very vitals, and the flesh shrinks from the sinews, he raises his last song of triumph, breathing the defiance of an unconquered heart, and invoking the spirits of his fathers to witness that he dies without a groan.

Notwithstanding the obloquy with which the early historians have overshadowed the characters of the unfortunate natives, some bright gleams occasionally break through, which throw a degree of melancholy lustre on their memories. Facts are occasionally to be met with in the rude annals of the eastern provinces, which, though recorded with the colouring of prejudice and bigotry, yet speak for themselves; and will be dwelt on with applause and sympathy, when prejudice shall have passed away.

In one of the homely narratives of the Indian wars in New England, there is a touching account of the desolation carried into the tribe of the Pequod Indians. Humanity shrinks from the cold blooded detail of indiscriminate butchery. In one place we read of the surprisal of an Indian fort in the night, when the wigwams were wrapped in flames, and the miserable inhabitants shot down and slain in attempting to escape, "all being dispatched and ended in the course of an hour."

After a series of similar transactions, "our soldiers," as the historian piously observes, "being resolved by God's assistance to make a final destruction of them," the unhappy savages being hunted from their homes and fortresses, and pursued with fire and sword, a scanty but gallant band, the sad remnant of the Pequod warriors, with their wives and children, took refuge in a swamp.

Burning with indignation, and rendered sullen by despair; with hearts bursting with grief at the destruction of their tribe, and spirits galled and sore at the fancied ignominy of their defeat, they refused to ask their lives at the hands of an insulting foe, and preferred death to submission.

As the night drew on they were surrounded in their dismal retreat, so as to render escape impracticable. Thus situated, their enemy "plied them with shot all the time, by which means many were killed and buried in the mire." In the darkness and fog that preceded the dawn of day some few broke through the besiegers and escaped into the woods: "the rest were left to the conquerors, of which many were killed in the swamp, like sullen dogs who would rather, in their self willedness and madness, sit still and be shot through, or cut to pieces," than implore for mercy. When the day broke upon this handful of forlorn but dauntless spirits, the soldiers, we are told, entering the swamp, "saw several heaps of them sitting close together, upon whom they discharged their pieces, laden with ten or twelve pistol bullets at a time; putting the muzzles of their pieces under the boughs, within a few yards of them; so as, besides those that were found dead, many more were killed and sunk into the mire, and never were minded more by friend or foe."

Can any one read this plain unvarnished tale, without admiring the stern resolution, the unbending pride, the loftiness of spirit, that seemed to nerve the hearts of these self taught heroes, and to raise them above the instinctive feelings of human nature? When the Gauls laid waste the city of Rome, they found the senators clothed in their robes and seated with stern tranquillity in their curule chairs; in this manner they suffered death without resistance or even supplication. Such conduct was, in them, applauded as noble and magnanimous; in the hapless Indians it was reviled as obstinate and sullen. How truly are we the dupes of show and circumstance! How different is virtue, clothed in purple and enthroned in state, from virtue naked and destitute, and perishing obscurely in a wilderness.

But I forbear to dwell upon these gloomy pictures. The eastern tribes have long since disappeared; the forests that sheltered them have been laid low, and scarce any traces remain of them in the thickly settled states of New England, excepting here and there the Indian name of a village or a stream. And such must sooner or later be the fate of those other tribes which skirt the frontiers, and have occasionally been inveigled from their forests to mingle in the wars of white men. In a little while, and they will go the way that their brethren have gone before. The few hordes which still linger about the shores of Huron and Superior, and the tributary streams of the Mississippi, will share the fate of those tribes that once spread over Massachusetts and Connecticut, and lorded it along the proud banks of the Hudson; of that gigantic race said to have existed on the borders of the Susquehanna; and of those various nations that flourished about the Patowmac and the Rappahanoc, and that peopled the forests of the vast valley of Shenandoah. They will vanish like a vapour from the face of the earth; their very history will be lost in forgetfulness; and "the places that now know them will know them no more for ever." Or if, perchance, some dubious memorial of them should survive, it may be in the romantic dreams of the poet, to people in imagination his glades and groves, like the fauns and satyrs and sylvan deities of antiquity. But should he venture upon the dark story of their wrongs and wretchedness; should he tell how they were invaded, corrupted, despoiled; driven from their native abodes and the sepulchres of their fathers; hunted like wild beasts about the earth; and sent down with violence and butchery to the grave; posterity will either turn with horror and incredulity from the tale, or blush with indignation at the inhumanity of their forefathers.—"We are driven back," said an old warrior, "until we can retreat no further—our hatchets are broken, our bows are snapped, our fires are nearly extinguished—a little longer and the white man will cease to persecute us—for we shall cease to exist!"

PHILIP OF POKANOKET

An Indian Memoir

As monumental bronze unchanged his look:
A soul that pity touch'd, but never shook:
Train'd, from his tree-rock'd cradle to his bier,
The fierce extremes of good and ill to brook
Impassive—fearing but the shame of fear—
A stoic of the woods—a man without a tear.

CAMPBELL.

It is to be regretted that those early writers who treated of the discovery and settlement of America, have not given us more particular and candid accounts of the remarkable characters that flourished in savage life. The scanty anecdotes which have reached us are full of peculiarity and interest; they furnish us with nearer glimpses of human nature, and show what man is in a comparatively primitive state, and what he owes to civilization. There is something of the charm of discovery in lighting upon these wild and unexplored tracts of human nature; in witnessing, as it were, the native growth of moral sentiment; and perceiving those generous and romantic qualities which have been artificially cultivated by society, vegetating in spontaneous hardihood and rude magnificence.

In civilized life, where the happiness, and indeed almost the existence, of man depends so much upon the opinion of his fellow men, he is constantly acting a studied part. The bold and peculiar traits of native character are refined away, or softened down by the levelling influence of what is termed good breeding; and he practises so many petty deceptions, and affects so many generous sentiments, for the purposes of popularity, that it is difficult to distinguish his real, from his artificial character. The Indian, on the contrary, free from the restraints and refinements of polished life, and, in a great degree, a solitary and independent being, obeys the impulses of his inclination or the dictates of his judgment; and thus the attributes of his nature, being freely indulged, grow singly great and striking. Society is like a lawn, where every roughness is smoothed, every bramble eradicated, and where the eye is delighted by the smiling verdure of a velvet surface; he, however, who would study nature in its wildness and variety, must plunge into the forest, must explore the glen, must stem the torrent, and dare the precipice.

These reflections arose on casually looking through a volume of early colonial history, wherein are recorded, with great bitterness, the outrages of the Indians, and their wars with the settlers of New England. It is painful to perceive, even from these partial narratives, how the footsteps of civilization may be traced in the blood of the aborigines; how easily the colonists were moved to hostility by the lust of conquest; how merciless and exterminating was their warfare. The imagination shrinks at the idea, how many intellectual beings were hunted from the earth; how many brave and noble hearts, of nature's sterling coinage, were broken down and trampled in the dust.

Such was the fate of PHILIP OF POKANOKET, an Indian warrior, whose name was once a terror throughout Massachusetts and Connecticut. He was the most distinguished of a number of cotemporary Sachems who reigned over the Pequods, the Narrhagansets, the Wampanoags, and the other Eastern tribes, at the time of the first settlement of New England: a band of native untaught heroes; who made the most generous struggle of which human nature is capable; fighting to the last gasp in the cause of their country, without a hope of victory or a thought of renown. Worthy of an age of poetry, and fit subjects for local story and romantic fiction, they have left scarcely any authentic traces on the page of history, but stalk, like gigantic shadows in the dim twilight of tradition.*

When the pilgrims, as the Plymouth settlers are called by their descendants, first took refuge on the shores of the New World, from the religious persecutions of the Old, their situation was to the last degree gloomy and disheartening. Few in number, and that number rapidly perishing away through sickness and hardships; surrounded by a howling wilderness and savage tribes; exposed to the rigours of an almost arctic winter, and the vicissitudes of an ever shifting climate; their minds were filled with doleful forebodings, and nothing preserved them from sinking into despondency but the strong excitement of religious enthusiasm. In this forlorn situation they were visited by Massasoit, chief Sagamore of the Wampanoags, a powerful chief, who reigned over a great extent of country. Instead of taking advantage of the scanty number of the strangers, and expelling them from his territories into which they had intruded, he seemed at once to conceive for them a generous friendship, and extended towards them the rites of primitive hospitality. He came early in the spring to their settlement of New Plymouth, attended by a mere handful of followers; entered

*While correcting the proof sheets of this article, the author is informed, that a celebrated English poet has nearly finished an heroic poem on the story of Philip of Pokanoket.

into a solemn league of peace and amity; sold them a portion of the soil, and promised to secure for them the good will of his savage allies. Whatever may be said of Indian perfidy, it is certain that the integrity and good faith of Massasoit, have never been impeached. He continued a firm and magnanimous friend of the white men; suffering them to extend their possessions and to strengthen themselves in the land; and betraying no jealousy of their increasing power and prosperity. Shortly before his death he came once more to New Plymouth, with his son Alexander, for the purpose of renewing the covenant of peace, and of securing it to his posterity.

At this conference he endeavoured to protect the religion of his forefathers from the encroaching zeal of the missionaries; and stipulated that no further attempt should be made to draw off his people from their ancient faith; but, finding the English obstinately opposed to any such condition, he mildly relinquished the demand. Almost the last act of his life was to bring his two sons, Alexander and Philip (as they had been named by the English,) to the residence of a principal settler, recommending mutual kindness and confidence; and entreating that the same love and amity which had existed between the white men and himself, might be continued afterwards with his children. The good old Sachem died in peace, and was happily gathered to his fathers before sorrow came upon his tribe; his children remained behind to experience the ingratitude of white men.

His eldest son, Alexander, succeeded him. He was of a quick and impetuous temper, and proudly tenacious of his hereditary rights and dignity. The intrusive policy and dictatorial conduct of the strangers excited his indignation; and he beheld with uneasiness their exterminating wars with the neighbouring tribes. He was doomed soon to incur their hostility, being accused of plotting with the Narrhagansets to rise against the English and drive them from the land. It is impossible to say whether this accusation was warranted by facts, or was grounded on mere suspicions. It is evident, however, by the violent and overbearing measures of the settlers, that they had by this time begun to feel conscious of the rapid increase of their power, and to grow harsh and inconsiderate in their treatment of the natives. They dispatched an armed force to seize at once upon Alexander, and to bring him before their court. He was traced to his woodland haunts, and surprised at a hunting house, where he was reposing with a band of his followers, unarmed, after the toils of the chase. The suddenness of his arrest, and the outrage offered to his sovereign dignity, so preyed upon the irascible feelings of this proud savage, as to throw him into a raging fever; he was permitted to return home on condition of sending his son as a pledge for his reappearance; but the blow he had received was fatal, and before he reached his home he fell a victim to the agonies of a wounded spirit.

The successor of Alexander was Metamocet, or King Philip, as he was called by the settlers, on account of his lofty spirit and ambitious temper. These, together with his well known energy and enterprise, had rendered him an object of great jealousy and apprehension, and he was accused of having always cherished a secret and implacable hostility towards the whites. Such may very probably, and very naturally, have been the case. He considered them as originally but mere intruders into the country, who had presumed upon indulgence, and were extending an influence baneful to savage life. He saw the whole race of his countrymen melting before them from the face of the earth; their territories slipping from their hands, and their tribes becoming feeble, scattered and dependent. It may be said that the soil was originally purchased by the settlers; but who does not know the nature of Indian purchases, in the early periods of colonization? The Europeans always made thrifty bargains through their superior adroitness in traffic; and they gained vast accessions of territory, by easily provoked hostilities. An uncultivated savage is never a nice inquirer into the refinements of law, by which an injury may be gradually and legally inflicted. Leading facts are all by which he judges; and it was enough for Philip to know, that before the intrusion of the Europeans his countrymen were lords of the soil, and that now they were becoming vagabonds in the land of their fathers.

But whatever may have been his feelings of general hostility, and his particular indignation at the treatment of his brother, he suppressed them for the present; renewed the contract with the settlers; and resided peaceably for many years at Pokanoket, or, as it was called by the English, Mount Hope,* the ancient seat of dominion of his tribe. Suspicions, however, which were at first but vague and indefinite, began to acquire form and substance; and he was at length charged with attempting to instigate the various eastern tribes to rise at once, and by a simultaneous effort, to throw off the yoke of their oppressors. It is difficult at this distant period to assign the proper credit due to these early accusations against the Indians. There was a proneness to suspicion, and an aptness to acts of violence, on the part of the whites, that gave weight and importance to every idle tale. Informers abounded where tale bearing met with countenance and reward; and the sword

*Now Bristol, Rhode Island.

was readily unsheathed when its success was certain and it carved out empire.

The only positive evidence on record against Philip is the accusation of one Sausaman, a renegado Indian, whose natural cunning had been quickened by a partial education which he had received among the settlers. He changed his faith and his allegiance two or three times, with a facility that evinced the looseness of his principles. He had acted for some time as Philip's confidential secretary and councillor, and had enjoyed his bounty and protection. Finding, however, that the clouds of adversity were gathering round his patron, he abandoned his service and went over to the whites; and in order to gain their favour, charged his former benefactor with plotting against their safety. A rigorous investigation took place. Philip and several of his subjects submitted to be examined, but nothing was proved against them. The settlers, however, had now gone too far to retract; they had previously determined that Philip was a dangerous neighbour; they had publicly evinced their distrust; and had done enough to ensure his hostility; according, therefore, to the usual mode of reasoning in these cases, his destruction had become necessary to their security. Sausaman, the treacherous informer, was shortly after found dead in a pond, having fallen a victim to the vengeance of his tribe. Three Indians, one of whom was a friend and councillor of Philip, were apprehended and tried, and on the testimony of one very questionable witness, were condemned and executed as the murderers.

This treatment of his subjects, and ignominious punishment of his friend, outraged the pride and exasperated the passions of Philip. The bolt which had fallen thus at his very feet awakened him to the gathering storm, and he determined to trust himself no longer in the power of the white men. The fate of his insulted and broken hearted brother still rankled in his mind; and he had a further warning in the tragical story of Miantonimo, a great Sachem of the Narrhagansets, who, after manfully facing his accusers before a tribunal of the colonists, exculpating himself from a charge of conspiracy, and receiving assurances of amity, had been perfidiously dispatched at their instigation. Philip, therefore, gathered his fighting men about him; persuaded all strangers that he could, to join his cause; sent the women and children to the Narrhagansets for safety; and wherever he appeared, was continually surrounded by armed warriors.

When the two parties were thus in a state of distrust and irritation, the least spark was sufficient to set them in a flame. The Indians, having weapons in their hands, grew mischievous, and committed various petty depredations. In one of their maraudings a warrior was fired upon and killed by a settler. This was the signal for open hostilities; the Indians pressed to revenge the death of their comrade, and the alarm of war resounded through the Plymouth colony.

In the early chronicles of these dark and melancholy times we meet with many indications of the diseased state of the public mind. The gloom of religious abstraction, and the wildness of their situation, among trackless forests, and savage tribes, had disposed the colonists to superstitious fancies, and had filled their imaginations with the frightful chimeras of witchcraft and spectrology. They were much given also to a belief in omens. The troubles with Philip and his Indians were preceded, we are told, by a variety of those awful warnings which forerun great and public calamities. The perfect form of an Indian bow appeared in the air at New Plymouth, which was looked upon by the inhabitants as a "prodigious apparition." At Hadley, Northampton, and other towns in their neighbourhood, "was heard the report of a great piece of ordnance, with a shaking of the earth and a considerable echo."* Others were alarmed on a still sunshiny morning by the discharge of guns and muskets; bullets seemed to whistle past them, and the noise of drums resounded in the air, seeming to pass away to the westward: others fancied that they heard the galloping of horses over their heads; and certain monstrous births which took place about the time, filled the superstitious in some towns with doleful forebodings. Many of these portentous sights and sounds may be ascribed to natural phenomena. To the northern lights which occur vividly in those latitudes; the meteors which explode in the air; the casual rushing of a blast through the top branches of the forest; the crash of falling trees or disruptured rocks; and to those other uncouth sounds and echoes which will sometimes strike the ear so strangely amidst the profound stillness of woodland solitudes. These may have startled some melancholy imaginations, may have been exaggerated by the love for the marvellous, and listened to, with that avidity with which we devour whatever is fearful and mysterious. The universal currency of these superstitious fancies, and the grave record made of them by one of the learned men of the day, are strongly characteristic of the times.

The nature of the contest that ensued was such as too often distinguishes the warfare between civilized men and savages. On the part of the whites it was conducted with superior skill and success; but with a wastefulness of the blood, and a disregard of the natural rights of their antagonists: on the part of the Indians it was waged

*The Rev. Increase Mather's History.

with the desperation of men fearless of death, and who had nothing to expect from peace, but humiliation, dependence and decay.

The events of the war are transmitted to us by a worthy clergyman of the time; who dwells with horror and indignation on every hostile act of the Indians, however justifiable, whilst he mentions with applause the most sanguinary atrocities of the whites. Philip is reviled as a murderer and a traitor; without considering that he was a true born prince, gallantly fighting at the head of his subjects to avenge the wrongs of his family; to retrieve the tottering power of his line; and to deliver his native land from the oppression of usurping strangers.

The project of a wide and simultaneous revolt, if such had really been formed, was worthy of a capacious mind, and, had it not been prematurely discovered, might have been overwhelming in its consequences. The war that actually broke out was but a war of detail; a mere succession of casual exploits and unconnected enterprizes. Still it sets forth the military genius and daring prowess of Philip; and wherever, in the prejudiced and passionate narrations that have been given of it, we can arrive at simple facts, we find him displaying a vigorous mind; a fertility in expedients; a contempt of suffering and hardship; and an unconquerable resolution; that command our sympathy and applause.

Driven from his paternal domains at Mount Hope, he threw himself into the depths of those vast and trackless forests that skirted the settlements and were almost impervious to any thing but a wild beast, or an Indian. Here he gathered together his forces, like the storm accumulating its stores of mischief in the bosom of the thunder cloud, and would suddenly emerge at a time and place least expected, carrying havoc and dismay into the villages. There were now and then indications of these impending ravages, that filled the minds of the colonists with awe and apprehension. The report of a distant gun would perhaps be heard from the solitary woodland, where there was known to be no white man; the cattle which had been wandering in the woods, would sometimes return home wounded; or an Indian or two would be seen lurking about the skirts of the forests, and suddenly disappearing; as the lightning will sometimes be seen playing silently about the edge of the cloud that is brewing up the tempest.

Though sometimes pursued and even surrounded by the settlers, yet Philip as often escaped almost miraculously from their toils, and plunging into the wilderness would be lost to all search or inquiry, until he again emerged at some far distant quarter, laying the country desolate. Among his strong holds were the great swamps or morasses, which extend in some parts of New England; composed of loose bogs of deep black mud; perplexed with thickets, brambles, rank weeds, the shattered and mouldering trunks of fallen trees, and overshadowed by lugubrious hemlocks. The uncertain footing and the tangled mazes of these shagged wilds, render them almost impracticable to the white man, though the Indian could thrid their labyrinths with the agility of a deer. Into one of these, the great swamp of Pocasset Neck, was Philip once driven with a band of his followers. The English did not dare to pursue him, fearing to venture into these dark and frightful recesses, where they might perish in fens and miry pits, or be shot down by lurking foes. They therefore invested the entrance to the neck, and began to build a fort, with the thought of starving out the foe; but Philip and his warriors wafted themselves on a raft over an arm of the sea, in the dead of night, leaving the women and children behind; and escaped away to the westward, kindling the flames of war among the tribes of Massachusetts and the Nipmuck country, and threatening the colony of Connecticut.

In this way Philip became a theme of universal apprehension. The mystery in which he was enveloped exaggerated his real terrors. He was an evil that walked in darkness; whose coming none could foresee, and against which none knew when to be on the alert. The whole country abounded with rumours and alarms. Philip seemed almost possessed of ubiquity; for, in whatever part of the widely extended frontier an irruption from the forest took place, Philip was said to be its leader. Many superstitious notions also were circulated concerning him. He was said to deal in necromancy, and to be attended by an old Indian witch or prophetess, whom he consulted, and who assisted him by her charms and incantations. This indeed was frequently the case with Indian chiefs; either through their own credulity, or to act upon that of their followers: and the influence of the prophet and the dreamer over Indian superstition has been fully evidenced in recent instances of savage warfare.

At the time that Philip effected his escape from Pocasset, his fortunes were in a desperate condition. His forces had been thinned by repeated fights, and he had lost almost the whole of his resources. In this time of adversity he found a faithful friend in Canonchet, Chief Sachem of all the Narrhagansets. He was the son and heir of Miantonimo, the great Sachem, who, as already mentioned, after an honourable acquittal of the charge of conspiracy, had been privately put to death at the perfidious instigations of the settlers. "He was the heir," says the old chronicler, "of all his father's pride and insolence, as well as of his malice towards the English;"—he certainly was the heir of his insults and injuries, and the legitimate avenger of his murder. Though he had forborne to take an active part in this hopeless war, yet he received Philip and his broken forces with open arms; and gave them the most generous countenance and support. This at once drew upon him the hostility of the English; and it was determined to strike a signal blow that should involve both the sachems in one common ruin. A great force was, therefore, gathered together from Massachusetts, Plymouth, and Connecticut, and was sent into the Narrhaganset country in the depth of winter, when the swamps, being frozen and leafless, could be traversed with comparative facility, and would no longer afford dark and impenetrable fastnesses to the Indians.

Apprehensive of attack, Canonchet had conveyed the greater part of his stores, together with the old, the infirm, the women and children of his tribe, to a strong fortress; where he and Philip had likewise drawn up the flower of their forces. This fortress, deemed by the Indians impregnable, was situated upon a rising mound or kind of island, of five or six acres, in the midst of a swamp; it was constructed with a degree of judgment and skill vastly superior to what is usually displayed in Indian fortification, and indicative of the martial genius of these two chieftains.

Guided by a renegado Indian, the English penetrated, through December snows, to this strong hold, and came upon the garrison by surprize. The fight was fierce and tumultuous. The assailants were repulsed in their first attack, and several of their bravest officers were shot down in the act of storming the fortress, sword in hand. The assault was renewed with greater success. A lodgement was effected. The Indians were driven from one post to another. They disputed their ground inch by inch, fighting with the fury of despair. Most of their veterans were cut to pieces; and after a long and bloody battle, Philip and Canonchet, with a handful of surviving warriors, retreated from the fort, and took refuge in the thickets of the surrounding forest.

The victors set fire to the wigwams and the fort; the whole was soon in a blaze; many of the old men, the women and the children perished in the flames. This last outrage overcame even the stoicism of the savage. The neighbouring woods resounded with the yells of rage and despair, uttered by the fugitive warriors as they beheld the destruction of their dwellings, and heard the agonizing cries of their wives and offspring. "The burning of the wigwams," says a contemporary writer, "the shrieks and cries of the women and children, and the yelling of the warriors, exhibited a most horrible and affecting scene, so that it greatly moved some of the soldiers." The same writer cautiously adds, "they were in *much doubt* then, and afterwards seriously inquired, whether burning their enemies alive could be consistent with humanity, and the benevolent principles of the Gospel."*

The fate of the brave and generous Canonchet is worthy of particular mention: the last scene of his life is one of the noblest instances on record of Indian magnanimity.

Broken down in his power and resources by this signal defeat, yet faithful to his ally and to the hapless cause which he had espoused, he rejected all overtures of peace, offered on condition of betraying Philip and his followers, and declared that "he would fight it out to the last man, rather than become a servant to the English." His home being destroyed; his country harassed and laid waste by the incursions of the conquerors; he was obliged to wander away to the banks of the Connecticut; where he formed a rallying point to the whole body of western Indians, and laid waste several of the English settlements.

Early in the spring he departed on a hazardous expedition, with only thirty chosen men, to penetrate to Seaconk, in the vicinity of Mount Hope, and procure seed corn to plant for the sustenance of his troops. This little band of adventurers had passed safely through the Pequod country, and were in the centre of the Narrhaganset, resting at some wigwams near Pautucket river, when an alarm was given of an approaching enemy. Having but seven men by him at the time, Canonchet dispatched two of them to the top of a neighbouring hill, to bring intelligence of the foe.

Panic struck by the appearance of a troop of English and Indians rapidly advancing, they fled in breathless terror past their chieftain, without stopping to inform him of the danger. Canonchet sent another scout, who did the same. He then sent two more, one of whom, hurrying back in confusion and affright, told him that the whole British army was at hand. Canonchet saw there was no choice but immediate flight. He attempted to escape round the hill, but was perceived and hotly pursued by the hostile Indians and a few of the fleetest of the English. Finding the swiftest pursuer close upon his heels, he threw off, first his blanket, then his silver laced coat and belt of peag, by which his enemies knew him to be Canonchet, and redoubled the eagerness of pursuit. At length, in dashing through the river, his foot slipped upon a stone, and he fell so deep as to wet his gun. This accident so struck him with despair, that, as he afterwards confessed, "his heart and his bowels turned within him, and he became like a rotten stick, void of strength."

To such a degree was he unnerved, that, being seized by a Pequod

---

*MS. of the Rev. W. Ruggles.

Indian within a short distance of the river, he made no resistance, though a man of great vigour of body and boldness of heart. But on being made prisoner the whole pride of his spirit arose within him; and from that moment we find, in the anecdotes given by his enemies, nothing but repeated flashes of elevated and prince like heroism. Being questioned by one of the English who first came up with him, and who had not attained his twenty second year, the proud hearted warrior, looking with lofty contempt upon his youthful countenance, replied, "You are a child—you cannot understand matters of war—let your brother or your chief come—him will I answer."

Though repeated offers were made to him of his life, on condition of submitting, with his nation, to the English, yet he rejected them with disdain, and refused to send any proposals of the kind to the great body of his subjects; saying, that he knew none of them would comply. Being reproached with his breach of faith towards the whites; his boast that he would not deliver up a Wampanoag, nor the paring of a Wampanoag's nail; and his threat that he would burn the English alive in their houses; he disdained to justify himself, haughtily answering that others were as forward for the war as himself, "and he desired to hear no more thereof."

So noble and unshaken a spirit, so true a fidelity to his cause and his friend, might have touched the feelings of the generous and the brave: but Canonchet was an Indian; a being towards whom war had no courtesy, humanity no law, religion no compassion—he was condemned to die. The last words of his that are recorded, are worthy of the greatness of his soul. When sentence of death was passed upon him, he observed "that he liked it well, for he should die before his heart was soft, or he had spoken any thing unworthy of himself." His enemies gave him the death of a soldier, for he was shot at Stonington, by three young sachems of his own rank.

The defeat at the Narrhaganset fortress, and the death of Canonchet, were fatal blows to the fortunes of King Philip. He made an ineffectual attempt to raise a head of war, by stirring up the Mohawks to take arms; but though possessed of the native talents of a statesman, his arts were counteracted by the superior arts of his enlightened enemies, and the terror of their warlike skill began to subdue the resolution of the neighbouring tribes. The unfortunate chieftain saw himself daily stripped of power, and his ranks rapidly thinning around him. Some were suborned by the whites; others fell victims to hunger and fatigue, and to the frequent attacks by which they were harassed. His stores were all captured; his chosen friends were swept away from before his eyes; his uncle was shot down by his side; his sister was carried into captivity; and in one of his narrow escapes he was compelled to leave his beloved wife and only son to the mercy of the enemy. "His ruin," says the historian, "being thus gradually carried on, his misery was not prevented, but augmented thereby; being himself made acquainted with the sense and experimental feeling of the captivity of his children, loss of friends, slaughter of his subjects, bereavement of all family relations, and being stripped of all outward comforts, before his own life should be taken away."

To fill up the measure of his misfortunes, his own followers began to plot against his life, that by sacrificing him they might purchase dishonourable safety. Through treachery a number of his faithful adherents, the subjects of Wetamoe, an Indian princess of Pocasset, a near kinswoman and confederate of Philip, were betrayed into the hands of the enemy. Wetamoe was among them at the time, and attempted to make her escape by crossing a neighbouring river: either exhausted by swimming, or starved with cold and hunger, she was found dead and naked near the water side. But persecution ceased not at the grave. Even death, the refuge of the wretched, where the wicked commonly cease from troubling, was no protection to this outcast female, whose great crime was affectionate fidelity to her kinsman and her friend. Her corpse was the object of unmanly and dastardly vengeance; the head was severed from the body and set upon a pole, and was thus exposed at Taunton, to the view of her captive subjects. They immediately recognised the features of their unfortunate queen, and were so affected at this barbarous spectacle, that we are told they broke forth into the "most horrid and diabolical lamentations."

However Philip had borne up against the complicated miseries and misfortunes that surrounded him, the treachery of his followers seemed to wring his heart, and reduce him to despondency. It is said that "he never rejoiced afterwards, nor had success in any of his designs." The spring of hope was broken—the ardour of enterprise was extinguished—he looked around, and all was danger and darkness; "there was no eye to pity, nor any arm that could bring deliverance." With a scanty band of followers, who still remained true to his desperate fortunes, the unhappy Philip wandered back to the vicinity of Mount Hope, the ancient dwelling of his fathers. Here he lurked about, like a spectre, among the desolated scenes of former power and prosperity, now bereft of home, of family, and friend. There needs no better picture of his destitute and piteous situation than that furnished by the homely pen of the chronicler, who is unwarily enlisting the feelings of the reader in favour of the hapless warrior whom he reviles. "Philip," he says, "like a savage wild beast, having been hunted by the English forces through the woods above a hundred miles backward and forward, at last was driven to his own den upon Mount Hope, where he retired with a few of his best friends, into a swamp, which proved but a prison to keep him fast till the messengers of death came by divine permission to execute vengeance upon him."

Even in this last refuge of desperation and despair a sullen grandeur gathers round his memory. We picture him to ourselves seated among his care worn followers, brooding in silence over his blasted fortunes, and acquiring a savage sublimity from the wildness and dreariness of his lurking place. Defeated, but not dismayed—crushed to the earth, but not humiliated—he seemed to grow more haughty beneath disaster, and to experience a fierce satisfaction in draining the last dregs of bitterness. Little minds are tamed and subdued by misfortune; but great minds rise above it. The very idea of submission awakened the fury of Philip, and he smote to death one of his followers, who proposed an expedient of peace. The brother of the victim made his escape, and in revenge betrayed the retreat of his chieftain. A body of white men and Indians were immediately despatched to the swamp where Philip lay crouched, glaring with fury and despair. Before he was aware of their approach, they had begun to surround him. In a little while he saw five of his trustiest followers laid dead at his feet; all resistance was vain; he rushed forth from his covert, and made a head-long attempt at escape, but was shot through the heart by a renegado Indian of his own nation.

Such is the scanty story of the brave, but unfortunate King Philip; persecuted while living, slandered and dishonoured when dead. If, however, we consider even the prejudiced anecdotes furnished us by his enemies, we may perceive in them traces of amiable and lofty character, sufficient to awaken sympathy for his fate, and respect for his memory. We find, that amidst all the harassing cares and ferocious passions of constant warfare, he was alive to the softer feelings of connubial love and paternal tenderness, and to the generous sentiment of friendship. The captivity of his "beloved wife and only son" are mentioned with exultation, as causing him poignant misery: the death of any near friend is triumphantly recorded as a new blow on his sensibilities; but the treachery and desertion of many of his followers, in whose affections he had confided, is said to have desolated his heart, and to have bereaved him of all further comfort. He was a patriot attached to his native soil—a prince true to his subjects, and indignant of their wrongs—a soldier, daring in battle, firm in adversity, patient of fatigue, of hunger, of every variety of bodily suffering, and ready to perish in the cause he had espoused. Proud of heart, and with an untameable love of natural liberty, he preferred to enjoy it among the beasts of the forests, or in the dismal and famished recesses of swamps and morasses, rather than bow his haughty spirit to submission, and live dependent and despised in the ease and luxury of the settlements. With heroic qualities and bold achievements that would have graced a civilized warrior, and have rendered him the theme of the poet and the historian; he lived a wanderer and a fugitive in his native land, and went down, like a lonely bark foundering amid darkness and tempest—without a pitying eye to weep his fall, or a friendly hand to record his struggle.

JOHN BULL

An old song, made by an aged old pate,
Of an old worshipful gentleman who had a great estate,
That kept a brave old house at a bountiful rate,
And an old porter to relieve the poor at his gate.

With an old study fill'd full of learned old books,
With an old reverend chaplain, you might know him by his looks,
With an old buttery-hatch worn quite off the hooks,
And an old kitchen that maintained half-a-dozen old cooks,
                    Like an old courtier, &c.
                                    OLD SONG.

There is no species of humour in which the English more excel, than
that which consists in caricaturing and giving ludicrous appellations,
or nick names. In this way they have whimsically designated, not merely
individuals, but nations; and in their fondness for pushing a joke, they
have not spared even themselves. One would think, that in personifying
itself, a nation would be apt to picture something grand, heroic, and
imposing; but it is characteristic of the peculiar humour of the English,
and of their love for what is blunt, comic, and familiar, that they have
embodied their national oddities in the figure of a sturdy, corpulent
old fellow, with a three cornered hat, red waistcoat, leather breeches,
and stout oaken cudgel. Thus they have taken a singular delight in
exhibiting their most private foibles in a laughable point of view,
and have been so successful in their delineations, that there is scarcely
a being in actual existence more absolutely present to the public mind,
than that eccentric personage, John Bull.

Perhaps the continual contemplation of the character thus drawn
of them, has contributed to fix it upon the nation; and thus to give
reality to what at first may have been painted in a great measure
from the imagination. Men are apt to acquire peculiarities that are
continually ascribed to them. The common orders of English seem
wonderfully captivated with the *beau ideal* which they have formed
of John Bull, and endeavour to act up to the broad caricature that is
perpetually before their eyes. Unluckily, they sometimes make their
boasted Bull-ism an apology for their prejudice or grossness; and this
I have especially noticed among those truly homebred and genuine
sons of the soil, who have never migrated beyond the sound of Bow
bells. If one of these should be a little uncouth in speech, and apt

to utter impertinent truths, he confesses that he is a real John Bull, and always speaks his mind. If he now and then flies into an unreasonable burst of passion about trifles, he observes, that John Bull is a choleric old blade, but then his passion is over in a moment, and he bears no malice. If he betrays a coarseness of taste, and an insensibility to foreign refinements, he thanks heaven for his ignorance—he is a plain John Bull, and has no relish for frippery and nick-nacks. His very proneness to be gulled by strangers, and to pay extravagantly for absurdities, is excused under the plea of munificence—for John is always more generous than wise.

Thus, under the name of John Bull, he will contrive to argue every fault into a merit, and will frankly convict himself of being the honestest fellow in existence.

However little, therefore, the character may have suited in the first instance, it has gradually adapted itself to the nation, or rather, they have adapted themselves to each other; and a stranger who wishes to study English peculiarities, may gather much valuable information from the innumerable portraits of John Bull, as exhibited in the windows of the caricature shops. Still, however, he is one of those fertile humourists, that are continually throwing out new portraits, and presenting different aspects from different points of view; and often as he has been described, I cannot resist the temptation to give a slight sketch of him, such as he has met my eye.

John Bull, to all appearance, is a plain, downright, matter of fact fellow, with much less of poetry about him than rich prose. There is little of romance in his nature, but a vast deal of strong natural feeling. He excels in humour, more than in wit; is jolly, rather than gay; melancholy, rather than morose; can easily be moved to a sudden tear, or surprised into a broad laugh; but he loathes sentiment, and has no turn for light pleasantry. He is a boon companion, if you allow him to have his humour, and to talk about himself; and he will stand by a friend in a quarrel, with life and purse, however soundly he may be cudgelled.

In this last respect, to tell the truth, he has a propensity to be somewhat too ready. He is a busy minded personage, who thinks not merely for himself and family, but for all the country round, and is most generously disposed to be every body's champion. He is continually volunteering his services to settle his neighbours' affairs, and takes it in great dudgeon if they engage in any matter of consequence without asking his advice, though he seldom engages in any friendly office of the kind without finishing by getting into a squabble with all parties, and then railing bitterly at their ingratitude. He unluckily took lessons in his youth in the noble science of defence, and having accomplished himself in the use of his limbs and his weapons, and become a perfect master at boxing and cudgel play, he has had a troublesome life of it ever since. He cannot hear of a quarrel between the most distant of his neighbours, but he begins incontinently to fumble with the head of his cudgel, and consider whether his interest or honour does not require that he should meddle in the broil. Indeed, he has extended his relations of pride and policy so completely over the whole country, that no event can take place, without infringing some of his finely spun rights and dignities. Couched in his little domain, with these filaments stretching forth in every direction, he is like some choleric, bottle bellied old spider, who has woven his web over a whole chamber, so that a fly cannot buzz, nor a breeze blow, without startling his repose, and causing him to sally forth wrathfully from his den.

Though really a good hearted, good tempered old fellow at bottom, yet he is singularly fond of being in the midst of contention. It is one of his peculiarities, however, that he only relishes the beginning of an affray: he always goes into a fight with alacrity, but comes out of it grumbling even when victorious; and though no one fights with more obstinacy to carry a contested point, yet, when the battle is over, and he comes to the reconciliation, he is so much taken up with the mere shaking of hands, that he is apt to let his antagonist pocket all that they have been quarrelling about. It is not, therefore, fighting that he ought so much to be on his guard against, as making friends. It is difficult to cudgel him out of a farthing, but put him in a good humour, and you may bargain him out of all the money in his pocket. He is like a stout ship, which will weather the roughest storm uninjured, but roll its masts overboard in the succeeding calm.

He is a little fond of playing the magnifico abroad; of pulling out a long purse; flinging his money bravely about at boxing matches, horse races, and cock fights, and carrying a high head among "gentlemen of the fancy;" but immediately after one of these fits of extravagance, he will be taken with violent qualms of economy; stop short at the most trivial expenditure; talk desperately of being ruined, and brought upon the parish; and in such moods, will not pay the smallest tradesman's bill, without violent altercation. He is, in fact, the most punctual and discontented paymaster in the world; drawing his coin out of his breeches' pocket with infinite reluctance, paying to the uttermost farthing, but accompanying every guinea with a growl.

With all his talk of economy, however, he is a bountiful provider, and a hospitable housekeeper. His economy is of a whimsical kind, its chief object being to devise how he may afford to be extravagant, for he will begrudge himself a beef steak and pint of port one day, that he may roast an ox whole, broach a hogshead of ale, and treat all his neighbours, on the next.

His domestic establishment is enormously expensive, not so much from any great outward parade, as from the great consumption of solid beef and pudding, the vast number of followers he feeds and clothes, and his singular disposition to pay hugely for small services. He is a most kind and indulgent master, and, provided his servants humour his peculiarities, flatter his vanity a little now and then, and do not peculate grossly on him before his face, they may manage him to perfection. Every thing that lives on him seems to thrive and grow fat. His house servants are well paid, and pampered, and have little to do. His horses are sleek and lazy, and prance slowly before his state carriage, and his house dogs sleep quietly about the door, and will hardly bark at a house breaker.

His family mansion is an old castellated manor house, grey with age, and of a most venerable though weather beaten appearance. It has been built upon no regular plan, but is a vast accumulation of parts, erected in various tastes and ages. The centre bears evident traces of Saxon architecture, and is as solid as ponderous stone and old English oak can make it. Like all the reliques of that style, it is full of obscure passages, intricate mazes, and dusky chambers; and though these have been partially lighted up in modern days, yet there are many places where you must still grope in the dark. Additions have been made to the original edifice from time to time, and great alterations have taken place; towers and battlements have been erected during wars and tumults; wings built in times of peace, and outhouses, lodges, and offices, run up according to the whim or convenience of different generations, until it has become one of the most spacious, rambling tenements imaginable. An entire wing is taken up with the family chapel, a reverend pile that must once have been exceedingly sumptuous, and, indeed, in spite of having been altered and simplified at various periods, has still a look of solemn religious pomp. Its walls within are storied with the monuments of John's ancestors, and it is snugly fitted up with soft cushions and well lined chairs, where such of his family as are inclined to church services, may doze comfortably in the discharge of their duties.

To keep up this chapel has cost John much money; but he is staunch in his religion, and piqued in his zeal, from the circumstance that many dissenting chapels have been erected in his vicinity, and several of his neighbours, with whom he has had quarrels, are strong papists.

To do the duties of the chapel, he maintains, at a large expense, a pious and portly family chaplain. He is a most learned and decorous personage, and a truly well bred christian, who always backs the old gentleman in his opinions, winks discreetly at his little peccadilloes, rebukes the children when refractory, and is of great use in exhorting the tenants to read their bibles, say their prayers, and above all, to pay their rents punctually, and without grumbling.

The family apartments are in a very antiquated taste, somewhat heavy, and often inconvenient, but full of the solemn magnificence of former times; fitted up with rich though faded tapestry, unwieldy furniture, and loads of massy gorgeous old plate. The vast fire places, ample kitchens, extensive cellars, and sumptuous banquetting halls, all speak of the roaring hospitality of days of yore, of which the modern festivity at the manor house is but a shadow. There are, however, complete suites of rooms apparently deserted and time worn; and towers and turrets that are tottering to decay, so that in high winds there is danger of their tumbling about the ears of the household.

John has frequently been advised to have the old edifice thoroughly overhauled, and to have some of the useless parts pulled down, and the others strengthened with their materials; but the old gentleman always grows testy on this subject. He swears the house is an excellent house—that it is tight and weather proof, and not to be shaken by tempests—that it has stood for several hundred years, and, therefore, is not likely to tumble down now—that as to its being inconvenient, his family is accustomed to the inconveniences, and would not be comfortable without them—that as to its unwieldy size and irregular construction, these result from its being the growth of centuries, and being improved by the wisdom of every generation—that an old family, like his, requires a large house to dwell in; new, upstart families may live in modern cottages and snug boxes, but an old English family should inhabit an old English manor house. If you point out any part of the building as superfluous, he insists that it is material to the strength or decoration of the rest, and the harmony of the whole, and swears, that the parts are so built into each other, that if you pull down one, you run the risk of having the whole about your ears.

The secret of the matter is, that John has a great disposition to protect and patronize. He thinks it indispensable to the dignity of an ancient and honourable family, to be bounteous in its appointments, and to be eaten up by dependants; and so, partly from pride, and partly from kind heartedness, he makes it a rule always to give shelter and maintenance to his superannuated servants.

The consequence is, that like many other venerable family establishments, his manor is incumbered by old retainers whom he cannot turn

off, and an old style which he cannot lay down. His mansion is like a
great hospital of invalids, and, with all its magnitude, is not a whit
too large for its inhabitants. Not a nook or corner but is of use in
housing some useless personage. Groups of veteran beef eaters, gouty
pensioners, and retired heroes of the buttery and the larder, are seen
lolling about its walls, crawling over its lawns, dozing under its trees,
or sunning themselves upon the benches at its doors. Every office and
out house is garrisoned by these supernumeraries and their families,
for they are amazingly prolific; and when they die off, are sure to
leave John a legacy of hungry mouths to be provided for. A mattock
cannot be struck against the most mouldering, tumble down tower,
but out pops, from some cranny or loop hole, the gray pate of some
superannuated hanger on, who has lived at John's expense all his life,
and makes the most grievous outcry, at their pulling down the roof
from over the head of a worn out servant of the family. This is an
appeal that John's honest heart never can withstand; so that a man,
who has faithfully eaten his beef and pudding all his life, is sure to be
rewarded with a pipe and tankard in his old days.

A great part of his park, also, is turned into paddocks, where his
broken down chargers are turned loose, to graze undisturbed for the
remainder of their existence—a worthy example of grateful recollection,
which, if some of his neighbours were to imitate, would not be to
their discredit. Indeed, it is one of his great pleasures to point out
these old steeds to his visiters, to dwell on their good qualities, extol their
past services, and boast, with some little vain glory, of the perilous
adventures and hardy exploits, through which they have carried him.

He is given, however, to indulge his veneration for family usages,
and family incumbrances, to a whimsical extent. His manor is infested
by gangs of gipsies, yet he will not suffer them to be driven off, because
they have infested the place time out of mind, and been regular
poachers upon every generation of the family. He will scarcely permit
a dry branch to be lopped from the great trees that surround the
house, lest it should molest the rooks, that have bred there for centuries.
Owls have taken possession of the dovecote; but they are hereditary
owls, and must not be disturbed. Swallows have nearly choked up
every chimney with their nests; martins build in every frieze and
cornice; crows flutter about the towers, and perch on every weather
cock; and old gray headed rats may be seen in every quarter of the
house, running in and out of their holes undauntedly, in broad daylight.
In short, John has such a reverence for every thing that has been long
in the family, that he will not hear even of abuses being reformed,
because they are good old family abuses.

All these whims and habits have concurred wofully to drain the old gentleman's purse; and as he prides himself on punctuality in money matters, and wishes to maintain his credit in the neighbourhood, they have caused him great perplexity in meeting his engagements. This too has been increased, by the altercations and heartburnings which are continually taking place in his family. His children have been brought up to different callings, and are of different ways of thinking; and as they have always been allowed to speak their minds freely, they do not fail to exercise the privilege most clamorously in the present posture of his affairs. Some stand up for the honour of the race, and are clear that the old establishment should be kept up in all its state, whatever may be the cost; others, who are more prudent and considerate, entreat the old gentleman to retrench his expenses, and to put his whole system of housekeeping on a more moderate footing. He has, indeed, at times seemed inclined to listen to their opinions, but their wholesome advice has been completely defeated by the obstreperous conduct of one of his sons. This is a noisy rattle pated fellow, of rather low habits, who neglects his business to frequent ale houses—is the orator of village clubs, and a complete oracle among the poorest of his father's tenants. No sooner does he hear any of his brothers mention reform or retrenchment, than up he jumps, takes the words out of their mouths, and roars out for an overturn. When his tongue is once going, nothing can stop it. He rants about the room, hectors the old man about his spendthrift practices, ridicules his tastes and pursuits, insists that he shall turn the old servants out of doors, give the broken down horses to the hounds, send the fat chaplain packing, and take a field preacher in his place—nay, that the whole family mansion shall be levelled with the ground, and a plain one of brick and mortar built in its place. He rails at every social entertainment and family festivity, and skulks away growling to the ale house whenever an equipage drives up to the door. Though constantly complaining of the emptiness of his purse, yet he scruples not to spend all his pocket money in these tavern convocations, and even runs up scores for the liquor over which he preaches about his father's extravagance.

It may readily be imagined, how little such thwarting agrees with the old cavalier's fiery temperament. He has become so irritable, from repeated crossings, that the mere mention of retrenchment or reform is a signal for a brawl between him and the tavern oracle. As the latter is too sturdy and refractory for paternal discipline, having grown out of all fear of the cudgel, they have frequent scenes of wordy warfare, which at times run so high, that John is fain to call in the aid of his son Tom, an officer who has served abroad, but is at present

living at home, on half pay. This last is sure to stand by the old gentleman, right or wrong; likes nothing so much as a racketing, roystering
life, and is ready, at a wink or nod, to out sabre, and flourish it over
the orator's head, if he dares to array himself against paternal authority.

These family dissensions, as usual, have got abroad, and are rare
food for scandal in John's neighbourhood. People begin to look wise,
and shake their heads, whenever his affairs are mentioned. They all
"hope that matters are not so bad with him as represented; but when
a man's own children begin to rail at his extravagance, things must
be badly managed. They understand he is mortgaged over head and
ears, and is continually dabbling with money lenders. He is certainly
an open handed old gentleman, but they fear he has lived too fast;
indeed, they never knew any good come of this fondness for hunting,
racing, revelling, and prize fighting. In short, Mr. Bull's estate is a
very fine one, and has been in the family a long while; but for all that,
they have known many finer estates come to the hammer."

What is worst of all, is the effect which these pecuniary embarrass-
ments and domestic feuds have had on the poor man himself. Instead
of that jolly round corporation, and smug rosy face, which he used
to present, he has of late become as shrivelled and shrunk as a frost
bitten apple. His scarlet gold laced waistcoat, which bellied out so
bravely in those prosperous days when he sailed before the wind, now
hangs loosely about him like a mainsail in a calm. His leather breeches
are all in folds and wrinkles, and apparently have much ado to hold up
the boots that yawn on both sides of his once sturdy legs.

Instead of strutting about, as formerly, with his three cornered hat
on one side, flourishing his cudgel, and bringing it down every moment
with a hearty thump upon the ground, looking every one sturdily in
the face, and trolling out a stave of a catch or a drinking song, he
now goes about, whistling thoughtfully to himself, with his head
drooping down, his cudgel tucked under his arm, and his hands thrust
to the bottom of his breeches' pockets, which are evidently empty.

Such is the plight of honest John Bull at present; yet for all this,
the old fellow's spirit is as tall and as gallant as ever. If you drop the
least expression of sympathy or concern, he takes fire in an instant;
swears that he is the richest and stoutest fellow in the country; talks
of laying out large sums to adorn his house, or to buy another estate;
and, with a valiant swagger and grasping of his cudgel, longs exceedingly to have another bout at quarter staff.

Though there may be something rather whimsical in all this, yet I
confess I cannot look upon John's situation, without strong feelings of
interest. With all his odd humours, and obstinate prejudices, he is a

sterling hearted old blade. He may not be so wonderfully fine a fellow as he thinks himself, but he is at least twice as good as his neighbours represent him. His virtues are all his own; all plain, homebred and unaffected. His very faults smack of the raciness of his good qualities. His extravagance savours of his generosity; his quarrelsomeness of his courage; his credulity of his open faith; his vanity of his pride; and his bluntness of his sincerity. They are all the redundancies of a rich and liberal character. He is like his own oak; rough without, but sound and solid within; whose bark abounds with excrescences in proportion to the growth and grandeur of the timber; and whose branches make a fearful groaning and murmuring in the least storm, from their very magnitude and luxuriance. There is something, too, in the appearance of his old family mansion, that is extremely poetical and picturesque; and as long as it can be rendered comfortably habitable, I should almost tremble to see it meddled with during the present conflict of tastes and opinions. Some of his advisors are no doubt good architects that might be of service; but many I fear are mere levellers, who when they had once got to work with their mattocks on the venerable edifice, would never stop until they had brought it to the ground, and perhaps buried themselves among the ruins. All that I wish is, that John's present troubles may teach him more prudence in future. That he may cease to distress his mind about other people's affairs; that he may give up the fruitless attempt to promote the good of his neighbours, and the peace and happiness of the world, by dint of the cudgel; that he may remain quietly at home; gradually get his house into repair; cultivate his rich estate according to his fancy; husband his income, if he thinks proper; bring his unruly children into order if he can; renew the jovial scenes of ancient prosperity, and long enjoy, on his paternal lands, a green, an honourable, and a merry old age.

THE
PRIDE OF THE VILLAGE

May no wolf howle; no screech owle stir
A wing about thy sepulchre!
No boysterous winds or stormes come hither,
      To starve or wither
Thy soft sweet earth! but like a spring
Love keep it ever flourishing.

HERRICK.

In the course of an excursion through one of the remote counties of
England, I had struck into one of those cross roads that lead through
the more secluded parts of the country, and stopped one afternoon at
a village, the situation of which was beautifully rural and retired. There
was an air of primitive simplicity about its inhabitants, not to be
found in the villages which lie on the great coach roads. I determined
to pass the night there, and having taken an early dinner, strolled out
to enjoy the neighbouring scenery.

My ramble, as is usually the case with travellers, soon led me to
the church, which stood at a little distance from the village. Indeed,
it was an object of some curiosity, its old tower being completely overrun with ivy, so that only here and there a jutting buttress, an angle
of grey wall, or a fantastically carved ornament, peered through the
verdant covering. It was a lovely evening. The early part of the day
had been dark and showery, but in the afternoon it had cleared up,
and though sullen clouds still hung over head, yet there was a broad
tract of golden sky in the west, from which the setting sun gleamed
through the dripping leaves, and lit up all nature into a melancholy
smile. It seemed like the parting hour of a good christian, smiling on
the sins and sorrows of the world, and giving, in the serenity of his
decline, an assurance that he will rise again in glory.

I had seated myself on a half sunken tombstone, and was musing,
as one is apt to do at this sober thoughted hour, on past scenes, and
early friends—on those who were distant, and those who were dead—
and indulging in that kind of melancholy fancying, which has in it
something sweeter even than pleasure. Every now and then, the stroke
of a bell from the neighbouring tower fell on my ear; its tones were
in unison with the scene, and instead of jarring, chimed in with my
feelings, and it was some time before I recollected, that it must be
tolling the knell of some new tenant of the tomb.

Presently I saw a funeral train moving across the village green; it wound slowly along a lane, was lost, and reappeared through the breaks of the hedges, until it passed the place where I was sitting. The pall was supported by young girls, dressed in white, and another, about the age of seventeen, walked before, bearing a chaplet of white flowers; a token that the deceased was a young and unmarried female. The corpse was followed by the parents. They were a venerable couple of the better order of peasantry. The father seemed to repress his feelings; but his fixed eye, contracted brow, and deeply furrowed face, showed the struggle that was passing within. His wife hung on his arm, and wept aloud with the convulsive bursts of a mother's sorrow.

I followed the funeral into the church. The bier was placed in the centre aisle, and the chaplet of white flowers, with a pair of white gloves, were hung over the seat which the deceased had occupied.

Every one knows the soul subduing pathos of the funeral service; for who is so fortunate as never to have followed some one he has loved to the tomb; but when performed over the remains of innocence and beauty, thus laid low in the bloom of existence—what can be more affecting? At that simple, but most solemn consignment of the body to the grave—"Earth to earth—ashes to ashes—dust to dust!" the tears of the youthful companions of the deceased flowed unrestrained. The father still seemed to struggle with his feelings, and to comfort himself with the assurance, that the dead are blessed which die in the Lord; but the mother only thought of her child as a flower of the field, cut down and withered in the midst of its sweetness; she was like Rachel, "mourning over her children, and would not be comforted."

On returning to the inn, I learnt the whole story of the deceased. It was a simple one, and such as has often been told. She had been the beauty and pride of the village. Her father had once been an opulent farmer, but was reduced in circumstances. This was an only child, and brought up entirely at home, in the simplicity of rural life. She had been the pupil of the village pastor, the favourite lamb of his little flock. The good man watched over her education with paternal care; it was limited, and suitable to the sphere in which she was to move, for he only sought to make her an ornament to her station in life, not to raise her above it. The tenderness and indulgence of her parents, and the exemption from all ordinary occupations, had fostered a natural grace and delicacy of character, that accorded with the fragile loveliness of her form. She appeared like some tender plant of the garden, blooming accidentally amid the hardier natives of the fields.

The superiority of her charms was felt and acknowledged by her companions, but without envy, for it was surpassed by the unassuming

gentleness and winning kindness of her manners. It might be truly
said of her,

> "This is the prettiest low-born lass, that ever
> Ran on the green-sward: nothing she does or seems,
> But smacks of something greater than herself;
> Too noble for this place."

The village was one of those sequestered spots, which still retain
some vestiges of old English customs. It had its rural festivals and
holyday pastimes, and still kept up some faint observance of the once
popular rites of May. These, indeed, had been promoted by its present
pastor; who was a lover of old customs, and one of those simple Christians
that think their mission fulfilled by promoting joy on earth and good
will among mankind. Under his auspices the May pole stood from
year to year in the centre of the village green; on May day it was
decorated with garlands and streamers; and a queen or lady of the
May was appointed, as in former times, to preside at the sports, and
distribute the prizes and rewards. The picturesque situation of the
village, and the fancifulness of its rustic fetes would often attract the
notice of casual visitors. Among these, on one May day, was a young
officer, whose regiment had been recently quartered in the neighbourhood. He was charmed with the native taste that pervaded this village
pageant; but, above all, with the dawning loveliness of the queen of
May. It was the village favourite, who was crowned with flowers, and
blushing and smiling in all the beautiful confusion of girlish diffidence
and delight. The artlessness of rural habits enabled him readily to
make her acquaintance; he gradually won his way into her intimacy;
and paid his court to her in that unthinking way in which young
officers are too apt to trifle with rustic simplicity.

There was nothing in his advances to startle or alarm. He never
even talked of love; but there are modes of making it, more eloquent
than language, and which convey it subtilely and irresistibly to the
heart. The beam of the eye, the tone of voice, the thousand tender-
nesses which emanate from every word, and look, and action—these
form the true eloquence of love, and can always be felt and understood, but never described. Can we wonder that they should readily
win a heart, young, guileless, and susceptible? As to her, she loved
almost unconsciously; she scarcely inquired what was the growing
passion that was absorbing every thought and feeling, or what were
to be its consequences. She, indeed, looked not to the future. When
present, his looks and words occupied her whole attention; when

absent, she thought but of what had passed at their recent interview. She would wander with him through the green lanes and rural scenes of the vicinity. He taught her to see new beauties in nature: he talked in the language of polite and cultivated life, and breathed into her ear the witcheries of romance and poetry.

Perhaps there could not have been a passion, between the sexes, more pure than this innocent girl's. The gallant figure of her youthful admirer, and the splendour of his military attire, might at first have charmed her eye; but it was not these that had captivated her heart. Her attachment had something in it of idolatry. She looked up to him as to a being of a superior order. She felt in his society the enthusiasm of a mind naturally delicate and poetical, and now first awakened to a keen perception of the beautiful and grand. Of the sordid distinctions of rank and fortune, she thought nothing; it was the difference of intellect, of demeanor, of manners, from those of the rustic society to which she had been accustomed, that elevated him in her opinion. She would listen to him with charmed ear and downcast look of mute delight, and her cheek would mantle with enthusiasm; or if ever she ventured a shy glance of timid admiration, it was as quickly withdrawn, and she would sigh and blush at the idea of her comparative unworthiness.

Her lover was equally impassioned; but his passion was mingled with feelings of a coarser nature. He had begun the connexion in levity; for he had often heard his brother officers boast of their village conquests, and thought some triumph of the kind necessary to his reputation as a man of spirit. But he was too full of youthful fervour. His heart had not yet been rendered sufficiently cold and selfish by a wandering and a dissipated life: it caught fire from the very flame it sought to kindle; and before he was aware of the nature of his situation, he became really in love.

What was he to do? There were the old obstacles which so incessantly occur in these heedless attachments. His rank in life—the prejudices of titled connexions—his dependance upon a proud and unyielding father—all forbad him to think of matrimony:—but when he looked down upon this innocent being, so tender and confiding, there was a purity in her manners, a blamelessness in her life, and a beseeching modesty in her looks, that awed down every licentious feeling. In vain did he try to fortify himself, by a thousand heartless examples of men of fashion, and to chill the glow of generous sentiment, with that cold derisive levity with which he had heard them talk of female virtue; whenever he came into her presence, she was still surrounded by that mysterious, but impassive charm of virgin purity, in whose hallowed sphere no guilty thought can live.

The sudden arrival of orders for the regiment to repair to the continent, completed the confusion of his mind. He remained for a short time in a state of the most painful irresolution; he hesitated to communicate the tidings, until the day for marching was at hand; when he gave her the intelligence in the course of an evening ramble.

The idea of parting had never before occurred to her. It broke in at once upon her dream of felicity; she looked upon it as a sudden and insurmountable evil, and wept with the guileless simplicity of a child. He drew her to his bosom, and kissed the tears from her soft cheek, nor did he meet with a repulse, for there are moments of mingled sorrow and tenderness, which hallow the caresses of affection. He was naturally impetuous, and the sight of beauty apparently yielding in his arms, the confidence of his power over her, and the dread of losing her forever, all conspired to overwhelm his better feelings—he ventured to propose that she should leave her home, and be the companion of his fortunes.

He was quite a novice in seduction, and blushed and faltered at his own baseness; but so innocent of mind was his intended victim, that she was at first at a loss to comprehend his meaning;—and why she should leave her native village, and the humble roof of her parents. When at last the nature of his proposals flashed upon her pure mind, the effect was withering. She did not weep—she did not break forth into reproach—she said not a word—but she shrunk back aghast as from a viper, gave him a look of anguish that pierced to his very soul, and clasping her hands in agony, fled, as if for refuge, to her father's cottage.

The officer retired, confounded, humiliated, and repentant. It is uncertain what might have been the result of the conflict of his feelings, had not his thoughts been diverted by the bustle of departure. New scenes, new pleasures, and new companions, soon dissipated his self reproach, and stifled his tenderness. Yet, amidst the stir of camps, the revelries of garrisons, the array of armies, and even the din of battles, his thoughts would sometimes steal back to the scene of rural quiet and village simplicity—the white cottage—the footpath along the silver brook and up the hawthorn hedge, and the little village maid loitering along it, leaning on his arm, and listening to him with eyes beaming with unconscious affection.

The shock which the poor girl had received, in the destruction of all her ideal world, had indeed been cruel. Faintings and hystericks had at first shaken her tender frame, and were succeeded by a settled and pining melancholy. She had beheld from her window the march of the departing troops. She had seen her faithless lover borne off, as if in triumph, amidst the sound of drum and trumpet, and the pomp of arms. She strained a last aching gaze after him, as the morning sun glittered about his figure, and his plume waved in the breeze: he passed away like a bright vision from her sight, and left her all in darkness.

It would be trite to dwell on the particulars of her after story. It was, like other tales of love, melancholy. She avoided society, and wandered out alone in the walks she had most frequented with her lover. She sought, like the stricken deer, to weep in silence and loneliness, and brood over the barbed sorrow that rankled in her soul. Sometimes she would be seen late of an evening sitting in the porch of the village church; and the milkmaids, returning from the fields, would now and then overhear her singing some plaintive ditty in the hawthorn walk. She became fervent in her devotions at church, and as the old people saw her approach, so wasted away, yet with a hectic bloom, and that hallowed air which melancholy diffuses round the form, they would make way for her, as for something spiritual, and, looking after her, would shake their heads in gloomy foreboding.

She felt a conviction that she was hastening to the tomb, but looked forward to it as a place of rest. The silver cord that had bound her to existence was loosed, and there seemed to be no more pleasure under the sun. If ever her gentle bosom had entertained resentment against her lover, it was extinguished. She was incapable of angry passions, and in a moment of saddened tenderness, she penned him a farewell letter. It was couched in the simplest language; but touching from its very simplicity. She told him that she was dying, and did not conceal from him that his conduct was the cause. She even depicted the sufferings which she had experienced; but concluded with saying, that she could not die in peace, until she had sent him her forgiveness and her blessing.

By degrees her strength declined, and she could no longer leave the cottage. She could only totter to the window, where, propped up in her chair, it was her enjoyment to sit all day and look out upon the landscape. Still she uttered no complaint, nor imparted to any one the malady that was preying on her heart. She never even mentioned her lover's name; but would lay her head on her mother's bosom and weep in silence. Her poor parents hung, in mute anxiety, over this fading blossom of their hopes, still flattering themselves that it might again revive to freshness, and that the bright unearthly bloom which sometimes flushed her cheek might be the promise of returning health.

In this way she was seated between them one Sunday afternoon; her hands were clasped in theirs, the lattice was thrown open, and the soft air that stole in, brought with it the fragrance of the clustering honeysuckle, which her own hands had trained round the window.

Her father had just been reading a chapter in the bible; it spoke of the vanity of worldly things, and of the joys of heaven; it seemed to have diffused comfort and serenity through her bosom. Her eye was fixed on the distant village church—the bell had tolled for the evening service—the last villager was lagging into the porch—and every thing had sunk into that hallowed stillness peculiar to the day of rest. Her parents were gazing on her with yearning hearts. Sickness and sorrow, which pass so roughly over some faces, had given to hers the expression of a seraph's. A tear trembled in her soft blue eye.—Was she thinking of her faithless lover?—or were her thoughts wandering to that distant church yard, into whose bosom she might soon be gathered?

Suddenly the clang of hoofs was heard—a horseman gallopped to the cottage—he dismounted before the window—the poor girl gave a faint exclamation, and sunk back in her chair:—it was her repentant lover! He rushed into the house, and flew to clasp her to his bosom; but her wasted form—her death like countenance—so wan, yet so lovely in its desolation, smote him to the soul, and he threw himself in an agony at her feet. She was too faint to rise—she attempted to extend her trembling hand—her lips moved as if she spoke, but no word was articulated—she looked down upon him with a smile of unutterable tenderness, and closed her eyes forever.

Such are the particulars which I gathered of this village story. They are but scanty, and I am conscious have little novelty to recommend them. In the present rage also for strange incident and high seasoned narrative, they may appear trite and insignificant, but they interested me strongly at the time; and, taken in connexion with the affecting ceremony which I had just witnessed, left a deeper impression on my mind than many circumstances of a more striking nature. I have passed through the place since, and visited the church again from a better motive than mere curiosity. It was a wintry evening; the trees were stripped of their foliage; the church yard looked naked and mournful, and the wind rustled coldly through the dry grass. Evergreens, however, had been planted about the grave of the village favourite, and osiers were bent over it to keep the turf uninjured.

The church door was open, and I stepped in. There hung the chaplet of flowers and the gloves, as on the day of the funeral: the flowers were withered, it is true, but care seemed to have been taken that no dust should soil their whiteness. I have seen many monuments, where art has exhausted its powers to awaken the sympathy of the spectator, but I have met with none that spoke more touchingly to my heart, than this simple, but delicate memento of departed innocence.

THE ANGLER

This day dame Nature seemed in love,
The lusty sap began to move,
Fresh juice did stir th' embracing vines,
And birds had drawn their valentines.
The jealous trout that low did lie,
Rose at a well dissembled flie,
There stood my friend, with patient skill,
Attending of his trembling quill.
                              SIR H. WOTTON.

It is said that many an unlucky urchin is induced to run away from
his family, and betake himself to a seafaring life, from reading the
history of Robinson Crusoe; and I suspect that, in like manner, many
of those worthy gentlemen, who are given to haunt the sides of pastoral
streams with angle rods in hand, may trace the origin of their passion
to the seductive pages of honest Izaak Walton. I recollect studying
his "Complete Angler" several years since, in company with a knot
of friends in America, and moreover that we were all completely bitten
with the angling mania. It was early in the year; but as soon as the
weather was auspicious, and that the spring began to melt into the
verge of summer, we took rod in hand and sallied into the country,
as stark mad as was ever Don Quixote from reading books of chivalry.

One of our party had equalled the Don in the fullness of his equipments; being attired cap-a-pie for the enterprize. He wore a broad
skirted fustian coat, perplexed with half a hundred pockets; a pair of
stout shoes, and leathern gaiters; a basket slung on one side for fish;
a patent rod; a landing net, and a score of other inconveniencies, only
to be found in the true angler's armoury. Thus harnessed for the field,
he was as great a matter of stare and wonderment among the country
folk, who had never seen a regular angler, as was the steel clad hero
of La Mancha among the goatherds of the Sierra Morena.

Our first essay was along a mountain brook, among the highlands
of the Hudson; a most unfortunate place for the execution of those
piscatory tactics which had been invented along the velvet margins
of quiet English rivulets. It was one of those wild streams that lavish,
among our romantic solitudes, unheeded beauties, enough to fill the
sketch book of a hunter of the picturesque. Sometimes it would leap
down rocky shelves, making small cascades, over which the trees
threw their broad balancing sprays, and long nameless weeds hung

in fringes from the impending banks, dripping with diamond drops. Sometimes it would brawl and fret along a ravine in the matted shade of a forest, filling it with murmurs; and after this termagant career, would steal forth into open day with the most placid demure face imaginable; as I have seen some pestilent shrew of a housewife, after filling her home with uproar and ill humour, come dimpling out of doors, swimming and curtseying, and smiling upon all the world.

How smoothly would this vagrant brook glide, at such times, through some bosom of green meadow land among the mountains; where the quiet was only interrupted by the occasional tinkling of a bell from the lazy cattle among the clover, or the sound of a woodcutter's axe from the neighbouring forest.

For my part, I was always a bungler at all kinds of sport that required either patience or adroitness, and had not angled above half an hour, before I had completely "satisfied the sentiment," and convinced myself of the truth of Izaak Walton's opinion, that angling is something like poetry—a man must be born to it. I hooked myself instead of the fish; tangled my line in every tree; lost my bait; broke my rod; until I gave up the attempt in despair, and passed the day under the trees, reading old Izaak; satisfied that it was his fascinating vein of honest simplicity and rural feeling that had bewitched me, and not the passion for angling. My companions, however, were more persevering in their delusion. I have them at this moment before my eyes, stealing along the border of the brook, where it lay open to the day, or was merely fringed by shrubs and bushes. I see the bittern rising with hollow scream as they break in upon his rarely invaded haunt; the kingfisher watching them suspiciously from his dry tree that overhangs the deep black mill pond, in the gorge of the hills; the tortoise letting himself slip sideways from off the stone or log on which he is sunning himself; and the panic struck frog plumping in headlong as they approach, and spreading an alarm throughout the watery world around.

I recollect also, that, after toiling and watching and creeping about for the greater part of a day, with scarcely any success, in spite of all our admirable apparatus, a lubberly country urchin came down from the hills with a rod made from a branch of a tree; a few yards of twine; and, as heaven shall help me! I believe a crooked pin for a hook, baited with a vile earth worm—and in half an hour caught more fish than we had nibbles throughout the day!

But above all, I recollect the "good, honest, wholesome, hungry" repast, which we made under a beech tree just by a spring of pure sweet water that stole out of the side of a hill; and how, when it was over, one of the party read old Izaak Walton's scene with the milk-maid, while I lay on the grass and built castles in a bright pile of clouds, until I fell asleep. All this may appear like mere egotism, yet I cannot refrain from uttering these recollections, which are passing like a strain of music over my mind and have been called up by an agreeable scene which I witnessed not long since.

In a morning's stroll along the banks of the Alun, a beautiful little stream which flows down from the Welsh hills and throws itself into the Dee, my attention was attracted to a group seated on the margin. On approaching, I found it to consist of a veteran angler and two rustic disciples. The former was an old fellow with a wooden leg, with clothes very much but very carefully patched, betokening poverty, honestly come by, and decently maintained. His face bore the marks of former storms, but present fair weather; its furrows had been worn into an habitual smile; his iron grey locks hung about his ears, and he had altogether the good humoured air of a constitutional philosopher, who was disposed to take the world as it went. One of his companions was a ragged wight, with the skulking look of an arrant poacher, and I'll warrant could find his way to any gentleman's fish pond in the neighbourhood in the darkest night. The other was a tall, awkward, country lad, with a lounging gait, and apparently somewhat of a rustic beau. The old man was busy in examining the maw of a trout which he had just killed, to discover by its contents what insects were seasonable for bait; and was lecturing on the subject to his companions, who appeared to listen with infinite deference. I have a kind feeling towards all "brothers of the angle," ever since I read Izaak Walton. They are men, he affirms, of a "mild, sweet and peaceable spirit"; and my esteem for them has been encreased since I met with an old "Tretyse of fishing with the Angle," in which are set forth many of the maxims of their inoffensive fraternity. "Take good hede," sayth this honest little tretyse, "that in going about your disportes ye open no man's gates but that ye shet them again. Also ye shall not use this forsayd crafti disport for no covetousness to the encreasing and sparing of your money only, but principally for your solace and to cause the helth of your body and specyally of your soule."*

---

*From this same treatise, it would appear that angling is a more industrious and devout employment than it is generally considered.—"For when ye purpose to go on your disportes in fishynge ye will not desyre greatlye many persons with you, which might let you of your game. And that ye may serve God devoutly in sayinge effectually your customable prayers. And thus doying, ye shall eschew and also avoyde many vices, as ydelnes, which is principall cause to induce man to many other vices, as it is right well known."

I thought that I could perceive in the veteran angler before me an exemplification of what I had read; and there was a chearful contentedness in his looks that quite drew me towards him. I could not but remark the gallant manner in which he stumped from one part of the brook to another; waving his rod in the air, to keep the line from dragging on the ground, or catching among the bushes; and the adroitness with which he would throw his fly to any particular place; sometimes skimming it lightly along a little rapid; sometimes casting it into one of those dark holes made by a twisted root or overhanging bank, in which the large trout are apt to lurk. In the meanwhile he was giving instructions to his two disciples; showing them the manner in which they should handle their rods, fix their flies, and play them along the surface of the stream. The scene brought to my mind the instructions of the sage Piscator to his scholar. The country around was of that pastoral kind which Walton is fond of describing. It was a part of the great plain of Cheshire, close by the beautiful vale of Gessford, and just where the inferior Welsh hills begin to swell up from among fresh sweet smelling meadows. The day, too, like that recorded in his work, was mild and sunshiny; with now and then a soft dropping shower, that sowed the whole earth with diamonds.

I soon fell into conversation with the old angler, and was so much entertained, that, under pretext of receiving instructions in his art, I kept company with him almost the whole day; wandering along the banks of the stream, and listening to his talk. He was very communicative, having all the easy garrulity of cheerful old age; and I fancy was a little flattered by having an opportunity of displaying his piscatory lore; for who does not like now and then to play the sage?

He had been much of a rambler in his day; and had passed some years of his youth in America, particularly in Savannah, where he had entered into trade and had been ruined by the indiscretion of a partner. He had afterwards experienced many ups and downs in life, until he got into the navy, where his leg was carried away by a cannon ball, at the battle of Camperdown. This was the only stroke of real good fortune he had ever experienced, for it got him a pension, which, together with some small paternal property, brought him in a revenue of nearly forty pounds. On this he retired to his native village, where he lived quietly and independently, and devoted the remainder of his life to the "noble art of angling."

I found that he had read Izaak Walton attentively, and he seemed to have imbibed all his simple frankness and prevalent good humour. Though he had been sorely buffeted about the world, he was satisfied that the world, in itself, was good and beautiful. Though he had been as roughly used in different countries as a poor sheep, that is fleeced by every hedge and thicket, yet he spoke of every nation with candour and kindness, appearing to look only on the good side of things; and above all, he was almost the only man I had ever met with, who had been an unfortunate adventurer in America, and had honesty and magnanimity enough, to take the fault to his own door, and not to curse the country. The lad that was receiving his instructions I learnt was the son and heir apparent of a fat old widow who kept the village inn, and of course a youth of some expectation, and much courted by the idle, gentleman like personages of the place. In taking him under his care, therefore, the old man had probably an eye to a privileged corner in the tap room, and an occasional cup of cheerful ale free of expense.

There is certainly something in angling, if we could forget, which anglers are apt to do, the cruelties and tortures inflicted on worms and insects, that tends to produce a gentleness of spirit, and a pure serenity of mind. As the English are methodical even in their recreations, and are the most scientific of sportsmen, it has been reduced among them to perfect rule and system. Indeed it is an amusement peculiarly adapted to the mild and highly cultivated scenery of England, where every roughness has been softened away from the landscape. It is delightful to saunter along those limpid streams which wander, like veins of silver, through the bosom of this beautiful country; leading one through a diversity of small home scenery; sometimes winding through ornamented grounds; sometimes brimming along through rich pasturage, where the fresh green is mingled with sweet smelling flowers; sometimes venturing in sight of villages and hamlets; and then running capriciously away into shady retirements. The sweetness and serenity of nature, and the quiet watchfulness of the sport, gradually bring on pleasant fits of musing; which are now and then agreeably interrupted by the song of a bird; the distant whistle of the pheasant; or perhaps the vagary of some fish, leaping out of the still water, and skimming transiently about its glassy surface. "When I would beget content," says Izaak Walton, "and increase confidence in the power and wisdom and providence of Almighty God, I will walk the meadows by some gliding stream, and there contemplate the lilies that take no care, and those very many other little living creatures that are not only created, but fed (man knows not how) by the goodness of the God of nature, and therefore trust in him."

I cannot forbear to give another quotation from one of those ancient champions of angling which breathes the same innocent and happy spirit:

Let me live harmlessly, and near the brink
　Of Trent or Avon have a dwelling-place;
Where I may see my quill, or cork, down sink,
　With eager bite of pike, or bleak, or dace;
And on the world and my creator think:
　Whilst some men strive ill-gotten goods t' embrace;
And others spend their time in base excess
　Of wine, or worse, in war or wantonness.

Let them that will, these pastimes still pursue,
　And on such pleasing fancies feed their fill;
So I the fields and meadows green may view
　And daily by fresh rivers walk at will,
Among the daisies and the violets blue,
　Red hyacinth and yellow daffodil.°

On parting with the old angler I inquired after his place of abode, and happening to be in the neighbourhood of the village a few evenings afterwards, I had the curiosity to seek him out. I found him living in a small cottage, containing only one room, but a perfect curiosity in its method and arrangement. It was on the skirts of the village, on a green bank, a little back from the road, with a small garden in front, stocked with kitchen herbs, and adorned with a few flowers. The whole front of the cottage was overrun with a honeysuckle. On the top was a ship for a weathercock. The interior was fitted up in a truly nautical style, his ideas of comfort and convenience having been acquired on the birth deck of a man of war. A hammock was slung from the ceiling, which, in the day time was lashed up so as to take but little room. From the centre of the chamber hung a model of a ship of his own workmanship. Two or three chairs, a table, and a large sea chest, formed the principal moveables. About the walls were stuck up naval ballads, such as Admiral Hosier's Ghost, All in the Downs, and Tom Bowling, intermingled with pictures of sea fights, among which the battle of Camperdown held a distinguished place. The mantle piece was decorated with sea shells; over which hung a quadrant, flanked by two woodcuts of most bitter looking naval commanders. His implements for angling were carefully disposed on nails and hooks about the room. On a shelf was arranged his library, containing a work on angling, much worn; a bible covered with canvass; an odd volume or two of voyages; a nautical almanack; and a book of songs.

°J. Davors.

His family consisted of a large black cat with one eye, and a parrot which he had caught and tamed, and educated himself, in the course of one of his voyages; and which uttered a variety of sea phrases with the hoarse brattling tone of a veteran boatswain. The establishment reminded me of that of the renowned Robinson Crusoe;—it was kept in neat order, every thing being "stowed away" with the regularity of a ship of war; and he informed me that he "scowred the deck every morning, and swept it between meals."

I found him seated on a bench before the door, smoking his pipe in the soft evening sunshine. His cat was purring soberly on the threshold, and his parrot describing some strange evolutions in an iron ring that swung in the centre of his cage. He had been angling all day, and gave me a history of his sport with as much minuteness as a general would talk over a campaign; being particularly animated in relating the manner in which he had taken a large trout, which had completely tasked all his skill and wariness, and which he had sent as a trophy to mine hostess of the Inn.

How comforting it is to see a cheerful and contented old age; and to behold a poor fellow, like this, after being tempest tost through life, safely moored in a snug and quiet harbour in the evening of his days. His happiness, however, sprung from within himself, and was independent of external circumstances; for he had that inexhaustible good nature, which is the most precious gift of heaven; spreading itself like oil over the troubled sea of thought, and keeping the mind smooth and equable in the roughest weather.

On inquiring further about him, I learnt that he was a universal favourite in the village, and the oracle of the tap room; where he delighted the rustics with his songs, and, like Sindbad, astonished them with his stories of strange lands, and shipwrecks, and sea fights. He was much noticed too by gentlemen sportsmen of the neighbourhood; had taught several of them the art of angling; and was a privileged visitor to their kitchens. The whole tenor of his life was quiet and inoffensive, being principally passed about the neighbouring streams when the weather and season were favourable; at other times he employed himself at home, preparing his fishing tackle for the next campaign, or manufacturing rods, nets, and flies for his patrons and pupils among the gentry.

He was a regular attendant at church on Sundays, though he generally fell asleep during the sermon. He had made it his particular request that when he died he should be buried in a green spot, which he could see from his seat in church, and which he had marked out ever since he was a boy, and had thought of when far from home on the raging sea, in danger of being food for the fishes—it was the spot where his father and mother had been buried.

I have done, for I fear that my reader is growing weary; but I could not refrain from drawing the picture of this worthy "brother of the angle;" who has made me more than ever in love with the theory, though I fear I shall never be adroit in the practice of his art: and I will conclude this rambling sketch, in the words of honest Izaak Walton, by craving the blessing of St. Peter's master upon my reader, "and upon all that are true lovers of virtue; and dare trust in his providence; and be quiet; and go a angling."

THE
LEGEND OF SLEEPY HOLLOW

(Found among the Papers of the late Diedrich Knickerbocker)

> A pleasing land of drowsy head it was,
> Of dreams that wave before the half-shut eye;
> And of gay castles in the clouds that pass,
> Forever flushing round a summer sky.
> CASTLE OF INDOLENCE.

In the bosom of one of those spacious coves which indent the eastern shore of the Hudson, at that broad expansion of the river denominated by the ancient Dutch navigators the Tappaan Zee, and where they always prudently shortened sail, and implored the protection of St. Nicholas when they crossed, there lies a small market town or rural port, which by some is called Greensburgh, but which is more generally and properly known by the name of Tarry Town. This name was given, we are told, in former days, by the good housewives of the adjacent country, from the inveterate propensity of their husbands to linger about the village tavern on market days. Be that as it may, I do not vouch for the fact, but merely advert to it, for the sake of being precise and authentic. Not far from this village, perhaps about two miles, there is a little valley, or rather lap of land among high hills, which is one of the quietest places in the whole world. A small brook glides through it, with just murmur enough to lull one to repose, and the occasional whistle of a quail, or tapping of a woodpecker, is almost the only sound that ever breaks in upon the uniform tranquillity.

I recollect that when a stripling, my first exploit in squirrel shooting was in a grove of tall walnut trees that shades one side of the valley. I had wandered into it at noon time, when all nature is peculiarly quiet, and was startled by the roar of my own gun, as it broke the sabbath stillness around, and was prolonged and reverberated by the angry echoes. If ever I should wish for a retreat, whither I might steal from the world and its distractions, and dream quietly away the remnant of a troubled life, I know of none more promising than this little valley.

From the listless repose of the place, and the peculiar character of its inhabitants, who are descendants from the original Dutch settlers, this sequestered glen has long been known by the name of SLEEPY HOLLOW, and its rustic lads are called the Sleepy Hollow Boys throughout all the neighbouring country. A drowsy, dreamy influence seems to hang over the land, and to pervade the very atmosphere. Some say that the place was bewitched by a high German doctor during the early days of the settlement; others, that an old Indian chief, the prophet or wizard of his tribe, held his powwows there before the country was discovered by Master Hendrick Hudson. Certain it is, the place still continues under the sway of some witching power, that holds a spell over the minds of the good people, causing them to walk in a continual reverie. They are given to all kinds of marvellous beliefs; are subject to trances and visions, and frequently see strange sights, and hear music and voices in the air. The whole neighbourhood abounds with local tales, haunted spots, and twilight superstitions; stars shoot and meteors glare oftener across the valley than in any other part of the country, and the night mare, with her whole nine fold, seems to make it the favourite scene of her gambols.

The dominant spirit, however, that haunts this enchanted region, and seems to be commander in chief of all the powers of the air, is the apparition of a figure on horseback without a head. It is said by some to be the ghost of a Hessian trooper, whose head had been carried away by a cannon ball, in some nameless battle during the revolutionary war, and who is ever and anon seen by the country folk, hurrying along in the gloom of night, as if on the wings of the wind. His haunts are not confined to the valley, but extend at times to the adjacent roads, and especially to the vicinity of a church at no great distance. Indeed, certain of the most authentic historians of those parts, who have been careful in collecting and collating the floating facts concerning this spectre, allege, that the body of the trooper having been buried in the church yard, the ghost rides forth to the scene of battle in nightly quest of his head, and that the rushing speed with which he sometimes passes along the hollow, like a midnight blast, is owing to his being belated, and in a hurry to get back to the church yard before day break.

Such is the general purport of this legendary superstition, which has furnished materials for many a wild story in that region of shadows; and the spectre is known, at all the country firesides, by the name of The Headless Horseman of Sleepy Hollow.

It is remarkable, that the visionary propensity I have mentioned is not confined to the native inhabitants of the valley, but is unconsciously imbibed by every one who resides there for a time. However wide awake they may have been before they entered that sleepy region, they are sure, in a little time, to inhale the witching influence of the air, and begin to grow imaginative—to dream dreams, and see apparitions.

I mention this peaceful spot with all possible laud; for it is in such little retired Dutch valleys, found here and there embosomed in the great state of New York, that population, manners, and customs, remain fixed, while the great torrent of migration and improvement, which is making such incessant changes in other parts of this restless country, sweeps by them unobserved. They are like those little nooks of still water, which border a rapid stream, where we may see the straw and bubble riding quietly at anchor, or slowly revolving in their mimic harbour, undisturbed by the rush of the passing current. Though many years have elapsed since I trod the drowsy shades of Sleepy Hollow, yet I question whether I should not still find the same trees and the same families vegetating in its sheltered bosom.

In this by place of nature there abode, in a remote period of American history, that is to say, some thirty years since, a worthy wight of the name of Ichabod Crane, who sojourned, or, as he expressed it, "tarried," in Sleepy Hollow, for the purpose of instructing the children of the vicinity. He was a native of Connecticut, a state which supplies the Union with pioneers for the mind as well as for the forest, and sends forth yearly its legions of frontier woodmen and country schoolmasters. The cognomen of Crane was not inapplicable to his person. He was tall, but exceedingly lank, with narrow shoulders, long arms and legs, hands that dangled a mile out of his sleeves, feet that might have served for shovels, and his whole frame most loosely hung together. His head was small, and flat at top, with huge ears, large green glassy eyes, and a long snipe nose, so that it looked like a weathercock perched upon his spindle neck, to tell which way the wind blew. To see him striding along the profile of a hill on a windy day, with his clothes bagging and fluttering about him, one might have mistaken him for the genius of famine descending upon the earth, or some scarecrow eloped from a cornfield.

His school house was a low building of one large room, rudely constructed of logs; the windows partly glazed, and partly patched with leaves of old copy books. It was most ingeniously secured at vacant hours, by a withe twisted in the handle of the door, and stakes set against the window shutters; so that though a thief might get in with perfect ease, he would find some embarrassment in getting out; an idea most probably borrowed by the architect, Yost Van Houten, from the mystery of an eelpot. The school house stood in a rather lonely but pleasant situation, just at the foot of a woody hill, with a brook running close by, and a formidable birch tree growing at one end of it. From hence the low murmur of his pupils' voices conning over their lessons, might be heard of a drowsy summer's day, like the hum of a bee hive; interrupted now and then by the authoritative voice of the master, in the tone of menace or command, or peradventure, by the appalling sound of the birch, as he urged some tardy loiterer along the flowery path of knowledge. Truth to say, he was a conscientious man, and ever bore in mind the golden maxim, "spare the rod and spoil the child."—Ichabod Crane's scholars certainly were not spoiled.

I would not have it imagined, however, that he was one of those cruel potentates of the school, who joy in the smart of their subjects; on the contrary, he administered justice with discrimination rather than severity; taking the burthen off the backs of the weak, and laying it on those of the strong. Your mere puny stripling, that winced at the least flourish of the rod, was passed by with indulgence; but the claims of justice were satisfied, by inflicting a double portion on some little, tough, wrong headed, broad skirted Dutch urchin, who sulked and swelled and grew dogged and sullen beneath the birch. All this he called "doing his duty by their parents;" and he never inflicted a chastisement without following it by the assurance, so consolatory to the smarting urchin, that "he would remember it and thank him for it the longest day he had to live."

When school hours were over, he was even the companion and playmate of the larger boys; and on holyday afternoons would convoy some of the smaller ones home, who happened to have pretty sisters, or good housewives for mothers, noted for the comforts of the cupboard. Indeed, it behooved him to keep on good terms with his pupils. The revenue arising from his school was small, and would have been scarcely sufficient to furnish him with daily bread, for he was a huge feeder, and though lank, had the dilating powers of an Anaconda; but to help out his maintenance, he was, according to country custom in those parts, boarded and lodged at the houses of the farmers, whose children he instructed. With these he lived successively a week at a time, thus going the rounds of the neighbourhood, with all his worldly effects tied up in a cotton handkerchief.

That all this might not be too onerous on the purses of his rustic patrons, who are apt to consider the costs of schooling a grievous burthen, and schoolmasters as mere drones, he had various ways of rendering himself both useful and agreeable. He assisted the farmers occasionally in the lighter labours of their farms, helped to make hay, mended the fences, took the horses to water, drove the cows from pasture, and cut wood for the winter fire. He laid aside, too, all the dominant dignity and absolute sway, with which he lorded it in his little empire, the school, and became wonderfully gentle and ingratiating. He found favour in the eyes of the mothers, by petting the children, particularly the youngest, and like the lion bold, which whilome so magnanimously the lamb did hold, he would sit with a child on one knee, and rock a cradle with his foot, for whole hours together.

In addition to his other vocations, he was the singing master of the neighbourhood, and picked up many bright shillings by instructing the young folks in psalmody. It was a matter of no little vanity to him on Sundays, to take his station in front of the church gallery, with a band of chosen singers; where, in his own mind, he completely carried away the palm from the parson. Certain it is, his voice resounded far above all the rest of the congregation, and there are peculiar quavers still to be heard in that church, and which may even be heard half a mile off, quite to the opposite side of the mill pond, of a still Sunday morning, which are said to be legitimately descended from the nose of Ichabod Crane. Thus, by diverse little make shifts, in that ingenious way which is commonly denominated "by hook and by crook," the worthy pedagogue got on tolerably enough, and was thought, by all who understood nothing of the labour of headwork, to have a wonderfully easy life of it.

The schoolmaster is generally a man of some importance in the female circle of a rural neighbourhood, being considered a kind of idle gentleman like personage, of vastly superior taste and accomplishments to the rough country swains, and, indeed, inferior in learning only to the parson. His appearance, therefore, is apt to occasion some little stir at the tea table of a farm house, and the addition of a supernumerary dish of cakes or sweetmeats, or, peradventure, the parade of a silver tea pot. Our man of letters, therefore, was peculiarly happy in the smiles of all the country damsels. How he would figure among them in the church yard, between services on Sundays; gathering grapes for them from the wild vines that overrun the surrounding trees; reciting for their amusement all the epitaphs on the tombstones, or sauntering, with a whole bevy of them, along the banks of the adjacent mill pond; while the more bashful country bumpkins hũng sheepishly back, envying his superior elegance and address.

From his half itinerant life, also, he was a kind of travelling gazette, carrying the whole budget of local gossip from house to house; so that his appearance was always greeted with satisfaction. He was, moreover, esteemed by the women as a man of great erudition, for he had read several books quite through, and was a perfect master of Cotton Mather's History of New England Witchcraft, in which, by the way, he most firmly and potently believed.

He was, in fact, an odd mixture of small shrewdness and simple credulity. His appetite for the marvellous, and his powers of digesting it, were equally extraordinary; and both had been increased by his residence in this spell bound region. No tale was too gross or monstrous for his capacious swallow. It was often his delight, after his school was dismissed of an afternoon, to stretch himself on the rich bed of clover, bordering the little brook that whimpered by his school house, and there con over old Mather's direful tales, until the gathering dusk of evening made the printed page a mere mist before his eyes. Then, as he wended his way, by swamp and stream and awful woodland, to the farm house where he happened to be quartered, every sound of nature, at that witching hour, fluttered his excited imagination: the moan of the whip-poor-will° from the hill side; the boding cry of the tree toad, that harbinger of storm; the dreary hooting of the screech owl; or the sudden rustling in the thicket, of birds frightened from their roost. The fire flies, too, which sparkled most vividly in the darkest places, now and then startled him, as one of uncommon brightness would stream across his path; and if, by chance, a huge blockhead of a beetle came winging his blundering flight against him, the poor varlet was ready to give up the ghost, with the idea that he was struck with a witch's token. His only resource on such occasions, either to drown thought, or drive away evil spirits, was to sing psalm tunes;— and the good people of Sleepy Hollow, as they sat by their doors of an evening, were often filled with awe, at hearing his nasal melody, "in linked sweetness long drawn out," floating from the distant hill, or along the dusky road.

Another of his sources of fearful pleasure was, to pass long winter evenings with the old Dutch wives, as they sat spinning by the fire, with a row of apples roasting and sputtering along the hearth, and listen to their marvellous tales of ghosts and goblins, and haunted fields and haunted brooks, and haunted bridges and haunted houses, and particularly of the headless horseman, or galloping Hessian of the Hollow, as they sometimes called him. He would delight them equally by his anecdotes of witchcraft, and of the direful omens and portentous sights and sounds in the air, which prevailed in the earlier times of Connecticut; and would frighten them wofully with speculations upon comets and shooting stars, and with the alarming fact that the world did absolutely turn round, and that they were half the time topsy-turvy!

°The whip-poor-will is a bird which is only heard at night. It receives its name from its note which is thought to resemble those words.

But if there was a pleasure in all this, while snugly cuddling in the chimney corner of a chamber that was all of a ruddy glow from the crackling wood fire, and where, of course, no spectre dared to show its face, it was dearly purchased by the terrors of his subsequent walk homewards. What fearful shapes and shadows beset his path, amidst the dim and ghastly glare of a snowy night!—With what wistful look did he eye every trembling ray of light streaming across the waste fields from some distant window!—How often was he appalled by some shrub covered with snow, which like a sheeted spectre beset his very path!—How often did he shrink with curdling awe at the sound of his own steps on the frosty crust beneath his feet; and dread to look over his shoulder, lest he should behold some uncouth being tramping close behind him!—and how often was he thrown into complete dismay by some rushing blast, howling among the trees, in the idea that it was the gallopping Hessian on one of his nightly scourings.

All these, however, were mere terrors of the night, phantoms of the mind, that walk in darkness; and though he had seen many spectres in his time, and been more than once beset by Satan in diverse shapes, in his lonely perambulations, yet daylight put an end to all these evils; and he would have passed a pleasant life of it, in despite of the Devil and all his works, if his path had not been crossed by a being that causes more perplexity to mortal man, than ghosts, goblins, and the whole race of witches put together, and that was—a woman.

Among the musical disciples who assembled, one evening in each week, to receive his instructions in psalmody, was Katrina Van Tassel, the daughter and only child of a substantial Dutch farmer. She was a blooming lass of fresh eighteen; plump as a partridge; ripe and melting and rosy cheeked as one of her father's peaches, and universally famed, not merely for her beauty, but her vast expectations. She was withal a little of a coquette, as might be perceived even in her dress, which was a mixture of ancient and modern fashions, as most suited to set off her charms. She wore the ornaments of pure yellow gold, which her great great grandmother had brought over from Saardam; the tempting stomacher of the olden time, and withal a provokingly short petticoat, to display the prettiest foot and ankle in the country round.

Ichabod Crane had a soft and foolish heart toward the sex; and it is not to be wondered at, that so tempting a morsel soon found favour in his eyes, more especially after he had visited her in her paternal mansion. Old Baltus Van Tassel was a perfect picture of a thriving, contented, liberal hearted farmer. He seldom, it is true, sent either his eyes or his thoughts beyond the boundaries of his own farm; but within those every thing was snug, happy, and well conditioned. He

was satisfied with his wealth, but not proud of it, and piqued himself
upon the hearty abundance, rather than the style in which he lived.
His strong hold was situated on the banks of the Hudson, in one of
those green, sheltered, fertile nooks, in which the Dutch farmers
are so fond of nestling. A great elm tree spread its broad branches
over it, at the foot of which bubbled up a spring of the softest and
sweetest water, in a little well, formed of a barrel, and then stole
sparkling away through the grass, to a neighbouring brook, that babbled
along among elders and dwarf willows. Hard by the farm house was
a vast barn, that might have served for a church; every window and
crevice of which seemed bursting forth with the treasures of the farm;
the flail was busily resounding within it from morning to night; swallows
and martins skimmed twittering about the eaves, and rows of pigeons,
some with one eye turned up, as if watching the weather, some with
their heads under their wings, or buried in their bosoms, and others,
swelling, and cooing, and bowing about their dames, were enjoying
the sunshine on the roof. Sleek unwieldy porkers were grunting in the
repose and abundance of their pens, from whence sallied forth, now
and then, troops of sucking pigs, as if to snuff the air. A stately
squadron of snowy geese were riding in an adjoining pond, convoying
whole fleets of ducks; regiments of turkeys were gobbling through the
farm yard, and guinea fowls fretting about it like ill tempered housewives, with their peevish discontented cry. Before the barn door strutted
the gallant cock, that pattern of a husband, a warrior, and a fine
gentleman, clapping his burnished wings, and crowing in the pride
and gladness of his heart—sometimes tearing up the earth with his
feet, and then generously calling his ever hungry family of wives and
children to enjoy the rich morsel which he had discovered.

The pedagogue's mouth watered, as he looked upon this sumptuous
promise of luxurious winter fare. In his devouring mind's eye, he
pictured to himself every roasting pig running about with a pudding
in his belly, and an apple in his mouth; the pigeons were snugly put
to bed in a comfortable pie, and tucked in with a coverlet of crust; the
geese were swimming in their own gravy; and the ducks pairing cosily
in dishes, like snug married couples, with a decent competency of
onion sauce; in the porkers he saw carved out the future sleek side
of bacon, and juicy relishing ham; not a turkey, but he beheld daintily
trussed up, with its gizzard under its wing, and, peradventure, a
necklace of savoury sausages; and even bright chanticleer himself lay
sprawling on his back, in a side dish, with uplifted claws, as if craving
that quarter, which his chivalrous spirit disdained to ask while living.

As the enraptured Ichabod fancied all this, and as he rolled his great green eyes over the fat meadow lands, the rich fields of wheat, of rye, of buckwheat, and Indian corn, and the orchards burthened with ruddy fruit, which surrounded the warm tenement of Van Tassel, his heart yearned after the damsel who was to inherit these domains, and his imagination expanded with the idea, how they might be readily turned into cash, and the money invested in immense tracts of wild land, and shingle palaces in the wilderness. Nay, his busy fancy already realized his hopes, and presented to him the blooming Katrina, with a whole family of children, mounted on the top of a waggon loaded with household trumpery, with pots and kettles dangling beneath; and he beheld himself bestriding a pacing mare, with a colt at her heels, setting out for Kentucky, Tennessee, or the Lord knows where!

When he entered the house, the conquest of his heart was complete. It was one of those spacious farm houses, with high ridged, but lowly sloping roofs, built in the style handed down from the first Dutch settlers. The low, projecting eaves formed a piazza along the front, capable of being closed up in bad weather. Under this were hung flails, harness, various utensils of husbandry, and nets for fishing in the neighbouring river. Benches were built along the sides for summer use; and a great spinning wheel at one end, and a churn at the other, showed the various uses to which this important porch might be devoted. From this piazza the wondering Ichabod entered the hall, which formed the centre of the mansion, and the place of usual residence. Here, rows of resplendent pewter, ranged on a long dresser, dazzled his eyes. In one corner stood a huge bag of wool ready to be spun; in another a quantity of linsey-woolsey just from the loom; ears of Indian corn, and strings of dried apples and peaches, hung in gay festoons along the walls, mingled with the gaud of red peppers; and a door left ajar, gave him a peep into the best parlour, where the claw footed chairs, and dark mahogany tables, shone like mirrors; andirons, with their accompanying shovel and tongs, glistened from their covert of asparagus tops; mock oranges and conch shells decorated the mantle-piece; strings of various coloured birds' eggs were suspended above it; a great ostrich egg was hung from the centre of the room, and a corner cupboard, knowingly left open, displayed immense treasures of old silver and well mended china.

From the moment Ichabod laid his eyes upon these regions of delight, the peace of his mind was at an end, and his only study was how to gain the affections of the peerless daughter of Van Tassel. In this enterprize, however, he had more real difficulties than generally fell to the lot of a knight errant of yore, who seldom had any thing but giants, enchanters, fiery dragons, and such like easily conquered adversaries, to contend with; and had to make his way merely through gates of iron and brass, and walls of adamant, to the castle keep, where the lady of his heart was confined; all which he achieved as easily as a man would carve his way to the centre of a Christmas pie, and then the lady gave him her hand as a matter of course. Ichabod, on the contrary, had to win his way to the heart of a country coquette, beset with a labyrinth of whims and caprices, which were for ever presenting new difficulties' and impediments, and he had to encounter a host of fearful adversaries of real flesh and blood, the numerous rustic admirers, who beset every portal to her heart, keeping a watchful and angry eye upon each other, but ready to fly out in the common cause against any new competitor.

Among these, the most formidable, was a burly, roaring, roystering blade, of the name of Abraham, or, according to the Dutch abbreviation, Brom Van Brunt, the hero of the country round, which rung with his feats of strength and hardihood. He was broad shouldered and double jointed, with short curly black hair, and a bluff, but not unpleasant countenance, having a mingled air of fun and arrogance. From his Herculean frame and great powers of limb, he had received the nick name of BROM BONES, by which he was universally known. He was famed for great knowledge and skill in horsemanship, being as dexterous on horseback as a Tartar. He was foremost at all races and cock fights, and with the ascendancy which bodily strength acquires in rustic life, was the umpire in all disputes, setting his hat on one side, and giving his decisions with an air and tone admitting of no gainsay or appeal. He was always ready for either a fight or a frolick; but had more mischief than ill will in his composition; and with all his overbearing roughness, there was a strong dash of waggish good humour at bottom. He had three or four boon companions, who regarded him as their model, and at the head of whom he scoured the country, attending every scene of feud or merriment for miles round. In cold weather he was distinguished by a fur cap, surmounted with a flaunting fox's tail, and when the folks at a country gathering descried this well known crest at a distance, whisking about among a squad of hard riders, they always stood by for a squall. Sometimes his crew would be heard dashing along past the farm houses at midnight, with whoop and halloo, like a troop of Don Cossacks, and the old dames, startled out of their sleep, would listen for a moment till the hurry scurry had clattered by, and then exclaim, "aye, there goes Brom Bones and his gang!" The neighbours looked upon him with a mixture of awe, admiration, and good will; and when any mad cap prank, or rustic brawl, occurred in the vicinity, always shook their heads, and warranted Brom Bones was at the bottom of it.

This rantipole hero had for some time singled out the blooming Katrina for the object of his uncouth gallantries, and though his amorous toyings were something like the gentle caresses and endearments of a bear, yet it was whispered that she did not altogether discourage his hopes. Certain it is, his advances were signals for rival candidates to retire, who felt no inclination to cross a lion in his amours; insomuch, that when his horse was seen tied to Van Tassel's paling, of a Sunday night, (a sure sign that his master was courting, or, as it is termed, "sparking," within,) all other suitors passed by in despair, and carried the war into other quarters.

Such was the formidable rival with whom Ichabod Crane had to contend, and, considering all things, a stouter man than he would have shrunk from the competition, and a wiser man would have despaired. He had, however, a happy mixture of pliability and perseverance in his nature; he was in form and spirit like a supple jack—yielding, but tough; though he bent, he never broke; and though he bowed beneath the slightest pressure, yet, the moment it was away—jerk!—he was as erect, and carried his head as high as ever.

To have taken the field openly against his rival, would have been madness; for he was not a man to be thwarted in his amours, any more than that stormy lover, Achilles. Ichabod, therefore, made his advances in a quiet and gently insinuating manner. Under cover of his character of singing master, he made frequent visits at the farm house; not that he had any thing to apprehend from the meddlesome interference of parents, which is so often a stumbling block in the path of lovers. Balt Van Tassel was an easy indulgent soul; he loved his daughter better even than his pipe, and like a reasonable man, and an excellent father, let her have her way in every thing. His notable little wife too, had enough to do to attend to her housekeeping and manage her poultry, for, as she sagely observed, ducks and geese are foolish things, and must be looked after, but girls can take care of themselves. Thus while the busy dame bustled about the house, or plied her spinning wheel at one end of the piazza, honest Balt would sit smoking his evening pipe at the other, watching the achievements of a little wooden warrior, who, armed with a sword in each hand, was most valiantly fighting the wind on the pinnacle of the barn. In the mean time, Ichabod would carry on his suit with the daughter by the side of the spring under the great elm, or sauntering along in the twilight, that hour so favourable to the lover's eloquence.

I profess not to know how women's hearts are wooed and won. To me they have always been matters of riddle and admiration. Some seem to have but one vulnerable point, or door of access; while others have a thousand avenues, and may be captured in a thousand different ways. It is a great triumph of skill to gain the former, but a still greater proof of generalship to maintain possession of the latter, for a man must battle for his fortress at every door and window. He who wins a thousand common hearts, is therefore entitled to some renown; but he who keeps undisputed sway over the heart of a coquette, is indeed a hero. Certain it is, this was not the case with the redoutable Brom Bones; and from the moment Ichabod Crane made his advances, the interests of the former evidently declined; his horse was no longer seen tied at the palings on Sunday nights, and a deadly feud gradually arose between him and the preceptor of Sleepy Hollow.

Brom, who had a degree of rough chivalry in his nature, would fain have carried matters to open warfare, and have settled their pretensions to the lady, according to the mode of those most concise and simple reasoners, the knights errant of yore—by single combat; but Ichabod was too conscious of the superior might of his adversary to enter the lists against him; he had overheard a boast of Bones, that he would "double the schoolmaster up, and lay him on a shelf of his own school house;" and he was too wary to give him an opportunity. There was something extremely provoking in this obstinately pacific system; it left Brom no alternative but to draw upon the funds of rustic waggery in his disposition, and to play off boorish practical jokes upon his rival. Ichabod became the object of whimsical persecution to Bones, and his gang of rough riders. They harried his hitherto peaceful domains; smoked out his singing school, by stopping up the chimney; broke into the school house at night, in spite of its formidable fastenings of withe and window stakes, and turned every thing topsy-turvy, so that the poor schoolmaster began to think all the witches in the country held their meetings there. But what was still more annoying, Brom took all opportunities of turning him into ridicule in presence of his mistress, and had a scoundrel dog, whom he taught to whine in the most ludicrous manner, and introduced as a rival of Ichabod's, to instruct her in psalmody.

In this way, matters went on for some time, without producing any material effect on the relative situations of the contending powers. On a fine autumnal afternoon, Ichabod, in pensive mood, sat enthroned on the lofty stool from whence he usually watched all the concerns of his little literary realm. In his hand he swayed a ferule, that sceptre of despotic power; the birch of justice reposed on three nails, behind the throne, a constant terror to evil doers; while on the desk before him might be seen sundry contraband articles and prohibited weapons, detected upon the persons of idle urchins, such as half munched apples, popguns, whirligigs, fly cages, and whole legions of rampant little paper game cocks. Apparently there had been some appalling act of justice recently inflicted, for his scholars were all busily intent upon their books, or slyly whispering behind them with one eye kept upon the master; and a kind of buzzing stillness reigned throughout the school room. It was suddenly interrupted by the appearance of a negro in tow cloth jacket and trowsers, a round crowned fragment of a hat, like the cap of Mercury, and mounted on the back of a ragged, wild, half broken colt, which he managed with a rope by way of halter. He came clattering up to the school door with an invitation to Ichabod to attend a merry making, or "quilting frolick," to be held that evening at Mynheer Van Tassel's, and having delivered his message with that air of importance, and effort at fine language, which a negro is apt to display on petty embassies of the kind, he dashed over the brook, and was seen scampering away up the hollow, full of the importance and hurry of his mission.

All was now bustle and hubbub in the late quiet school room. The scholars were hurried through their lessons, without stopping at trifles; those who were nimble, skipped over half with impunity, and those who were tardy, had a smart application now and then in the rear, to quicken their speed, or help them over a tall word. Books were flung aside, without being put away on the shelves; inkstands were overturned, benches thrown down, and the whole school was turned loose an hour before the usual time; bursting forth like a legion of young imps, yelping and racketing about the green, in joy at their early emancipation.

The gallant Ichabod now spent at least an extra half hour at his toilet, brushing and furbishing up his best, and indeed only suit of rusty black, and arranging his looks by a bit of broken looking glass, that hung up in the school house. That he might make his appearance before his mistress in the true style of a cavalier, he borrowed a horse from the farmer with whom he was domiciliated, a choleric old Dutchman, of the name of Hans Van Ripper, and thus gallantly mounted, issued forth like a knight errant in quest of adventures. But it is meet I should, in the true spirit of romantic story, give some account of the looks and equipments of my hero and his steed. The animal he bestrode was a broken down plough horse, that had outlived almost every thing but his viciousness. He was gaunt and shagged, with a ewe neck and a head like a hammer; his rusty mane and tail were tangled and knotted with burrs; one eye had lost its pupil, and was glaring and spectral, but the other had the gleam of a genuine devil in it. Still he must have had fire and mettle in his day, if we may judge from the name he bore of Gunpowder. He had, in fact, been a favourite steed of his master's, the cholerick Van Ripper, who was a furious rider, and had infused, very probably, some of his own spirit into the animal, for, old and broken down as he looked, there was more of the lurking devil in him than in any young filly in the country.

Ichabod was a suitable figure for such a steed. He rode with short stirrups, which brought his knees nearly up to the pommel of the saddle; his sharp elbows stuck out like grasshoppers'; he carried his whip perpendicularly in his hand, like a sceptre, and as his horse jogged on, the motion of his arms was not unlike the flapping of a pair of wings. A small wool hat rested on the top of his nose, for so his scanty strip of forehead might be called, and the skirts of his black coat fluttered out almost to the horse's tail. Such was the appearance of Ichabod and his steed, as they shambled out of the gate of Hans Van Ripper, and it was altogether such an apparition as is seldom to be met with in broad day light.

It was, as I have said, a fine autumnal day, the sky was clear and serene, and nature wore that rich and golden livery which we always associate with the idea of abundance. The forests had put on their sober brown and yellow, while some trees of the tenderer kind had been nipped by the frosts into brilliant dyes of orange, purple, and scarlet. Streaming files of wild ducks began to make their appearance high in the air; the bark of the squirrel might be heard from the groves of beech and hickory nuts, and the pensive whistle of the quail at intervals from the neighbouring stubble field.

The small birds were taking their farewell banquets. In the fullness of their revelry, they fluttered, chirping and frolicking, from bush to bush, and tree to tree, capricious from the very profusion and variety around them. There was the honest cock robin, the favourite game of stripling sportsmen, with its loud querulous note; and the twittering blackbirds flying in sable clouds; and the golden winged woodpecker, with his crimson crest, his broad black gorget, and splendid plumage; and the cedar bird, with its red tipt wings and yellow tipt tail, and its little monteiro cap of feathers; and the blue jay, that noisy coxcomb, in his gay light blue coat and white under clothes, screaming and chattering, nodding and bobbing, and bowing, and pretending to be on good terms with every songster of the grove.

As Ichabod jogged slowly on his way, his eye, ever open to every symptom of culinary abundance, ranged with delight over the treasures of jolly autumn. On all sides he beheld vast store of apples, some hanging in oppressive opulence on the trees, some gathered into baskets and barrels for the market, others heaped up in rich piles for the cider press. Further on he beheld great fields of Indian corn, with its golden ears peeping from their leafy coverts, and holding out the promise of cakes and hasty pudding; and the yellow pumpkins lying beneath them, turning up their fair round bellies to the sun, and giving ample prospects of the most luxurious of pies; and anon he passed the fragrant buckwheat fields, breathing the odour of the bee hive, and as he beheld them, soft anticipations stole over his mind of dainty slap jacks, well buttered, and garnished with honey or treacle, by the delicate little dimpled hand of Katrina Van Tassel.

Thus feeding his mind with many sweet thoughts and "sugared suppositions," he journeyed along the sides of a range of hills which look out upon some of the goodliest scenes of the mighty Hudson. The sun gradually wheeled his broad disk down into the west. The wide bosom of the Tappaan Zee lay motionless and glassy, excepting that here and there a gentle undulation waved and prolonged the blue shadow of the distant mountain: a few amber clouds floated in the sky, without a breath of air to move them. The horizon was of a fine golden tint, changing gradually into a pure apple green, and from that into the deep blue of the mid-heaven. A slanting ray lingered on the woody crests of the precipices that overhung some parts of the river, giving greater depth to the dark grey and purple of their rocky sides. A sloop was loitering in the distance, dropping slowly down with the tide, her sail hanging uselessly against the mast, and as the reflection of the sky gleamed along the still water, it seemed as if the vessel was suspended in the air.

It was toward evening that Ichabod arrived at the castle of the Heer Van Tassel, which he found thronged with the pride and flower of the adjacent country. Old farmers, a spare, leathern faced race, in homespun coats and breeches, blue stockings, huge shoes and magnificent pewter buckles. Their brisk withered little dames in close crimped caps, long waisted short gowns, homespun petticoats, with scissors and pincushions, and gay calico pockets, hanging on the outside. Buxom lasses, almost as antiquated as their mothers, excepting where a straw hat, a fine ribband, or perhaps a white frock, gave symptoms of city innovation. The sons, in short square skirted coats with rows of stupendous brass buttons, and their hair generally queued in the fashion of the times, especially if they could procure an eel skin for the purpose, it being esteemed throughout the country as a potent nourisher and strengthener of the hair.

Brom Bones, however, was the hero of the scene, having come to the gathering on his favourite steed Daredevil, a creature, like himself, full of mettle and mischief, and which no one but himself could manage. He was in fact noted for preferring vicious animals, given to all kinds of tricks, which kept the rider in constant risk of his neck, for he held a tractable well broken horse as unworthy of a lad of spirit.

Fain would I pause to dwell upon the world of charms that burst upon the enraptured gaze of my hero, as he entered the state parlour of Van Tassel's mansion. Not those of the bevy of buxom lasses, with their luxurious display of red and white: but the ample charms of a genuine Dutch country tea table, in the sumptuous time of autumn. Such heaped up platters of cakes of various and almost indescribable kinds, known only to experienced Dutch housewives. There was the doughty dough nut, the tenderer oly koek, and the crisp and crumbling cruller; sweet cakes and short cakes, ginger cakes and honey cakes, and the whole family of cakes. And then there were apple pies and peach pies and pumpkin pies; besides slices of ham and smoked beef; and moreover delectable dishes of preserved plums, and peaches, and pears, and quinces; not to mention broiled shad and roasted chickens; together with bowls of milk and cream, all mingled higgledy-piggledy, pretty much as I have enumerated them, with the motherly tea pot sending up its clouds of vapour from the midst—Heaven bless the mark! I want breath and time to discuss this banquet as it deserves, and am too eager to get on with my story. Happily, Ichabod Crane was not in so great a hurry as his historian, but did ample justice to every dainty.

He was a kind and thankful creature, whose heart dilated in proportion as his skin was filled with good cheer, and whose spirits rose with eating, as some men's do with drink. He could not help, too, rolling his large eyes round him as he ate, and chuckling with the possibility that he might one day be lord of all this scene of almost unimaginable luxury and splendour. Then, he thought, how soon he'd turn his back upon the old school house; snap his fingers in the face of Hans Van Ripper, and every other niggardly patron, and kick any itinerant pedagogue out of doors that should dare to call him comrade!

Old Baltus Van Tassel moved about among his guests with a face dilated with content and good humour, round and jolly as the harvest moon. His hospitable attentions were brief, but expressive, being confined to a shake of the hand, a slap on the shoulder, a loud laugh, and a pressing invitation to "fall to, and help themselves."

And now the sound of the music from the common room or hall, summoned to the dance. The musician was an old grey headed negro, who had been the itinerant orchestra of the neighbourhood for more than half a century. His instrument was as old and battered as himself. The greater part of the time he scraped away on two or three strings, accompanying every movement of the bow with a motion of the head; bowing almost to the ground, and stamping with his foot whenever a fresh couple were to start.

Ichabod prided himself upon his dancing as much as upon his vocal powers. Not a limb, not a fibre about him was idle, and to have seen his loosely hung frame in full motion, and clattering about the room, you would have thought Saint Vitus himself, that blessed patron of the dance, was figuring before you in person. He was the admiration of all the negroes, who, having gathered, of all ages and sizes, from the farm and the neighbourhood, stood forming a pyramid of shining black faces at every door and window, gazing with delight at the scene, rolling their white eye balls, and showing grinning rows of ivory from ear to ear. How could the flogger of urchins be otherwise than animated and joyous; the lady of his heart was his partner in the dance; and smiling graciously in reply to all his amorous oglings, while Brom Bones, sorely smitten with love and jealousy, sat brooding by himself in one corner.

When the dance was at an end, Ichabod was attracted to a knot of the sager folks, who, with old Van Tassel, sat smoking at one end of the piazza, gossiping over former times, and drawling out long stories about the war.

This neighbourhood, at the time of which I am speaking, was one of those highly favoured places which abound with chronicle and great men. The British and American line had run near it during the war; it had, therefore, been the scene of marauding, and been infested with refugees, cow boys, and all kinds of border chivalry. Just sufficient time had elapsed to enable each story teller to dress up his tale with a little becoming fiction, and in the indistinctness of his recollection, to make himself the hero of every exploit.

There was the story of Doffue Martling, a large, blue bearded Dutchman, who had nearly taken a British frigate with an old iron nine pounder from a mud breastwork, only that his gun burst at the sixth discharge. And there was an old gentleman who shall be nameless, being too rich a mynheer to be lightly mentioned, who in the battle of Whiteplains, being an excellent master of defence, parried a musket ball with a small sword, insomuch that he absolutely felt it whiz round the blade, and glance off at the hilt: in proof of which, he was ready at any time to show the sword, with the hilt a little bent. There were several more who had been equally great in the field, not one of whom but was persuaded that he had a considerable hand in bringing the war to a happy termination.

But all these were nothing to the tales of ghosts and apparitions that succeeded. The neighbourhood is rich in legendary treasures of the kind. Local tales and superstitions thrive best in these sheltered, long settled retreats; but are trampled under foot, by the shifting throng that forms the population of most of our country places. Besides, there is no encouragement for ghosts in most of our villages, for they have scarce had time to finish their first nap, and turn themselves in their graves, before their surviving friends have travelled away from the neighbourhood, so that when they turn out of a night to walk the rounds, they have no acquaintance left to call upon. This is perhaps the reason why we so seldom hear of ghosts except in our long established Dutch communities.

The immediate cause, however, of the prevalence of supernatural stories in these parts, was doubtless owing to the vicinity of Sleepy Hollow. There was a contagion in the very air that blew from that haunted region; it breathed forth an atmosphere of dreams and fancies infecting all the land. Several of the Sleepy Hollow people were present at Van Tassel's, and, as usual, were doling out their wild and wonderful legends. Many dismal tales were told about funeral trains, and mournful cries and wailings heard and seen about the great tree where the unfortunate Major André was taken, and which stood in the neighbourhood. Some mention was made also of the woman in white, that haunted the dark glen at Raven Rock, and was often heard to shriek on winter nights before a storm, having perished there in the snow. The chief part of the stories, however, turned upon the favourite spectre of Sleepy Hollow, the headless horseman, who had been heard several times of late, patroling the country; and it was said, tethered his horse nightly among the graves in the church yard.

The sequestered situation of this church seems always to have made it a favourite haunt of troubled spirits. It stands on a knoll, surrounded by locust trees and lofty elms, from among which its decent, whitewashed walls shine modestly forth, like Christian purity, beaming through the shades of retirement. A gentle slope descends from it to a silver sheet of water, bordered by high trees, between which, peeps may be caught at the blue hills of the Hudson. To look upon its grass grown yard, where the sunbeams seem to sleep so quietly, one would think that there at least the dead might rest in peace. On one side of the church extends a wide woody dell, along which raves a large brook among broken rocks and trunks of fallen trees. Over a deep black part of the stream, not far from the church, was formerly thrown a wooden bridge; the road that led to it, and the bridge itself, were thickly shaded by overhanging trees, which cast a gloom about it, even in the day time; but occasioned a fearful darkness at night. Such was one of the favourite haunts of the headless horseman, and the place where he was most frequently encountered. The tale was told of old Brouwer, a most heretical disbeliever in ghosts, how he met the horseman returning from his foray into Sleepy Hollow, and was obliged to get up behind him; how they gallopped over bush and brake, over hill and swamp, until they reached the bridge, when the horseman suddenly turned into a skeleton, threw old Brouwer into the brook, and sprang away over the tree tops with a clap of thunder.

This story was immediately matched by a thrice marvellous adventure of Brom Bones, who made light of the gallopping Hessian as an arrant jockey. He affirmed, that on returning one night from the neighbouring village of Sing-Sing, he had been overtaken by this midnight trooper; that he had offered to race with him for a bowl of punch, and should have won it too, for Daredevil beat the goblin horse all hollow, but just as they came to the church bridge, the Hessian bolted, and vanished in a flash of fire.

All these tales, told in that drowsy under tone with which men talk in the dark, the countenances of the listeners only now and then receiving a casual gleam from the glare of a pipe, sunk deep in the mind of Ichabod. He repaid them in kind with large extracts from his invaluable author, Cotton Mather, and added many very marvellous events that had taken place in his native state of Connecticut, and fearful sights which he had seen in his nightly walks about Sleepy Hollow.

The revel now gradually broke up. The old farmers gathered together their families in their wagons, and were heard for some time rattling along the hollow roads, and over the distant hills. Some of the damsels, mounted on pillions behind their favourite swains, and their light hearted laughter mingling with the clatter of hoofs, echoed along the silent woodlands, sounding fainter and fainter until they gradually died away—and the late scene of noise and frolick was all silent and deserted. Ichabod only lingered behind, according to the custom of country lovers, to have a tête-a-tête with the heiress; fully convinced that he was now on the high road to success. What passed at this interview I will not pretend to say, for in fact I do not know. Something, however, I fear me, must have gone wrong, for he certainly sallied forth, after no very great interval, with an air quite desolate and chopfallen—Oh these women! these women! Could that girl have been playing off any of her coquettish tricks?—Was her encouragement of the poor pedagogue all a mere sham to secure her conquest of his rival?—Heaven only knows, not I!—Let it suffice to say, Ichabod stole forth with the air of one who had been sacking a hen roost, rather than a fair lady's heart. Without looking to the right or left to notice the scene of rural wealth, on which he had so often gloated, he went straight to the stable, and with several hearty cuffs and kicks, roused his steed most uncourteously from the comfortable quarters in which he was soundly sleeping, dreaming of mountains of corn and oats, and whole valleys of timothy and clover.

It was the very witching time of night that Ichabod, heavy hearted and crest fallen, pursued his travel homewards, along the sides of the lofty hills which rise above Tarry Town, and which he had traversed so cheerily in the afternoon. The hour was as dismal as himself. Far below him the Tappaan Zee spread its dusky and indistinct waste of waters, with here and there the tall mast of a sloop, riding quietly at anchor under the land. In the dead hush of midnight, he could even hear the barking of the watch dog from the opposite shore of the Hudson; but it was so vague and faint as only to give an idea of his distance from this faithful companion of man. Now and then, too, the long drawn crowing of a cock, accidentally awakened, would sound far, far off, from some farm house away among the hills—but it was like a dreaming sound in his ear. No signs of life occurred near him, but occasionally the melancholy chirp of a cricket, or perhaps the guttural twang of a bull frog, from a neighbouring marsh, as if sleeping uncomfortably, and turning suddenly in his bed.

All the stories of ghosts and goblins that he had heard in the afternoon, now came crowding upon his recollection. The night grew darker and darker; the stars seemed to sink deeper in the sky, and driving clouds occasionally hid them from his sight. He had never felt so lonely and dismal. He was, moreover, approaching the very place where many of the scenes of the ghost stories had been laid. In the centre of the road stood an enormous tulip tree, which towered like a giant above all the other trees of the neighbourhood, and formed a kind of land mark. Its limbs were gnarled, and fantastic, large enough to form trunks for ordinary trees, twisting down almost to the earth, and rising again into the air. It was connected with the tragical story of the unfortunate André, who had been taken prisoner hard by; and was universally known by the name of Major André's tree. The common people regarded it with a mixture of respect and superstition, partly out of sympathy for the fate of its ill starred namesake, and partly from the tales of strange sights, and doleful lamentations, told concerning it.

As Ichabod approached this fearful tree, he began to whistle; he thought his whistle was answered: it was but a blast sweeping sharply through the dry branches. As he approached a little nearer, he thought he saw something white, hanging in the midst of the tree: he paused and ceased whistling; but on looking more narrowly, perceived that it was a place where the tree had been scathed by lightning, and the white wood laid bare. Suddenly he heard a groan—his teeth chattered, and his knees smote against the saddle: it was but the rubbing of one huge bough upon another, as they were swayed about by the breeze. He passed the tree in safety, but new perils lay before him.

About two hundred yards from the tree, a small brook crossed the road, and ran into a marshy and thickly wooded glen, known by the name of Wiley's Swamp. A few rough logs, laid side by side, served for a bridge over this stream. On that side of the road where the brook entered the wood, a group of oaks and chestnuts, matted thick with wild grape vines, threw a cavernous gloom over it. To pass this bridge, was the severest trial. It was at this identical spot that the unfortunate André was captured, and under the covert of those chestnuts and vines were the sturdy yeomen concealed who surprised him. This has ever since been considered a haunted stream, and fearful are the feelings of the schoolboy who has to pass it alone after dark.

As he approached the stream, his heart began to thump; he, however, summoned up all his resolution, gave his horse half a score of kicks in the ribs, and attempted to dash briskly across the bridge; but instead of starting forward, the perverse old animal made a lateral movement, and ran broadside against the fence. Ichabod, whose fears increased with the delay, jerked the reins on the other side, and kicked lustily with the contrary foot: it was all in vain; his steed started, it is true, but it was only to plunge to the opposite side of the road into a thicket of brambles and alder bushes. The schoolmaster now bestowed both whip and heel upon the starvelling ribs of old Gunpowder, who dashed forward, snuffling and snorting, but came to a stand just by the bridge with a suddenness that had nearly sent his rider sprawling over his head. Just at this moment a plashy tramp by the side of the bridge caught the sensitive ear of Ichabod. In the dark shadow of the grove, on the margin of the brook, he beheld something huge, misshapen, black and towering. It stirred not, but seemed gathered up in the gloom, like some gigantic monster ready to spring upon the traveller.

The hair of the affrighted pedagogue rose upon his head with terror.

What was to be done? To turn and fly was now too late; and besides, what chance was there of escaping ghost or goblin, if such it was, which could ride upon the wings of the wind? Summoning up, therefore, a show of courage, he demanded in stammering accents—"who are you?" He received no reply. He repeated his demand in a still more agitated voice.—Still there was no answer. Once more he cudgelled the sides of the inflexible Gunpowder, and shutting his eyes, broke forth with involuntary fervour into a psalm tune. Just then the shadowy object of alarm put itself in motion, and with a scramble and a bound, stood at once in the middle of the road. Though the night was dark and dismal, yet the form of the unknown might now in some degree be ascertained. He appeared to be a horseman of large dimensions, and mounted on a black horse of powerful frame. He made no offer of molestation or sociability, but kept aloof on one side of the road, jogging along on the blind side of old Gunpowder, who had now got over his fright and waywardness.

Ichabod, who had no relish for this strange midnight companion, and bethought himself of the adventure of Brom Bones with the galloping Hessian, now quickened his steed, in hopes of leaving him behind. The stranger, however, quickened his horse to an equal pace; Ichabod pulled up, and fell into a walk, thinking to lag behind—the other did the same. His heart began to sink within him; he endeavoured to resume his psalm tune, but his parched tongue clove to the roof of his mouth, and he could not utter a stave. There was something in the moody and dogged silence of this pertinacious companion, that was mysterious and appalling. It was soon fearfully accounted for. On mounting a rising ground, which brought the figure of his fellow traveller in relief against the sky, gigantic in height, and muffled in a cloak, Ichabod was horror struck, on perceiving that he was headless! but his horror was still more increased, on observing, that the head, which should have rested on his shoulders, was carried before him on the pommel of the saddle! His terror rose to desperation; he rained a shower of kicks and blows upon Gunpowder, hoping, by a sudden movement, to give his companion the slip—but the spectre started full jump with him. Away, then, they dashed, through thick and thin; stones flying, and sparks flashing, at every bound. Ichabod's flimsy garments fluttered in the air, as he stretched his long lank body away over his horse's head, in the eagerness of his flight.

They had now reached the road which turns off to Sleepy Hollow; but Gunpowder, who seemed possessed with a demon, instead of keeping up it, made an opposite turn, and plunged headlong down hill to the left. This road leads through a sandy hollow shaded by trees for about a quarter of a mile, where it crosses the bridge famous in goblin story, and just beyond swells the green knoll on which stands the whitewashed church.

As yet the panic of the steed had given his unskilful rider an apparent advantage in the chace, but just as he had got half way through the hollow, the girths of the saddle gave way, and he felt it slipping from under him; he seized it by the pommel, and endeavoured to hold it firm, but in vain; and had just time to save himself by clasping old Gunpowder round the neck, when the saddle fell to the earth, and he heard it trampled under foot by his pursuer. For a moment the terror of Hans Van Ripper's wrath passed across his mind—for it was his Sunday saddle; but this was no time for petty fears: the goblin was hard on his haunches; and (unskilful rider that he was!) he had much ado to maintain his seat; sometimes slipping on one side, sometimes on another, and sometimes jolted on the high ridge of his horse's back bone, with a violence that he verily feared would cleave him asunder.

An opening in the trees now cheered him with the hopes that the Church Bridge was at hand. The wavering reflection of a silver star in the bosom of the brook told him that he was not mistaken. He saw the walls of the church dimly glaring under the trees beyond. He recollected the place where Brom Bones' ghostly competitor had disappeared. "If I can but reach that bridge," thought Ichabod, "I am safe." Just then he heard the black steed panting and blowing close behind him; he even fancied that he felt his hot breath. Another convulsive kick in the ribs, and old Gunpowder sprung upon the bridge; he thundered over the resounding planks; he gained the opposite side, and now Ichabod cast a look behind to see if his pursuer should vanish, according to rule, in a flash of fire and brimstone. Just then he saw the goblin rising in his stirrups, and in the very act of hurling his head at him. Ichabod endeavoured to dodge the horrible missile, but too late. It encountered his cranium with a tremendous crash—he was tumbled headlong into the dust, and Gunpowder, the black steed, and the goblin rider, passed by like a whirlwind.———

The next morning the old horse was found without his saddle, and with the bridle under his feet, soberly cropping the grass at his .master's gate. Ichabod did not make his appearance at breakfast—dinner hour came, but no Ichabod. The boys assembled at the schoolhouse, and strolled idly about the banks of the brook; but no schoolmaster. Hans Van Ripper now began to feel some uneasiness about the fate of poor Ichabod, and his saddle. An inquiry was set on foot, and after diligent investigation they came upon his traces. In one part of the road leading to the church, was found the saddle trampled in the dirt; the tracks of horses' hoofs deeply dented in the road, and evidently at furious speed, were traced to the bridge, beyond which, on the bank of a broad part of the brook, where the water ran deep and black, was found the hat of the unfortunate Ichabod, and close beside it a shattered pumpkin.

The brook was searched, but the body of the schoolmaster was not to be discovered. Hans Van Ripper, as executor of his estate, examined the bundle which contained all his worldly effects. They consisted of two shirts and a half; two stocks for the neck; a pair or two of worsted stockings; an old pair of corduroy small clothes; a rusty razor; a book of psalm tunes, full of dog's ears; and a broken pitch pipe. As to the books and furniture of the schoolhouse, they belonged to the community, excepting Cotton Mather's History of Witchcraft, a New England Almanack, and a book of dreams and fortune telling, in which last was a sheet of foolscap much scribbled and blotted, in several fruitless attempts to make a copy of verses in honour of the heiress of Van Tassel. These magic books and the poetic scrawl were forthwith consigned to the flames by Hans Van Ripper, who from that time forward determined to send his children no more to school, observing, that he never knew any good come of this same reading and writing. Whatever money the schoolmaster possessed, and he had received his quarter's pay but a day or two before, he must have had about his person at the time of his disappearance.

The mysterious event caused much speculation at the Church on the following Sunday. Knots of gazers and gossips were collected in the church yard, at the bridge, and at the spot where the hat and pumpkin had been found. The stories of Brouwer, of Bones, and a whole budget of others, were called to mind; and when they had diligently considered them all, and compared them with the symptoms of the present case, they shook their heads, and came to the conclusion, that Ichabod had been carried off by the gallopping Hessian. As he was a bachelor, and in nobody's debt, nobody troubled his head any more about him, the school was removed to a different quarter of the hollow, and another pedagogue reigned in his stead.

It is true, an old farmer, who had been down to New York on a visit several years after, and from whom this account of the ghostly adventure was received, brought home the intelligence that Ichabod Crane was still alive; that he had left the neighbourhood partly through fear of the goblin and Hans Van Ripper, and partly in mortification at having been suddenly dismissed by the heiress; that he had changed his quarters to a distant part of the country; had kept school and studied law at the same time; had been admitted to the bar, turned politician, electioneered, written for the newspapers, and finally had been made a Justice of the Ten Pound Court. Brom Bones too, who, shortly after his rival's disappearance, conducted the blooming Katrina in triumph to the altar, was observed to look exceedingly knowing whenever the story of Ichabod was related, and always burst into a hearty laugh at the mention of the pumpkin; which led some to suspect that he knew more about the matter than he chose to tell.

The old country wives, however, who are the best judges of these matters, maintain to this day, that Ichabod was spirited away by supernatural means; and it is a favourite story often told about the neighbourhood round the winter evening fire. The bridge became more than ever an object of superstitious awe, and that may be the reason why the road has been altered of late years, so as to approach the church by the border of the millpond. The schoolhouse being deserted, soon fell to decay, and was reported to be haunted by the ghost of the unfortunate pedagogue; and the plough boy, loitering homeward of a still summer evening, has often fancied his voice at a distance, chanting a melancholy psalm tune among the tranquil solitudes of Sleepy Hollow.

POSTSCRIPT

Found in the Handwriting of Mr. Knickerbocker

The preceding Tale is given, almost in the precise words in which I heard it related at a corporation meeting of the ancient city of Manhattoes, at which were present many of its sagest and most illustrious burghers. The narrator was a pleasant, shabby, gentlemanly old fellow, in pepper and salt clothes, with a sadly humourous face, and one whom I strongly suspected of being poor, he made such efforts to be entertaining. When his story was concluded, there was much laughter and approbation, particularly from two or three deputy aldermen, who had been asleep the greater part of the time. There was, however, one tall, dry looking old gentleman, with beetling eye brows, who maintained a grave and rather severe face throughout; now and then folding his arms, inclining his head, and looking down upon the floor, as if turning a doubt over in his mind. He was one of your wary men, who never laugh but upon good grounds—when they have reason and the law on their side. When the mirth of the rest of the company had subsided, and silence was restored, he leaned one arm on the elbow of his chair, and sticking the other akimbo, demanded, with a slight, but exceedingly sage motion of the head, and contraction of the brow, what was the moral of the story, and what it went to prove.

The story teller, who was just putting a glass of wine to his lips, as a refreshment after his toils, paused for a moment, looked at his inquirer with an air of infinite deference, and lowering the glass slowly to the table, observed, that the story was intended most logically to prove,

"That there is no situation in life but has its advantages and pleasures, provided we will but take a joke as we find it:

"That, therefore, he that runs races with goblin troopers, is likely to have rough riding of it:

"Ergo, for a country schoolmaster to be refused the hand of a Dutch heiress, is a certain step to high preferment in the state."

The cautious old gentleman knit his brows tenfold closer after this explanation, being sorely puzzled by the ratiocination of the syllogism; while methought the one in pepper and salt eyed him with something of a triumphant leer. At length he observed, that all this was very well, but still he thought the story a little on the extravagant—there were one or two points on which he had his doubts.

"Faith, sir," replied the story teller, "as to that matter, I don't believe one half of it myself."   D.K.

L'ENVOY*

Go, little booke, God send thee good passage,
And specially let this be thy prayere,
Unto them all that thee will read or hear,
Where thou art wrong, after their help to call,
Thee to correct in any part or all.
                CHAUCER's *Belle Dame sans Mercie.*

In concluding a second volume of the Sketch Book, the Author cannot
but express his deep sense of the indulgence with which his first has
been received, and of the liberal disposition that has been evinced
to treat him with kindness as a stranger. Even the critics, whatever
may be said of them by others, he has found to be a singularly gentle
and good natured race: it is true that each has in turn objected to some
one or two articles,—and that these individual exceptions, taken in
the aggregate, would amount almost to a total condemnation of his
work; but then he has been consoled by observing, that what one
has particularly censured, another has as particularly praised; and
thus, the encomiums being set off against the objections, he finds his
work, upon the whole, commended far beyond its deserts.

He is aware that he runs a risk of forfeiting much of this kind
favour by not following the counsel that has been liberally bestowed
upon him; for where abundance of valuable advice is given gratis, it
may seem a man's own fault if he should go astray. He can only
say, in his vindication, that he faithfully determined, for a time, to
govern himself in his second volume by the opinions passed upon
his first; but he was soon brought to a stand by the contrariety of
excellent counsel. One kindly advised him to avoid the ludicrous; another to shun the pathetic; a third assured him that he was tolerable
at description, but cautioned him to leave narrative alone; while a
fourth declared that he had a very pretty knack at turning a story,
and was really entertaining when in a pensive mood, but was grievously
mistaken if he imagined himself to possess a spirit of humour.

Thus perplexed by the advice of his friends, who each in turn closed
some particular path, but left him all the world beside to range in,
he found that to follow all their counsels would, in fact, be to stand
still. He remained for a time sadly embarrassed; when, all at once,
the thought struck him to ramble on even as he had begun: that his

*Closing the second volume of the London edition,

work being miscellaneous, and written for different humours, it could not be expected that any one would be pleased with the whole; but that if it should contain something to suit each reader, his end would be completely answered. Few guests sit down to a varied table with an equal appetite for every dish. One has an elegant horror of a roasted pig; another holds a curry or a devil in utter abomination; a third cannot tolerate the ancient flavour of venison and wild fowl; and a fourth, of truly masculine stomach, looks with sovereign contempt on those knick-knacks, here and there dished up for the ladies. Thus each article is condemned in its turn; and yet, amidst this variety of appetites, seldom does a dish go away from the table without being tasted and relished by some one or other of the guests.

With these considerations he ventures to serve up this second volume in the same heterogeneous way with his first; simply requesting the reader, if he should find here and there something to please him, to rest assured that it was written expressly for intelligent readers like himself; but intreating him, should he find any thing to dislike, to tolerate it, as one of those articles which the author has been obliged to write for readers of a less refined taste.

To be serious.—The author is conscious of the numerous faults and imperfections of his work; and well aware how little he is disciplined and accomplished in the arts of authorship. His deficiencies are also increased by a diffidence arising from his peculiar situation. He finds himself writing in a strange land, and appearing before a public which he has been accustomed, from childhood, to regard with the highest feelings of awe and reverence. He is full of solicitude to deserve their approbation, yet finds that very solicitude continually embarrassing his powers, and depriving him of that ease and confidence which are necessary to successful exertion. Still the kindness with which he is treated encourages him to go on, hoping that in time he may acquire a steadier footing; and thus he proceeds, half venturing, half shrinking, surprized at his own good fortune, and wondering at his own temerity.

THE END.

APPENDIX A

[This "Prospectus" introduced *Sketch Book* Number I in the first three American editions.]

PROSPECTUS

The following writings are published on experiment; should they please they may be followed by others. The writer will have to contend with some disadvantages. He is unsettled in his abode, subject to interruptions, and has his share of cares and vicissitudes. He cannot therefore promise a regular plan, nor regular periods of publication. Should he be encouraged to proceed, much time may elapse between the appearance of his numbers; and their size must depend on the materials he has on hand. His writings will partake of the fluctuations of his own thoughts and feelings; sometimes treating of scenes before him; sometimes of other purely imaginary, and sometimes wandering back with his recollections to his native country. He will not be able to give them that tranquil attention necessary to finished composition, and as they must be transmitted across the Atlantic for publication, he must trust to others to correct the frequent errors of the press. Should his writings, however, with all their imperfections, be well received, he cannot conceal that it would be a source of the purest gratification; for though he does not aspire to those high honours that are the rewards of loftier intellects; yet it is the dearest wish of his heart to have a secure, and cherished, though humble, corner in the good opinions and kind feelings of his countrymen.

London, 1819

APPENDIX B

[This "Advertisement" was printed at the beginning of Volume I of the first British edition, 1820, and continued to introduce *The Sketch Book* until replaced by the "Preface to the Revised Edition" in 1848.

ADVERTISEMENT

The following desultory papers are part of a series written in this country, but published in America. The author is aware of the austerity with which the writings of his countrymen have hitherto been treated by British critics: he is conscious, too, that much of the contents of his papers can be interesting only in the eyes of American readers. It was not his intention, therefore, to have them reprinted in this country. He has, however, observed several of them from time to time inserted in periodical works of merit, and has understood that it was probable they would be republished in a collective form. He has been induced, therefore, to revise and bring them forward himself, that they may at least come correctly before the public. Should they be deemed of sufficient importance to attract the attention of critics, he solicits for them that courtesy and candour which a stranger has some right to claim, who presents himself at the threshold of a hospitable nation.

February, 1820.

NOTES

(A somewhat abridged and slightly modified version of the "Explanatory Notes" compiled by Haskell Springer, editor of *The Sketch Book of Geoffrey Crayon, Gent.* (Boston: Twayne Publishers, 1978)—vol. VIII of *The Complete Works of Washington Irving*—and included in that volume, pp. 305–39. Used with permission. Quotations and allusions that are unexplained in the notes have yet to be identified.)

The numbers before all notes indicate page and line respectively. Chapter numbers, chapter or section titles, epigraphs, author's chapter or section summaries, text quotations, and footnotes are included in the line count. Only running heads and rules added by the printer to separate the running head from the text are omitted from the count. The quotation from the text, to the left of the bracket, is the matter under discussion.

epigraph "I have no wife. . . ." Burton.]   Robert Burton's *The Anatomy of Melancholy*, 1621. The quotation is from the introductory section entitled "Democritus Junior to the Reader."

PREFACE TO THE REVISED EDITION

5.5 'And for my love . . .']   *The Merchant of Venice*, I, iii.

5.10 *crimp*]   To impress soldiers or seamen; hence, to entrap.

5.29 Don Cossack]   The Don Cossacks are so called because the river Don flows through their homeland in southwest Russia.

6.23 John Bunyan's Holy War]   Published in 1682.

6.30 Lockhart]   John Gibson Lockhart (1794–1854), a contributor to *Blackwood's Edinburgh Magazine*, who married Scott's daughter, Sophia. His *Life of Scott* was published in 1838.

6.36 "nigromancy"]   A form of "necromancy," not a slur on "Negro."

7.33 *Sunnyside*]   In 1835 Irving bought twenty-four acres on the Hudson River near Tarrytown, and gradually remodeled the small cottage he found there into Sunnyside, a fine house of romantic architecture.

THE AUTHOR'S ACCOUNT OF HIMSELF

8.8 LYLY's EUPHUES] John Lyly (1554–1606) published *Euphues, The Anatomy of Wit* in 1578, and *Euphues and His England* in 1580. "Euphuism" derives from the title of the book and describes its style.

10.4–5 the cascade of Terni] The artificially created falls of the river Velino near the town of Terni in the Italian province of Perugia.

THE VOYAGE

11.12 OLD POEM] The fourth stanza of a song, "Halloo my fancie," given in *English Minstrelsy*, 2d ed. (Edinburgh: Ballantyne & Co., 1810), vol. II, song 13.

11.25–26 'a lengthening chain'] Oliver Goldsmith, *The Traveller* (1764), line 10.

14.6 Deep called unto deep.] "Deep calleth unto deep" (Ps. 42:7).

ROSCOE

16.1 *ROSCOE*] William Roscoe (1753–1831). His most important works are: *The Life of Lorenzo de'Medici*; and *The Life and Pontificate of Leo the Tenth*. Irving met him in 1815 when Roscoe was at the peak of his fame, and the two became well acquainted.

16.7 THOMSON] James Thomson (1700–1748), wrote *The Seasons* and *The Castle of Indolence*. This quotation is from a tragedy, *Sophonisba*, II, i.

16.9 the Athenaeum] Originally "the temple of Athena" at Athens, in which poets and learned men read their works. In modern times a literary and scientific club.

17.3–4 stony places of the world] See Matt. 13:5.

17:31 living streams of knowledge] See Cant. 4:15 and Rev. 7:17.

17.31 "daily beauty in his life,"] *Othello*, V, i.

18.3 Lorenzo De Medici] (1449–1492), called "il Magnifico"; Florentine statesman, patron of arts and letters, scholars, poet.

18.42 *Address on the opening of the Liverpool Institution.] The Royal Institution. Roscoe was the prime mover behind its establishment in 1817. It was the central literary institution in Liverpool.

19.22 ". . . dispersed about the country"] Irving apparently did not know that Roscoe's friends purchased £600 of his books at the sale, and offered them to him as a gift. He refused it, and they gave them to the Liverpool Athenaeum to form a "Roscoe Collection."

19.31–32 black letter]   A heavy-faced type used in the earliest printed books.

20.23 Pompey's column at Alexandria]   Erected in honor of the Emperor Diocletian in 302.

THE WIFE

22.8 MIDDLETON]   Thomas Middleton (1570–1627), dramatist. The quotation is from *Women, Beware Women*, III, i.

RIP VAN WINKLE

Irving reportedly wrote "Rip Van Winkle" at great speed in June, 1818, at the home of his sister, Sarah Van Wart, in Birmingham. His immediate literary source was "Peter Klaus" in Otmar's *Volkssagen*, but his own observation of Dutch families in New York, his reading from Riesbeck's *Travels Through Germany*, and his interest in American and European folklore are also apparent in the story.

28.13 a history of the province]   Irving's *A History of New York . . . by Diedrich Knickerbocker*.

28.28 ". . . more in sorrow than in anger,"]   *Hamlet*, I, ii.

28.34 Waterloo medal]   Issued by George IV as regent to every officer and soldier who took part in the actions of June 16, 17, and 18, 1815.

28.34–35 Queen Anne's farthing]   These farthings were struck in 1713–1714 on the recommendation of Jonathan Swift. They are falsely thought to be very rare.

29.6 thylke]   *The*, or *that same*.

29.8 CARTWRIGHT]   William Cartwright (1611–1643), clergyman, poet, and dramatist. The quotation is unidentified.

29.28 Peter Stuyvesant]   Governor of New Netherlands from 1647 to 1664.

29.38 Fort Christina]   See the *History of New York*, bk. 6, chap. 7.

30.6 curtain lecture]   "A reproof given by a wife to her husband in bed" (Johnson's *Dictionary*).

31.8 galligaskins]   Loose breeches.

34.23 hanger]   A kind of short sword, originally hung from the belt.

34.43 hollands]   A gin manufactured in Holland.

37.9–10 a red night cap]   The Phrygian cap, worn by slaves freed by the Romans and later adopted as the symbol of liberty in the French Revolution.

40.12 Hendrick Hudson]   Henry Hudson (d. 1611) was English, not Dutch as Irving's rendering of the name is meant to imply.

41.23–24 emperor Frederick *der Rothbart*, and the Kypphauser mountain]   Holy Roman Emperor Frederick I (1152–1190), also known as Frederick Barbarossa, sleeps, according to legend, in a cave of the Kyffhäuser mountain in central Germany. When Barbarossa's red beard has thrice encircled the table at which he sleeps, he will awake and make Germany the preeminent state of the world.

42.1 POSTSCRIPT]   Irving added this section in 1848.

ENGLISH WRITERS ON AMERICA

43.6 ON THE LIBERTY OF THE PRESS]   That is, *Areopagitica* (1644).

48.21 Knowledge is power]   ("Nam et ipsa scientia potestas est.") The quotation is from Francis Bacon's *Essayes, Religious Meditations. Places of Perswasion and Disswasion* (1597).

RURAL LIFE IN ENGLAND

50.5 COWPER]   William Cowper (1731–1796); the quotation is from *The Task*, bk. III, lines 290–92; "pleasure" should be "leisure."

50.11 wakes]   These were annual festivals to commemorate the completion of the parish church.

53.28 "The Flower and the Leaf"]   Dryden attributed it to Chaucer, but its authorship is still unknown.

THE BROKEN HEART

56.6 MIDDLETON]   from *Blurt, Master Constable*, III, i.

56.37–38 the wings of the morning]   Ps. 139:9.

56.38 "fly to the uttermost part of the earth, and be at rest."]   Pss. 139:10, 55:6.

57.18 "dry sorrow drinks her blood,"]   *Romeo and Juliet*, III, v, "Dry sorrow drinks our blood."

57.22 "darkness and the worm."]   "The deep damp vault, the darkness, and the worm" (Edward Young, *Night Thoughts*, Night IV, line 11).

57.41 young E————]   Robert Emmet (1778–1803) planned to capture Dublin Castle and the lord lieutenant; after his failure he was tried and hanged. He made moving speeches before being sentenced, and on the gallows.

58.11–12 the daughter of a late celebrated Irish Barrister]   Sarah, the youngest daughter of John Philpot Curran, a famous Irish lawyer and judge.

59.2 "heeded not the song of the charmer. . . ."]   "Which will not hearken to the voice of charmers, charming never so wisely" (Ps. 58:5).

59.34 Moore]   Thomas Moore (1779–1852). The poem, whose first line is also its title, is in *Irish Melodies*.

THE ART OF BOOK MAKING

61.2 Synesius]   A bishop of Cyrene at the time of Theodosius the younger, ca. 375–413.

62.23 "pure English undefiled"]   The allusion is to Spenser, *The Faerie Queen*, bk. 2, canto 2, stanza 32: "Dan Chaucer, well of English undefiled," but may also owe something to the Bible. See James 1:27: "Pure religion and undefiled. . . ."

63.1–2 line upon line, precept upon precept, here a little and there a little.]   See Isa. 28:10.

63.3–5 witches' caldron . . . "slab and good."]   *Macbeth*, IV, i, is the source for these lines, which are somewhat inaccurately quoted.

64.22 "The Paradise of dainty Devices,"]   (1576) A popular verse miscellany.

64.36 an arcadian hat]   Any rustic hat. Arcadia, a pastoral region in the Peloponnesus, is supposed to be typical of rural simplicity.

64.38 Primrose hill]   North of Regent's Park, it commands a fine view of London.

64.41 "babbling about green fields."]   *Henry V*, II, iii. Falstaff on his deathbed "babbled of green fields."

65.15 Beaumont and Fletcher]   Francis Beaumont (ca. 1584–1616), and John Fletcher (1579–1625), Elizabethan dramatists chiefly noted for the plays they wrote together.

65.15–16 Castor and Pollux] The Dioscuri or Twins. Perhaps the reference is to the battle of Lake Regillus (see Macaulay's *Lays of Ancient Rome*).

65.16 Ben Jonson] (1572–1637). The famous playwright and poet is supposed to have killed an enemy in single-handed combat while serving with the English army in the Netherlands.

65.20 the dead body of Patroclus.] See the *Iliad*, bks. 16–18.

65.28–29 "chopped bald shot."] *Henry IV, Part II*, III, ii. Falstaff: "O, give me always a little, lean, old, chapt, bald shot."

65.31–32 learned Theban] *King Lear*, III, iv.

A ROYAL POET

67.25 Sir Peter Lely] (1618–1680), a Dutch artist; First Painter to Charles II.

67.26 "large green courts,"] Surrey's "Prisoned in Windsor, he recounteth his pleasure there passeth," line 6.

67.28–29 hapless Surrey] Henry Howard, earl of Surrey (ca. 1517–1547). He was beheaded on a charge of treason.

67.30 the Lady Geraldine] The "Fair Geraldine" of Surrey's poetry was apparently inspired by Lady Elizabeth Fitzgerald, but she was a child at the time, and the lady in the poetry is no doubt largely imaginary.

67.31–32 "With eyes cast up. . . ."] "Prisoned in Windsor . . . ," lines 7, 8.

67.34 James the First] (1394–1437). He became king in 1406, and was assassinated on February 20 or 21, 1437. His widow, Joan Beaufort, a granddaughter of John of Gaul, had no difficulty bringing the murderers to justice. Irving's picture of him, though romanticized, is, in historical detail, largely correct.

68.41 °Buchanan] George Buchanan (1506–1582), *Rerum Scotticarum Historia*, bk. 10.

68.42 †Ballenden's Translation of Hector Boyce.] bk. 16, chap. 16. A free translation into the Scottish vernacular, by John Ballenden or Ballentyne (1533–1587), of a history of Scotland written in ancient Latin by Hector Bocce, or Boethius (1465–1536).

69.22 Tasso in his dismal cell] The Italian poet (1544–1595) was confined for seven years in a hospital for lunatics because he offended the duke of Ferrara.

69.40 †Roger l'Estrange] This is stanza 11 of "Loyalty Confined," found in David Lloyd's *Memoirs of Those that Suffered in the Cause of Charles I* (London, 1668), and reprinted in Bishop Percy's *Reliques of Ancient English Poetry*, vol. II, bk. 3, song 12. Percy attributes it to Sir Roger L'Estrange (1616–1704). His authorship of this song, though, has not been proven.

70.17–18 "Cynthia rinsing. . . ."]   A very free translation.

71.21–22 . . . his perpetual blindness]   See the sonnets "When I consider how my light is spent" and "Cyriac, this three years' day"; see also *Paradise Lost*, bk. 3, lines 1–55.

74.28 gilliflower]   Used to designate any of several flowers, including the stock and clove pink.

75.24 Gower]   John Gower (ca. 1330–1408) wrote the *Confessio Amantis*.

75.41–42 morning stars]   "When the morning stars sang together, and all the sons of God shouted for joy." Job 38:7.

76.1–2 captivating fiction]   The allusion is to Sir Walter Scott.

77.37 "Christ's Kirk of the Green,"]   Its authorship is uncertain.

78.6 Vaucluse]   Near Avignon, it was for many years the home of Petrarch.

78.6–7 the shrine at Loretto]   The Santa Casa at Loreto, Italy, according to tradition, is the house in which Mary had been born, brought up, and received the Annunciation. Because of threatened destruction by the Turks in the thirteenth century the building was supposedly carried away by angels and ultimately placed where it now stands.

THE COUNTRY CHURCH

79.6 BEGGAR'S BUSH]   A comedy (1615–1622) by John Fletcher and Philip Massinger. The quotation is from II, iii.

82.42 rapt out of sight in a whirlwind]   See Elijah in 2 Kings 2:1.

THE WIDOW AND HER SON

83.4 MARLOWE'S TAMBURLAINE]   The preceding passage is from part I, V, ii, in C. F. Tucker Brooke's edition.

83.14–15 Sweet day, so pure. . . .]   Lines 1 and 2 of "Virtue" in *The Temple*, by George Herbert (1593–1633).

87.20–21 "that looked on his childhood,"]   Unidentified.

A SUNDAY IN LONDON

89.40 *Part of a sketch. . . .]   The manuscript of this piece gives no clue about the "sketch" to which Irving refers. It apparently never became part of *The Sketch Book*.

THE BOAR'S HEAD TAVERN, EAST CHEAP

91.7 MOTHER BOMBIE]   John Lyly's last comedy.

91.37 a great German critick]   No doubt August Wilhelm von Schlegel, whose *Lectures on Dramatic Art and Literature* appeared in English in 1815.

92.18–19 old Jack Falstaff. . . .]   Falstaff describes himself in these terms in *Henry IV, Part I*, II, iv.

92.26 Dame Quickly]   Hostess of the Boar's Head Tavern. She appears in *The Merry Wives of Windsor*, both parts of *Henry IV*, and *Henry V*.

92.32 haunted regions of Cock-lane]   Alluding to the reported appearance of a ghost in a Cock Lane house in 1762. Samuel Johnson was instrumental in exposing the spirit as a fraud.

92.33–34 Cateaton Street and Oly Jewry]   Cateaton Street is now Gresham Street. The name "Old Jewry" derives from their Jewish quarter which existed there before the expulsion of the Jews from England in 1290.

92.34–35 Guildhall and its two stunted Giants]   The council hall of the city of London; its "giants" are large figures of Gog and Magog. (See Ezekiel 38–39, and Rev. 20:8. See also Caxton's translation of the *Recuyell of the Historyes of Troye* [ca. 1474] for the mythical connection of Gog and Magog with the history of Britain.)

92.36 London Stone]   Probably a fragment of the great central milestone of the Romans, from which all distances were measured.

92.37 Jack Cade]   The leader of a rebellion in 1450, during the reign of Henry VI.

92.41 old Stow]   John Stowe, or Stow, historian and antiquary, published a *Survey of London* in 1598. It is our most valuable source book on medieval and Renaissance London.

93.1 sawtrie]   psaltry.

93.22 the Monument]   A stone column built by Sir Christopher Wren to commemorate the great fire of 1666.

93.29–30 the great fire of London]   It began on September 2, 1666, lasted five days, and virtually destroyed the city.

94.15 Milton's angels] The allusion is no doubt to *Paradise Lost*, bk. 2. lines 557–61: "Others apart sat on a Hill retir'd, / In thoughts more elevate, and reason'd high / Of Providence, Foreknowledge, Will, and Fate, / Fixt Fate, Free will, Foreknowledge absolute, / And found no end, in wand'ring mazes lost."

94.29 Turenne] Henri Vicomte de Turenne (1611–1675); French general.

94.32–33 William Walworth . . . Wat Tyler] Walworth, Mayor of London, in 1381 killed Wat Tyler, one of the leaders of a revolt, while Tyler was speaking to the King.

94.35 Sovereigns of Cockney] Irving uses "Cockney" here to mean London. More exactly, it refers to someone born "within the sound of Bow Bells," the bells of the church of St. Mary le Bow, Cheapside.

95.15–16 the "mirre garland of captain Death"] Unidentified.

95.16 sundry train-band captains] The train-bands or trained-bands were a militia established in 1327. They were discontinued in 1662, except for those of London, which were reorganized in 1794 as the City of London Militia.

96.23 Miles Lane] A corruption of St. Michael's Lane.

96.25 "bully Rock"] Or "bully-rook," now archaic. *The Merry Wives of Windsor*, I, iii; II, i. Bully-rock apparently means either (1) a jovial comrade or (2) a blustering gallant.

98.3 the learned Scriblerius. . . .] See Chapter 3 of *Memoirs of the Extraordinary Life, Works and Discoveries of Martinus Scriblerus*, a burlesque on pedantry, written by members of the Scriblerus Club which included Pope, Arbuthnot, Gay, and Swift. Published by Pope in 1741.

98.14 Bardolph] He appears in *Henry IV*, parts 1 and 2, *Henry V*, and *The Merry Wives of Windsor*.

98.42 II^d Part. Henry IV.] II, i.

99.18 a "tedious brief" account] *A Midsummer Night's Dream*, V, i.

99.35 the far famed Portland vase.] An ancient funeral urn, loaned in 1810 to the British Museum by the duke of Portland.

THE MUTABILITY OF LITERATURE

100.11 DRUMMOND OF HAWTHORNDEN] William Drummond of Hawthornden (1585–1649). The quotation (inaccurate in several places) consists of lines 1–3 and 5–8 of an untitled sonnet from his *Poems* (1616). The last line should read: "And that nought lighter is than airy praise."

100.25 doomsday book]   Properly *Domesday Book*. The great survey of England, ordered by William the Conqueror.

100.33 An ancient picture]   Apparently of John Williams (1582–1650), dean of Westminster and a key political figure before the Puritan Revolution.

102.40 Robert Grosteste of Lincoln]   Usually spelled Grosseteste (ca. 1175–1253). He was bishop of Lincoln, and wrote many works on theology, philosophy, and husbandry.

103.2–3 Gyraldus Cambrensis]   Gerald of Wales (1146–1220?). A turbulent churchman and topographer who wrote a number of works on various subjects.

103.5–6 Henry of Huntingdon]   (1084?–1155), archdeacon. He wrote a *Historia Anglorum* and *De Contemptu Mundi*.

103.8 Joseph of Exeter]   (ca. 1190). Author of a Latin poem in six books, *De Bello Trojano*, and a number of other works in Latin. Some of the writings with which he is credited may never have existed.

103.13 John Wallis, the Franciscan]   John Waleys or Wallensis, regent master of the Franciscan schools at Oxford before 1260, and author of theological works. He also taught in Paris, where he was known as "Arbor Vitae" ("The Tree of Life").

103.14 William of Malmsbury]   (ca. 1090–1143). Librarian of Malmesbury Abbey. His *Gesta Regum Anglorum* is based on ballads which he collected.

103.14 Simeon of Durham]   (ca. 1130), precentor of Durham. He wrote a history of Durham Cathedral and other compilations.

103.14–15 Benedict of Peterborough]   (d. 1193), abbot of Peterborough. He wrote histories of the Passion, and of the miracles of St. Thomas à Becket.

103.15 John Hanvill of St. Albans]   Born probably before 1180, and known as John of St. Giles, John Giles, or John of St. Albans. He was a Dominican monk and physician, and archdeacon of Oxford. His only extant work is *Experimenta Joannis de S. Aegideo*.

103.20 Wynkyn de Worde]   (d. 1534). He was a Belgian pupil of William Caxton, and became the second printer in London.

103.32 Robert of Gloucester]   (ca. 1260–1300). Known only from the metrical *Chronicle* of England (to 1270) which bears his name.

103.37 *Chaucer's Testament of Love*]   The *Testament of Love* was actually written by Thomas Usk, a contemporary of Chaucer.

103.38 Holinshed]   Raphael Holinshed (d. 1580) published his *Chronicles of England, Scotland, and Ireland* in 1577. The passage is unlocated.

103.40 John Scogan]   (ca. 1480). Fool at the court of Edward IV. "It is not improbable that his biography, which is supplied in his 'Jests,' said to have been compiled by Andrew Boorde . . . is apocryphal and that Scogan is a fictitious hero" (*Dictionary of National Biography*).

103.40 John Lydgate, monke of Berrie]   (ca. 1370–1449). He wrote well over 100,000 lines of poetry, much of it justly forgotten. At the age of fifteen he became a monk at the abbey of Bury St. Edmunds.

103.42 John Jewell, Bishop of Sarum]   John Jewel (1522–1571) was bishop of Salisbury (formerly Sarum). Hooker was among his protégés, and Fuller edited his works.

103.42–43 John Fox]   John Foxe wrote *The Acts and Monuments of the Church* (1563), better known as "The Book of Martyrs."

104.1 . . . Spenser's 'well of pure English undefiled,']   See note 62.23.

104.18 As unintelligible . . . as an Egyptian obelisk]   Champollion's discovery of the meaning of Egyptian hieroglyphics was not made public until 1822, at least three years after Irving wrote the sketch.

104.22 Xerxes]   See Herodotus, *The Histories*, bk. 7, par. 44–46.

104.28–29 Sackville's stately plays, and Mirror for Magistrates]   Thomas Sackville, earl of Dorset (1536–1608), wrote an "Induction" and one of the stories for the second edition of the collection of rhymed narratives called *A Mirror for Magistrates* (1563). The "Induction" is one of the best English poems between the *Canterbury Tales* and *The Faerie Queen*. He also collaborated in the first blank verse tragedy, *Gorboduc*, later entitled *Ferrex and Porrex*.

104.30 "unparalelled John Lyly."]   In 1632 Edward Blount collected six of Lyly's plays, and published them as *Sixe Court Comedies* . . . Written By the onely Rare Poet of that Time, The Witie, Comicall, Facetiously-Quicke and Unparalelld: John Lilly, Master of Arts. See note 8.8.

104.42 Bellona]   Roman goddess of war.

104.42 Suada]   Roman goddess of persuasion.

104.43 *Harvey's Pierces's Supererogation*]   Gabriel Harvey (1545?–1630), fellow of Cambridge, friend of Spenser, lecturer, rhetorician. *Pierce's Supererogation* (1593) was one of his contributions to a long and vicious pamphlet war between Gabriel and his brother Richard on one side, and Robert Greene and Thomas Nashe on the other.

105.15 groan with rank and excessive vegetation]   See *Comus*, lines 720–31.

105.31 fountains of thought . . . broken up]   See Gen. 7:11.

106.3 checks on population . . . economists]   Thomas Malthus published his much discussed *Essay on Population* in 1798.

106.17 knew little of Latin, and nothing of Greek]   See Ben Jonson's poem,

"To the Memory of Mr. W. Shakespeare," which was prefaced to the First Folio.

107.7 faithful portrayer of nature] See *Hamlet*, III, ii: "to hold, as 't were, the mirror up to nature."

107.44 CHURCHYARD] Thomas Churchyard (1520?–1604), soldier and minor poet. The quotation is unidentified.

RURAL FUNERALS

109.7 CYMBELINE] IV, ii.

109.23–27 White his shroud. . . .] *Hamlet*, IV, v (inaccurately quoted).

110.1 says Bourne] in *Antiquitates Vulgares*, chap. 3. Henry Bourne (1696–1733), divine and antiquary. See Acts 20:24.

110.25 Sir Thomas Overbury] (1581–1613). The brief description in prose of different character types which were appended to Overbury's didactic poem, *A Wife*, were known as "characters," and were written by a number of other authors as well as by Overbury. The sketch of "the faire and happy milkmaid" is most likely by John Webster, the dramatist.

110.30 "The Maid's Tragedy,"] First published in 1619. The lines quoted are in I, i. The maid cannot marry her lover and so laments.

110.38 Herrick] Robert Herrick (1591–1674), major Cavalier poet and apparently one of Irving's favorite authors. The passage is stanza 2 of "The Dirge of Jephthah's Daughter," Number 83 in *Noble Numbers*.

111.4 says Evelyn, in his Sylva] John Evelyn (1620–1706), famous for the *Diary* which bears his name. His *Sylva* (1664) is a plea for reforestation in England.

111.31 "Corydon's Doleful Knell,"] Stanzas 5 to 7. See Percy's *Reliques*. vol. II, bk. 2, song 27.

112.14 Camden . . . Britannia] William Camden (1551–1623), antiquary, historian, and teacher of Ben Jonson. The *Britannia* is a Latin survey of the British Isles. The passage quoted by Irving was apparently added by Bishop Gibson in his edition of the *Britannia* (1772).

112.21 Thomas Stanley, Esq.] (1625–1678), lyric poet.

112.29 "The Maid's Tragedy,"] The passage is in II, i.

113.13–16 "Lay her i' the earth," . . . violets spring!] *Hamlet*, V, i.

113.17 "Dirge of Jephtha,"] "The Dirge of Jephtha's Daughter," stanzas 11 and 13. See note 110.38.

114.3–9 With fairest flowers. . . .] *Cymbeline*, IV, ii.

114.27 Jeremy Taylor] (1613–1667). Bishop and author of *Holy Living*,

Holy Dying, The Liberty of Prophesying, and some outstanding sermons. The quotation is from his *Funeral Sermon on the Countess of Carbery.*

115.9–12 Each lonely place shall him restore. . . .] A free rendering of the last stanza of a poem by William Collins (1721–1759), entitled "Dirge in Cymbeline."

117.32 Bright, in his travels in Lower Hungary] Richard Bright, M.D. (1789–1858), discoverer of Bright's disease, and physician to Queen Victoria, author of *Travels from Vienna through Lower Hungary* (Edinburgh, 1818).

118.1 Iffland] August Wilhelm Iffland (1759–1814). German actor and dramatist.

THE INN KITCHEN

119.2 Shall I not take mine ease in mine inn?] *Henry IV, Part I*, III, iii. See also 209.19–20.

119.5 *Pomme d'Or*] Golden Apple.

119.6 *table d'hote*] A fixed-price meal at a specified time.

120.24 *écume de mer*] meerschaum.

THE SPECTRE BRIDEGROOM

121.8 SIR EGER, SIR GRAHAME, AND SIR GRAY-STEEL] The story appears in *Early Metrical Tales, &c.* (Edinburgh: W. and D. Laing, 1826). Irving's source is unknown.

122.12 the Heldenbuch] Collection of thirteenth century German epic poetry. Its literary value is not great.

122.18 Minne-lieders] Irving means *Minnesingers*, the German troubadours of the twelfth and thirteenth centuries who sang *Minnelieder*, or love songs.

122.32 wasting their sweetness] See Gray's "Elegy Written in A Country Church-Yard," line 56.

124.14 the fatted calf had been killed] An allusion to Luke 15:11–32, the parable of the prodigal son.

124.16 *Rhein-wein*] Rhein wine.

124.17 *Ferne-wein*] Properly *Firne-wein*, old but inferior wine, tasting of the barrel. Irving apparently mistook the meaning of the term.

124.17 the great Heidelburg tun] The Great Tun (20 feet high by 31 feet long, and holding 49,000 gallons) is kept in the castle of Heidelberg, the German university town. It was built in 1751, and is thus an anachronism in the story.

124.19 *Saus und Braus*] revelry and riotous living.

128.14 Hoch-heimer] Hochheimer is a famous Rhine wine.

128.38–40 Leonora . . . world] Lenore is the name of the heroine of a popular ballad by Gottfried August Bürger (1747–1794), who is carried off by the ghost of her dead lover.

129.42 the wild huntsman] See Bürger's "Der Wilde Jäger," which was translated by Sir Walter Scott.

WESTMINSTER ABBEY

134.16 CHRISTOLERO'S EPIGRAMS, by T. B. 1598.] *Chrestoleros: Seven Bookes of Epigrams*, written by Thomas Bastard (1566–1618), depicts the manners of the time and is sometimes very bitter.

135.14–15 Vitalis . . . Gislebertus . . . Laurentius. . . .] Vitalis was a Norman; Gislebertus (Gilbert Crispin) exhumed the body of Edward the Confessor in 1102; Laurentius obtained the canonization of Edward in 1163. "Abbas" means "Abbot."

136.11 Addison] Joseph Addison (1672–1719). He and Richard Steele wrote *The Tatler* and *The Spectator*.

137.32–33 "all the brothers. . . ."] See the full inscription on p. 146.

137.36–37 the tomb of Mrs. Nightingale, by Roubillac] Lady Elizabeth Nightingale (d. 1731). Louis Roubillac (1695–1762) was a French sculptor, whose monument for Mrs. Nightingale was erected in 1758.

140.33 Edward the Confessor] Edward, king of England and later a saint, ruled from 1042 to his death in 1066, the year of the Norman Conquest.

140.40 "beds of darkness."] See Job 17:13: "I have made my bed in the darkness."

142.7–9 "Our fathers," says Sir Thomas Brown. . . .] *Hydriotaphia, Urne Buriall* (1658), chap. 5. Sir Thomas Browne (1605–1682), a physician, also wrote *Religio Medici*.

142.16–18 "The Egyptian mummies. . . ."] Browne, *Hydriotaphia*, chap. 5.

142.17 Cambyses] Son of Cyrus the Great, king of Persia. In 525 B.C. he conquered Egypt.

142.17 Mizraim] One of the sons of Ham. See Gen. 10:6. The name signifies Egypt.

142.28 as a tale that is told.]   Ps. 90:9.

142.30 NOTES CONCERNING WESTMINSTER ABBEY]   Irving added this section in 1848.

142.33–34 Pope Gregory the Great]   Pope from 590–604. One of the four great doctors of the Western Church. He sent Augustine to England in 596.

144.18 A curious narrative]   *A True and Perfect Narrative of the Strange and Unexpected Finding the Crucifix and Gold-Chain of that Pious Prince, St. Edward, the King and Confessor, which was found after 620 Years' Interment: and Presented to His Most Sacred Majesty, King James the Second,* by Charles Taylour, Gent. (London, 1688). Irving follows the narrative closely.

144.19 Paul Pry]   A busybody in a comedy of the same name by John Poole, which was produced at Haymarket on September 13, 1825.

145.41 Malcolm. Lond. Rediv.]   *Londinium Redivivum,* by James Peller Malcolm, 1802 (in four volumes). The quoted passage is supposedly in vol. I, p. 94.

146.1 *Inscription on a monument. . . .*]   The allusion is on p. 137. The orthography and punctuation are generally modernized.

146.29 one of the Pultneys.]   Daniel Pulteney, a lord of the Admiralty, who died in 1731.

CHRISTMAS

147.5 HUE AND CRY AFTER CHRISTMAS]   From the anonymous pamphlet "Arraignment, Conviction and Imprisoning of Christmas: . . . with An Hue and Cry after Christmas. . . ." (London, 1645).

148.10 OLD SONG]   This is reported to be stanza 7 of "Time's Alteration," found in Joseph Ritson's *Select Collection of English Songs* (1783).

150.36 sherris sack]   a dry white Spanish wine; sherry.

151.21 Waits]   Bands of musicians and singers who at Christmas time went from house to house.

151.24 "when deep sleep falleth upon man,"]   See Job 4:13 and 33:15.

151.31 "telling the night watches . . ."]   *Comus,* line 34, "Count the night watches to his feathery Dames." See note 105.15.

151.33–39 "Some say that ever . . ."]   *Hamlet,* act I, sc. 1.

152.9 Stranger and sojourner]   See Ps. 39:12. There are several similar combinations of the words, as in Lev. 25:23.

THE STAGE COACH

153.2–7 Omne benè . . . deponendi.]   Unknown origin; similar to the verses in the *Carmina Burana*, set to music by Carl Orff. A rendering which catches the spirit of the piece might be as follows: Every pleasure / No more pain / Now it's time for play. / The hour has come / To set aside / Our books without delay.

153.35 Bucephalus]   Favorite horse of Alexander the Great.

156.1–11 "Now capons and hens . . . lick his fingers."]   The passage quoted is from the December section in Nicholas Breton's *The Fantasticks* (1626).

156.9–10 Dice and cards benefit the butler]   It was customary for the players to give part of their winnings to the butler.

157.8 a smoke jack]   A device for turning a roasting-spit.

157.39 Poor Robin's Almanack, 1684]   *Poor Robin* was one of many prophetical almanacs originating in the seventeenth and eighteenth centuries, and differs from most in its humorous attitude toward its own prophecies.

CHRISTMAS EVE

159.10 CARTWRIGHT]   These lines are from *The Ordinary*, III, i, a comedy by Cartwright. See 29.8.

159.23 Peacham]   Henry Peacham (1576–1644?). His *Compleat Gentleman* (1622) deals with manners, geometry, poetry, music, military arts, and other matters thought relevant to the education of a gentleman.

159.24 Chesterfield]   Philip Dormer Stanhope, fourth earl of Chesterfield (1694–1773) wrote *Letters to His Son* (1774) addressed to his illegitimate son, Philip. The letters, not originally intended for publication, counsel sophistication and the keeping up of appearances rather than normal behavior.

161.3 'merrie disport.']   Stow's *Survey of London*, 1603 edition, p. 98. See note 92.41.

161.8 "mongrel, puppy, whelp. . . ."]   From "An Elegy on the Death of a Mad Dog," in Chapter 17 of *The Vicar of Wakefield* (1766), by Oliver Goldsmith (1730–1774).

161.11–12 "—The little dogs and all. . . ."]   *King Lear*, III, vi.

162.9–11 the old games of hoodman blind, shoe the wild mare, hot cockles, steal the white loaf, Bob apple, and snap dragon]   *Hoodman blind*: Blind Man's Buff. *Shoe the wild mare*: The player chosen to be the wild mare was allowed a head start, and then chased by the other players. In trying to escape, the mare probably kicked enthusiastically. In a Scottish version the player chosen had to perform stunts upon a beam strung between two ropes. If he did not fall off he successfully shod the "auld" mare. *Hot cockles*: One player had to kneel down blindfolded, and, being struck, had to guess who hit him. *Bob apple*: The player had to try to catch in his mouth an apple swinging at the end of a string. (A bob is the weight at the end of a plumb-line.) *Snap dragon*: The object is to snatch raisins from a tray of blazing brandy, and eat them without burning oneself.

163.33–38 Come, bring with a noise. . . .] Robert Herrick, "Ceremonies for Christmasse," stanza 1, from *Hesperides* (1648).

164.15–16 perfectly orthodox] Minced pie, also called "Christmas pie," was in disfavor with those of Puritan predilections, who did not observe Christmas.

167.27–28 "no spirit dares stir abroad,"] *Hamlet*, I, i.

168.1 waits] See note 151.21.

CHRISTMAS DAY

169.2–10 Dark and dull night. . . .] From stanzas 1, 3, and 4 of Herrick's "A Christmas *Caroll* sung to the King in his Presence at *White-Hall*," Number 96 in *Noble Numbers*.

169.18–19 Rejoice . . . morning.] The varying refrain of a carol, "The Sunny Bank," found in *Songs of the Nativity*, pp. 23–24, published without a date by J. C. Hotten.

170.31–38 'Tis thou that crown'st. . . ."] "A Thanksgiving to God, for His House," *Noble Numbers*, 47, lines 37–44. See note 110.38.

171.36 Sir Anthony Fitzherbert] (1470–1538), judge and author. His *Booke of Husbandrie* is a practical manual for farmers.

172.21 Markham's Country Contentments] Gervase (or Jervaise) Markham (1568–1637), scholar, poet, dramatist, horsebreeder, and agriculturist. *Country Contentments* (1611) is a book for sportsmen.

172.21–22 the Tretyse of Hunting, by Sir Thomas Cockayne, Knight] Sir Thomas Cokayne (1519?–1592), a country gentleman who devoted himself to hunting, published *A Short Treatise of Hunting, compyled for the Delight of Noblemen and Gentlemen* in 1591.

172.22–23 Isaac Walton's Angler] Izaak Walton (1593–1683) wrote *The Compleat Angler* (1653) and a collection of lives of his contemporaries. See note 264.2–10 in "The Angler," where Walton is repeatedly cited.

172.35 old Tusser] Thomas Tusser (ca. 1525–1580) became the poet laureate of the farm. He composed a *Hundred Good Points of Husbandry Married to as Many of Good Huswifery*. The verse is unlocated.

173.4–6 'deep, solemn mouths,' . . .] The passage Irving quotes from concerns choosing dogs for "sweetness of cry."

173.33 Caxton] William Caxton (ca. 1422–1491) set up the first printing press in England in 1476. Among his best productions are the *Morte d'Arthur* and *Canterbury Tales*.

173.33 Wynkin de Worde] See note 103.20.

175.24 . . . Theophilus of Cesarea] It is not at all clear which Theophilus Irving is referring to. The most likely candidate is Theophilus, patriarch of Alexandria (385–428).

175.24 St. Cyprian] (ca. 200–258), bishop of Carthage.

175.24 St. Chrysostom] (345?–407), archbishop of Constantinople; the most famous Greek father.

175.25 St. Augustine] (354–430), bishop of Hippo. The greatest of the Latin fathers of the Church. Author of the *City of God* and *Confessions*.

175.25 a cloud more] See Heb. 12:1: "a cloud of witnesses."

176.8 Prynne] William Prynne (1600–1669), Puritan pamphleteer who compiled an enormous book attacking the theater, entitled *Histrio-Mastix*.

176.9 round heads] That is, Puritans.

176.40–42 *"Ule! Ule! / Three puddings in a pule; / Crack nuts and cry ule!"] Unidentified.

177.18–23 Poor Robin . . . catch 'em] See note 157.39.

177.22 duke Humphry] To dine with Duke Humphrey meant to fast.

177.23 Squire Ketch] Usually "Jack Ketch," meaning the hangman, after a famous one of the seventeenth century.

177.37 black jacks] Large leather beer cups or jugs, coated with tar.

177.41 *Round about our Sea-coal Fire*] The quotation is from *Round about our Coal Fire, or Christmas Entertainments* (chap. 1, p. 1), an eighteenth-century pamphlet.

178.35 a Christmas box] An earthenware box in which apprentices and others collected contributions at Christmas. The box was later broken and the contents shared.

179.23 oil and wine] A frequently repeated biblical phrase.

THE CHRISTMAS DINNER

180.14 WITHER'S JUVENILIA] George Wither or Withers (1588–1667), poet and pamphleteer. This is the first stanza of "A Christmas Carol," *Juvenilia*, 1622, pt. 3.

180.21–26 Just in this nick. . . .] Stanza 15 of "A Ballad upon a wedding," published in *Fragmenta Aurea* (1646). Sir John Suckling (1609–1642), royalist poet and playwright.

181.8–9 Belshazzar's parade of the vessels. . . .] The incident, but not the quotation, is found in Dan. 5:1–4.

181.22 Holbein's portraits] Hans Holbein the Younger (1497–1543), German painter who painted the portraits of many of the chief men of England, including King Henry VIII.

181.22 Albert Durer's prints] Albrecht Dürer (1471–1528), German painter and graphic artist.

182.8–13 Caput apri defero . . . convivio] One of at least four known versions of the "Boar's Head Carol." This one was first printed in Wynkyn de Worde's *Christmasse Carolles* (1521). Translation: "The boar's head I bring, giving praises to the Lord . . . who are present at the feast."

183.5 full of expectation] *Henry IV, Part I*, II, iii, "a good plot, good friends, and full of expectation."

183.25 servire cantico] Serve with a song.

183.30 In Reginensi Atrio] In the king's hall.

183.38 . . . ancient oath, used by Justice Shallow, "by cock and pye."] *Henry IV, Part II*, v, i, and *Merry Wives of Windsor*, I, i, "Cock" is a corruption of "God," and "pye" is the service book of the pre-Reformation church.

183.39 Massinger in his City Madam] Philip Massinger (1583–1640), the dramatist. The quotation is from *City Madam*, II, i.

184.37–42 Next crowne . . . a swinger] From Herrick's "Twelfe night, or King and Queen," lines 19–24. F. Max Patrick's *Complete Poetry of Robert Herrick* annotates "Lamb's Wool" as "apple pulp," and "a swinger" as "a whopper."

185.5–18 The brown bowle, / The merry brown bowle, / . . . . / And sound a lusty laugh-a.*] The second stanza of a poem for June beginning "The Black Jack, / The merry Black Jack," in Tutin's *Poor Robin's Almanack: Selected Verses* (n.d.) (see note 157.39).

185.24 slow hound] sleuth hound.

185.38 ARCHAEOLOGIA] *Archaeologia: or, Miscellaneous Tracts Relating to Antiquity, Published by the Society of Antiquaries of London*, was first published in 1773.

186.31–32 an "alphabet of faces,"] Thomas Nashe, *Pierce Penilesse His Supplication to the Divell* (1592); R. W. McKerrow, ed., *The Works of Thomas Nashe*, I, 167, line 35.

186.42–187.1 "Cupid's Solicitor for Love;"] The verse is from "Song upon the wooing of a Widow," in *Cupid's Solicitor of Love* (ca. 1640), by Richard Crimsall.

187.8 Joe Miller] (1684–1738) was a comic actor at Drury Lane, but *Joe Miller's Jests, or the Wit's Vade Mecum*, published after his death, was a collection of jokes by John Motley, a dramatist.

187.26 mock fairies about Falstaff] *Merry Wives of Windsor*, V, v.

187.40 STOW] The note is from Stow's *Survey of London*, 1603 edition, p. 98. See note 92.41.

189.34 Covenanters] Those who supported the Scottish National Covenant of 1638, or the English Parliament's Solemn League and Covenant of 1643, which were directed toward the extirpation of Catholicism and Episcopacy.

190.37 Sir John Hawkins] (1719–1789). His *General History of the Science and Practice of Music* appeared in 1776.

191.25–30 At the time of . . . Newstead Abbey.] Irving spent Christmas of 1831 at Barlborough Hall, Derbyshire, and then visited at Newstead Abbey, formerly Byron's home.

LONDON ANTIQUES

192.2–6 ————I do walk . . . FLETCHER] I cannot find which of the many poets named Fletcher wrote this verse. "Guido Vaux" is Guy Fawkes, a chief conspirator in the Gunpowder Plot, which almost succeeded in blowing up both houses of Parliament and King James I on November 5, 1605. "William o'the Wisp" (or Will-o'-the-wisp) is a malicious sprite who misled travelers; Robin Goodfellow (Puck) is a mischievous elf.

192.39 Knights Templars] The most famous of the three great military orders founded in the twelfth century. They originated in the Holy Land after the first crusade, and took their name from the so-called Temple of Solomon in Jerusalem where they were quartered.

195.27 Sir Thomas Sutton] (1532–1611). He made a fortune from coal mines.

195.35–196.5 Stow . . . brotherly love."]   Stow died six years before the hospital was founded. The quotations are not from Stow but from John Strype's edition of Stow's *Survey* (London, 1754), bk. 1, chap. 27. See note 92.41.

LITTLE BRITAIN

197.2–5 What I write. . . . NASHE]   From Thomas Nashe's prose work, *Christ's Tears Over Jerusalem. Whereunto is annexed a comparative admonition to London*, published in 1593. See also note 94.35.

198.29 eat pan cakes on Shrove Tuesday]   Shrove Tuesday is the day before Ash Wednesday, on which, in the middle ages, sins were confessed in preparation for Lent. The eating of pancakes derives from the need to use up eggs and fat, which were prohibited during Lent.

198.30 Michaelmas]   The feast of the archangel Michael, September 29.

198.31–32 burn the Pope on the Fifth of November]   November 5 is Guy Fawkes Day, celebrating the discovery of the Gunpowder Plot. See note 192.2–6.

198.38–39 the figures that strike the hours at St. Dunstan's clock]   One of London's most popular sights were the two savages (or Hercules) which struck the hours of the clock of St. Dunstan's-in-the-West. When the church was razed in 1630, the figures were sold to the marquis of Hertford and taken to his villa at Regent's Park, still known as St. Dunstan's.

198.39 the Monument]   See note 93.22.

198.39; 199.1 lions in the Tower]   Stow's *Survey of London* says: "Henry I build his manor of Woodstock. . . . He placed therein . . . divers strange beasts . . . such as . . . lions, leopards, lynxes . . . and such other." Since the time of Henry III "these lions and others have been kept in a part of this bulwark, now called the Lion Tower. . . ." For Stow see note 92.41.

199.1 the wooden giants in Guildhall]   See note 92.34–35.

199.27–28 Robert Nixon]   Known as the Cheshire prophet, he was apparently an idiot who at intervals delivered oracles. His dates and even his existence are in doubt.

199.28 Mother Shipton]   She was a supposed witch and prophetess who, according to tradition, lived in the late fifteenth century in Yorkshire.

199.34–35 the grasshopper on the top of the Exchange]   The grasshopper was the crest of Sir Thomas Gresham, who founded the Royal Exchange, and a figure of one stood on top of the building.

199.38–40 repairs . . . workshop]   These took place in 1820. On the church of St. Mary le Bow, see note 94.35.

200.4–6 The good old king . . . had all at once given up the ghost; another king had mounted the throne]   George III died January 29, 1820, and his son was crowned George IV.

200.6 a royal duke had died suddenly]   Edward, duke of Kent, fourth son of George III, and father of Queen Victoria, died January 23, 1820.

200.6–7 another, in France, had been murdered]   The Duc de Berri, son of Charles X, was murdered as he left the Paris Opera House on February 14, 1820.

200.7 there had been radical meetings]   Agitation for reform, on such issues as universal suffrage and annual parliaments, led to frequent radical meetings between 1816 and 1819, especially in northern England.

200.8 the bloody scenes at Manchester]   The Manchester or "Peterloo" massacre of August 16, 1819, when a huge meeting of working people, held to demand Parliamentary reform, was charged by cavalry. A dozen people were killed and hundreds were injured.

200.8–9 the great plot in Cato Street]   The foiled conspiracy of Arthur Thistlewood and twenty-three other Radicals to assassinate the members of the English Cabinet, while they were at dinner on February 23, 1820, resulted in the hanging of Thistlewood and four others.

200.9 the Queen had returned to England]   Caroline, wife of George IV, had been excluded from court while her husband was regent, and had been living in Italy. On George's accession to the throne in 1820 she returned to England to claim her rights as queen.

200.17–18 that steeple . . . Wittington and his Cat]   Richard Whittington (d. 1423) was an extremely wealthy man, and several times mayor of London. Popular legend has him a poor orphan who makes his fortune by capitalizing on the rat-catching abilities of his cat, and by heeding the sound of Bow bells. See note 94.35.

200.26 Gentleman's Magazine]   Founded by its publisher, Edward Cave, in 1731. Samuel Johnson later joined the staff. The bulk of the magazine, which appeared monthly until 1907, consisted of excerpts and condensations from the newspapers.

200.26 Rapin's History of England]   Paul de Rapin (1661–1725) wrote a *History of England* (1723–1725) to the time of William and Mary.

200.27 Naval Chronicle]   A history of the Royal Navy, containing original papers on nautical matters. It appeared between 1799 and 1818.

201.1 Margate]   A seaside report on the Isle of Thanet, in Kent.

201.25–26 "Truman, Hanbury, and Co's. Entire,"]   "Entire" or "Entire butt" was a mixture of ale, beer, and twopenny, similar to what is now referred to in England as "Porter."

201.26 Old Tom]   A strong English gin.

201.27 Bacchus and Momus]   In classical mythology Bacchus is god of wine and intoxication while Momus is god of mockery and censure.

202.7 trowle]   Now spelled troll. A round. "Trowle" in the third stanza of the song means "pass."

202.7 Gammer Gurton's Needle]   One of the earliest English comedies, written probably by William Stevenson about 1559, and performed at Christ's College, Cambridge. The "Confession of Faith" opens act 2.

202.18–25; 203.28–41 I cannot eate. . . .]   Nut browne toste: "nut browne and tost: ale"; crab: crab apple; mault-worme: "malt worm: one who loves malt liquor." (Definitions are from the *Oxford English Dictionary*.)

203.8 St. Bartholomew's Fair]   King Henry I granted a charter to Royer or Rahere, the king's minstrel, founder and first prior of the Priory and Hospital of St. Bartholomew, Smithfield, to hold an annual fair and use the proceeds for his institution. In the early eighteenth century the Fair became notoriously immoral. Ben Jonson's comedy, *Bartholomew Fair*, gives a fine picture of the event. The following notes on shows at the Fair come from H. Morley's *Memoirs of Bartholomew Fair* (1859).

203.8–9 Lord Mayor's day]   November 9, the date of inauguration of the Lord Mayor of London.

203.21 the Flying Horses]   Horse shows were quite popular at such fairs, but this particular act is unidentified. See, for example, Dickens' *Hard Times*.

203.22 Signior Polito]   The owner of a famous menagerie or Wild Beast Show.

203.22 the Fire Eater]   Madame Josephine Girardelli, the "Fireproof Lady" or the "Female Salamander," was a well-known "fire-eater" at the Fair in the years before Irving wrote "Little Britain."

203.22 the celebrated Mr. Paap]   The Dutch dwarf, Sampoeman, known as Simon Paap. He was shown at the Fair in 1815, and later presented to the Royal Family. At the time, he was 26 years old, weighed 27 pounds, and measured 28 inches in height.

203.22–23 the Irish Giant]   Perhaps Patrick O'Brien, who was last exhibited in 1804.

204.5 Temple Bar]   One of the gates of the city of London, at the junction of the Strand and Fleet Street. The last actual gateway was removed in 1878. The sovereign ceremonially halts there to receive permission from the Lord Mayor to enter the City.

204.17 train bands]   See note 95.16.

204.34 All-Fours]   a card game.

204.34 Pope-Joan]   Unidentified.

204.34–35 Tom-come-tickle-me]   Apparently a kind of a tag game.

204.38 Epping Forest]   About 16 miles from Little Britain.

205.35 Kean]   Edmund Kean (1787–1833), perhaps England's greatest tragic actor. His portrayals of Shylock and Lear in particular are landmarks in theatrical history.

STRATFORD-ON-AVON

209.6 GARRICK]   David Garrick (1717–1779), the famous actor. The quotation is the first stanza of Air VI of his "Ode" composed for the Stratford Jubilee of 1769, which he was instrumental in organizing.

209.19–20 "Shall I not take mine ease in mine inn?"]   *Henry IV, Part I*, III, iii.

209.31–32 the Jubilee, and David Garrick]

210.10 a garrulous old lady]   Mrs. Mary Hornby, who lived at the birthplace from 1793 to 1820.

210.20 Shakespeare's mulberry tree]   This tree stood in the garden of Shakespeare's house, New Place, though there is no proof that he himself planted it. It was cut down in 1758 and numerous artifacts made from the wood.

210.36–37 the Santa Casa of Loretto]   See note 78.6–7.

210.37 the flying chair of the Arabian enchanter]   Possibly a reference to King Housain's magic Persian carpet in the *Arabian Nights*.

210.38 sold . . . to a northern princess]   Known as Shakespeare's chair, the original relic was sold in 1790 to Princess Czartoryska, who took it to Poland. But there were at least three other oak chairs for sale among Mrs. Hornby's relics.

211.8 a play of her own composition]   *The Battle of Waterloo*, a tragedy (Stratford-upon-Avon, 1819)

212.1 grand daughter]   Sally Kite (afterward Trinder).

212.3 John Ange]   Joseph Ainge, an almsman of the borough.

213.7–10 Good friend. . . .]   The spelling is modernized here.

213.36–37 Mrs. Hall]   His first child. She was actually buried in the churchyard, not in the church.

213.38 John Combe, of usurious memory]   The charge of usury probably derives from John Aubrey (1626–1697), collector of anecdotes, and appears to be unfair. John Combe, a wealthy Stratford bachelor, died in 1614 and left Shakespeare £5 in his will. The "ludicrous epitaph" supposedly written by Shakespeare can be found in Aubrey's *Brief Lives*.

214.17–18 Sir Thomas Lucy] (1532–1600), owner of Charlecote Hall. The Lucys did not own a deer park during Shakespeare's youth, though they did much later. The legend owes most to Nicholas Rowe's biography of Shakespeare prefaced to his six-volume edition of the plays (1709).

214.31 revenged himself in his writings] This supposed revenge is in *The Merry Wives of Windsor*, I, i. See 220.12.

214.34–42 A parliament member. . . .] Although these lines were attributed to the poet by an old man who lived near Stratford and died in 1703, they are probably not authentic.

215.32–33 a traditionary anecdote . . . Avon."] *Picturesque Views on the Warwickshire Avon* was published in 1795 by Samuel Ireland after a visit to Stratford to gather material for the book. His escort, John Jordan, Stratford poet and forger of Shakespeariana, apparently invented numerous village customs for his benefit, such as this one.

216.21–27; 217.1–2 song in Cymbeline . . . lady sweet arise!] II, iii.

217.9–11 "to sit round the fire . . . goblins, and friars."] Unidentified.

217.35 *Scot, in his "Discoverie of Witchcraft,"] Published in 1584, this scholarly work was written by Reginald Scot (d. 1599) to reveal the folly of persecuting witches. Shakespeare's witches in *Macbeth* in part derive from it. The passage is from bk. 7, chap. 15.

218.19 meditations of Jaques] See *As You Like It*, II, vii.

218.30–37 Under the green wood tree . . . winter and rough weather.] *As You Like It*, II, v. The second and third lines should read: "And turn his merry note / Unto the sweet bird's throat."

219.18–20 "*Falstaff* . . . good air."] *Henry IV, Part II*, V, iii.

220.38–39 a portrait by Sir Peter Lely] The portrait is actually by Sir Godfrey Kneller, a native of Holstein, who was invited to England in 1674. He was court painter from 1680 until his death in 1723. For Lely, see note 67.25.

221.16 as Master Slender would say, "a cane-coloured beard."] It is Simple, not Slender, who, in *The Merry Wives of Windsor*, I, iv, speaks of a "cane [or 'Cain'] coloured beard."

221.41 *Bishop Earle] John Earle (1601–1665), chaplain to Charles II in exile, wrote *Micro-cosmographie, or, A Peece of The World Discovered; In Essayes and Characters* (1628). The quotation is from Number 17, An Upstart Knight.

222.17 with that pity "that dwells in womanhood."] Unidentified.

222.18–19 brief authority]   "Man, proud man! dressed in a little brief authority." *Measure for Measure*, II, ii.

222.25–26 "to a last year's pippin of his own graffing, with a dish of carraways;"]   *Henry IV, Part II*, V, iii.

222.36 description of a Mr. Hastings]   Henry Hastings (1551–1650) son of the fourth earl of Huntingdon. Anthony Ashley Cooper, the first earl of Shaftesbury, inscribed on Hastings' portrait an account of his life, which was later reprinted in various publications. The passage in Shaftesbury's account is practically identical to the one quoted.

223.1–6 "By cock and pye, Sir. . . ."]   See note 183.38.

223.13–14 " 'Tis merry in hall. . . ."]   *Henry IV, Part II*, V, iii.

223.18 "working day world"]   *As You Like It*, I, iii.

223.24 airy nothings]   "The poet's pen . . . gives to airy nothing / A local habitation and a name." *A Midsummer Night's Dream*, V, i.

223.26 I had heard Jaques soliloquize beneath his oak]   *As You Like It*, II, vii.

223.27–28 the fair Rosalind . . . woodlands]   In *As You Like It*.

223.29–30 Falstaff . . . Justice Shallow . . . Master Slender . . . Anne Page]   They are all characters in *The Merry Wives of Windsor*; and, as the preceding quotations indicate, the three men also appear in *Henry IV*, Parts I and II.

TRAITS OF INDIAN CHARACTER

225.6 SPEECH OF AN INDIAN CHIEF]   Logan, or Tahgahjute (ca. 1725–1780), a Cayuga who acquired great influence with the Shawnee after marrying into their tribe, supposedly sent this speech to a peace council after a battle with the British at Point Pleasant on the Ohio in 1774. Its authenticity has been questioned.

226.37–42 The American government has been indefatigable. . . .]   The government's sincerity and fairness have in recent times been seriously questioned.

227.9–15 "For," says an old historian. . . . meanly of."]   The passage is quoted almost word for word from Thomas Morton's *New English Canaan* (1637), bk. 1, p. 178.

228.12–13 an old record of the early settlement]   Morton's *New English Canaan*. The incident occurs in bk. 3, pp. 169–71, and Irving's report of the sachem's speech closely follows Morton's.

230.32–33 glorious "pomp and circumstance of war,"]   *Othello*, III, iii: "pomp and circumstance of glorious war!"

231.36–38 one of the homely narratives . . . Pequod Indians.]   *A Narrative of the Troubles with the Indians in New-England* (Boston, 1677) by the Reverend William Hubbard (1621–1704), who emigrated to New England in 1635.

233.9–10 that gigantic race said to have existed on the borders of the Susquehanna]   Unidentified.

233.14–15 "the places that now know them will know them no more for ever."]   Unidentified.

233.25–28 "We are driven back . . . to exist."]   Source unidentified.

PHILIP OF POKANOKET

234.9 CAMPBELL]   Thomas Campbell (1777–1844), Scottish poet. The quotation is from "Gertrude of Wyoming" (1809), a poem focusing on a Mohawk raid on the Pennsylvania settlement of Wyoming. See pt. 1, stanza 23, lines 3–9.

235.11 PHILIP OF POKANOKET]   He died in 1676. Irving is essentially correct in the details of his life.

235.41 a celebrated English poet]   Robert Southey (1774–1843), who became poet laureate of England in 1813. The poem Irving refers to is "Oliver Newman, A New England Tale" (1837).

237.4 Metamocet]   Actually Metacomet.

239.34 one of the learned men of the day]   That is, Increase Mather.

239.41 *The Rev. Increase Mather's History]   *A Brief History of the War with the Indians in New England* (1676) by Increase Mather (1639–1723), the father of Cotton Mather, for whom see note 276.41.

240.3–4 a worthy clergyman of the time]   The Reverend William Hubbard. See note 231.36–38.

241.39–41 "He was . . . English;"]   Hubbard.

243.9–10 "he would fight it out . . . English."]   Hubbard.

243.33 peag]   Beads made from shell, strung together and used by the Indians as money.

243.38–39 "his heart and his bowels . . . of strength."]   Hubbard.

244.5–10 Being questioned . . . answer."]   Hubbard.

244.19–20 "and he desired to hear no more thereof."]   Hubbard.

244.27–28 "that he liked it well . . . himself."]   Hubbard.

244.29 Stonington]   in Connecticut.

245.2–8 "His ruin . . . away."]   Hubbard.

245.18–19 where the wicked . . . troubling]   Job 3:17: "There the wicked cease from troubling; and there the weary be at rest."

245.26 "most horrid and diabolical lamentations."]   Hubbard.

245.29–33 "he never rejoiced afterwards . . . deliverance."]   Hubbard.

245.41–246.5 "Phillip," he says . . . upon him."]   Hubbard.

246.33 "beloved wife and only son"]   Hubbard.

JOHN BULL

248.1 *JOHN BULL*]   *Law is a Bottomless Pit, or the History of John Bull* (1712), a satire by Dr. John Arbuthnot (1667–1735), contained a character named "John Bull" who allegorically stood for England. The name soon gained popularity and was applied to the nation or a particular Englishman. Irving's friend James K. Paulding wrote *The Diverting History of John Bull and Brother Jonathan*, and sent Irving a copy of it in 1812.

248.37–38 beyond the sound of Bow bells.]   See note 94.35.

250.31–32 "gentlemen of the fancy;"]   Those who fancy a particular sport or amusement, especially boxing.

253.4 beef eaters]   Here referring to soldiers.

254.16–17 obstreperous conduct of one of his sons]   Perhaps an allusion to "Orator Hunt," a popular agitator of the time who always managed to keep himself out of trouble.

254.42 Tom, an officer]   Tommy Atkins, the nickname given to British soldiers. At the end of the Napoleonic Wars in 1815, many British officers were on half pay.

255.10–11 he is mortgaged over head and ears]   The national debt had grown from a hundred and thirty million pounds before the American Revolution to seven hundred million after the Napoleonic Wars.

255.32 pockets . . . empty]   From 1797 to 1821 Bank of England notes were not redeemable in gold.

THE PRIDE OF THE VILLAGE

257.3–9 May no wolfe howle. . . . HERRICK]   Stanza 12 of "The Dirge of Jephthah's Daughter." See note 110.38.

258.24 flower of the field]   Ps. 103:15; Isa. 40:6.

258.25–26 Rachel, "mourning . . . comforted."]   See Jer. 31:15 and Matt.
  2:18.

259.3–6 "This is the prettiest . . . place."]   *The Winter's Tale*, IV, iv.

262.19 the silver cord]   Eccles. 12:6.

THE ANGLER

264.2–10 This day dame Nature. . . . Sir H. Wotton]   Sir Henry Wotton
  (1568–1639), ambassador, poet, provost of Eton College. His works are
  collected under the title *Reliquiae Wottonianae*. These lines are from a
  poem quoted by Izaak Walton in *The Compleat Angler*, pt. 1, chap. 1.
  See note 172.22–23.

264.16–17 Izaak Walton . . . "Complete Angler"]   See note 172.22–23.

264.31 La Mancha . . . Sierra Morena]   *Don Quixote*, pt. 1, bk. 3, chap.
  9.

265.40–41 "good honest, wholesome, hungry" repast]   *The Compleat Angler*, pt. 1, chap. 4.

266.1–2 Izaak Walton's scene with the milkmaid]   *The Compleat Angler*,
  in pt. 1, chap. 2.

266.26 "brothers of the angle,"]   A reiterated phrase in *The Compleat
  Angler*.

266.27 "mild, sweet and peaceable spirit"]   *The Compleat Angler*, pt. 1,
  chap. 1.

266.28–29 "Tretyse of fishing with the Angle,"]   *A Treatyse of Fysshynge
  wyth an Angle*, by Dame Juliana Berners (about whom nothing is known),
  was the first English book on fishing. It was printed by Wynkyn de Worde
  in 1496. This quotation is from the next-to-last page, and is followed by
  the passage quoted in Irving's note.

267.14 instructions of the sage Piscator to his scholar]   In *The Compleat
  Angler*.

267.33 battle of Camperdown]   On October 11, 1797, Admiral Duncan
  defeated the Dutch fleet off Camperdown on the Dutch coast.

267.38 the "noble art of angling."]   Irving is presumably quoting again from
  Walton.

268.33–39 "When I would . . . him"]   *The Compleat Angler*, pt. 1, end of
  chap. 21.

269.1–14 Let me live . . . daffodil.]   The opening lines of a poem quoted
  in *The Compleat Angler*, pt. 1, chap. 1. The book from which the quo-

tation comes was published in 1613 and was written by John Dennys (d. 1609), not J. Davors.

269.30–31 naval ballads, such as Admiral Hosier's Ghost] Richard Glover (1712–1785) wrote this ballad. It is printed in Percy's *Reliques*, vol. 2, bk. 3, song 25.

269.31 All in the Downs] Better known as "Sweet William's Farewell to Black-eyed Susan," by John Gay (1685–1732).

269.31 Tom Bowling] A song by Charles Dibdin (1745–1814), playwright and songwriter. It is based on Lieutenant Tom Bowling, Roderick's uncle in Tobias Smollett's *Roderick Random*.

271.8 St. Peter's master] That is, Jesus.

271.9–10 "and upon all that . . . go a angling."] A similarly worded passage closes Chapter 13 of Part 1 of *The Compleat Angler*.

THE LEGEND OF SLEEPY HOLLOW

"The Legend of Sleepy Hollow" has literary antecedents transmuted by the author's imagination. Bürger's "Der wilde Jäger" is an important literary source, while the chase and throwing of the false head are found in the Rübezahl legends of Germany.

272.8 CASTLE OF INDOLENCE] By James Thomson; canto 1, stanza 6. See also note 16.7.

272.12–13 implored the protection of St. Nicholas] St. Nicholas was the protector of shipwrecked sailors, and others in hazardous trades.

273.6 Hendrick Hudson] See note 40.12.

273.14–15 the night mare, with her whole nine fold] See *King Lear*, III, iv.

275.5–6 "spare the rod and spoil the child."] Samuel Butler's *Hudibras* (1663–1678), bk. 2, canto 1, line 844. See Prov. 13:24, "He that spareth the rod hateth his son."

276.2–3 the lion bold . . . hold] In the *New England Primer* (ca. 1683) the couplet accompanying the letter L read, "The lion bold / The lamb doth hold."

276.17–18 "by hook and by crook,"] The phrase apparently dates back to the fourteenth century, but its origin is unknown.

276.41 Cotton Mather's History of New England Witchcraft] Cotton Mather (1663–1728) was the most famous of the Mather dynasty of ministers. Irving's reference is probably to *Memorable Providences Relating to Witchcrafts and Possessions* (1689), though Mather also wrote on witch-craft in two other major works: *Magnalia Christi Americana,* and *The Wonders of the Invisible World.*

277.21 token]   Apparently a sign or warning.

277.25 "in linked sweetness . . ."]   "Of linked sweetness long drawn out," Milton, *L'Allegro,* line 140.

278.33 Saardam]   A town about five miles northwest of Amsterdam; also called Zaandam.

281.37 Don Cossacks]   See note 5.29.

282.3 rantipole]   wild, disorderly.

282.17 supple jack]   A climbing shrub with strong stems from which walk-ing sticks are often made.

285.36 monteiro]   *Montero,* a round huntsman's cap with a flap.

287.14–15 oly koek, and . . . cruller]   oly koek: sweetened dough fried in lard; kruller: dough twisted into various shapes, and crisply fried in lard or oil.

288.38 Whiteplains]   General Howe was defeated by the Americans at White Plains, north of New York City, on October 28, 1776.

289.23 Major André]   The British officer (1751–1780) who was involved in Benedict Arnold's attempt to betray West Point. Despite much popular sympathy for the personable André, he was hanged as a spy.

291.11 the very witching time of night]   *Hamlet,* III, ii.

294.23 "If I can but reach that bridge,"]   Alluding to the belief that super-natural beings could not cross running water.

296.3 Ten Pound Court]   That is, small claims court.

L'ENVOY

298.7 CHAUCER'S *Belle Dame sans Mercie*]   Although formerly attributed to Chaucer, *La Belle Dame sans Mercie* is a mid-fifteenth-century trans-lation by Sir Richard Ros of a poem by Alain Chartier.

SUGGESTIONS FOR FURTHER READING

The Complete Works of Washington Irving. 29 volumes. Gen. eds. Henry
A. Pochmann, Herbert L. Kleinfield, Richard D. Rust. Madison, Wis.:
University of Wisconsin Press, and Boston: Twayne Publishers, 1969–88.

GENERAL STUDIES OF IRVING'S LIFE, WORKS, TIMES

Bowden, Mary Weatherspoon. *Washington Irving* (Twayne's United States
Authors Series, no. 379). Boston: G. K. Hall, 1981.

Brodwin, Stanley, ed. *The Old and New World Romanticism of Washington
Irving.* Westport, Conn.: Greenwood Press, 1986.

Brooks, Van Wyck. *The World of Washington Irving.* Cleveland: The World
Publishing Co., 1944.

Hedges, William L. *Washington Irving: An American Study, 1802–1832.*
Baltimore: The Johns Hopkins Press, 1965.

Kasson, Joy S. *Artistic Voyagers: Europe and the American Imagination in
the Works of Irving, Cooper, Hawthorne, Allston, and Cole.* Westport,
Conn.: Greenwood Press, 1982.

Lynen, John F. "The Fiction in the Landscape: Irving and Cooper," in *The
Design of the Present: Essays on Time and Form in American Literature.*
New Haven; Yale University Press, 1969. Pp. 153–204.

Myers, Andrew B., ed. *A Century of Commentary on the Works of Washington Irving.* Tarrytown, N. Y.: Sleepy Hollow Restorations, 1976.

Pochmann, Henry A., ed. *Washington Irving: Representative Selections.*
New York: American Book Co., 1934.

Reichart, Walter. *Washington Irving and Germany.* Ann Arbor: University
of Michigan Press, 1957.

Ringe, Donald A. *American Gothic: Imagination and Reason in Nineteenth-
Century Fiction.* Lexington: University Press of Kentucky, 1982.

———. *The Pictorial Mode: Space and Time in the Act of Bryant, Irving
and Cooper.* Lexington: University Press of Kentucky, 1971.

Roth, Martin. *Comedy and America: The Lost World of Washington Irving.*
Port Washington, N. Y.: Kennikat Press, 1976.

Rubin-Dorsky, Jeffrey. *Adrift in the Old World: The Pilgrimage of Washington Irving.* Chicago: University of Chicago Press, 1988.

Wagenknecht, Edward. *Washington Irving: Moderation Displayed.* New
York: Oxford University Press, 1962.

Williams, Stanley T. *The Life of Washington Irving.* 2 vols. New York:
Oxford University Press, 1935.

THE SKETCH BOOK: LITERARY HISTORY, CRITICISM, AND INTERPRETATION

Bone, Robert. "Irving's Headless Hessian: Prosperity and the Inner Life." *American Quarterly*, 15 (1963), 167–75.

Clendenning, John. "Irving and the Gothic." *Bucknell Review*, 12 (1964), 90–98.

Daigrepont, Lloyd M. "Ichabod Crane: Inglorious Man of Letters." *Early American Literature*, 19 (1984), 68–81.

Dawson, William P. " 'Rip Van Winkle' as Bawdy Satire: The Rascal and the Revolution." *ESQ: A Journal of the American Renaissance*, 27 (1981), 198–206.

Fetterly, Judith. *"An American Dream: 'Rip Van Winkle,' "* in *The Resisting Reader: A Feminist Approach to American Fiction*. Bloomington: Indiana University Press, 1978. Pp. 1–11.

Heiman, Marcel. "Rip Van Winkle: A Psychoanalytic Note on the Story and its Author." *American Imago*, 16 (1959), 3–47.

Hoffman, Daniel. "Prefigurations: 'The Legend of Sleepy Hollow,' " in *Form and Fable in American Fiction*. New York: Oxford University Press, 1961. Pp. 83–96.

Kann, David J. " 'Rip Van Winkle': Wheels within Wheels." *American Imago*, 36 (1979), 178–96.

Leary, Lewis. "The Two Voices of Washington Irving," in *From Irving to Steinbeck: Studies in American Literature in Honor of Harry R. Warfel*, ed. Motley Deakin, Peter Liska. Gainesville: University of Florida Press, 1972. Pp. 13–26.

LeFevre, Louis. "Paul Bunyan and Rip Van Winkle." *Yale Review*, 36 (1946), 66–76.

Martin, Terence. "Rip, Ichabod, and the American Imagination." *American Literature*, 31 (1959), 137–49.

Pajak, Edward F. "Washington Irving's *Ichabod Crane*: American Narcissus." *American Imago*, 38 (1981), 127–35.

Pattee, Fred Lewis. *The Development of the American Short Story*, ch. 1. New York: Harper and Brothers, 1923.

Pochmann, Henry A. "Irving's German Sources in *The Sketch Book*." *Studies in Philology*, 37 (1930), 477–507.

Ringe, Donald A. "New York and New England: Irving's Criticism of American Society." *American Literature*, 38 (1967), 455–67.

Rubin-Dorsky, Jeffrey. "Washington Irving and the Genesis of the Fictional Sketch." *Early American Literature*, 21 (1986/87), 226–47.

Seelye, John. "Root and Branch: Washington Irving and American Humor." *Nineteenth-Century Fiction*, 38 (1984), 415–25.

Shear, Walter. "Time in 'Rip Van Winkle' and 'The Legend of Sleepy Hollow.'" *Midwest Quarterly*, 15 (1976), 158–72.

Springer, Haskell. "Creative Contradictions in Irving," in *Washington Irving Reconsidered: A Symposium*, ed. Ralph M. Aderman. Hartford, Conn.: Transcendental Books, 1969. Pp. 14–18.

Young, Philip. "Fallen from Time: The Mythic Rip Van Winkle." *Kenyon Review*, 22 (1960), 547–73.

Zlogar, Richard J. "'Accessories that Covertly Explain': Irving's Use of Dutch Genre Painting in 'Rip Van Winkle.'" *American Literature*, 54 (1982), 44–62.

FOR THE BEST IN PAPERBACKS, LOOK FOR THE

In every corner of the world, on every subject under the sun, Penguin represents quality and variety—the very best in publishing today.

For complete information about books available from Penguin—including Pelicans, Puffins, Peregrines, and Penguin Classics—and how to order them, write to us at the appropriate address below. Please note that for copyright reasons the selection of books varies from country to country.

In the United Kingdom: For a complete list of books available from Penguin in the U.K., please write to *Dept E.P., Penguin Books Ltd, Harmondsworth, Middlesex, UB7 0DA.*

In the United States: For a complete list of books available from Penguin in the U.S., please write to *Dept BA, Penguin,* Box 999, Bergenfield, New Jersey 07621-0999.

In Canada: For a complete list of books available from Penguin in Canada, please write to *Penguin Books Canada Ltd, 2801 John Street, Markham, Ontario L3R 1B4.*

In Australia: For a complete list of books available from Penguin in Australia, please write to the *Marketing Department, Penguin Books Australia Ltd, P.O. Box 257, Ringwood, Victoria 3134.*

In New Zealand: For a complete list of books available from Penguin in New Zealand, please write to the *Marketing Department, Penguin Books (NZ) Ltd, Private Bag, Takapuna, Auckland 9.*

In India: For a complete list of books available from Penguin, please write to *Penguin Overseas Ltd, 706 Eros Apartments, 56 Nehru Place, New Delhi, 110019.*

In Holland: For a complete list of books available from Penguin in Holland, please write to *Penguin Books Nederland B.V., Postbus 195, NL–1380AD Weesp, Netherlands.*

In Germany: For a complete list of books available from Penguin, please write to *Penguin Books Ltd, Friedrichstrasse 10–12, D–6000 Frankfurt Main 1, Federal Republic of Germany.*

In Spain: For a complete list of books available from Penguin in Spain, please write to *Longman Penguin España, Calle San Nicolas 15, E–28013 Madrid, Spain.*

In Japan: For a complete list of books available from Penguin in Japan, please write to *Longman Penguin Japan Co Ltd, Yamaguchi Building, 2-12-9 Kanda Jimbocho, Chiyuoda-Ku, Tokyo 101, Japan.*